FROM NOW
UNTIL
FOREVER

*"Jesus Christ the same yesterday,
and today, and forever."*
Hebrews 13:8

Laura L. Drumb

Nov, 2022

To Steven ❀ + Rachel,

Hope you all enjoy this! Laura

Remember always that Jesus Christ is the same from now until forever! Laura L. Drumb

Called To Hope ~ To Live + Enjoy! Eph. 1:18 — Rom. 15:13

www.lonemesapublishing.com

From Now Until Forever
Laura L. Drumb
ISBN: 978-0996752978

Contact the author at lauradrumb@gmail.com.

†TABLE OF CONTENTS†

✝ DEDICATION ✝

From Now Until Forever is lovingly dedicated to my dear friend Ann Buscarino who always believed in me no matter what dream I was pursuing. The last thing she said to me before she went Home to be with the Lord was that she couldn't wait to read this manuscript when I finished it; unfortunately, she never got the chance to do so. But I know she is flashing that famous smile at me now and thanking me for telling a story that honors the Native American heritage of her own blood. An incurable romantic, she adored love stories with happy endings and, of course, anything that glorifies how God works in this world. I believe she would have enjoyed the story of Mandy and Ken-ai-te and their love for each other and for our Heavenly Father. You are my hero, Ann!

Laura L. Drumb

†ACKNOWLEDGEMENTS†

To the many that deserve my gratitude for their contributions in the creation of the story of Mandy and Ken-ai-te, the simple words "thank you" hardly seem enough but, nevertheless, I will try.

First and foremost, of course, is our mighty God who conceived of the plot long before He gave it to me to write and then taught me to listen to my characters tell the story in their own words. And I pray fervently that any glory which might come out of this book will go directly and solely to Him alone!

Next would have to be my husband and daughters, who have lived with this story as long as I have. It has taken roughly twenty years to complete this project and they have had to listen to me talking about it all that time! This requires great patience and love, and Gary certainly has had that. For all those times I was glued to the computer or too tired to be good company or fix dinner or get housework done in a timely manner, I thank you for loving me through it. And for Holly and Angela, who listened countless times as I worked out plot points or talked as though these people were my next-door neighbors, I thank the two of you from the bottom of my heart. It wouldn't have happened without your encouragement and prayers!

Some time back God gave me the idea of creating a Prayer Team to pray for me as I finished writing this novel. He showed me clearly who to ask and each woman eagerly agreed to pray faithfully for me on a regular basis. To these precious ladies, I say thanks from the bottom of my heart. When I became too weary or preoccupied to pray through something as thoroughly as I should regarding the plot, it was humbling to know you were lifting me up for that wisdom and strength. Thank you, Dianne, Lynn, Kay, Linda, JoAnn and Brandy. Although most of you all don't know each other, you have prayed for one another as well, even as I prayed for you also. I couldn't have done this without a prayer covering and you all graciously offered this for me.

In addition, I had a number of friends who agreed to read my manuscript when it was done to give me feedback, as well as helping to catch little inaccuracies or omissions along the way. You know who you are and each is deeply appreciated. My fellow members of Fellowship of Christian Writers here in Tulsa (OK) have been my encouragers from the word go and I am indebted to our FCW online Critique Group members who also gave me thoughtful guidance early on. Now I have a Rave to report, folks!

Several other friends also have been there for me along the way and I would be remiss if I did not mention them. Linda, who has given me so much in the way of the vision for this project as well as invaluable practical advice not to mention being the one who helped me link up with a primary source that proved invaluable to the success of this project; Janice, who loves "everything Indian" and endured countless hours of walking through museums and art galleries with me to find any mention of the Kiowa which might enhance details in the book, and also accompanied me on a trip to the Tallgrass Prairie Reserve in Pawhuska where we literally had the exciting privilege of being surrounded up close by buffalo roaming free on the range—right next to our car, in fact; and, help of a different nature with some of the medical techniques mentioned in Chapter Thirty Two from my dear friend and former physician, Dr. Terrence L. Moore. He served two volunteer tours of duty in Vietnam as a battlefield doctor and witnessed many such injuries in places where normal medical protocols were next to impossible to follow. Such was the case with this incident and I appreciated his in-depth explanation of how to make the situation more believable.

When I began seeking a primary source for some of my research questions, God led me to a well-respected Kiowa elder, Dorothy Whitehorse DeLaune, in a way only He could have orchestrated. She quickly became a priceless resource with her depth of knowledge about the Kiowa people, their language, culture, and history. In addition, she loves Jesus Christ and has been most supportive of this book and its purpose. Dorothy, I am most grateful to you for your encouragement every step of the way and for allowing me to call you my friend. Through you, I have come to love and respect the Kiowa people even though I have not one drop of Kiowa blood in my veins. Learning about them from you has made me wish I did!

And last but certainly not least, where would I be without you, my readers? Thank you for joining Mandy and Ken-ai-te on their journey of faith and adventure. I hope to see each of you again soon in the pages of my next book!

With deepest gratitude,
Laura L. Drumb
Called to Hope... To live in Joy!
Ephesians 1:18, Romans 15:13

† CHAPTER ONE †

"Be of good courage, and he shall strengthen your heart,
all ye that hope in the LORD."
Psalm 31:24

"What is it, Pete? Why have we stopped?"
Mandy glanced at Pete's face and felt the color drain from her own. He put his fingers to his lips, eyes darting everywhere. The throbbing in her ears grew louder and she grasped the handle of the buckboard seat with both hands until her knuckles ached with the effort, as though that could afford her some measure of security.

She looked across the river at the ridge in front of them, then twisted slightly on the wooden bench to get a glimpse of the one behind but saw nothing out of the ordinary. A hawk circled lazily in the cloudless sky and Mandy wished she could be up there with him for a moment to see if the danger Pete had sensed was real or not. It could be simply a prairie chicken scurrying little ones under her wings for protection. Or something more sinister.

It wasn't the first time Pete had scared her to death with fears about a possible Indian attack. His constant prudence, even to the point of becoming stifling, had ended a perfectly good day teaching a Bible lesson to some Kiowa children in a village not far from the mission a few weeks before. He rode into the camp all in an uproar to inform them a raiding party had burned a farm nearby and demanded she and her father accompany him back to safety immediately. All Mandy's plans were ruined and the children had been disappointed.

She knew they were in Indian Territory, had heard all the horror stories about savages murdering settlers, but it just seemed so far-fetched to consider this kind of evil might touch them in some way. She had reminded Pete they were there in the first place due to a calling from God for ministry to the Indians who lived in the area. And therefore, how could anything that might happen to them lie beyond His control?

However, Pete took his job as foreman seriously. While he didn't disagree with her point he wouldn't allow them to leave the house the rest of the afternoon, where they all hunkered down with shutters drawn and rifles at the ready. Even though they stayed there all that time without anything resembling an Indian attack at the mission, he kept saying it could happen, at any minute. They were safe, all right—safe and sound and bored. Like now...

A sigh escaped from her lips and she wished Pete would quit being such a worrier. Finally, she could hold her silence no longer, though she whispered in case she was wrong.

"Pete, I don't think anything is there except that hawk up in the sky. The sun is hot. Could we please go ahead and get the water we came for so we can leave and get out of this heat?"

After another moment he visibly relaxed a little and said in a more normal voice, "Sorry, Miss Mandy. Just trying to be careful. Never know when them savages could be sneakin' up on you around here."

"Oh, Pete, for heaven's sake! There's not a hostile Indian within miles and miles of us. You worry too much."

"Guess so. But it could be what's kept me alive this long, you know. And now I'm responsible for you, too."

"Please don't start that again, Pete. Remember our conversation the other night? I told you and Jesse that you weren't responsible for me, that we are partners, as it were, and that since I am an adult now I am perfectly capable of making my own decisions and living with the consequences."

He opened his mouth, then clamped his lips shut. Had he been about to argue with her but thought better of it?

"Besides, God hasn't changed my calling to the Indians in this area just because my father is no longer living. I simply have to push forward if I want to accomplish the dream we had for the mission. Nothing happens without effort and sacrifice. It is a small way I can honor his memory, you know? Perhaps I'm not being quite reasonable about this in some ways. I mean, I know it will be hard doing it all by myself. But when you two try to persuade me differently, you fellows really aren't paying attention to what brought me here in the first place, you know."

He glanced at her with an odd look on his face, eyebrows raised, a slight grin playing with the corners of his mouth.

"What, are you surprised that I can be this determined?"

"Yep, I suppose I am, Miss Mandy. You are your father's daughter, aren't you?"

She laughed softly. "Yes, I am, Pete. Both my earthly father's and my Heavenly Father's, in fact. Though my heart is broken that Papa won't be there to share with me in the victory I know is ahead, I also know that he would be proud of me for not giving up and running home to Aunt Ida. I'd never live that down, you know. Oh, my, I could just *never* go back to Ohio now that I've experienced this place. The smells, the sights, the wonder of it all, especially in the dark eyes of those precious children I've been teaching about the Bible. I would miss it terribly, even after only a few months. This is 'home' now, not Ohio."

She hoped her words were more than just that—words. *Please, God, make them real to me in the days to come. Don't let me lose that resolve to carry on Your work here.*

Pete still didn't move a muscle, just watched on every side cautiously. Mandy sighed and leaned back against the seat. Best not to disturb him until he was satisfied they were safe. Mandy felt only a little guilty about what she had said to her friend. She understood why he was being so protective and genuinely appreciated it. But it was still her life and she was not the child everyone seemed to think she was! Getting here had not been easy and neither had the weeks since they arrived. Wasn't that proof enough to others that, although still very young in some ways, she was mature beyond her years in others?

She had to admit she had begged to accompany him on this outing, eager to be away from the mission even for something mundane like collecting water for the week. But he was going too far by spoiling the beautiful spring day with this excessive caution.

Still, her mind briefly flashed back to one horrible day not long past when the soldiers arrived bearing her father's body. Graphic evidence her grand-sounding philosophy was incorrect to some extent, certainly. Where was God when he died? She still wrangled with that question, not to mention what would happen to her now. Once again Mandy fought the persistent nagging voice reminding her she should listen to Pete more and her own heart less. Be more practical and get her head out of the clouds. She shuddered and threw off the memory of that devastating day and turned her attention back to the moment.

Silence tiptoed in the still air around them. Pete remained motionless a few more moments, his face a frozen mask of tension. Finally to the delight of his young charge he urged the team of horses on over to the river's edge so they could get to the task they came for. She pushed all doubts aside as the two began the job of filling the various canteens and pots in addition to the barrel on the back of the wagon, their attention focused on their duties for several minutes.

While Mandy worked, her thoughts drifted back to the day her father announced his imminent return to Indian Territory. She and her Aunt Ida had been chatting about an upcoming church social during dinner when she noticed her father was quieter than usual that evening. Before she could ask him if he felt all right, he cleared his throat and they stopped in mid-sentence to look in his direction.

"I've made a decision and wanted the two of you to know about it."

"What, Papa?"

"I'm going back to Indian Territory to resume the ministry with the Kiowa people your mother and I began before you were born. God apparently isn't through with me there. These years have been good ones here in Trenton with you, Ida, and words cannot express my gratitude to you for helping me rear Amanda. But now He has called me back. And I must go."

"You mean permanently?" Mandy's eyes were wide with excitement.

"Yes, I do, sweets," he replied.

All three of them had begun talking at once, and Mandy smiled, remembering how her father at first strenuously protested the idea of her coming along. But in the end, as he always did when dealing with his little girl, he lost the battle. His sister was furious he would even consider taking her niece away from civilization to that wilderness, but Mandy assured her this had also been her dream ever since she could remember. And now it had become a reality. She couldn't wait!

And come they did, claiming Deuteronomy 31:6 as they went. Mandy had memorized the verse as a child and was now living it: "Be strong and of good courage, fear not nor be afraid of them: for the LORD thy God, he it is that doth go with thee; he will not fail thee, nor forsake thee." It had been quite a whirlwind of an adventure, all crammed into a few short months. First, the long journey west from Ohio; then the rebuilding of the original mission and hiring Pete and Jesse to help run things; and finally befriending the Indians from various tribes who lived nearby. In the same way Josiah and Lily had done years before, Mandy took her mother's place to teach Bible stories to the children while her father talked to the men of each village, to make friends first and later hopefully share Christ. And the two handymen had quickly become like uncles to Mandy and were quite overprotective. Especially since Josiah's death.

15

Mandy winced at that thought and stopped to take a drink of the cool water from the canteen she had just filled. She noticed her companion had been keeping a sharp eye out as he worked while she had allowed her mind to wander a bit. Something triggered an unsettled feeling in the pit of her stomach she couldn't explain yet could not ignore. *I'll certainly be relieved when this is done and we are safely back at the mission.*

Suddenly, a flurry of wings startled them both when a covey of quail rose from the ridge above them. Mandy's eyes were immediately drawn in that direction and her breath caught in her throat. Staring in mute horror at the sight of a lone Indian standing there with his lance raised over his head, she let the canteen in her hand drop with a thud to the ground.

Breathlessly she whispered, "Oh, dear Lord, have mercy on us!"

†CHAPTER TWO†

"What time I am afraid, I will trust in thee."
Psalm 56:3

"Pete!" Mandy tried to scream. Only a hoarse whisper came out. "I see him. Don't—move—a—muscle."

The lone warrior up on the ridge watched the helpless pair below without a sound. Mandy hoped he was alone. Although a relative newcomer to this frontier, she knew better. Time seemed to have stopped. Had her heart ceased to beat, too?

Seconds later shrill war cries sounded from all around them. Pete screamed at her, "Mandy, *run*! Get to the wagon—*now*!"

She whirled on her heels and they both raced for the wagon where the rifle lay on the seat. The instant he reached out to grab hold of it, Mandy heard an odd thump. With a soft groan Pete crumpled to the ground a couple of feet in front of her, an arrow stuck in his chest.

"Pete!" Mandy ran to where he lay in the dust. In her panic she forgot all about the weapon. She heard more war screams and pounding hooves of horses and her blood turned to ice. Several warriors charged down the bank. She only saw Pete's face as she vainly searched it for any sign of life. The shrieks of the savages split the otherwise calm April air. Somewhere in the back of her mind she heard the team of horses whinnying in fear and it crossed her mind that they sounded as afraid as she was. Her tears fell on the weathered face that held her attention and she gently wiped them away.

Although she tried to ignore the din, a furtive glance sideways did reveal bright dashes of red and yellow paint on the legs of the four ponies that circled her. The grip of fear left her breathless and she steeled her eyes on Pete, unwilling to look any higher into the faces of the Indians.

Instead, she held the lifeless body close in spite of the arrow protruding from his chest and wailed, "Don't leave me, Pete! Wake up! Do you hear me?" Gently Mandy cradled him in her arms and tried to will him back to life, rocking to and fro. "Oh, God, help us! Don't let Pete die!"

Her voice broke. Sobs choked her. She squeezed her eyes shut and prayed silently. *Maybe they will leave me alone if I don't look at them or try to defend myself. Father, please make them go away! And if they aren't going to go away, at least let them kill me quickly while my eyes are closed!*

However, the arrow never came. Mandy heard the sound of another horse joining the group and reluctantly opened her eyes and looked up in time to see the lone warrior she had first spotted rein his brown and white pony to a stop next to the others. She trembled at the wild colors splashed across the faces and bodies of all the savages, recognizing war paint though she'd not seen it before. The face of the one continued to hold her stare, her stomach clenched tight and her throat dry with terror.

None of the Indians had dismounted and it appeared the five of them were having a bit of an argument among themselves about something. Mandy could only imagine the reason and at the same time wasn't sure she wanted to know. One of them in particular kept eyeing her with such hatred it made her shiver. He had a fearsome scar that went from his forehead across the bridge of his nose and down his cheek to the chin. Suddenly he dismounted and strode to where Mandy sat on the ground. A second warrior jumped off his horse as well. The scar-faced one grabbed her by the hair and jerked her onto her feet which forced her to release Pete's lifeless form. He pulled her backward a couple of steps and the other one ran to kneel over the body, yanking his knife from the sheath at his side. The young woman's eyes widened in horror as she realized what was about to take place, right in front of her. Clamping her eyes shut, she screamed in protest. "Noooo!"

Too late. Mandy would never forget the ripping sound, not even in her dreams, and it made her stomach lurch. The constant and almost unbearable pain in her head overrode everything else, including her nausea. The one who held her captive was tall enough that no matter how much she tried to stand up straight it didn't ease the pressure on her scalp. He half dragged her by the hair in the direction of his horse which threw her completely off balance and she stumbled repeatedly, struggling to stay on her feet. She feared if the excruciating pain lasted much longer he would pull her hair out by the roots. It seemed to take an eternity to cover such a short distance; even under the circumstances she knew it to be only seconds.

Any moment Mandy expected to suffer the same fate as Pete and she swallowed hard, blinking back tears of both agony and fear. In dismay she watched the warrior kneeling by the body empty Pete's pockets, cut off the belt buckle, and stuff the items into a small pouch tied at his waist.

To take her mind off the immediate danger she tried to focus a moment on the men themselves. Were they Kiowa or perhaps Comanche? Would they listen if she tried to explain she had come to them in peace? But her mind had gone blank, their words gibberish to her ears. They couldn't be Kiowa because she didn't understand a thing they were saying.

Whichever one didn't really matter for Mandy could taste the terror of her dire predicament, regardless. She had heard all the stories out here in the West about raids by roving bands from many tribes, revenge against the whites driving their savagery. Somehow, they had never seemed real to her. Now she had come face to face with them, could not deny any longer that they did happen. She had never felt so helpless in her whole life.

In an effort to ease her suffering Mandy tried to pry Scar-face's fingers out of her hair. With his free hand he slapped hers away. He stopped beside his pony, swiftly drew his knife, and whipped the blade up to her throat. She gasped and bit her lip, trying not to cry and doing her best to remain absolutely still, hardly daring to breathe. If she moved even a fraction of an inch the huge knife might slip and her life would end. Maybe it was all a horrible nightmare and would be over soon. She closed her eyes to shut everything out and make it all go away. Another prick from the knife shattered her pretense, a jarring reminder of its urgent reality. Mandy was convinced with each breath it would be her last. So she silently took the fear to her Father in Heaven.

God, I know You could send a legion of angels or maybe soldiers from the fort to rescue me, I don't care who. If You are going to save me it better happen soon before they decide to kill me—or worse, take me with them. Grant me the courage to accept death with grace if my life cannot be spared. I ask only that it be without further pain or indignity.

A deep sense of calm settled over her while she waited to find out her fate.

With a shrill scream of triumph the warrior rose from Pete's body and leapt onto his horse, holding the bloody scalp high in the air for all to see. And the momentary peace she had felt crumbled as her vision blurred.

It was not a nightmare! And there would be no rescue. The best she could hope for might be a swift death—better than the alternative of being taken captive by these Indians.

The harsh words resumed with a vengeance. Again, one part of Mandy wished that she could understand what they were saying. On the other hand, maybe it was best *not* to know. She had the eerie feeling their disagreement centered on her. The lone warrior kept pointing at her, then gesturing to the ridge behind them. But the other four became more and more incensed at his arguments, especially the one with the knife at Mandy's throat. She gulped hard and tried to avert her eyes from Pete's body, also trying to avoid looking at the one shaking his trophy with every angry word.

Each time she shifted her head back enough to ease the pressure of the blade, Scar-face pressed it harder into the tender flesh. And the angrier her captor became, the more keenly she felt the sharp edge of the steel on her neck. Certainly he had drawn blood by now. There was no real pain at her throat, only in her scalp where her captor cruelly twisted her hair tighter and tighter in his grip. With his face so close to hers she could smell his foul breath with every word, making her feel faint with revulsion and terror.

Oh God, I can't take any more. Get this over with!

⸸ CHAPTER THREE ⸸

"Yet in thy manifold mercies forsookest them not
in the wilderness..."
Nehemiah 9:19

"Lord, I know You can hear me! Help—"

Mandy's words were cut short by a severe jerking of her head by Scar-face. Tears blurred her sight and she blinked them back. The lone Indian continued to shout at Scar-face who never let up the string of harsh words coming out of his mouth. Another warrior joined in and his face contorted in rage and seemed to crack the jagged lines of red and yellow war paint across his cheeks and down his chest when he gestured emphasis with every sound.

Why doesn't he go ahead and shove the blade into my neck? Will it hurt for long? At least the waiting will be over. Bile rose again and she fought to hold it down. He twisted his fingers ever tighter in her hair. She was nearly breathless from the agonizing pain in her scalp.

More shouts. More gestures. Mandy shut them out for a moment but couldn't ignore them for long.

Without warning Scar-face shoved her to the ground, waving the knife in the air. Sharp pain exploded in her shoulder when she landed in a heap at his feet. She cried out and gagged on the grit in her mouth.

The warrior glared down at her and spat. He turned on his heel and in one smooth movement mounted his horse, stopping only once to gesture in the direction of the lone warrior sitting tall on his pony. The one who had mutilated Pete nudged his mount over to the wagon & reached down for the rifle lying there, lifting it on high with a cry of victory. Scar-face never took his eyes off the one with whom he'd been arguing, shrieking one more time at him as the four turned and rode away in a cloud of red dust.

Mandy's pulse throbbed in her head. She was now alone with the one warrior. What would happen to her? With a groan she pushed herself up to a sitting position and eyed her new captor.

The man swung down off his horse, grabbed a rope and strode over to her.

She gulped a deep breath. "What—what are you going to do to me?" One hand shaded her eyes against the bright sunlight and she squinted, trying to read the expression on his painted face. "Please, let me go!"

Without a word he pulled Mandy up by one arm and tied her wrists together. He yanked it tight and she winced as the rawhide cut into her flesh.

Her shoulder ached and she wanted to rub it. With her wrists bound she could do little except move the muscles around and twist her head a bit.

The warrior growled at her and yanked hard on the rope and she stumbled and almost fell. Mandy glared at him in disbelief. Did he think she had tried to pull loose? She watched while he walked back to his horse, remounted, and prodded the pony into a brisk walk.

Mandy blinked, unsure what was about to happen. Then the rope jerked taut, throwing her to the ground.

"Wait!" she cried while being dragged several feet. Spitting dust out of her mouth she pleaded, "Stop!"

Couldn't he hear? Why did he keep going? At first she just lay there limp and let him pull her along. Surely he would slow down in a moment so she could get back on her feet. Her chin stung from bouncing along the ground when she fell and she knew she wouldn't last long being subjected to this brutal treatment. Then she saw a large cactus plant clinging to the slope right in front of her. She must regain her footing and now!

Mandy managed to roll to one side at the last instant, and coming to the top of the ridge somehow she was able to scramble to her feet. Good thing. Much more bumping along the ground and she would be black and blue all over. Pain shot out through her entire body. Muscles she hadn't known were there screamed in protest. She tasted blood and her elbows burned from scraping across the ground even that short distance. Helpless to ease any of her suffering, she focused on putting one foot in front of the other to keep going.

Stay on your feet, Mandy. Nothing else matters. You can't fall again! The words echoed repeatedly through her brain as the minutes stretched on and on with no end in sight. At least a breeze had picked up, providing a minimum of relief from the heat, then swiftly turned into strong gusts.

In spite of her resolve, though, she discovered it to be tougher than she had imagined and soon her fury spilled over.

"Stop, you brute savage!" Her pleas seemed to fall on deaf ears. "I should have grabbed the rifle when you killed Pete and used it on you and your friends. At least I'd be dead right now instead of being tortured like this! And I would have had the pleasure of knowing I took some of you with me." Still nothing. Her throat rasped from the screams yet produced no reaction whatsoever. Unbelievable! Could he hear her with all the wind? What if he couldn't understand English? What else could she do? Or did he fully comprehend every word and simply chose to ignore her?

Reluctantly, Mandy had to admit once again her focus must be on survival, not on her outrage at how she was being treated. Without knowing how long this might go on yet fully aware she needed every ounce of strength simply to stay on her feet, she managed to swallow her anger for the moment in order to preserve her dwindling supply of energy. Sidestepping a large boulder in her path, she kept her eyes on the few feet in front of her to avoid other obstacles. *After all, what did*

I expect to happen to me as the captive of an Indian?

Topping the next ridge, Mandy gasped at the view. All she could see in any direction were waist-high grasses moving in the breeze, much like the ocean waves she'd seen in pictures in books. Her tattered dress suffered numerous tears whenever she stumbled over rocks obscured from view in the dense vegetation. With each step a new dread mounted. Shivering in spite of the heat from the sun overhead, she felt her mouth grow even drier.

Oh, God, please help me! What if there is a rattlesnake hiding in the tall prairie grass? You know how petrified I am of being bitten. And the Indian wouldn't even know if it happened. I guess he would continue to drag my lifeless body along behind his pony and never know the difference! The fear compounded each moment until it became almost unbearable.

Tears stung her eyes and she numbly plodded on in response to the tugging on her wrists. Everything from wild desperation to calm acceptance and all in between jumbled through her brain. She couldn't feel her fingers any longer. Would this never end? *Are You listening to me?*

Suddenly they descended into a gully which had been hidden from sight and changed direction slightly as they came back up and somehow the taller grasses disappeared. The plateau area they were now on was covered with sparse grass only a few inches deep. With a sigh of relief, she realized she would be able to spot rocks and snakes alike much more easily here than before. She could feel the tension drain markedly when her terror eased. Taking a deep breath, she prayed again.

"Heavenly Father, thank You for hearing me in my panic. I'm sorry I'm not reacting in a way honoring of You, because of my fear. I ask for peace in my heart rather than turmoil. You have promised I can do all things through You, and I know You are the One who gives me strength to face this ordeal. I am aware You are with me and I know

You care. Give me courage with every step I take."

The hot sun bore down on Mandy's arms and face and she longed for the sunbonnet so carelessly left behind on her bed that morning. Pete had reminded her she might need it but she had brushed his caution aside, relishing the warm sun when they set out.

Oh, Pete! The memory of his last moments was too much to endure and she gulped hard at the burning sensation in her throat.

Long black tresses swirled around her face making it difficult at times to watch where she stepped. The bow tied at the nape of her neck had been lost somewhere along the way and she hadn't realized it until now.

"Probably happened when that horrible scar-faced brute grabbed me by the hair," she muttered half under her breath.

Once more thoughts of happier times flashed through her mind. Mandy recalled how her father had always loved it when she wore the blue calico dress with the matching ribbon, whether as a band close to her face or tied back in a bow. Grief tore at her heart in considering the fact his death had come at the hands of the very people for whom he came to this place to share the love of Christ. And again tears dimmed her sight.

Because her hands were drawn out so far in front of her, Mandy couldn't reach her face to wipe the tears much less prevent hair from sticking in her mouth and eyes. Completely at the whim of the hot prairie winds, her dark strands whipped back and forth mercilessly.

With the combination of heat and exhaustion, Mandy was quickly reaching what she believed to be her limit of endurance. Would lunch time never come? Surely the savage would have to stop and rest at some point, if not for himself then certainly for his pony. Several times she felt she couldn't go another step. At those moments God's strength seemed to surge in her and in spite of her fatigue she found the ability to continue a little longer.

Overriding all her determination to continue was the human drive to satisfy her thirst. Mandy knew if she didn't get something to drink very soon, she would collapse. Ironically the day had begun with a trip to the river for water. How she wished for one sip from the canteen she dropped in her panic!

She glanced up at the sky. "You know, Lord, some rain would help. Maybe a few clouds at least to shield me from the sun, if not the hope of showers?"

However, the deep blue color overhead contradicted her prayer, offering no promise of relief. And the anger surged until she couldn't contain it any longer, regardless of what she told herself.

"Hey, you! Listen to me!" she croaked from between cracked lips. "I've got to have something to drink!" No response. The warrior started down into another small gulley when she called out to him and coming back up the ridge the rope had some slack in it, just enough for her to try to get his attention. Mandy summoned up the strength to yank as hard as possible on both wrists, ignoring the sharp pain it caused. Startling both of them, the rope fell loose from her captor's hand.

"Oh!" she cried out. "I'm free!"

✝CHAPTER FOUR✝

"The eternal God is thy refuge and underneath
are the everlasting arms..."
Deuteronomy 33:27

I can't believe I'm free! Mandy whirled around and ran as fast as she could back the way they came. She stumbled a time or two over her skirts but there wasn't time to attempt to gather them up between her bound hands. Pushing her legs mercilessly she jumped over rocks, sidestepped cactus quills, and scrambled up one small rise in her effort to get away from her captor.

Could she elude him long enough he might give up the chase? No hiding places in sight. If only she had the tall grasses again. Her breaths became more ragged by the second. Maybe, just maybe...

The thought of escape fueled her frantic pace and her hopes soared briefly. All too soon, however, Mandy heard the thudding of horse's hooves in back of her and glanced over her shoulder without breaking stride. In horror she saw the warrior had hopped off his pony, sprinting only a few steps behind now. She gave it all she had in one last burst of energy, in the vain hope it would be enough.

Mandy never heard a single footstep, only the gentle swishing of the grasses. Suddenly he knocked her down with the full weight of his body hitting hers and she cried out as the air was forced out of her lungs.

The two rolled together several times, Mandy flailing her arms and legs in every direction at once, trying desperately to hit him over and over. She managed to land several solid blows in spite of being bound.

"Let go of me!" she hollered again and again, until, breathless, she could no longer speak.

It was all to no avail. Within moments, he had easily overpowered her and had thrown a leg over her body, sitting on top of her before she could stop him. He pinned both arms over her head with one hand and with the free one slapped her hard across the mouth, grunting something from between clenched teeth. Her head reeled from the blow and she squinted against the bright sunlight that pierced her eyes and intensified the spinning motion, causing her to close them briefly. A few seconds later Mandy opened her eyes and glared at him with all the hatred she could muster.

"Why don't you go ahead and kill me and get it over with? Anything is better than this torture!"

He raised his hand as though to hit her again but oddly, stopped in midair. Abruptly he jumped up and dragged her to her feet by one arm, then turned and walked away toward his horse. She gagged from the dust on her tongue and hastily pushed her hair back out of her face, knowing she didn't have much time to catch her breath before they resumed their trek. At least she was standing and this time knew to brace herself when the rope jerked tight against her wrists.

However, Mandy had used whatever reserve of energy she had before the failed escape and now found herself in worse shape physically. Twinges shrieked at her from all over her body because of the hard fall, especially that troublesome shoulder she'd injured earlier. Her lips were bleeding again and at least it provided a tiny bit of moisture for her mouth. The taste of it, though, made her stomach churn and she swallowed hard to fight back her growing nausea.

In the end, the warrior had gotten what he wanted: a compliant captive. Numbly she put one foot in front of the other as she followed him without being able to form a cohesive thought for quite a while. There would be no further escape attempts. For now.

Eventually, though, she began to pray again. *God, I truly don't think I can last any longer without something to drink. Couldn't you prevail upon this savage to—*

Her thoughts were interrupted when the warrior came to an abrupt halt. They were at the foot of a rather steep hill and the very sight of it made her weary muscles ache. Rather than heading up as she expected her captor to do, he dismounted and pulled her toward him with the rope until she was a few feet away from him. *What on earth—*

Suddenly he jerked on the rope, forcing her down to the ground where she fell in an exhausted heap. Grateful for the respite, Mandy laid down flat to rest the pounding in her head. The combination of heat and fatigue had taken its toll on her and her vision blurred. She paid little attention to the warrior, desperately wanting to give in to her heavy eyelids demanding sleep. Through flickering eyelashes, she vaguely noted the man slowly creeping up the hill on his belly.

In that instant, she smelled smoke. Her eyes popped open. A campfire! People! She was saved!

In spite of Mandy's exhaustion, the thought of rescue called too strongly to simply lie there and do nothing. Whoever had built the fire would surely take pity on her and exact revenge on her captor. And then she could go back home! She gritted her teeth, took a deep breath, and began to inch up the hillside behind the warrior. Although she attempted to imitate his cautious movements, she yearned to run up there yelling for help the whole way.

Before she had gone even half way Mandy already regretted her decision not to take advantage of the time to rest. Crawling through the grass like a snake was harder than it appeared to be and she wondered how Indians managed with all their bare skin. Her raw elbows scraped along the ground and she kept stirring up enough dust to choke a horse. *My dress is a disaster but it will be worth it when I see those white people in a few seconds. And then this savage will be sorry he tangled with me!*

Mandy finally reached the top of the ridge and lay motionless beside her captor. They were well hidden in the grass yet had a full view of the meadow below. Several figures were huddled around a campfire. Her heart fell. Even from this distance, their copper skin could be readily distinguished. *Why isn't he eagerly riding toward these Indians instead of hiding here? I don't understand.*

He rolled to face her and Mandy looked intently into his dark eyes for the first time. The thought flitted through her mind that he was actually rather handsome, in a rugged sort of way, quickly regretting the observation when the ropes on her wrists abruptly brought her back to the moment.

"Comanch," he growled with a frown. Apparently then, as she had suspected, this man must be Kiowa and therefore had no desire to confront a band of Comanche warriors while dragging a white captive behind him. Cold chills crawled up her sunburned arms and she shuddered. Somehow, she sensed she was better off with him than with the ones below them.

The two quickly slithered back down the hill the way they'd come up, to where the pony grazed nonchalantly in the hot sun. To her shock, Mandy realized the warrior had not been holding onto her rope the whole time. She'd been free and could have taken advantage of his preoccupation to get away.

Where on earth would she go? Like her father used to say, from the frying pan into the fire? With a strange sense of resignation, she resumed her position at the end of the rope when they began the roundabout route away from the area where the Comanches were camped. She sighed with relief that at least her captor had protected her from more danger. However, she knew it to be a hollow victory because the stories about Kiowa treachery were as common and terrifying as those about the Comanches.

I know you protected me from those savages, Lord, I feel it deep in my soul in a way I cannot explain. But why?

How could God allow one tragedy to overwhelm her and then turn around and save her from another one? Might her captor be a coward and that's why he avoided a confrontation with the Comanches? It was all more than her fatigued mind could possibly comprehend, so she shoved it away into a corner to focus once more on each step ahead of her to...where were they were headed? In truth, it didn't really matter. Nothing mattered to her except the all-consuming drive to satisfy her thirst. Mandy obediently followed the Kiowa who now controlled her every move with little resistance from her.

Once they safely eluded the Comanches, the warrior picked up the pace considerably. Each torturous step increased her suffering many times over. Inside she wailed but had no tears left to shed. From the position of the sun, Mandy was certain it had to be late in the afternoon. Rivulets of sweat traced a path down the middle of her back, bathed her face, and tickled the end of her nose as it dripped. Her eyes stung so badly she couldn't focus them properly. *If only I could reach my face to wipe it!*

Amazed the warrior could go this far without water or rest, it struck her she had done so, too. *Of course, he got to ride while I have walked every step—or been dragged, I should say. I have no idea how on earth I managed to have enough strength to keep going. It has to have come from You, Father, and You alone.*

They topped yet another ridge in the endless prairie and Mandy saw below them what at first she believed to be an illusion: a stream with trees nearby. No, this was real! The warrior urged his pony down the hill and Mandy had to run to keep up. The glistening waters ahead pulled her along with no care given to aching muscles. She licked her lips in anticipation and knew she had to stay on her feet no matter what. Relief was in sight!

Just as she got within a few feet of the bank of the stream, however, her captor suddenly yanked on the rope and stopped her short of what she so craved. She fell to her knees and cried out in pain and frustration, tugging on the rope with all her might, to no avail.

"No! Tell me this can't be happening! Don't you have any mercy at all?"

⨾CHAPTER FIVE⨾

"And they that know thy name will put their trust in thee:
for thou, LORD, hast not forsaken them that seek thee."
Psalm 9:10

"You can't do this to me!" Mandy lay helplessly where she'd fallen, her body wracked by dry sobs.

The Kiowa calmly tied the rope to a nearby tree without giving her a single glance. Then he turned his back on her and led his horse down into the water. She vaguely watched him scrub the war paint off his horse's body and then off his own. Mandy turned her head away when she could no longer bear the sight of him enjoying what she so craved and desperately needed to survive.

It was a few minutes before she realized shade from the trees overhead sheltered her from the sun's worst heat. She took small comfort in its relief and from the cool grass beneath her as she again watched her captor leisurely drinking and reveling in the refreshing water. And Mandy knew in those moments she would not be able to take another step unless first allowed to do the same. In despair, she closed her eyes to shut out the sight of him enjoying what she could not have. At some point, she drifted off to sleep, only to be rudely awakened a few minutes later when the warrior jerked her rope and suddenly dragged her into the water.

Mandy felt as though she had died and gone to Heaven! She drank greedily, not sure how long she would be permitted to stay there nor how long before she was given any more water. Vaguely she noticed the warrior filling a water skin of some sort and figured it would probably be a long wait for another rest stop.

Dipping down under the surface, she relished the sensation of the layers of red dust washing out of her hair and off her skin and clothing. She shook her head vigorously over and over when she returned to the surface, then repeated the process several more times. To her great relief she was able to smooth her hair back somewhat out of her face. If only she had the ribbon.

Sitting waist deep in the cool water she became entranced at how the rays of sunlight twinkled across the surface like dew drops on a spider's web. *Maybe I could just slip underwater and swim away!* As quickly as the thought formed, though, it dissolved when she saw out of the corner of her eye that her captor watched every move she made from the bank where he stood, rope in hand. She deliberately turned her head away and took another long drink in spite of the fact the stream had muddied with her movements in it. All too soon, the familiar pull on her wrists signaled her time of refreshment had ended and she rose to her feet.

Coming up out of the water, she saw the Kiowa eying her with a smirk on his lips. She glanced down and realized with her dress soaking wet it revealed every curve of her body! Horrified but helpless to cover herself up in any way, she averted her eyes and refused to look at him while he led her back to the stand of trees. She felt the hot burn on her cheeks and wished fervently she could prevent him from seeing the embarrassment she felt inside. There was nothing she could do except deliberately avoid his stare.

Surprisingly, her captor gave her a few more minutes to rest in the shade. He squatted down a short distance away with the rope securely in his hands and took something out of a bag at his waist, chomping on it while his pony grazed nearby. He did not offer her anything to eat. Nor did he take his eyes off his prisoner.

Mandy tried to ignore the warrior by curling up into a ball hopefully to prevent him from seeing more than he had a right to see.

Finally, she rolled over so she didn't have to look at him anymore. *Let him stare at my back and see how much pleasure he gets out of that!* In spite of the emptiness in her stomach, Mandy's body demanded sleep more than food. Resting on the cool grass she again drifted off to sleep momentarily, all too soon awakened by the rope tugging at her hands once more.

Mandy scrambled to get to her feet before the slack in the rope was entirely gone and glanced back at the stream with longing in her heart. How she wished she could have just one more drink before they continued the arduous trek!

The refreshment of being able to slake her thirst somewhat and have the opportunity to wash off the dust in the stream in addition to a short rest had energized Mandy to some extent. However, it also presented a new problem. The ropes cut into her wrists with a new ferocity as the sun dried the rawhide. In addition to everything else, the extra weight from her wet dress slapped against her legs with every step and weighed her down even more. She knew it would soon dry out in this heat. Unfortunately, that didn't help right now.

Father, I may be more miserable now in some ways but I know my strength has all come from You. And I am deeply grateful for Your mercy. Along with her prayer of thanksgiving, Mandy tried to recall some Bible verses to give additional encouragement and keep her from focusing on the anger she felt toward her captor. Nothing. Not one word. What happened? Stunned, she felt as though all the years of memorizing Scripture had never taken place. When she needed it the most, she was unable to access the greatest resource she owned: her knowledge of the Bible.

"God in Heaven," she cried, "please help me! I need to hear from You, to help me endure this awful nightmare. Without it, I know I won't survive!"

Almost immediately, a flood of words came back to her and she began feeding on those precious verses during the long afternoon ahead. With each step, she found renewed strength for the next one. And fresh hope she hadn't been forgotten.

Sometime later, while preoccupied with a passage from the Psalms, Mandy suddenly felt one of her feet squish into something soft and, at the same moment, her nose confirmed what happened. She apparently had stepped into a cow patty. And a fresh one, at that. Cows meant white people were somewhere close by! Excited she twisted every which way, hoping to see signs of civilization her captor had missed, to no avail.

Disappointment swept over her. Slowly the realization dawned—the patty was too large for an ordinary cow. Instead, it must have been from a buffalo. And now she saw there were many such patties everywhere and concluded they must be on a buffalo trail of some kind. She'd heard the Indians sometimes followed these to find the herds when on a hunt. Her hopes of rescue once more evaporated.

She pulled her thoughts back to avoid another misstep and also tried to brush her shoe off a bit in the grass while walking. It didn't work very well, however, since keeping up with the steady pace set by her captor didn't allow her the luxury. After a short distance, she gave up the futile effort and tried vainly to ignore the stench coming from the direction of her feet.

Suddenly something startled Mandy by running right in front of her and she stumbled but quickly regained her footing. The creature sat up and looked at her from a short distance away and emitted a sharp barking sound accompanied by a bobbing motion she would have found humorous under other circumstances.

"It's a prairie dog! In fact, there are several of them." All at once, they were everywhere, about ten or so of them, and for the first time she noticed the small mounds of dirt piled up here and there. Each one she knew indicated an entrance to their underground burrows. Pete had explained to her about these animals when she spotted them all around the mission while unloading the wagons to move in.

With a hint of a smile on her cracked lips, Mandy recalled often watching them bravely dart in and out of their holes, yipping in excitement and daring the people who had invaded their territory to come any closer. Could that really have been only a few weeks ago? Seemed more like a lifetime.

The tiny brown bodies dotted the area. Most gazed warily at the pair disrupting their lazy afternoon while others in obvious alarm plunged headfirst into the ground as quickly as they had appeared. *Wish I could disappear like they are! Wouldn't it be funny if the Kiowa found himself without a captive when he arrived at wherever he is going?*

Somehow, the sight brought comfort, a reminder life continues here on the prairie in spite of anything that might threaten to interrupt the routine. In the midst of the most abnormal event in Mandy's life, for a brief time she had been a part of something completely normal.

Within minutes, the prairie dogs were gone, she assumed deep into the earth in their burrows. Too bad they didn't follow along behind her because she would have enjoyed the company of the cute little animals. *What amusing creatures they are. In spite of everything they are kind of fun to watch, even if only for a moment or two. I just need to be careful not to step into one of their holes, else I could break an ankle easily. And I'm certain that savage dragging me along wouldn't hear me scream for help.* Her dark mood returned.

"The sun doesn't seem quite so unbearable now," she remarked to herself a short time later. "Oh, joy. Now I'm talking to myself again. I think the heat has addled my brain for sure."

Instantly the reason for her observation about the sun hit her and she gasped. Sundown. Nighttime was coming fast, and with it the certain threat of assault by her captor! Fear tingled from the roots of her hair down to her toes and it threatened to strangle her. *What am I going to do? What's going to happen to me when we stop for the night?*

From deep within, a chilling calm took hold that formed the resolve in Mandy's heart. "I will never let that man touch a hair on my head as long as I breathe! The thought is more than I can bear to consider. I swear before You, Almighty God, I will kill him before I allow him near me. Or slit my own throat. But I will never, *ever*, submit to a physical assault by him or any other heathen savage! You have to protect me—somehow!"

╀ CHAPTER SIX ╀

"Thou shalt not be afraid for the terror by night;
nor for the arrow that flieth by day."
Psalm 91:5

I *really do mean what I said, Father. You simply have to give me the*
strength to face what I know is coming.

Topping a ridge some minutes later, Mandy spotted a small lake below them. Water! Finally, rest!

"What am I thinking?" Her lip trembled and she knew the weakness in her knees had nothing whatsoever to do with her fatigue. Sheer terror enveloped her, mixed with a powerful dread that grew by the second. Nighttime loomed like a giant monster hovering overhead and threatening to devour her.

In spite of this, the promise of an end to her thirst and sleep before long provided strong medicine to Mandy's mind and body alike, enabling her to stay on her feet to their destination. She pushed the panic down deep and tried to dismiss it. First things, first. One step at a time. Literally. No sense borrowing trouble before it erupts...maybe nothing would come of the long hours ahead.

Mandy didn't have to wait long to find out her captor's plans. Arriving on the banks of the lake, the process from earlier in the day was repeated. Mandy had to wait her turn for a drink, hobbled under a nearby stand of trees like an animal, until the warrior and his horse were both finished. Finally, her turn came to refresh herself in the cooling waters and she relished every single moment. Once the Kiowa decided she had been in there long enough, he dragged her back onto dry ground and tied the rope onto a tree branch.

"Don't you dare touch me!" Her helpless situation didn't deter her one whit from protesting at the top of her lungs. "I know what you are thinking; I can read it in your eyes. And don't you dare come near me. I'll kill you if you do!"

When he reached out to grab one of her feet, Mandy became hysterical. She kicked at him with all her might, twisted to get away from his grasp, and frantically pummeled his head and arms with her fists. The ropes restricted her effectiveness, though. With his superior strength, he easily overpowered her. Ignoring her shrieks, he managed to take hold of both feet at the same time. In one smooth motion, he wrapped a second rope several times around her ankles, knotted it, then quickly secured it to the tree trunk.

As he did so, she stopped resisting and watched in shock when the warrior calmly walked away. All he'd done was tie her up for the night so she couldn't escape.

Mandy felt a little sheepish over the fury of her reaction. The warrior had left her a little slack in both ropes, though not much, and after tugging on them for a few moments, she gave up and surrendered to great gasping sobs, in part due to her exhaustion and in part due to her fear. When would he return to finish what he started?

Oddly, however, without a glance in her direction the Kiowa squatted down and began piling up twigs and small branches to start a fire. She could hear him speak softly to his horse, grazing nearby, and the gentle whinny in response. A brutal warrior yet tender with his pony?

Little by little, the sun sank toward the horizon and then slipped out of sight. Still sniffling, Mandy noticed the streaks of the sunset splashed across the sky in brilliant red, orange, and purple. But it was impossible to enjoy the beauty of God's majesty displayed above her when totally focused on every movement of her captor. Like a trapped animal, she kept her eyes on him constantly.

Eventually the fatigue took over and she finally stopped crying. She felt her entire body begin to relax, her neck and shoulders and legs all reacting to the rest they were now experiencing after the long and difficult day. Sleep sounded more and more attractive in order to forget the nightmare she now inhabited, a good thing since there were few other options. If only she could feel confident in her safety if she closed her eyes! Mandy studied the flames of the small campfire and soon became mesmerized by the intoxicating sight. Her eyelids drooped lower and lower.

Suddenly her captor rose and walked toward her. Instantly she was awake with every nerve on alert. Although she could do little to protect herself, given her predicament, by instinct she tried to draw herself into a ball, to give her legs room to maneuver some strong kicks at her attacker, should it be necessary. May not be much help but what else could she do? Her muscles tensed and she prayed. *God, help me!*

The Kiowa towered over her for a moment while Mandy's heart pounded. Then he extended something toward her mouth and nodded, offering her some type of food. Feeling very foolish, she opened her mouth eagerly. After the first bite, she uncoiled just a bit and reached out to take the rest of it from his hand. Tearing another chunk off with her teeth, she decided it must be a jerky of some kind, with a strong yet tasty flavor. What had he given her? At that moment, she didn't care. While it didn't begin to fill her stomach, at least she felt a little less empty. Without some type of nourishment, she could not make it through another day of walking so being choosy right now would not be wise.

The Kiowa nodded at her again, apparently satisfied she had eaten, and patted his chest.

"Ken-ai-te," he said very slowly.

"Your name is Ken-ai-te?" she asked, her tongue stumbling over the unfamiliar syllables.

He nodded in response. When she said nothing more, he pointed at her.

"My name?"

Again, the silent nod.

"My name is Mandy."

"Man-dee." He seemed to savor the sound and even smiled at her. She carefully chewed the last bite of her so-called dinner, determined not to return the kind gesture because there was no way she would ever *smile* at the savage. In fact, she fixed a scowl on her face designed to chase away all who saw it.

This is crazy! I'm having a civilized conversation with the man who has been torturing me all day and now is about to rape me! Why am I even talking to him?

He grunted and turned away. Staring at his back, she swallowed the jerky and wondered if she dared to ask for a drink.

"Thank you," she called to him as he stretched out on the blanket he had laid out on the other side of the campfire. He gazed at her and nodded in acknowledgement. *So you do understand some English. Wonder how much more you know.*

Mandy took a deep breath for courage. "Would it be possible for me to have a drink of water? The jerky made me thirsty."

He stared at her blankly for a moment. It hit her then she had invited him to come back to her side of the camp. She averted her eyes and half hoped he wouldn't get up. Again, she didn't really care what he thought. Her survival was at stake and, so far, he really hadn't been all that violent with her, except when she tried to escape. And even then he didn't beat her, only slapped her once. With his strength, she knew he could have done much more, had he chosen to do so. Now there was this bizarre exchanging of names thing. She puzzled over his kindness in some ways and his indifference or brutality in most and in so doing failed to notice when he rose and circled the crackling fire. In the space of one breath of inattention, he stood before her. Mandy gasped in fear and drew back a few inches instinctively. When she spotted the water skin in his hand, however, relief flooded her entire body.

While she gulped the precious water, Mandy became aware of his intense stare. Her dress had ripped on one shoulder and after returning the bag to him, she tried to pull the torn area up some to reveal a little less skin.

"Thank you, again. Your kindness is appreciated. But hopefully you can also understand me when I say," enunciating each word carefully, "*please—let—me—go. The soldiers will come and hunt you down if you don't and I promise they will hang you when they catch you."

His frown told her he'd understood enough at least. He glared at her for a long silent moment and she rolled over with her back to him, lying motionless in protest of his obvious rejection of her pleas and threat as she silently petitioned God. *Please make him go away!*

Hearing nothing for several moments, Mandy finally dared to glance over her shoulder and saw he had returned to his blanket and sat there cross-legged staring into the flames. She shuddered. It unnerved her he could silently move around the camp without her being able to hear a thing. He caught her eye and she turned away abruptly, her cheeks blazing. *The last thing I need is him thinking I'm watching him!*

On every side in the dark around them wolves howled at the moon and Mandy shivered at the mournful yips as each echo died out, to be replaced by several more and repeated again and again. She was grateful for the safety of the fire close by. *Could have used some of this cool air earlier today. Wish I could store up some of it for tomorrow, too. Oh, God, please give me strength to endure what is ahead.*

Another yowl sounded in the distance and the horse reared his head on alert, stamping his feet nervously. Would the wolves attack in spite of the campfire? If they did, she would be completely helpless to defend herself against them. Could the Kiowa protect her from them and the other wild animals prowling around out there on the prairie? How she longed to embrace the black nothingness of sleep, shut it all out and pretend today had never happened!

Apparently, God wasn't ready for the day to end, though, much as Mandy's body demanded the rest. He had one more gift to offer before she closed her eyes. Tiny dots of light glittered through the canopy of leaves above her and they captivated her with their beauty. She couldn't help getting caught up in admiring the night sky overhead and to her surprise the tension slowly drained away.

Amazing to recall Your Word says You know how many stars are out there and call each of them by name! You are truly awesome, Father. And off to the east, the half-moon shone brightly. Indeed, a perfect late spring night, with just a touch of a chill in the air. Fortunately, there wasn't a breeze or she might have been cold, especially with her clothing still damp, an irony not lost on her in spite of the fatigue and anxiety.

Softly, so the Kiowa couldn't hear her, Mandy began praising God aloud for His incredible handiwork. "Those twinkling lights are a powerful reminder You are watching over me tonight. I'm so grateful You care that I'm frightened and alone and facing a terrible future. At least I know You are there because You have shared your stars with me this night, and I can sleep in peace in spite of my fears."

✝CHAPTER SEVEN✝

*"The eyes of the LORD are upon the righteous,
and his ears are open unto their cry."*
Psalm 34:15

Why won't you leave me alone so I can sleep? I don't want to get up yet, Aunt Ida.

A gentle tug quickly turned into a harsh jerk and she sat upright. It was morning, but she most definitely was not in her bed back in Ohio!

Mandy shook her head in disbelief. This nightmare was real and she was living it. She thought she would be sick for a moment as reality returned and she tried to shake off the effects of sleeping on the hard ground without even a blanket against the cold. Mandy's captor had already untied her feet. How had he managed to do so without her feeling a thing?

Before her head had completely cleared, the Kiowa offered her some more of the jerky and water and gestured for her to hurry. After gulping down the few bites and drinking greedily from the water skin, she managed to get on her feet while he took the rope and mounted his horse. And they moved out of the makeshift camp toward—what? His village somewhere out there in the vast wilderness? Perhaps she had not experienced the worst yet.

Setting out across the prairie that morning, Mandy focused her heart on praise for the beauty of the day and tried not to think any further than her next steps.

"Thank You, Father, for protecting me last night. I still can't believe that savage didn't attack me. I know You prevented him from doing so. As You say in Psalm 41, I know You have blessed with Your favor because my enemy did not triumph over me. You have upheld my integrity and set me before Your face this beautiful morning. Glorious are You, my Lord forever! I am also deeply grateful for the food, water, and night's rest and I thank You for this mercy. Now please go before me and grant courage and strength for the day to come."

Before the sun rose fully into the sky, Mandy began experiencing something that hadn't bothered her much the day before—mosquitoes and flies buzzed everywhere around her head and body. She was helpless to fend them off and soon felt a number of bites on her exposed arms and neck. It didn't take long for the heat to begin to drain her energy and she yearned for a time to rest.

"If yesterday is any example, I doubt if you stop for lunch again. You aren't even human, being able to go without food or water for hours on end!" On the other hand, she had to admit having observed him hopping off his pony several times the day before, presumably to allow the horse to walk without a rider for a bit, and saw him offering water to his mount at those times. So perhaps he had endured at least some of the same grueling experience she had. Of course, he never walked for long. Regardless, it didn't seem fair to expect her to go through it. And now for a second day, too. Mandy knew her words were probably lost on the warrior but that didn't stop her.

"Who cares if you can't understand what I'm saying? You know, I'm used to men being courteous to women, not treating them like dogs!" she growled at the Kiowa's back.

Mandy chided herself for losing her concentration on where she was going as she stumbled over a hole and slightly twisted her ankle. The satisfaction of giving in to the temptation to rail against her treatment wasn't worth the price if she injured herself in the process. Better to shut up and remain quiet, keeping her eyes on the ground in front of her.

Her shoulders cramped already from the effort of extending her arms out in front of her far enough to prevent the rawhide from cutting further into her wrists. In addition, the rope burns from the previous day screamed at her every time her bonds jerked at her hands. No matter how she adjusted her steps, it wasn't possible to relieve the tension enough to ease the pain. Her situation seemed more hopeless by the minute.

The terrain had changed again, and now they were on a flat plain of some kind. There were fewer gullies and no hills in sight. She assumed it would be a little easier to travel across, not like yesterday. But she was wrong. The grass had thinned out some, revealing many rocks of all sizes and quite a few large prickly pear cactus plants in her path. This made staying on her feet while avoiding these obstacles much more difficult. Mandy continued to focus on the few feet in front of her and she paid little attention to anything else for most of the morning.

Except for one majestic sight, that is. They had come back up from another one of the countless hidden gullies when her captor came to an abrupt halt on top of a rise overlooking a broad valley. Suddenly she could *feel* even as she *saw* an enormous herd of buffalo in the distance below them, the ground shaking from their hooves pounding the dirt in a thunderous roar. They ran almost like a wave of the sea, first one way and then another and back again, giving the appearance someone had sent them a signal to change directions each time, in eerie precision. Truly breathtaking! Mandy was grateful they were not up close to the huge beasts. Pete had told her one time about the danger when they stampeded and the damage that could cause, and she had no desire to experience it for herself.

The Kiowa stopped to admire them for a moment, granting a short break in the arduous pace. Mandy collapsed on the ground when he dismounted and watched him begin to chant softly. Then he raised his arms over his head and seemed to be oblivious to everything else around him. He arched his back with his face to the sky and it startled Mandy to see his eyes were closed. He appeared to be *worshipping* these magnificent animals! She held her breath, not wanting to disturb him and mar the unusual moment. In spite of herself, she had to admit the scene awed her—a true marvel of prairie life, of both man and beast. As the last one disappeared over the horizon, leaving behind clouds of red dust swirling where they'd been only seconds before, the world somehow seemed an emptier place than before. The magical moment gone, her captor remounted and rode away.

Mandy moaned and scrambled to her feet. Here we go again. *The breather was nice while it lasted. You know, you ought to be worshipping the Creator of those buffalo, not the animals themselves. God, please show him that truth somehow.*

She caught her breath and stumbled a couple of steps. *I can't believe I just prayed for him—the one who is responsible for all my suffering!* Mandy didn't like the uncomfortable feeling that had suddenly sprung up. How could she pray for someone who subjected her to such torture? This was not the time or place to consider such deep thoughts so she pushed it all aside as her captor suddenly sped up a little.

"Hey, slow down, will you? You're plain crazy to expect me to keep going at this pace!"

Without warning, something pierced her heart like a bolt of lightning, stabbing her as surely as if the Kiowa had thrust his lance deep into her body. She had spent last night with an Indian! Mortified, she let the hideous thought seep into the very marrow of her bones. Her terror was so real she could taste it, the gritty twang causing her tongue to stick to the roof of her mouth and the nausea to rise in her throat. Tears trailed down her face in spite of her extreme thirst, evidence of the distraught emotions twisting in her mind.

"How on earth will any white man ever want me now?" she wailed. "No matter what I say about the circumstances, the truth is that

I camped last night with this Kiowa. Who is going to believe he didn't assault me?" She had heard the tales, even back East, about what Indians do to white women they capture. Her aunt and father shielded her from most of the details but she still managed to hear some of them and could imagine the rest.

Mandy also remembered those she'd heard about who had been kidnapped by Indians and later were released. For the most part, they were painfully ostracized by white society, living miserable lives because of having been with the savages. Jesse had told her not long before her father died about a family whose daughter was returned to them after several months with the Comanche. She had gone out of her mind from her ordeal, however, and just couldn't adjust, finally shooting herself to death. *Will that be my fate, too? Or worse?*

Mandy's mind went numb and even when she whacked her shin on a large rock in the path the discomfort hardly registered. Silently she continued to put one foot in front of the other without taking note of the obstacles or direction she walked. In truth, she wanted God to ease the anguish and fear threatening to strangle her, to feel His peace once more. But for some reason she felt completely incapable of reaching out to Him to receive it when she needed it the most.

She desperately desired to let go of the images filling her brain. But they wouldn't stop. Of people whispering about her. Of young men refusing to speak to her. Of a lonely life cut off from all human contact, simply because this warrior had abducted her. In spite of the fact she had done nothing to encourage it and in fact had tried her best to prevent it from happening, that wouldn't matter to *them*. It wasn't her fault, yet they would make it hers.

"I'll never get married now, have a family, live the dream I have always had of a ministry where I can share my faith with others! Why have You abandoned me like You have, Father, allowed this horrible event to befall me when I was only trying to be obedient to You?" Mandy choked back a sob as a cloud of red dust sent her into a fit of coughing.

"With Pete dead I'm sure Jesse has found another job by now and moved on. So that means no one will even be out looking for me! Is the honorable thing truly to kill myself, though doing so goes against Your Word? Or keep my head up and learn to accept my fate with the Kiowa, however ghastly it might be?"

Several minutes of emptiness passed with no relief for Mandy's anguish.

"God!" she cried aloud, the sight of the empty horizon stretching out endlessly before them blurred by her tears. "Are You listening to me? How will I survive without the dream of going home? If I can't go back and I can't go forward, what am I to do? Please help me!"

† CHAPTER EIGHT †

"They that hate me without a cause are more
than the hairs of mine head..."
Psalm 69:4

*T*here is just no hope for me any longer, no way You can use me
now to further Your kingdom, given my circumstances. Why do
You not rescue me from the certain living death I am facing?

No voice from Heaven echoed in answer and no mysterious angel
appeared with a flaming sword to pluck Mandy out of her dire
predicament. Her shoulders drooped lower and lower with each
agonizing step, while her heart ached with longing for a swift end to
the torture she was enduring.

What is ahead for me, if I am to believe Your Word when it says
every day of my life has been planned since before the foundation of
the world? How will I survive?

Several harsh jerks on the rope sharpened Mandy's awareness that
the pace of the warrior had increased once more. In a daze, she walked
faster in response. Why not let herself fall right here and die, get it over
with before being forced to go through any more pain?

They topped a ridge and off in the distance Mandy spotted a large
cluster of trees as the sound of rushing waters broke through into her
conscious thoughts. In spite of the heat, her heart chilled. Off to one
side in a large clearing a number of Indian tipis clustered around a fire
area nestled in the middle. It must be the warrior's village. She gulped
hard, biting on her lip to keep from crying out in fear when they started
down the embankment.

Within moments several dogs ran out to greet them, yipping on every side in excitement at the Kiowa's return. Right behind them was a crowd of children, everyone chattering and yelping in celebration of the returning warrior with his trophy. Without warning, a rock hit Mandy on the shoulder and she stumbled from the impact.

"Ouch!"

Unable to defend herself against the attack, she was pelted with stones of all sizes thrown by the children the rest of the way into the village. Some were large enough to really hurt. After only a few steps more, she could see bruises rising on her arms and blood oozed from several of the scrapes. One pebble landed on her left cheek as the pair came to a stop by the central campfire. Women quickly surrounded them and joined in a chorus of jeers and taunts directed at her. Some spat on Mandy but at least the stoning had stopped. She stood there with her head bowed, afraid to move or look up at anyone for fear more abuse would start.

She saw out of the corner of her eye that Ken-ai-te had jumped down from his pony and held his end of the rope high in the air as though in triumph. The cheers quieted as he began speaking in Kiowa to the crowd.

Mandy glanced sideways a time or two at the faces of some of the people and was shocked to see the fury in their eyes. What had she ever done to them? Yet they despised her without even knowing anything about her. Words filtered into her mind from the Bible though she couldn't recall more than a couple of phrases, "in wrath they hate me" and "horror has overwhelmed me." She bowed her head again and tears fell. Never had she experienced such hatred prior to this moment and she felt helpless to protect her heart from its impact. Fearing any moment she might pass out, Mandy's knees trembled.

Oh, God, please have mercy! What is going to happen to me?

Mandy kept her eyes lowered so she didn't have to look into the copper faces surrounding her, lips moving in silent prayer. What if they decided to kill her right here and now? Would that be such an awful thing?

Suddenly the crowd erupted in angry rants. She jerked her head up and saw they were all glaring at her, punching the air with their fists. Mandy raised her chin defiantly and met their stares with what she hoped they would interpret as courage. She recalled her father telling her one time that Indians respect courage but detest cowardice. She didn't *feel* courageous; fortunately, they didn't know the truth and maybe she could fool them into believing otherwise. However, the din only increased. Apparently, she had done the wrong thing.

Who cares? What is the worst they can do to me—kill me? Death would be a welcome relief to the prospect of living with these savages!

With a shock, Mandy spotted the scar-faced warrior who had participated in her capture as he pushed his way through the crowd to stand beside Ken-ai-te. What was he doing here? The last time she had seen his ugly face her captor had been arguing with this monster over possession of her, then watched as he exploded furiously when forced by him to leave without her. Shaken she quickly looked away, losing what little self-confidence she had left.

Mandy wondered if all the others who had joined in the attack lived here as well. So why had her captor argued so vehemently with them if they were all from the same village? They obviously had wanted to take her in a different direction from the one desired by Ken-ai-te, but why? Her mind raced with dozens of unanswered questions and she tried to force herself to claim courage once more instead of giving in to defeat. It wasn't working.

Now it appeared these two were continuing the same argument, only this time in front of an older warrior—perhaps the chief of these Kiowa? *What if he gives me to the one with the scar?* The thought repulsed her and her legs threatened to give way.

Scar-face screamed wildly and gestured toward Mandy, then shouted at her captor and in turn at the chief. She shivered at the harsh words though of course she could not understand what was being said. Gazing at the faces in the crowd around her, she wondered if the one who scalped Pete also was there somewhere.

Honestly, I don't think I could recognize him again. It's odd; I don't recall ever looking at his face. I only remember the one with the terrible scar...

Mandy tried to read the expression in the chief's eyes but he showed no emotion, simply looked from one warrior to the other and back at Mandy, not saying a word. He had on a huge bear-claw necklace that covered his entire chest and Mandy's eyes widened at the size of those claws. She had seen a smaller one on a chief recently, never one so immense. Three feathers were fastened somehow into his grey hair, which flowed about his bare shoulders. He wasn't as tall as either of the other braves, but no one could doubt who was in charge. Mandy kept her attention riveted on him so she didn't have to look at Scar-face. The thought flickered that the chief wasn't nearly as handsome as Ken-ai-te, yet certainly a far cry better than the other one. She wondered how many battles he had fought in order to win the position of chief of these people, how many whites he had killed. *Wish I knew what his name is.*

A Bible verse elbowed its way into Mandy's consciousness, from somewhere in Matthew she thought; in her near panic couldn't recall exactly. Jesus' own words, not man's: "Love your enemies, bless them that curse you, do good to them that hate you, and pray for them which despitefully use you and persecute you." *God, You've got to be kidding me! I can't pray for these people. They want to kill me! Why, of all the verses You could have brought to mind right now, did You choose this one? I just can't, it's asking too much. Maybe not hate them, but* pray *for them?*

She knew she was directly defying a command from Jesus Himself and in a singularly rebellious moment didn't care. There might have been some instances, she conceded, in which the Indians were justified in their killing, but never in their torture. And besides, didn't they start most of it? Even the women and children today had shown their hatred for her, and she hadn't done a thing to any of them. How on earth could she hope to escape from harm with all the violence on every side?

Her attention drew sharply back to the chief when abruptly the crowd grew quiet, all eyes on their leader. Ken-ai-te handed the rope to him. *Does this mean he's presenting me to the chief?* Mandy fervently wished she had paid more attention to the Kiowa words her father had shared with her from time to time, so she might be able to understand their words better. Still, perhaps it was best she could not. It appeared soon enough now she would know her fate. She held her breath.

Please God, don't let Scar-face win! No matter how much I detest this Ken-ai-te who captured me, I don't think he would harm me like the other one would. You've got to help me. Just get me away from all these Kiowa savages as soon as possible!

The chief uttered a few brief words and handed the rope back to her captor. Mandy sighed in relief and offered a quick prayer of thanks. She was safe, for the moment at least. When the warrior who had been so cruel to her earlier whirled around and glared at her, she noted the anger burning on his face as he then disappeared into the crowd. Apparently, whatever the chief had said didn't set well with him.

Before Mandy had any more time to consider what would happen to her now, her captor jerked on the rope binding her wrists and she flinched as pain shot out. Obediently she followed him to where he stopped in front of one of the tipis. He whipped out his knife and Mandy's eyes were transfixed on it. *What is he going to do with that?* Before she could think to pull away from him, he sliced through the rope binding her wrists. A gasp escaped from her lips but no blood gushed and she felt no new pain. *How did he manage without cutting me?* She rubbed her wrists tenderly for a moment, flexing her fingers to restore the full circulation to her hands and winced at the discomfort as feeling came back. Sure enough, there were no cuts except for the deep rope burns rubbed there from two days of being dragged across the prairie.

Without a word, he shoved her into the tipi and Mandy fell to her knees on the hard dirt floor inside. Immediately she gagged from the stench that met her nostrils. The hide flap covering the opening of the tipi was closed behind her. Mandy's eyes rebelled in the dim light. She blinked quickly several times and slowly began to distinguish a few shapes here and there. No one lurked in the shadows and she heaved a sigh of relief. But the smell immediately overpowered her. Mandy tried to breathe through her mouth to lessen the instinctive reaction to empty her stomach on the spot. She recognized sweat and leather and a faint hint of smoke but there was also something stronger, quite unfamiliar and quite unpleasant.

Feeling her way around the floor of the tipi, Mandy crawled to the opposite side of the campfire ring in the center, noting the one beam of sunlight bearing down on it from above. She glanced upward and saw the blue sky through the small opening. *Wonder what happens when it rains?* Odd, how the mind works at difficult moments.

Her fingers recoiled when she touched something rough and scratchy, then reached out again and decided it was some kind of furry blanket. Must be a buffalo robe. She recalled seeing them in some of the villages she had visited with her father but never got close enough to feel of them. Or smell them. Part of the stench came from there, so she moved around it and pushed herself into a corner up against the hide wall, as far away from the door of the tipi as she could manage. With a shock, she realized that her own body provided much of the strong smell around her but there was little she could do about that.

For a few minutes, she gently massaged her wrists, trying to ignore the pain from them. Using a corner of her skirt Mandy dabbed at the raw skin to remove some of the dirt and blood, hoping the wounds wouldn't fester. Then she pulled her knees up to her chest and rested her head on them and sat there sweltering in the heat.

Not sure how long I can take this. I'm suffocating in here, feeling dizzy...maybe if I lie down for just a minute I'll feel better. Not over there on that smelly buffalo rug but here on the dirt, will put my head down and...maybe go to sleep for a little bit...

✝CHAPTER NINE✝

"For the eyes of the LORD run to and fro
throughout the whole earth, to shew himself strong
in the behalf of them whose heart is perfect toward him..."
II Chronicles 16:9

Where—am I? Mandy's head swam and she couldn't focus her eyes at first.

With a start, recollection came crashed in. She glanced overhead at the hide walls. *Oh, yes, I'm in that warrior's tipi, Ken-ai-te, wasn't it? I wonder how long I slept?* Voices outside the tipi were muffled and she wished she could hear them more clearly.

She stretched a little and felt every muscle in her body ache with the strain of the torturous walk she had been on for the past couple of days. Suddenly the door flap was thrown open and a stooped figure bowed to enter, then rose to reveal an older Kiowa woman bearing a couple of bowls. Mandy scrambled to sit up and face her.

"Eat."

Mandy didn't have to be told twice. She took the bowls from the woman and saw one contained water, the other some food. She gulped all the water in one long swallow, then turned her attention to the second bowl. It contained some berries and a few bites of meat. The berries were sweet and delicious and the meat more of the same jerky she had tasted on the trek here. The older woman stood and watched in silence until she finished. With a start, Mandy realized she had understood the woman's command.

"You speak English!"

59

"No speak."

"Does that mean you don't want me to speak?"

"I say no speak!" Her words were harsher this time, and Mandy complied. The woman gathered up the bowls and without another word left the tipi, closing the flap behind her.

With her eyes now more attuned to the half-light, Mandy was able to make out additional features of the tipi from those she had noticed upon first entering earlier. Piled in one corner were what looked like buffalo hides—or perhaps bear? Did they even hunt bear hereabouts? Then she recalled the chief's elaborate necklace and figured they probably did. But she knew they did hunt buffalo. A long spear stood deep in the shadows in one corner across the tipi and she peered at it to try to make out the feathers on it. Suddenly it dawned on her that those were not feathers. They were scalps!

She retched at the sight of the offensive lance and the significance of it, fighting to keep her meal down since she didn't know when she might have another. Tears spilled over.

"Oh, God, please forgive these horrible people for their inhumane acts of violence to others. I know they don't understand how to be civilized, but the idea of keeping scalps in their homes as trophies is repulsive. What kind of evil place have You brought me to? I beg You not to abandon me here. Let me know You are still beside me through this ghastly ordeal."

Just then, the flap went up again and she swiped at the tears. No way she wanted the warrior to see her crying over his scalps. However, it was the woman again, and Mandy felt relieved. Until the older woman spoke.

"You Kiowa now. I teach how speak Kiowa, be Kiowa woman, understand? You learn fast or Ken-ai-te beat you. Understand?"

"Well, you know I've already experienced some of this Ken-ai-te's 'beating' and it wasn't so bad. I—"

"No speak! First rule to learn. No speak, head down, do work."

"Well, how am I supposed to learn if I can't ask questions?" She looked at the woman with a smug smile on her face. *Let her answer that one!*

"If you not obey, he beat me as well as you. So you obey, understand?"

Mandy's smile faded and she nodded in compliance. She had no desire to cause this woman any pain, certainly. The woman returned the gesture, apparently satisfied the captive would obey without question now. Inside Mandy seethed with bitterness.

This is only an outer obedience. No way I'm doing it in my heart! And she glared at her, hoping she would comprehend her unspoken statement of rebellion. *I'm only obeying to keep you from receiving a beating at the hands of that savage. I don't care about myself but I don't want to be responsible for your suffering, too.*

Something about the woman was odd. Her white hair framed a wrinkled face, darkened to a leathery appearance probably by years in the sun. She didn't look as though she had ever smiled in her entire life. Mandy wondered how old she might be. And who she was. Perhaps the warrior's mother? No, too old, maybe his grandmother? All of a sudden, it hit Mandy: the woman's eyes were blue!

"You—you're not Kiowa. You're white, aren't you? I mean, you have to be white because of your blue eyes, right?" The throbbing in Mandy's ears almost drowned out her own words.

"No speak!"

"But—"

The woman raised her fist as though to strike Mandy, who flinched slightly.

"Okay, 'no speak' it is."

Breathless with excitement in spite of the woman's hostility, Mandy longed to ask her name and how long she had been held captive. The woman's older age concerned her but she hoped that maybe the woman had been captured recently, meaning she hadn't been here a long time. She pushed aside the nagging voice telling her that if it appeared she had spent a great deal of time in the sun she probably was not a new captive. A hope buoyed her spirits. Maybe the two of them could escape together!

The woman turned and picked up a bowl she had sat down upon entering the tipi and held it out. Mandy frowned, not sure what she was supposed to do with the water in it. Another drink maybe?

"Clean face. Hair. Now."

"I'm supposed to clean my face? Oh, that would be wonderful. Do you have a comb for—" And she stopped at the scowl on the older woman's face. *Oops. Guess that was too much for Miss No Speak!*

The woman dipped her fingers in the water and began working them through Mandy's hair. She scrunched up her face.

"Ouch, that hurts! It's too tangled for that. I need a comb or brush. And it desperately needs to be washed."

"Kiowa way." And she proceeded to spit on her fingers and repeat her actions.

"You've got to be kidding! Okay, just please stop doing that, it's disgusting. I'll use the water. I don't like the 'Kiowa way,' as you put it, with your spit in my hair! Now I'll have to wash it for sure."

The older woman retreated from the tipi and Mandy attempted to complete untangling her hair, to no avail. Finally, with great reluctance she tried spit and was amazed how her fingers slid through the knots.

"Humph. She did know what she was talking about. Never would have believed it. If you can stand the thought that spit is all over your hair, that is. But it's still a lost cause for the most part. Wonder when they will allow me to wash it?"

She searched for a rag of some sort with which to clean her face. Finding nothing, she tore a corner off the hem of her dress and soaked it in the water, dabbing at her cheeks gently. The place where one of the stones thrown by the children had hit her left cheek was quite tender. She imagined it would leave a nasty bruise.

"Oh, who cares? At least I don't have to look at myself in a mirror. A good thing—I must be a sight by now."

Mandy glanced down at the stains and tears and missing parts of her once-beautiful dress and sighed. No need to try to stand on dignity at this point, just accept the inevitable. It was ruined, no question. But the important thing right now was getting herself cleaned up a bit. It surprised her that the woman allowed her to do this, but she assumed it had nothing to do with compassion.

"Probably more with making me presentable for that savage's pleasure." Her contentment in such a menial task was shattered and her shoulders slumped. "Oh, well, might as well finish. Not like I have anything else to do right now and goodness knows, I certainly need it. This is not for him, though, it's for *me*."

Mandy wiped down her neck and arms with the blue rag, relishing the feel of the cool water on her sunburned skin. The insect bites itched furiously and she scrubbed at them with it as well to hopefully ease that discomfort but, in all honesty, it did little good. She scratched for a couple of moments but knew for the most part she would have to learn to ignore them.

"Now that I'm finished I wonder what I'm supposed to do with the rest of this water?" Her eyes came to rest on her filthy shoes & she decided her feet could use some refreshment, too. "What on earth can I use for a buttonhook, though, to get these buttons on my shoes undone?" She looked around the tipi but saw nothing that might work so gave up the idea.

Disappointed, Mandy had to settle for resting her feet instead of cleaning them. She wiggled her toes around inside the stiff leather. Tiny pinpricks of pain came to her attention and she figured those must be the blisters she most certainly had rubbed on various parts of her feet during the long walk. "Certainly hope I don't have to live in these things for the rest of the time I'm here. That would be awful."

Just then, the warrior burst through the doorway carrying

something over his arm. Mandy jumped up and backed away from him.

"Take off clothes."

So this was it, finally. What she had dreaded for two days. Just like that, no warning whatsoever. Gulping back her fear, Mandy defiantly lifted her chin and said the first thing that came to her muddled mind, as calmly as she could manage.

"So you do speak English."

He glared but said nothing.

"And I most certainly will *not* take off my clothes! I dare you to make me." She put her hands on her hips to emphasize her words. "Touch one hair on my head and I will kill you, I swear it!"

✝ CHAPTER TEN ✝

"Whosoever therefore shall confess me before men,
him will I confess also before my Father which is in heaven."
Matthew 10:32

"Take off. Now." The warrior's voice grew harsher with each syllable while he gestured toward her dress. Mandy supposed he wasn't used to someone quite as stubborn. Well, she would show him!

"No, I will not!

And he tossed down at her feet what she thought was a blanket and said between clenched teeth, "Put on. Now."

Without taking her eyes off the man, she reached down and picked up the "blanket" and slowly brought it up to where she could see what it was. Not a blanket but instead a buckskin dress.

"Well, if you wanted me to put something else on, why didn't you say so? I thought you just wanted me to take my clothes off, and I wasn't about to help you, uh, do whatever it is you were thinking about doing."

He continued to stare at her without another word.

"Well, if you want me to change my clothes, you are going to have to leave. Or at least turn around. I'm certainly not going to do this in front of you, with you staring at me!" She gestured at him and hoped he got the gist of what she meant so she wouldn't have to repeat it.

The warrior turned and stood with his back to her, feet apart and arms folded across his chest. Mandy sighed and quickly removed what was left of her blue calico as well as her dingy petticoat. She refused to remove her camisole, however, testament to the stubborn rebellion dueling in her heart with anxiety over her disobedience. *What he doesn't know won't hurt him. But it will make me feel much better.* Then she slipped the buckskin over her head. It fit her perfectly and was cool and smooth against her body. At least it wouldn't show her curves off too much if it got wet like the other one did, especially with the camisole underneath.

She picked up her old dress and held it against her cheek, the last vestige of life with her people. The sadness was overwhelming and unexpected as it washed over her. Tears slipped out but she brushed them away before her captor could turn around and notice them. *I can't let him see my weakness!*

After a few seconds, the Kiowa faced her again and stared. Mandy was irritated he didn't wait for her to give him permission. She supposed having the privacy of dressing alone was a luxury she would soon give up altogether, so under the circumstances she had better be grateful for even this little bit. His eyes flickered approval briefly, then he frowned.

Pointing at her neck, he said gruffly, "Off."

Mandy glanced down to see what he wanted "off" and saw her gold cross gleaming in the dim light.

"This?" And she grasped it in her fingers gently.

"Off. Now."

"No! My father gave this to me several years ago and it means everything to me. It is the symbol of my God and I never take it off." The warrior scowled. "Do you not understand the word 'God'? Um, the Great Spirit. I know you Kiowa are familiar with that at least. Don't stand there frowning at me like that. It's only a piece of jewelry. It's not hurting a thing. Please don't take it away from me."

Silence.

"What is your problem? A small gold necklace got you spooked? Well, I'm not giving it up! You will have to rip it off my dead body to get it away from me. But I warn you, I'm stronger than I look and I'm not tied up now. So you'd better just go ahead and kill me if you are going to try to take this off my neck!" She stood with her feet apart and her hands on her hips once again to emphasize her defiance.

The warrior glared at her but finally motioned that she should put it inside her dress, which Mandy quickly decided she could live with and obeyed. And that seemed to satisfy him. At least she had won the battle—more or less—and she got to keep her beloved cross. It was also the only thing she had left to remind her of her Savior and, right now, she needed that even more than the memory of her father giving it to her. Maybe her captor would think twice about trying to harm her after this scene. At least she hoped so.

Those hopes were dashed in the next second, however. The warrior again frowned at her and stared at her shoes.

"I know; they are pretty awful, aren't they?" she asked with a touch of sarcasm. "I don't have a buttonhook or I would have taken them off earlier. You wouldn't happen to have—"

He whipped out his knife and advanced on her as she backed up a couple of steps, her eyes wide with terror. What did he intend to do with that knife?

"What—what are you doing?"

In one movement, he grabbed her arm and pulled her to the ground, then knelt down beside her and poked at the top of the right shoe with his knife.

"Stop, please!" Was he going to cut off her foot?

With one swipe of the razor-sharp blade, he proceeded to rip through all the buttons and Mandy watched in shock as they went flying in every direction. Then he turned to the left one to repeat his motion. She stared in horror at her ruined shoes while he replaced the knife in the sheath at his waist. It seemed unbelievable he could do that much damage so quickly without harming her feet. At least she could breathe easier now that the knife was out of his hand.

"All right, bright one. What am I supposed to do now for shoes? Go barefoot?"

He ripped the shreds off both feet before she could stop him and she scooted backwards a little, desperately hoping he didn't mean to chop off her feet as well. However, she knew he probably would have done so without destroying the shoes, had that been his intention. She had to admit being free of the rigid leather was a relief.

The warrior rose and walked over to a corner of the tipi with his back to her. Gleefully, she wiggled her toes and then gently massaged her weary feet, feeling the blisters even more now.

After a couple of moments, he turned back with a pair of moccasins in his hand and tossed them down beside Mandy.

"Put on."

Mandy did as told with the first one but he squatted down and jerked it off before she could stop him. Then he ripped at her stocking until it came loose at the ankle and tossed it aside. He replaced the moccasin while she looked on, uncomfortable with the feel of his rough fingers on her foot yet powerless to prevent it. She recovered quickly, however, and also tore the other stocking off at the ankle so he wouldn't have reason to touch her again. Then she put on the second moccasin while he stood up and eyed her closely. Later she could remove the remnant of the stockings when alone, since she wasn't about to do that in front of him. For now, he seemed satisfied. And Mandy was relieved. She stood up and relished the feel of the soft buckskin on her tired feet as the older woman came back into the tipi.

The warrior turned to leave and without thinking Mandy blurted out, "Wait—Ken-ai-te, remember when I told you my name was Mandy? Well, it's *Miss Amanda Clark* to you." She all but spit the name out at him with an arrogant glare in her eyes. "Only my closest friends are allowed to call me Mandy."

He swung around and glared at her, barked something to the woman in Kiowa, and left the tipi. Mandy turned to look at the older woman, who stared at her curiously.

"What's your name?" Mandy asked. "What am I supposed to call you?"

"Sleeping Bird. And you no speak! You have great honor, belong to Ken-ai-te. Very wealthy warrior, have big tipi," and here she gestured at the expanse around them, "also five horses. You give respect, obey him. Understand?"

Silently Mandy nodded and started to sit down, though inside she seethed with resentment at Sleeping Bird's speech. This was not the time and place to defy her. It had been a trying few minutes and her knees were wobbly. Perhaps the combination of the heat inside the tipi and lack of food and water recently—she wasn't sure; in any case, she wanted only to collapse and be left alone.

But just as she sank to her knees, Sleeping Bird grabbed her by the arm and jerked her back on her feet. "No time for rest. Much to do before light gone. Much to learn, how to be Kiowa woman. Come, now."

The afternoon stretched endlessly before Mandy and she sighed while following her out of the tipi and into the village. She glanced around as they walked and wrinkled up her nose.

God, what kind of a pit have you delivered me to? This is horrible! The smells, the primitive conditions, these people who are so uncivilized and hostile to You and Your values—

Mandy's thoughts were interrupted by a blow to her shoulder. "Too slow! Walk faster."

"All right, all right. You don't have to hit me! Sorry, um, Sleeping Bird, is it?"

The woman didn't respond, just kept moving. *I don't care if I got it right or not. Your name could be Flying Bird or Leaping Bird or some other stupid thing for all I care. At least it's not some unpronounceable gibberish. Oh, I'm so tired right now; I would give anything if I could just sit down for a little while.*

The older woman stopped when they reached a large clearing between two of the tipis on the edge of the village. A gigantic hide was staked out on the ground and several Kiowa women were on their knees all around it. Sleeping Bird indicated where Mandy should kneel down to join them. *Good, I finally get to sit down, or at least not be on my feet any longer.* As she knelt, an offensive odor hit her nostrils and her stomach lurched—again. *Seem to be doing a great deal of that lately. Oh, my goodness, what on earth is that smell?*

Sleeping Bird set a large gourd beside her filled with a green goo, and the stench that was causing her insides such distress grew even stronger.

"What—is—*that*?"

"Buffalo, um—" She stopped and pointed at her temple.

"Head?" A scowl on her face told Mandy her guess had been incorrect. The woman continued to jab at the side of her head.

"Don't tell me it's the brains?" Mandy figured her face must match the condition of her stomach right then. And probably the color of the gooey mess in the gourd.

Sleeping Bird nodded, then pointed to her middle.

"*And* the stomach?" This was getting worse by the second.

She shook her head vigorously and seemed to dismiss the questioning by turning her back to her. A moment later, she turned around with a large mushy mass in her hands, blood dripping from between her fingers. Mandy gawked and her jaw dropped open. Could it be a liver? Or more than one since it was bigger by far than any animal's liver she'd ever seen before. And messier. And smellier. Revolting would be a better word.

Instinctively her face twisted into a disgusted mask and she muttered almost reluctantly, "Liver. It's made from a buffalo's brains and liver?"

Sleeping Bird nodded and uttered a couple of words in Kiowa but Mandy didn't even pretend to repeat them. It would forever be "goo" to her. And if she didn't get her queasiness under control soon, she would be adding her own contribution to the mixture in the gourd, she was quite certain. She swallowed hard and closed her eyes briefly, trying to breathe through her mouth instead of her nose.

Oh, God, please don't tell me I'm supposed to eat this stuff! While waiting for those dreaded orders she stared wide-eyed at it. *How on earth will I ever manage to swallow that vile concoction?*

✝CHAPTER ELEVEN✝

"And many nations shall be joined to the LORD...
and shall be my people: and I will dwell in the midst of thee,
and thou shalt know that the LORD of hosts
hath sent me unto thee."
Zechariah 2:11

I didn't see that huge cauldron until now. Glad it's way over there instead of closer to us. The smell is bad enough from this distance. I'd much prefer to be here rather than helping the women around it with whatever they are doing.

Mandy watched as Sleeping Bird dumped the liver back in and wiped her fingers off in the grass. Apparently, the goo was being mixed there. With the women hunched over it like they were, it reminded her of a picture she'd seen one time in a book of a group of witches who were surrounding their evil brew and uttering curses over it while they stirred.

Glancing around the circle Mandy noticed each woman had her own gourd of the green mess and they were smearing it all over the animal skin—not eating it! Relief flooded her and the hint of a smile flirted with her lips. *Oh, thank You, Lord! That I can do, just so I don't have to put that stuff in my mouth!*

Sleeping Bird settled beside her, then nudged Mandy to follow her circular motions working it into the hide. *This should be a snap, rather like painting with your hands except I don't have to make any sense out of it or even think, and that's a good thing as tired as I am right now. Must remember to breathe through my mouth, though. In and out,*

Mandy, in and out, and don't give a thought to what is all over your fingers.

Within minutes, however, Mandy discovered this task was much more difficult than it appeared to be, in fact, backbreaking work that stretched muscles she wasn't sure were even usable in those positions. It didn't take long before her neck and shoulders cramped up and she had to sit back on her heels a moment. Sleeping Bird elbowed her hard in the ribs.

"No stop. Keep working."

"I will. Just let me catch my breath a second. Good grief, I—"

Sleeping Bird scowled and pursed her lips, eyes flashing. "Work. Now."

"Okay, don't get in a huff," Mandy snapped. "No need to be so impatient," and she scooped up another handful of the goo.

"No speak."

The glowering look on the older woman's face pushed Mandy's thoughts inside and she clamped her lips together. *Wonder how many times I'm going to hear 'no speak' while I'm here. Better not be too many more times or I'll go crazy hearing those words. How would she like to have a face full of this mess?* She had to grit her teeth to keep from finding out!

Mandy slowed her movements a bit in order to accommodate the aches she had developed and shifted her weight to take the pressure off her knees as well. As she copied the other women's motions, she looked at each one. *Some of them are hardly more than young girls, while others have grey hair like Sleeping Bird. How do they keep at this without taking a break and moving around?*

No one seemed to object to the smell or the feel of the goo on their fingers. No one, that is, except for Mandy. *Well, you know what, ladies? We white women are tough, just like you Kiowa women. I can do anything you can do, and longer and better! You watch me.* She forced her mind to go numb and simply function automatically to keep from thinking much about anything. And for some time it seemed to help as the routine dictated her movements.

The women chattered quietly to each other as they worked but, of course, no one spoke to Mandy except the one guarding her. And mostly she used blows—or the threat of them—rather than words to let her know if she did something incorrectly or not quickly enough.

Pricks of loneliness grew deep inside as Mandy contemplated how rapidly her life had turned topsy-turvy. Even more ominous was how her future stretched out in front of her like a speeding train about to veer off a tall trestle and plunge into a bottomless chasm below. *Oh, God, are You even here in this place?*

Tears welled up, then trickled down Mandy's cheeks in little rivulets. When she reached up to wipe them away, she forgot about the green mess all over her hands.

"Oh, great! Now I have this stuff all over my face, too!" One of the younger girls snickered at the sight, which only made things worse. Mandy ignored the scowls from the others after her outburst but she didn't care. It stung her face and eyes and she used the sleeve of her dress to rub it off, with some success. *At least it's not burning quite so badly. Wonder why it does that?* She had noticed her fingers were tingling a bit but chalked it up to the repetitious circles she was making. Now she wasn't so sure.

A short time later one of the younger women got up and left the group and Mandy watched as she took a drink from a water skin hanging nearby, then washed her hands with some of the water, drying them on a rag of some kind. As she walked out of sight, it crossed Mandy's mind that perhaps she should just get up and do the same. *I'm thirsty and tired of this nonsense. How fast would Sleeping Bird follow me if I did that? Maybe I could get over there and at least get a drink before she stopped me!* But in the long run, it wasn't worth the effort or the risk. Maybe in a few minutes.

Mandy refocused her attention on the task at hand. Obviously, they were working on a buffalo hide but its immense size awed her. She recalled having watched the buffalo racing across the prairie earlier that day and shuddered to think how powerful these animals are, being of such a size.

Wonder if it is hard to chase them down for the kill? Papa told me of buffalo hunts he had watched from afar when he lived here before, of how the Kiowa butchered them for the meat and other parts after they killed them. I just don't understand how they could kill such a magnificent animal. Or why. Surely, they have other sources of meat besides these beasts.

A few minutes later, the woman who had left earlier returned with a baby on her hip. She knelt down, settled the infant on her lap, and opened the side of her dress in order to nurse him. Mandy was stunned! *Right here, in front of everyone? Decent women don't do such a thing. Why, I've never even seen that, much less in public.* Her jaw dropped as she stared. *What if one of the men came by?*

As soon as the baby was actively nursing, the mother resumed her work on the hide, propping him up on her lap and paying him no further mind. No one seemed to find this unusual in the least, and she noticed that a couple of the women smiled kindly at the young mother who flashed a grin in return.

These people are so strange. I can't imagine the stir it would cause if a mother tried to nurse her baby in public back in Ohio! Good grief, there would be an awful scandal if this happened at the weekly quilting bee Aunt Ida used to have in her home. I believe some of those old biddies would not only swoon but also probably have a heart attack! And there were only women present, in a private home, yet it would be considered offensive nevertheless. Mandy shook her head. Would she ever cease to be shocked at the behavior of these Kiowa?

Sleeping Bird finally rose but pushed Mandy back down with her elbow when she tried to do the same. She uttered a word in Kiowa but, of course, Mandy didn't understand. Assuming it meant something like "stay put" she obediently complied. But she couldn't help wondering where the woman was going and why.

It was nerve wracking to be left on her own with these women. Certainly, they were among the ones who had greeted her entry into the village earlier with such anger and hate-filled looks. Would they try to harm her? Would any of them speak to her now that Sleeping Bird had left? She supposed not, considering it was obvious to everyone she was a captive and not doing this of her own free will.

What if the situation were reversed? Would I try to be friendly to a Kiowa who had been captured by whites and brought to civilization? Blushing, Mandy had to admit in all honesty she most likely would not. *And she, a woman called to minister to these people! But these savages don't—*

They don't what, Mandy? The voice, clear as a lark's song, had been almost audible. Did others hear it, too? *Don't count? Don't have a soul? Don't have feelings? They don't what?*

Cold chills crept up her arms and she shivered. She was grateful these Kiowa women couldn't read her mind. Although she had never heard God's voice speak to her before in this manner, Mandy knew for certain that He had, and her hands trembled. Jesus died for these women, too. And she had no business arguing with God over whether they deserved it or not. That's why it was called grace.

But, Father, have You seen what they have done to me? And much worse to many other white people, for that matter. Like Pete—he didn't deserve to die like he did. How can You say that is fair or right? And she knew deep in her soul He had seen and was of course displeased. *Then why don't You put a stop to it? Why do You allow it to go on and on? I really don't understand all this. I just feel so much anger right now.*

Or maybe equal parts fatigue. It had been a very long two days and this one wasn't over yet. She pushed her fury deep to keep it under control. It was neither the time nor the place to continue this argument, but she knew, at some point, she would have to do more than merely avoid it. God would never settle for that.

Her mind drifted back to her original curiosity about whether anyone would acknowledge her or not. *Do any of them speak English? Wonder how Ken-ai-te learned, maybe from Sleeping Bird?* Instinctively she wanted to speak to the women and find out if any of them understood her, but then she soberly reminded herself they were her *enemies*. She had no intentions of giving them the satisfaction of thinking she wished to be friendly in any way. Tiny daggers of bitterness embedded themselves deep in her heart and though she tried to ignore them, she could feel their sting in spite of her effort to pretend they were not there. She stared down at her hands and, getting a whiff of the goo, reminded herself harshly to keep breathing through her mouth.

Just then, Sleeping Bird returned and pulled Mandy abruptly to her feet. When she tried to stand, she collapsed and fell against the older woman. Her legs were asleep! She stomped them several times and the feeling slowly returned as she leaned on the other one's arm for support. Mandy was grateful that she didn't just let her fall to the ground, at least.

After leading her to the water skin, she allowed Mandy to clean her hands. She was relieved to get that stuff off her fingers and wiped her face with the damp rag as well to remove the traces of the goo that still clung there.

Sleeping Bird growled a Kiowa phrase at her—maybe "follow me"—because she walked briskly away and disappeared behind one of the tipis. Mandy rushed to catch up and, as she rounded what she thought was the right tipi, she realized she had apparently turned the wrong way. Sleeping Bird was nowhere in sight. Which way should she go?

She glanced around for something familiar and tried to determine what to do now. *How can I get lost in this village, no bigger than it is?*

A low growl sounded from behind her. Mandy whirled to face the source and felt as though someone had thrown a bucketful of cold water in her face. She gulped and did her best to steady her knees. With that same vicious blade in his hand from yesterday, Scar-face was bearing down on her with an expression that terrified her.

"Help! Someone help me!" she screamed and backed up a couple of steps. But she knew no one would come to her rescue. That left her with only seconds to act.

However, without a weapon with which to defend herself, what could she do? A flash of courage washed over her and she knew she could not cower before this animal.

"Stop!" she shouted without considering whether or not the savage understood English. "You'd better not come one step nearer or you will have to answer to Ken-ai-te. And you and I both know that you will lose once more if you defy him again!"

†CHAPTER TWELVE†

"Blessed is the man that trusteth in the LORD,
and whose hope the LORD is."
Jeremiah 17:7

"You take one more step and you will be sorry!" Mandy's heart throbbed and she held her breath. She stared directly into those evil eyes. Would Scar-face listen? Were her threats enough to stop him?

The warrior hesitated for a split second, long enough that Mandy noticed. *So you understand English, too. Good. You didn't expect me to fight back, did you?*

Slowly he lowered the knife but the expression on his ugly face made Mandy shudder.

"Mine!" he suddenly growled, pointing at her, taking her off guard.

What on earth was he talking about? His? God forbid! Should she ignore him and walk away or wait until he moved? She didn't want to turn her back on him so she hesitated.

Before she could act, however, Sleeping Bird rushed up and stepped between the two, planting her feet right in front of his. Though considerably shorter than the warrior, she didn't seem at all intimidated by him. Wagging her finger in his face, she shrieked something in Kiowa and he visibly paled in spite of his copper skin. Finally, he turned on his heel and disappeared out of sight.

"That was impressive, Sleeping Bird. I don't know what you said to him but—"

"No talk to Black Feather. No speak anyone."

Mandy stood there a moment with her mouth open, then shut it in disbelief. Did she actually believe Mandy had engaged in a conversation with this "Black Feather"—is that what she called him? She had to be kidding! Obviously, she did not notice the size of the blade he had brandished. And, she didn't know Mandy's history with it and how close she came to losing her life from it the day before.

"Did you see what he did? He pulled his knife on me!"

"Follow. Eyes down." And once more, she walked away. Mandy had no intentions of falling behind this time and hurried to stay close. The day was getting worse by the minute. Would it never end?

When they arrived back at the tipi, Mandy took a moment to look around. She saw bright colors splashed across the sides and along with them some strange drawings and curiously wondered about their significance—perhaps just random scrawls of paint? Who did the tipi belong to, her captor or Sleeping Bird? They both seemed to live there. It couldn't be Sleeping Bird's, though, because Kiowa women didn't have their own. *Now how on earth did I know that? Must have heard it from Papa.*

In any case, her sense of relief mixed with confusion. For some strange reason Mandy felt a level of safety in simply being close to the tipi, even in the few hours she had been here in the village. Rather like the security she sensed in the Kiowa when they encountered the Comanche camp out on the trail.

Apparently, he can protect me from that horrible Black Feather who's been harassing me. Even the mention of my captor's name seems to strike fear into him. Wish I knew what Sleeping Bird said to make him leave me alone. I'm grateful, but not at all sure I like feeling indebted to either of them for anything. Yet I'm completely dependent upon them for everything right now.

Mandy was ordered to help prepare dinner, delighted it would be a hot meal instead of more of the jerky. The grumbling in her stomach reminded her how little she had eaten over the past two days. She licked her lips in anticipation of whatever she would be cooking in the large pot that hung from a three-legged stick contraption over the fire. Had to be better than starving!

Sleeping Bird quickly piled up a few twigs and branches from a nearby stack of wood and, rubbing two sticks together vigorously, soon had fanned a few sparks into flames in the pit next to the tipi while Mandy watched. She gestured for her to kneel down and feed the fire, which she did.

"Why here and not inside the tipi?" Mandy asked, nodding toward the fire.

"Too hot there."

Makes sense. I guess the inside one is used when the weather gets colder. A shiver snaked down her spine at the thought of still being here when the snows came, and it was most decidedly not from considering the cold that would accompany the snowfalls. *God, you have to get me out of here before then, else I believe I shall die of a broken heart. I just can't bear the thought of having to live here that long! And I must have Your help to get away.*

Fighting back tears, she continued to stoke the fire with more twigs as it burned stronger. *Maybe if I can get it big enough I could manage to burn the whole village down and then escape while they all run for their lives! By the time they missed me I would already be home.*

While occupied with ecstatic thoughts about escape, another reason for having a fire inside the tipi pushed its way forward and sucked the air right out of her chest. At night! Mandy thought she would suffocate. She reminded herself to breathe, though it came in short gasps. And she tried to ignore the prickle in her heart about the next few hours.

Suddenly her thoughts were interrupted when Sleeping Bird shoved a large knife in her hand. She stared at it numbly for a few seconds. Then her instincts kicked in and she had to fight an overwhelming urge to use it on the older woman and run off. *Maybe I can hide it somewhere and when the right opportunity presents itself to get away, I would have a weapon to use. Or at least find out where it is kept so I could steal it when I need it. Wait a moment—what am I thinking?*

Mandy's heart was crushed with the weight of having entertained, however briefly, the idea of stealing an item that didn't belong to her. And using violence on others in order to be free. Regardless of the reason, her reaction remained in direct opposition to everything she knew about God's Word. At the same time, she rationalized it as being all right, given her unique circumstances. *Surely, God wouldn't hold that against me knowing it might mean the difference in my freedom or further enslavement here with the Kiowa.*

Unaware of these dark thoughts, Sleeping Bird instructed Mandy to chop some strange looking vegetables. She was to do the task on a large rock apparently used for food preparation. Suddenly her appetite diminished. *Why don't these savages all die from food poisoning, living in such primitive conditions?* She clenched her teeth to control the lurching in her stomach and did as told.

While she worked, Mandy glanced at the copper water bucket and noticed it was similar to the one they had at the mission. Had it been stolen from some unfortunate white people? And then she looked over at the stewpot, expecting it to be metal as well. Surprisingly, it seemed to be made from some kind of animal skin. Wouldn't it burn up hanging over a fire? She shook her head in amazement, tossing the chunks into the pot.

Slap! The sound interrupted her thoughts. Sleeping Bird had thrown down a chunk of raw meat on the rock on which Mandy was working, splattering blood in every direction. Mandy instinctively jumped back, relieved the blood drops hadn't soiled her clothes or moccasins. Growling a Kiowa word, Sleeping Bird pantomimed a chopping motion. *So I'm making stew. Wonder what kind? Certainly not squirrel, judging by the size of it.*

"What kind of meat is this?" she asked as she worked.

"Buffalo. No speak!" *There she goes again with that insane command! I'm going to 'no speak' her here in a moment. I have a knife in my hand and she'd better watch out, is all I can say.* Silent, Mandy's imagination took her down yet another dark path for a few moments, where she used the knife to steal a horse and ride across the prairie to freedom. It was ridiculous she knew. And added to her earlier guilt over stealing. But it kept her hope afloat a little longer.

When Mandy finished with the knife, Sleeping Bird took it, wiped it off on the grass under her feet, and returned it to a leather sheath tied to her belt. Mandy hadn't paid attention to it until now, thought it was only the warriors who had those. Her heart sank. There would be no getting it away from her unnoticed.

Several moments later, the fact the blade had been wiped clean on the grass crept into her conscious mind and she flirted with the thought that maybe she should stick with jerky. *How ridiculous! I'm sure she used the same knife on it, too.* A soft groan escaped her lips and her stomach rumbled as the delicious aroma of the stew simmering over the fire filled the air. Her resistance collapsed. How soon would it be ready?

The two women busied themselves with numerous tasks for some time, which annoyed Mandy because they had nothing whatsoever to do with finishing up the meal. Her resentments boiled right along with the stew. *How about a little rest? Do you have any idea what I've been through this day already?* Exhaustion made her knees wobbly and she wished their dinner would hurry up and cook so they could eat. Maybe then, she could sit down for a while and not have to face yet another repulsive task, but simply let her weary mind and achy bones calm a bit while she filled her stomach.

Sometime later Ken-ai-te strode into sight and sat down cross-legged close to the fire. He glanced at the western sky and Mandy's eyes were drawn there as well, with nature's breathtaking beauty displayed against the setting sun. However, she simply did not have the energy to appreciate it, her eyes shifting quickly back again to the cooking pot over the fire.

Sleeping Bird tasted the stew, then shoved a gourd at Mandy and said something in Kiowa—maybe ladle up food for Ken-ai-te? She begrudgingly did as told. *Why can't he serve his own dinner? What am I, his slave or something?*

She gulped. *I* am *his slave! Probably the main reason he stole me, to fix his meals and take care of him. Not to mention other things he will expect me to do for him.*

Fear threatened to strangle her at that thought and she almost missed the smile he gave her when she handed him the full gourd. Instinctively she wanted to return the smile. Then anger recoiled in full force. *What is he smiling at me for? I'm his slave, right? It's an absolute insult for him to kidnap me like he did and then have the audacity to sit there and* smile *at me!* She wanted to slap him but knew better than to provoke his fury—at least until she had eaten.

Instead, she averted her eyes; a furtive glance revealed the scowl on his face when she did so. *He wants my eyes lowered, he shall have it. But I refuse to smile at this savage while he holds me captive!*

┤CHAPTER THIRTEEN ├

"For the LORD...forsaketh not his saints;
they are preserved forever..."
Psalm 37:28

Wonder how I'm supposed to eat this without a spoon or fork?
Surely not with my fingers!

However, Mandy noticed the other two were doing exactly that with the chunks of meat and vegetables and sopping up the rest with the pieces of bread Sleeping Bird had torn off and tossed into each gourd. Seems she had little choice. They ate in silence, which suited Mandy just fine.

When she had been shown how to clean the gourds—if you could call it such—and where they were kept, the thought crossed her mind about what they were supposed to do now. The sun was sinking quickly and a soft breeze had picked up. Ken-ai-te rose and sniffed the air, then spoke to Sleeping Bird and she scurried about picking up odds and ends from around the tipi. Ken-ai-te scooped up some dirt to douse the fire, then kicked at it to ensure the embers had died.

"Bring things into tipi, hurry. Rain comes." Sleeping Bird's command was sharp.

"Rain, are you kidding? With a sunset like that?" And she gestured toward the sky behind them. When they both ignored her question, she shrugged and hurried to help gather the things Sleeping Bird indicated needed to be brought inside. Suddenly the breeze gusted around them in a flurry and with it came cooler air. Now she had to admit the smell of rain was heavy around them. Apparently, the older woman knew something Mandy did not! Before she could duck into the tipi with her arms full, the first drops splashed around her.

Mandy had noticed with irritation that Ken-ai-te hadn't helped bring anything into the tipi as he ducked in right behind her. He did, however, immediately grab two tall poles resting to one side and proceed to close a previously hidden flap in the top of the tipi. *So that answers my question earlier about what happens when it rains. Hmm, they actually have designed something that makes sense. Only thing I've found so far that does.*

While Mandy had her back turned to the warrior, she smelled a whiff of smoke. Sure enough, when she turned around he had a good fire going in the center of the tipi. She wondered what would happen when the interior filled with smoke, since it had nowhere to go now the vent was closed.

Ken-ai-te sat down on the buffalo robe while the women stashed everything out of the way. Mandy worked under Sleeping Bird's instructions. It amazed her that even after everything had been stored in its proper place; the three of them still had plenty of room to sit down. The tipi had seemed so small earlier, yet now she could envision how several people could easily be housed in one this size. Had Ken-ai-te had a family at one time? Is that the reason he had women's clothing handy for her to wear?

It didn't take long for Mandy to get her silent question answered about the smoke as her eyes rapidly filled with tears from the acrid smell. However, it didn't seem to bother the other two at all. She rubbed her eyes and wondered how long it would take to get used to it because not breathing was definitely out of the question!

Mandy couldn't take her gaze off the bed, adjacent to the area where they were sitting, yet she tried not to let either of the two catch her looking at it. After several glances, she decided it seemed to be more a place to stash robes and skins of various types rather than the purpose for which it was intended, and she sighed in relief. A low wooden structure with some kind of dried brush crammed underneath, it certainly didn't look too inviting. Cold chills skittered down her arms as she contemplated what would happen when bedtime came. And silently renewed her vow never to let this savage touch one hair on her head!

Sleeping Bird joined Ken-ai-te on the robe and pulled a large bag from her waistband. Pouring brightly colored beads out in front of her, she pushed them around in the deep fur into some sort of obscure pattern. The two completely ignored Mandy and she stood there for a moment, unsure what to do next. Since they didn't seem to care, she chose to retreat to the corner where she'd been earlier in the afternoon, as far away from them as possible. She sat down and pulled her legs up to her chest after ensuring her ankles were completely covered by her dress and stared at them for some time. Only her spells of coughing broke the silence and after a few minutes, they grew more infrequent and finally stopped.

With no pretense whatsoever of including Mandy, the two began chattering away between them in Kiowa. The warrior picked up a stack of arrows and placed them in front of him, then selected one from the group and began scraping it with something. Ken-ai-te continued to work intently on his arrows, one at a time, though why remained a mystery—perhaps part of the arrow-making process? Sleeping Bird became engrossed in her beadwork and never looked in Mandy's direction. Occasionally Mandy glanced over at them but in general tried to ignore them as well. She didn't want to give either one the impression she might be interested in what they were doing or saying nor the satisfaction of knowing how infuriating their treatment of her was.

She turned her attention to the sound of the raindrops pounding the hide on every side at once, feeling deep gratitude for the shelter over her head. *I'm thankful it didn't rain like this last night.*

Sleeping Bird smiled broadly and laughed at something Ken-ai-te said to her and he joined in. *Glad they are having such a wonderful time this evening.* Were they talking about her? In spite of herself, she wished she could understand their guttural sounds. None of them sounded remotely like the Kiowa words her father had taught her as she grew up. *Oh, who cares? I'm not about to learn their foul language, no matter what they say. Sleeping Bird may have forgotten her English but I never shall! Besides, I'm not planning to stick around long enough to learn Kiowa fluently.*

How could they sit there and talk to each other using words they knew she didn't understand and not include her in the conversation? That was just plain rude! But did she really expect them to do so? Dare she invite their attention by protesting? Absolutely not!

I can outlast their silence. Just because I am a captive doesn't mean I don't have ears, you know. Or do you? I'm not sure if either one of you has even looked at me in these last few hours closely enough to determine that I do, indeed, have ears like you do. I wish I had the courage to go over there and jerk your ears!

Finally, Mandy could control her fury no longer. She had read one time about how a volcano spews out hot lava when it can't contain it anymore and though she'd only seen pictures of this in books, that's precisely how she felt at that moment. About to explode all over them! Without further considering the consequences, that is what she did.

"You know, you could set me free anytime." Both looked up at her and stared. "If you don't, the soldiers will hunt you down and hang you when they catch you. If you will release me so I can go home, they will leave you alone. Please let me go!"

Dead silence.

"Well?" Still nothing. "Are you both deaf? I know you understand enough English to know what I'm saying. Answer me!" She slammed her fist into the hard ground beside her feet for emphasis, glaring at the pair steadily. When neither moved, she jumped up and put her hands on her hips.

"Listen to me, you two, and listen well. I'm white, do you hear? White! That's how I was born and it's how I shall die. And no heathen savage can ever make me any different from how God created me! Not the clothes, hairstyle, food, or even living in a tipi can turn me into a Kiowa. Not ever, do you understand? Is that clear enough for you?"

Ken-ai-te leapt to his feet, eyes flashing, and Mandy flinched, taking a tentative step backward. Was he going to strike her? But instead, he spoke gruffly to Sleeping Bird in Kiowa, then turned to see Mandy's expression as the older woman translated.

"You belong him now. No talk to leave."

Mandy frowned and Sleeping Bird realized she had made some sort of mistake in her English.

"No talk about my leaving here? Is that what you are trying to say? Or rather, what he said?"

"Yes. For...never—no, wrong word." And haltingly, the words that were about to change Mandy's life for all time to come emerged. "Belong him. From now to forever."

"From now until forever? I belong to him?" and she gestured toward the warrior, who nodded in affirmation.

Hesitantly, his tongue twisted around the strange words. "From now, for-ev-er."

"In the first place, sir, I don't 'belong' to anyone except my God. And since both my parents are deceased now, I answer to no one but Him. What's more, I have absolutely zero intentions of being held accountable to you as long as I breathe! You would be wise to let me go, else you are liable to be in for a whirlwind of fury you didn't even know existed!"

†CHAPTER FOURTEEN†

"I will both lay me down in peace, and sleep;
for thou, LORD, only makest me dwell in safety."
Psalm 4:8

"Good riddance! Let him stay out there in the rain, for all I care. The audacity of that man infuriates me!" After Mandy's furious outburst the angry warrior had stomped out into the storm without another word. So much for threats.

Sleeping Bird just glared at her for a moment, then quietly gathered her beads and replaced them in the leather pouch at her waist. Rising, she stepped to the door of the tipi, then turned to look at Mandy.

"Tomorrow you do all work yourself, start before sun come up. Sleep now." And she grabbed a blanket from the pile in the corner and threw it over her head as she silently padded out of the tipi, leaving the astonished Mandy staring behind her.

"Fine! You go, too. I'd rather be by myself, thank you very much." She shivered slightly from the cold seeping in under the tipi sides and decided to move away from the edge, closer to the fire. Warming her hands over the flames, she once more felt the sting from the smoke. Or was it her tears? She couldn't hold them back any longer and they spilled over as she covered her face with her fingers and wept.

"Why, God? Why have You done this to me? You abandon me to a pagan place and expect me to be happy about it? Well, I'm not! It is simply more than I can bear. Much more. You promised never to give me more than I can handle, but You don't seem to understand—I'm not strong enough for a nightmare of such magnitude. And to think that I might be here forever? This just can't be happening to me. Why have You withdrawn Your love and protection right when I need it the most? God, get me out of here! I want to go home—please! Or anywhere else except living in a tipi with a Kiowa savage."

Sobs broke her solitude for quite some time, then slowed, and finally ended. She needed to wipe away her tears and blow her nose. Peering around the tipi for something to use, her eye caught a flash of blue sticking out from under a blanket. Frowning, she recognized it but couldn't quite place why at first. Mandy crawled over and pulled it out and gasped. It was the tiny fragment of her blue dress that she had torn off earlier to clean her face and arms. The rest of her clothing had disappeared while she was out of the tipi working; apparently, this piece had been overlooked. She held it against her nose and inhaled deeply, hoping to catch at least a faint scent of "home" from it, but mostly all she smelled was dirt. However, the feel of it against her cheek was comforting and another tear trickled down her face as she wiped it away gently. *I'm going to stash this somewhere neither of those two will ever find it and when I'm feeling homesick and lonely I can pull it out and touch its precious threads. And maybe I won't miss home quite so much.*

Something filtered into Mandy's consciousness but it took a moment for it to register. The fire! It had almost gone out.

"Sleeping Bird should have shown me how to manage the fire before she stormed out. I don't now to keep it going. Um, I guess just like I kept the one going at the mission, except it was in a *real* fireplace in a *real* house." Gulping against the memory, she glanced around the tipi and spotted a few pieces of kindling wood and one small branch. "Won't keep it going all night, I'm sure, though it might be enough to keep me warm until I can fall asleep at least." With the torrential rains there would be no dry wood anywhere outside so she had no other option for now.

Slowly she pushed the kindling into embers and soon a flame rose up from them. After letting it burn for a moment, she then broke the branch in two and laid those pieces on top. Before long, the flames were higher again.

Mandy inched away from the fire a bit, to avoid the stench of the buffalo rug. She had no desire to battle its scratchy hairs, either. As she lay back down on the hard earthen floor and tried to make her mind go numb enough in order for sleep to overtake her weary body and mind, fear clutched at her heart. A tear slipped out of one eye and trickled down her cheek onto the hand under her head.

"Lord, I'm just a hopeless mess! Please don't let that warrior come back and try to attack me. My body aches and my heart aches and even my brain aches from everything that has happened to me in these last two days. You've promised me peace at night but there doesn't seem any possibility of it when I'm surrounded by fear on every side. What am I going to do when he comes back? Help me!"

⚔

Ooh, this feels so good! Mandy snuggled deeper under the covers and smiled in anticipation of the delicious breakfast Aunt Ida was cooking up for her in the kitchen. The incredible aroma caused her nose to twitch with excitement. Her day promised to be delightful— and she wasn't even out of bed yet. *Wonder what I should wear today? Maybe my new yellow dress trimmed in the blue...*

Suddenly her eyes popped open and in the dim light, she was disoriented for a moment. *Where am I? Certainly not in my room!*

She rose up on one elbow and saw a dark form a few feet away lying across the entrance to the tipi. Memory crushed her heart as awareness returned. Her Kiowa captor had his back to her and soft snores indicated even breathing so he wasn't awake yet.

A blanket covered her and she fingered it curiously. *How did this get here? Did he put it on me last night while I slept? How could he have done it and I remain unaware of him touching me?* Mandy shuddered and threw it off. If it came from him, she definitely didn't want it touching her skin. Still, it represented an obvious act of kindness. The whole thing didn't make sense to her. First, he kidnaps, starves, and tortures her, and then covers her with a blanket so she won't get cold? She shook her head in disbelief.

At least another night went by without him assaulting me. That's a huge relief. I can't believe it, though I'm certainly grateful. Then she remembered she hadn't thought to praise God in her first waking moments, in her usual custom. But today was different. Far different, as yesterday had been. And besides, insofar as her wounded heart could determine she had precious little to praise Him about this morning. Although being protected from unwanted advances was definitely a big one, all right. *I prayed God would do so before I went to sleep last night and I guess I owe Him a thank you for answering that prayer at least. So—thanks.*

Mandy sat up and rubbed her eyes while shaking her hair out, running her fingers through the long black strands to untangle them. *Good grief, it's a mess this morning! What did I do in my sleep, wrestle a bear?* The vague memories of a restless night came back in a rush but she discarded them as irrelevant. *Who wouldn't be uncomfortable after sleeping on the hard ground?* She stretched her arms and moved her neck around to get the kinks out of her muscles, wishing fervently for a hot bath in which she could soak to her heart's content.

A shaft of dim light danced over the fire pit while swirls of dust played in it. *At least it appears the sun will be shining today once it's fully risen, that's something to be grateful for. Guess Ken-ai-te reopened the flap at some point after it stopped raining.* Embers from the fire still glowed from under the pile of grey ash but not enough to generate any real heat in the tipi. Mandy shivered. *Perhaps I was a little hasty in discarding that blanket. She reached out and touched it. No! I would rather freeze to death than accept anything from that brute.* And she shoved it even further away from her. Then she pulled her legs up under her dress as she had done the night before, tucking in the hem around her ankles and putting her arms around her knees in the hopes of staying warm in the cool air. How she longed for the comfort and safety of her bed back home!

Obviously, he chose to sleep next to the entrance to prevent my escape. As though I would venture out into a terrible storm in the middle of the night and try to walk out of here. I may want to leave bad but I'm not stupid! He's the foolish one for passing up sleeping in his bed for that reason. I hope his back aches like mine does this morning!

Mandy brushed some red dirt off the front of her dress and once more admired the handiwork that had gone into it. It was stunning in its intricate design, though simple overall. Red and yellow beads alternated to form a series of star-like formations splashed across the neckline on a background of soft blue. *Each bead is so tiny. There must be several hundred of them here.*

After removing the remnants of her stockings the night before once she was alone, she had decided to sleep in the moccasins to help keep her feet warm. Now she wanted to examine the design on the shoes more closely as well so quietly removed one of them. Similar colors decorated them, too, and when she turned them over in her hand, she realized they appeared to have barely been worn. *Was yesterday the first time anyone has had them on? I wish I knew whose clothes these are.*

The stirring of her captor brought her thoughts back to reality and she held her breath to see what he would say or do upon awakening. Mandy replaced the shoe and, in spite of her earlier reluctance to accept the blanket, instinctively pulled it up to her chin, as though it might protect her should he decide to attack her.

Ken-ai-te sat up and faced her. He nodded at her and she hesitantly returned the gesture. Then he got up and left without a word.

A few seconds later Sleeping Bird slipped in with two bowls

again. She offered them to the young woman who gratefully tossed the blanket to one side in order to drink the water and gulp down the berries and jerky.

While she munched Sleeping Bird deftly took several strands of Mandy's hair and began forming a braid on one side of her head. Surprisingly, she did it with a minimum of pulling, considering all the knots she had to work through.

"Better for work." When she had finished, she moved to the other side and quickly braided it, too. "You do now." Mandy assumed this meant she would be responsible for doing it from now on and shrugged. No need to create a fight over how she wears her hair. She sensed it would be a battle she would lose if she did.

In between bites, Mandy asked, "Did you put the blanket over me last night?"

Sleeping Bird shook her head. "Ken-ai-te. Night cool, you not on robe."

"That thing?" And she pointed at the buffalo rug.

"Sleeping robe. For you and Ken-ai-te."

Mandy blushed deeply and averted her eyes. Apparently, this woman was under the mistaken impression that the two were sleeping together.

"Well, maybe for him but not for me," she said with as much disgust as she could muster. "Right here on the dirt is fine with me. He will never touch my body as long as I have breath!"

⸶CHAPTER FIFTEEN⸷

"And whatsoever ye do, do it heartily, as to the Lord,
and not unto men...for ye serve the Lord Christ."
Colossians 3:23-24

"Did you hear what I said?"

Mandy was disappointed Sleeping Bird hadn't reacted to her declaration of death being preferable to her captor touching her body. Her emotions were running high this morning, which put her in the mood for a good fight, and she figured this would be a perfect topic. She would not back down and it was high time the older woman knew where Mandy stood on the subject. Did she comprehend the words and pretend ignorance due to their sensitive nature or truly not grasp what Mandy had said?

Sleeping Bird frowned but said nothing.

"Well, just so you understand my position. And that goes double for the others in the camp, by the way. They all need to know the truth rather than believing a lie. Glad that's settled between us. It is not something I wish to talk about in the future, now we've—"

"Come, much work before heat of day."

"Uh, yes, that's a good idea. It does get pretty warm when the sun is—"

Abruptly Sleeping Bird left and with a sigh, Mandy rose and followed her, to begin learning her new daily schedule as a Kiowa woman.

First up was learning how to gather firewood, a backbreaking task Mandy quickly decided she wouldn't wish on her worst enemy. It was obvious why the women did this before the sun got too high, as the heat would have made the task much more difficult.

Wonder why the men don't do this job. Back at the mission, Pete and Jesse would chop the wood and haul it up next to the house, then bring in the pieces as I needed them to keep the house warm or the stove hot for cooking our meals. Mandy blinked back tears at the fond memory and the pain further fed her resentment. God, every time I recall something about home, my heart just breaks in two. Will I never be able to remember without tears?

"Work faster. Too slow."

Sleeping Bird's sharp words jerked Mandy's mind back to the present. She glanced around and noticed that all the other women had disappeared.

"I'm working as fast as I know how. It's not my fault I'm new to this and can't do it as quickly as everyone else. They do this every day and I—"

"No speak!"

She shut her mouth and stomped her feet in frustration which caused her to drop a couple of branches and made her even more upset. Before she could stop it, a word escaped her lips that horrified Mandy with its venom. Although she'd heard it from time to time from workmen her father used to hire to work on Aunt Ida's house, she'd never used it before, wasn't even entirely certain of its meaning. Just seemed appropriate at the time, yet quickly she felt the humiliation of failing to maintain self-control over her tongue. She blushed and pressed her lips tight, begging for God's forgiveness as she took deep breaths in an effort to calm herself down.

Sleeping Bird frowned. Mandy said, "Don't Kiowa ever swear? I know I shouldn't have but white men do it all the time. And—"

"Kiowa no say this."

"Really, the Kiowa don't? I'll bet you're wrong. In fact, I would imagine they have plenty of profanity from which to choose."

The smirk on Mandy's face faded as Sleeping Bird shook her head.

"No words for that. Now work. No speak!"

"I'm so tired of—" The scowl on Sleeping Bird's face choked off her words.

Ooh, what I wouldn't say to you if given the chance! You are a disgrace to your race, you know. Here you are, a white woman choosing to live as a Kiowa and now forcing me to do the same. I don't have a choice but I'm quite certain you do. And I still say you are wrong that the Kiowa have no profane words in their language. You may never hear them but I'm quite certain they are there.

When Mandy had put the wood in its place next to the tipi, Sleeping Bird handed her the copper bucket and gestured for her to follow. Obviously they were going after water from, she guessed, a river that although hidden could be easily heard. The further they walked down the slope toward a stand of trees, the more excited Mandy became at the idea of getting out of the village even if only for a short time. The background noise from the rushing waters soon became deafening, the further they went. When they cleared one of the thickets, she could see why.

The powerful waters of the somewhat narrow river tumbled over large boulders in its relentless path, creating numerous tiny waterfalls and clear pools in between each area. The sound itself refreshed Mandy's weary ears and the sparkling water stirred something deep in Mandy's heart as she gazed upon it. How she longed to go swimming in its depths!

Proper ladies didn't usually know how to swim but her father had taught her one summer when his sister was away visiting some friends for a few weeks. They had spent many happy hours together in the river that ran through Trenton until Ida returned home. And both somehow managed to keep it from her aunt, who would have been scandalized had she known what her little brother had done to her niece. As often as possible after that, Mandy would sneak away to go swimming again with her father. It surprised her no one ever told her aunt about the secret but to her knowledge, she never knew.

Mandy supposed the Kiowa wouldn't appreciate her swimming in their water supply, but maybe downstream a short distance? Perhaps in time she would be permitted to come here unaccompanied and then...

Once more, the thought of *time* left her short of breath. *God, please tell me I'm not going to have to stay here for long, certainly not forever. You can work it out to get me home soon. I know You can!*

Sleeping Bird was scowling at her again and Mandy realized that she must have missed something she had said to her about collecting water. The bank sloped down gently into the swirling current in one place and it was here the women of the village were gathering to fill their water buckets and skins.

"Get water." And she rattled out a couple of Kiowa words, unrecognizable gibberish to Mandy.

Shivers crawled up her spine as she recalled the last time she had done so, the day Pete died. *Was that really only two days ago? Seems like a lifetime has passed by already.*

Hauling the heavy bucket required a great deal of physical effort and mental concentration on Mandy's part to scramble back up the river bank without spilling any of the water or stepping in one of the numerous mud puddles in her path. To her shock she managed, at least until she glanced up the hill in front of her. All thought of congratulating herself on her small success faded with her smile. It had been a pleasant stroll down here; back up would obviously be another matter.

I suppose I will eventually develop my muscles for these tasks like the Kiowa women apparently have done, but I swear these people feel no pain! They make it look so effortless, it's disgusting. The whole way she watched the backs of the other women carrying their heavy loads and chattering amongst themselves while walking as casually as though going for a morning stroll. All this, while Mandy struggled just to keep going, much less keep up.

When she finally joined Sleeping Bird at the top of the rise, she could see by the expression on the older woman's face how she felt about Mandy's slow pace. She didn't care; it was all she could do to gasp in enough air to keep from passing out after the long climb. The harsh Kiowa words were lost on her, yet not their intensity. Mandy resolved next time she would beat Sleeping Bird up the hill!

By the time the two women got back to the tipi, Ken-ai-te already sat cross-legged by the cold fire ring, apparently waiting on his breakfast. He seemed amused to see the sweat pouring off Mandy's face but not amused in the least by the fact he would not have a hot breakfast this day. She couldn't care less how he felt, frankly. No longer than it had been since she awoke, Mandy was ready for the day to be over. How she longed to wipe that smug expression off his face! To avoid further scolding, however, she swallowed the urge to do so and mutely followed her instructions on how quickly to put together a meal that didn't have to be cooked.

Sleeping Bird retrieved some jerky from a bag hanging beside the tipi and shoved it into Mandy's hands with a gesture to offer it to Ken-ai-te. She handed her a bowl and indicated she should give him some water to go with it, which Mandy did, a sour look on her face as the only way to indicate her inward rebellious spirit. Sleeping Bird then took some berries from yet another pouch and put them into a gourd bowl and Mandy offered it to her captor as well.

For a brief second, his hand brushed against hers and Mandy's skin crawled with revulsion at his touch. Drawing back her hand, she lowered her eyes so she wouldn't have to face him with the coloring she felt on her cheeks. Yet she saw the hint of a smile playing with his lips and that deepened her disgust and embarrassment even further. *That's it!*

"Now is a good time to bring this up, before we go another step.

Because in spite of what you said earlier, I have no intentions of remaining her forever!" Mandy's words startled the two as Ken-ai-te glanced up from his food and Sleeping Bird stopped in her tracks as she hustled about the area.

Clearing her throat, she looked the warrior in the eye and said as firmly as possible, "If you have any sense of decency at all in you, please let me go! I promise I won't tell anyone where your village is, not even sure I could lead them here if I wanted to since I haven't a clue where we are right now. But I want to go home! You can't mean to keep me here permanently!"

The only response was a soft grunt out of the man's mouth. Sleeping Bird resumed her tasks as though that answered that. It most certainly did *not* as far as Mandy was concerned!

"For-ever. You stay here, now until forever."

"Excuse me? You can't mean that!"

"No speak!" came the terse command from Sleeping Bird. And she raised her fist as though to strike Mandy on the arm if she dared to disobey. Tears filled her vision but she swiped them away and turned to fill her own bowls so she wouldn't have to look at either person. *Forever? God, they can't be serious! Why do they keep saying this? I can't stay here for the rest of my life! I can't stay here the rest of the day! You have to get me out of this place now!*

By this time, Ken-ai-te had finished eating and he tossed aside his bowls and stalked away without a backward glance in Mandy's direction. Clapping her jaw shut, Mandy fumed silently.

Good, I didn't want to talk to you, either! See if I care. Just leave me alone is all I ask and I'll do the same for you. But if the soldiers ever catch you, you will wish the word forever had never been invented!

While Mandy chewed as slowly as possible on her meal of berries and dried meat, something occurred to her about the river. *I didn't see any canoes anywhere along the shoreline; maybe they keep them hidden. Perhaps I could steal one of those for my escape. Surely the river leads back to civilization. If only I knew the name of it.* She continued her mental discussion on the subject for some time, tuning everything and everyone else out.

Escape was never far from her thoughts, because already she sensed the futility of hoping for rescue. It would be up to her own resourcefulness to get away from here, not sitting around and waiting for someone to swoop down and take her home.

The rest of the morning passed with Mandy learning various tasks for her new way of life. Whenever she failed to do so quickly enough, Sleeping Bird would threaten a blow to her arm or back to sharpen her focus and push her to hurry. At least it helped Mandy to realize as the day wore on she was subjected to this treatment less often and sometimes only received a tongue lashing to express Sleeping Bird's displeasure. Kiowa words were sprinkled in everywhere, with Mandy ordered to repeat them back as she worked. In her stubbornness, she adamantly refused to do so much of the time and when she did, she would deliberately mangle the words. It became almost a joke to her but she noted Sleeping Bird didn't seem to appreciate the humor.

Late afternoon with the sun sinking lower in the western sky, a thought suddenly dug its talons deep into her mind, like a hawk does with his prey, and her anguish was so great the result was as keen as if sharp claws had actually pierced her skull.

"Oh, no! It's Sunday!" she cried out without thinking. Her tears blurred the scowl on Sleeping Bird's face but Mandy didn't care one bit, didn't even resist them at first when they slid down her cheeks. She might have to keep on working but inside she rebelled with every breath.

This is the first Sabbath Day in my life I haven't been able to attend services. Even on the long journey west, we celebrated with the other people on the wagon train on Sunday mornings with a short worship time before setting out again for the day. Oh, Papa, I'm so sorry that I have been forced to disobey you and God today. It's just so unfair!

Her demeanor changed abruptly after this revelation and the sadness pulled her down until she could hardly bear its weight. She was weepy the rest of the afternoon, talking often to her beloved father about the pain she was feeling. However, never once did she take her broken heart to the Lord in prayer. The verse about rejoicing in the day God has made came to mind once or twice but she couldn't bear the thought of "rejoicing" in her present circumstances. What was there to rejoice about? *Papa, will all my life be this void of joy and happiness now? I just can't go on like this one more step!*

✝ CHAPTER SIXTEEN ✝

"My flesh and my heart faileth;
but God is the strength of my heart, and my portion forever."
Psalm 73:26

"Wrong way. Do right!" The harsh words from Sleeping Bird settled on Mandy's heart like a heavy blanket, smothering the breath out of her. *Will I ever do anything to please her? Wonder of wonders, I didn't mouth off to her this time. And she didn't hit me, just scolded. Guess I'm making some progress, at least.*

As Mandy once more attempted to start the fire using two twigs the way she had been shown countless times, she gritted her teeth and determined to light a spark. A moment later, to her great surprise, one appeared. Her hand shook with excitement as she dropped the twigs onto the tiny flame that had caught on the grasses she'd laid there earlier. She glanced up to see if Sleeping Bird noticed but she had disappeared again. *Where is she when I need her attention?*

"The past several days," she muttered to herself, "have been a blur. Everyone has ignored me for the most part except for Sleeping Bird. Don't know where she got her name but it certainly wasn't from all the *sleeping* she does because I honestly don't think she ever closes her eyes!"

Mandy finally got the fire going with more sticks and a couple of good-sized branches and was rather proud of her accomplishment. "You are my first real triumph, you know," she said to the fire. "Don't you dare go out!"

Then she scurried to finish the rest of the preparations for the morning meal. The sun peered over the distant horizon and she paused a moment to look at its bright rays. A perfect spring day was dawning, just over the wrong place. "If only—"

She stopped in mid-sentence and sighed. "Won't do any good going on like that, Mandy. Keep your focus on the here and now. Forget about home. It no longer exists."

Despair weighed her heart down all morning as she went through the motions she had been taught. Inside—another matter. Mandy seethed with anger and resentment yet not once did she pray concerning her emotional turmoil. It had been a long couple of weeks. At least, she thought only two weeks had passed since her captor brought her here. Could have been more, without any way to keep track of time.

"I'll have to figure something out to mark the days, else I won't know when it's the Sabbath Day again; in fact, I have already missed another one. Maybe with the various colors of beads? I'll think that through later."

Most evenings she and Ken-ai-te were able to stumble through some semblance of conversation with each other. Against her will, the Kiowa words were sinking in, little by little. At the same time, she sensed his desire to know more English. At least he understood her better now and sometimes would repeat words after her. Depending on her mood at the moment, sometimes she would also do the same with Kiowa phrases. Her stubbornness prevented her from even attempting most of them, a fact that pleased neither her captor nor Sleeping Bird.

The older woman, of course, knew a great deal more English than did Ken-ai-te, though she was more stubborn than he in insisting that Mandy use only Kiowa as much as possible. However, in the last couple of days Mandy had often been able to speak to her in English when they were alone without being reprimanded. It appeared to her that Sleeping Bird struggled with wanting to remember the foreign words of her long-ago memory, yet also insisted that Mandy learn

Kiowa right away. The whole thing left her confused and frustrated.

One afternoon Mandy had fleshed maybe half of a large portion of a deerskin when Sleeping Bird approached and told her she needed more water and directed her to go to the river to fetch it for her. *Anything to get out of this nasty job.* And she took up the extra bucket and walked away, expecting Sleeping Bird to follow. But she did not.

Mandy's heart jumped as each step took her closer to the river. For the first time she had been allowed to leave the village on her own! She felt exhilarated not to have every movement watched. Now she stood at the edge of the mighty waters that perhaps offered a chance for escape. Glancing from side to side nervously, she saw no one nearby.

"This is the perfect opportunity to look for a boat or a raft of some kind which might be hidden somewhere close." Mandy poked around for several minutes without any luck—no canoes. Another hope dashed to pieces. "Better get the water before they miss me and think I took off."

After filling the bucket, she turned to start up the hill and gasped. Black Feather stood a few feet away staring at her, an unpleasant sneer on his ugly face. How had he snuck up on her like that, without her hearing a sound? Eyes wide with fear, Mandy shifted the bucket to the left hand so she might use the other for defense if needed. She had no other weapon though the bucket, had it been empty, might have been a good one. *I can always throw the water at him and then use the bucket to bash his head in. God, give me courage! No one will hear my screams from down here.*

She took a deep breath and glared at him as evenly as she could manage. Her knees were shaking and she was grateful he couldn't see them.

"Get out of my way, please." She had managed to learn the word "now" in Kiowa and used it to punctuate the English words with as harsh a voice as she could produce. He didn't budge but did spout several words in Kiowa that made her flinch with their venom, though she hadn't a clue what he said. If she tried, she could imagine their meaning but she preferred to remain in ignorance.

"Mine!" he barked at her.

Again, that word. Shivers crept down her arms.

"No Ken-ai-te!" His dark eyes narrowed and bore into her.

She frowned and realized she must make the first move because obviously he wasn't going to comply with her demand.

Mandy took one step toward him, then side stepped to go wide, trying to stay out of his reach. He suddenly grabbed her free arm and caught her off balance, causing some of the water to splash out.

"Let go of me!" She tried to jerk her arm loose from his grasp when suddenly Sleeping Bird appeared out of the bushes. Had she been watching the whole time? If so, why didn't she intervene right off?

The older woman spoke angrily to him in Kiowa and he released Mandy's arm. Taking one step back, his eyes locked in a stare down with Sleeping Bird.

"Go," she muttered to Mandy in Kiowa.

Another word Mandy had learned well. And this time didn't hesitate to obey. Although she knew she ought to lower her eyes, she couldn't help a smug smile as she passed by the warrior. He had lost again. Couldn't be too happy about that. Too bad!

One of these days, you are going to learn to leave me alone. Just hope it's sooner rather than later. What on earth makes you believe I belong to you instead of Ken-ai-te? I guess I was the focus of your argument with him the day of my capture, as I suspected—but why?

Her heart pounded as she climbed the bank and started up the hill toward the village. Half way, Sleeping Bird joined her and Mandy struggled to keep up with her long strides while not spilling any of the precious water. She had no desire to repeat the trip down to the river for more all alone.

For such a short woman, you certainly walk fast. Don't know if I

107

will ever be able to do that. And up this steep slope, no less. Nervously she glanced over her shoulder a time or two, relieved to see Black Feather did not appear to be following them.

The pace of the climb left Mandy breathless by the time they reached the tipi. Sleeping Bird took the bucket of water and gestured for Mandy to return to the task she had been doing, then left her alone once more. Mandy sank to the ground, as her knees simply wouldn't hold her any longer. Picking up the fleshing tool, she gazed at a gleam of sunlight as it glinted off the blade.

"Wish I'd had you a few minutes ago! That whole scene would have ended quite differently. What does he have against me? No one else bothers me that way. They all simply ignore me. I'm going to ask Sleeping Bird when she comes back."

"Ask what?" Sleeping Bird stood there, an empty bucket in one hand. Chalk one up to another Kiowa able to move without a sound. This was getting annoying.

"Why Black Feather hates me like he apparently does. What have I ever done to him to warrant such anger?"

Sleeping Bird took out her knife and sliced through the hide Mandy was holding. Then she picked up another fleshing tool and sat down beside her before she spoke, handing one piece to her and keeping the second one for herself.

"Black Feather good man once. White soldiers cut his face, kill sister and her son. He not forget. Hate all white men now. You most."

"Why does he hate me the most? I don't understand that kind of bitterness. I haven't done anything to him, yet from the first moment he laid eyes on me, his hatred has been overwhelming. He frightens me."

Sleeping Bird paused a moment and stared at her. "Ken-ai-te reason."

"What does Ken-ai-te have to do with Black Feather's irrational anger with me?"

"His wife and son who die."

Her jaw dropped open as the truth sank in. "Black Feather and Ken-ai-te are brothers-in-law—or rather were?"

Sleeping Bird frowned. "Not know this word."

"In other words, Ken-ai-te's wife was Black Feather's sister?" She nodded.

"No wonder he hates me so much. He wants to kill me, doesn't he? As revenge for his sister's death."

Again, she nodded her head, avoiding Mandy's eyes.

"What, there's more? There's something else you're not telling me."

After several moments of silence, Sleeping Bird gazed evenly at Mandy. "Ken-ai-te take you for revenge. Black Feather want you more. They now fight, maybe to death. For you."

⊹CHAPTER SEVENTEEN⊹

"A good name is rather to be chosen than great riches,
and loving favour rather than silver and gold."
Proverbs 22:1

"To the *death*? Are you kidding me? They would actually fight each other, men of the same family, over a white captive? That doesn't make sense."

"Kiowa way." Mandy sat in stunned silence. "Chief Twin Fox give you to Ken-ai-te, not Black Feather, cause more anger."

"Chief Twin Fox? Is that the chief's name, then?" Sleeping Bird nodded in reply. Mandy didn't appreciate being treated like a ball being bounced from one warrior to another but she was grateful for the chief's apparent wisdom in awarding her to the one he did.

Minutes crept by. They worked without a word except those necessary to complete their task.

Finally, Mandy asked quietly, "Do the clothes I'm wearing belong to his wife?"

"Not hers, yours now."

So that was who had done all the intricate beading on her dress and moccasins. Ken-ai-te's dead wife. Killed by white men. And Mandy was now his slave, to be used for revenge for this death. Or deaths—there had also been a son. How awful for Ken-ai-te, to lose his family like he did. How long had it been? Wounds like that go deep and don't heal quickly or easily. She didn't have to be married or a parent to comprehend his pain.

What really left her baffled came as an unsettled feeling, almost compassion; whatever, it made her uncomfortable. Sympathy, perhaps. But caring beyond that? Why on earth should she feel like she did? Ken-ai-te kidnapped her and killed Pete, or at least condoned his murder. And she felt certain he must have killed other whites in the past; the hated scalp lance was proof of that. She squirmed but it wasn't because her legs were going to sleep again. This whole thing would take some time to digest, to consider it carefully from every angle, because it was a bit overwhelming.

A silent voice nagged deep to also pray, but she tried to push it aside. What more could God say to her than the silence between them now?

Later that night she and Ken-ai-te were both in the tipi and her curiosity concerning what she had learned earlier got the best of her.

"Sleeping Bird told me today white soldiers killed your wife and son. What were their names?"

His eyes flashed briefly, then he averted his gaze and replied with a hard edge in his voice, "No speak names of dead."

Mandy nodded and let it go. She understood if he found it painful to speak of them. After a few minutes, however, she couldn't resist probing further.

"How long ago were they killed?"

Silence. Mandy shrugged, trying again to drop the subject and instead focus on her beadwork. *Aunt Ida would be proud to see what a good job I'm doing and she would be amazed at how much tiny detail there is in—*

Her thoughts trailed off. Aunt Ida...home...safety. She squeezed back tears and took a deep breath to control her emotions.

"What cross mean?" It took Mandy a couple of moments to realize Ken-ai-te had spoken to her.

"My cross? Oh, you mean this one," and she pulled the gold chain out from under her dress and fingered the tiny symbol. "It is the sign of my God. His Son's name was Jesus. He died on a cross so I have my

111

necklace to remember Him by."

Ken-ai-te frowned. "Die on cross?"

"Yes, some men hated Him and wanted to kill Him so they nailed Him to a cross and He bled to death."

He didn't seem to understand "nailed" so it took Mandy several moments to explain using mostly sign language. Kiowa people didn't use nails. But they did use wooden pegs to hold the tipis together and for other purposes. Suddenly he jumped up, his face a red and angry mask.

"Son die and father not stop?" he yelled.

Mandy gasped and realized he had compared this situation to his own feelings when his son was killed. Wrong thing to say, for certain!

She hastily tried to explain God could have stopped His Son's death but chose not to; however, every word she uttered made things worse. Her frustration quickly slid into irritation. Why could he not just accept this and quit making it so personal? She didn't mean God should have intervened, just that it happened. It was in the Bible. How else could she explain it?

Again, a gentle voice reminded her she should have prayed before opening her mouth. To add fuel to the fire, her words rang a bit hollow, given the barrenness of her soul right now. Unfortunately, she couldn't take back her words or find a kinder way to explain the event. The damage had already been done.

He grew more angry with each word until, exasperated, she snapped at him, "Look, that's how it happened and I can't help it if you don't like it. I—"

Without warning Ken-ai-te stormed out of the tipi and left her alone and miserable in the middle of her sentence. Why did she feel she had failed him so? What did she care if he understood or not? Mandy wasn't sure even *she* understood this complicated point. Indeed, why *would* God have sat back and done nothing when His Son was being tortured and killed?

112

The thought slowly formed amidst the turmoil in her mind. *Same reason He stood by while I was being tortured, I guess. I know it wasn't because He didn't love Jesus. And I know He loves me. But why when He can do something, does He choose not to?*

"You know, God, if I just had my Bible, maybe the bitterness I have in my heart would go away. You've always told me to depend on Your Word, only now I don't have it any more. I should depend on You alone, I know, but I don't know how to do it any longer. I'm so weary of trying and battling my fears and being so lonely! Why do You sit there and do *nothing*? Don't You want me to read the Bible again? Ever?"

She sighed and put her beading away. The system she had invented for keeping track of the days wasn't working and she couldn't figure out how to do it. Her brain couldn't function any longer this evening. Another long night sleeping on the cold, hard ground loomed in front of her. The buffalo robe looked more attractive every day.

"You don't suppose I'm getting used to the smell, do you? It doesn't bother me like it did at first. Oh, please tell me I'm not smelling like that, too!" She wrinkled up her nose, groaned softly, and laid her head down on the fur. "I appreciate your continued protection from Ken-ai-te not assaulting me, Lord. It is confusing, though. Does he not find me attractive enough?"

"Oh, good grief, Mandy!" She sat up abruptly. "I don't care if he finds me attractive or not, would prefer if he did not. You *must* be lonely if you are having thoughts like this. I just want him to stay away and leave me alone."

She rose and grabbed her scrap of blue fabric out from its hiding place, then plopped back down again in her usual spot. Hugging it might mean she was behaving like a small child but at times she felt like one. In any case, she knew sleep would not be pleasant tonight.

†

Mandy didn't have an opportunity to speak with Ken-ai-te at any length until the next evening. She hoped to untangle some of the anger he had expressed regarding the Cross.

"Ken-ai-te, could you please tell me how to say a few Kiowa words?" She figured that would please him and take him off his guard so she could bring up the subject once more.

He proceeded to explain a few of the words she asked for, carefully enunciating each one so she could attempt to replicate the guttural sounds and lilt of his voice. For the most part, though, she remained pretty hopeless at this. The Kiowa words her father had taught her growing up didn't sound anything like these and she found that curious. He had learned them from the people to whom he had ministered and she always believed they were Kiowa. Maybe there were various dialects within the complicated language?

The warrior smiled and nodded vigorously to encourage her with the successful attempts and patiently repeated the words for her when she didn't get them right. In spite of herself, Mandy's heart warmed at pleasing him. After several minutes, she collapsed into a fit of giggles over the way she mangled the difficult syllables. It was enough to break the ice between them, at least, as they laughed together and she felt the tension between them drain away. Deep inside, however, she felt a twinge of hypocrisy because in truth she didn't care if she learned to say them or not. She was just making conversation with him.

After several minutes, she said quietly, "Ken-ai-te, yesterday when I said my God's Son died on the Cross you were upset. And I understand why, because of your own son. How old was he when he died?"

Silence. Failure reared its ugly head and Mandy's mood deflated.

"Three moons."

"Three months old? That's horrible! Why would anyone kill a young mother with such a tiny baby, especially US Army soldiers?"

More silence.

"I'm sorry, you know. I'm embarrassed people of my race would do such a horrible thing. It makes me sad white people and Kiowa cannot get along better. We have much in common, actually."

He frowned and she continued. "Many things are the same between Kiowa and whites, I mean." The expression on his face made Mandy believe he was considering what she had said. At least he didn't find the idea offensive, so she continued. "Like our God, for instance. He wants us to pray to Him, as you prayed that day out on the prairie when we saw the buffalo herd running."

Ken-ai-te smiled at the memory. "Yes, pray. You pray your God?"

"Yes, I pray to my God. All the time."

"Never see."

"Because I pray to Him in my heart," and she gestured toward her chest. "I pray out loud as well but since I can't go to church any more I usually just pray in my heart."

"Chur-ch?" His tongue twisted around the unfamiliar word.

"That is the place where I worship my God with others. We sing hymns and pray to Him and read the Bible."

"Bi-ble?"

"That's my holy book, Ken-ai-te. It is very special to me and I miss not having my Bible very much."

"Ho-ly book?"

"Yes. It has my God's words in it, messages to me from Him. And stories of people from long ago times who lived when Jesus lived."

"Where this book?"

"Where is it?" And he nodded. "I left it in my bedroom at the mission the morning when—" Her voice broke at the painful memory. She cleared her throat and continued. "When Pete and I went to collect water. When you abducted me."

"Pete husband?"

Mandy laughed. "Oh my goodness, no! He is, uh, that is, he *was* the foreman at the mission where I lived. More like an uncle to me, especially since my father died."

"Father die?"

"Yes, he was killed by Indians a few weeks ago. We never found out who did it or why. Soldiers brought his body back to the mission so we could bury him there."

"That same, too."

"You mean because we each have lost someone very dear to us in a violent manner by the other's people?"

Ken-ai-te nodded and gazed intently at her face. Mandy lowered her eyes because she was concerned he might see sympathy in them and she didn't want to be that vulnerable to him, to show weakness to this man. Besides, she found it difficult to look him in the eye for it stirred strange feelings deep within she didn't want to have, couldn't quite put a name to, didn't understand and wasn't sure she wanted to. After all, he was her enemy and she needed to keep that uppermost in her mind.

After a few minutes, he rose and left the tipi without saying another word. Mandy sighed and put aside the sewing she had been working on. She couldn't concentrate.

"What's the matter with me? I've simply got to keep my hands and mind busy, else I shall go out of my mind for sure." Reluctantly, she picked it up again, sighed and simply stared numbly at it.

Sleeping Bird had told her she would need a second dress soon so she had attempted to sew three deer hide pieces together, without much luck. This sewing was so different from what she had learned from her Aunt Ida, much more primitive, but in spite of its simplicity, she was becoming quite discouraged. She poked at the fire and roused the embers into flames, feeling the heat on her face. Moving her fingers through the hairs on the buffalo robe under her, she imagined again, what it would be like to sleep in its warmth instead of on the ground, then quickly dismissed the thought.

Suddenly Ken-ai-te reappeared. "Give you Kiowa name now."

"But I like Mandy and I want to keep this name," she said as her voice rose in panic. "My parents gave it to me. You can't take that away from me, too!"

"You Prayer Woman now. *Daw-t'sai-mah*. You say."

"Dow-sigh-mah?"

"Close, Prayer Woman. No talk. Sleep." And he strode out once more.

"Prayer Woman? Where on earth did he get that, I wonder? Prayer Woman...I rather like it. At least it's not some gibberish I can't pronounce. Suppose I should be grateful for small favors. What were the Kiowa words—*dow-sigh-mah*, or something like that? Yes, I like it, not as much as Mandy, but it will do."

Like a bolt of lightning, a piece of Scripture pierced her heart and took her breath away. She couldn't recall precisely its location but thought it might be in Isaiah; however, she clearly remembered the words that now brought tears to her eyes as she proclaimed them aloud. "Thou shalt be called by a new name, which the mouth of the LORD shall name."

"*You* have proclaimed me 'Prayer Woman'? You're telling me You managed somehow to inspire this heathen to give me a new name, and not just any new name but this particular one? He said he'd never seen me pray. Are you reminding me, Father, that I need to let him see me in prayer rather than only doing it when I'm alone? How humbled I am and ashamed to admit my rebellion once again. Give me the courage to live the responsibility You've placed before me. 'Prayer Woman'. What do You think, God?"

✝ CHAPTER EIGHTEEN ✝

"And ye shall know the truth, and the truth shall make you free."
John 8:32

"Sleeping Bird, where is Ken-ai-te? I wanted to ask him something but I can't find him anywhere in the camp."

"Gone."

"Obviously! That's my point. Where did he go?"

"Not say."

"Well, how long will he be gone? Do you know when he'll return?"

"Not say."

"Warriors can do that, just take off and not tell anyone where they are going or when they will be back? What if something happens and they are needed here?"

"Kiowa way. No speak more."

Mandy sighed in frustration. *Wish I could do the same—run away and no one would even care where I'd gone or if I'd be back. It's not fair! I don't care if I am considered a slave around here, when I need the man he should be close by.* Her question, as important as it might seem to her at the moment, would have to wait.

She put her focus back on learning how to make Indian bread. It had turned out to be a much harder task than she thought at first and every one of her attempts ended up more like pancakes than bread! Sleeping Bird's wasn't much thicker but at least it had some substance to it and filled the stomach. Mandy's, on the other hand, was quite unappetizing, even she had to admit that. She'd not had difficulty making bread back home; in fact, she had been quite proud of her ability to do so. However, these circumstances were so different and she hadn't gotten the hang of cooking it over a campfire like they did. Kneading it, she slapped it as she would have liked to do the face of her captor, taking all her irritation out on it.

Slowing her actions a bit Mandy pictured in her mind what by anyone's standards would definitely be considered handsome features, much as she hated to agree. Rugged, with a few copper canyons but otherwise smooth skin on his face, he of course had the distinctive broad nose, high cheekbones, and strong chin of a Kiowa warrior. He wore his hair in a heavy braid on each side of his head, with the hair in between left loose down his back. The braids were wrapped with rawhide strips and adorned with a few small feathers as well. Ken-ai-te wore two larger feathers wound into the hair on the back of his head with rawhide strips so they stood straight up above his head.

How on earth they stayed there so perfectly, day after day, lay beyond her comprehension. Or it seemed that way, for she had watched just that morning in fascination as he removed them and then replaced them again, working deftly without the benefit of a mirror, all by feel and done smoothly without much apparent effort. Mandy had never seen him redo the braids; however, she noticed they always looked freshly done and how the smaller feathers changed quite often.

His muscles rippled in his chest and shoulders when he moved, displaying for all to see his obvious strength of body. His thighs were the same way, and she blushed a bit thinking about how muscled they were, too. She'd never seen his calves. He wore moccasins that came up almost to his knees, which she found odd. Many of the men in the village did the same but quite a few others wore the more traditional style like the women did. *Wonder why the difference? Maybe just personal preference, I suppose. They would help protect his legs when riding or walking in the prairie grasses, though.*

119

And she had never seen them off his feet, even at night. Surely, he took them off occasionally, but never in front of her. He wore only a breechcloth and thinking about it once more brought color to Mandy's cheeks. She wished he would wear more clothing, because it made her uncomfortable to stare at his bare chest and legs especially when they were alone.

Sleeping Bird told Mandy one of her duties would be to make all of Ken-ai-te's clothes so maybe she could make him a shirt at least when the weather became cooler. *I would assume he will dress more warmly when it's winter than now but if I offer to make him some leggings and a shirt perhaps he will cover himself up before then. It's worth a try.*

That night during the evening meal Sleeping Bird announced she would stay overnight with Mandy in the tipi since Ken-ai-te had not yet returned. It was the first time he'd been gone overnight. Mandy immediately felt enormous relief. At least this one night, she wouldn't have to wonder if the time had come he would choose to exercise his right over her body.

"That's great, because I get a little lonely at night by myself. Ken-ai-te usually stays at the campfire with the other men until long after I am asleep and I never even hear him come in. And tonight I will get to sleep on the buffalo robe instead of on the ground." She glanced at the other woman's face after her last statement to see if she registered any surprise but she did not. And Mandy sighed in relief. No nagging reminder of her duty to Ken-ai-te at least for today.

After they finished dinner, the two women joined everyone at the campfire. Mandy had never been invited before and her excitement bubbled at being included.

"What does everyone do at the campfire in the evening, Sleeping Bird?"

"No speak. Eyes down. Women quiet unless singing."

Disappointed, Mandy nevertheless quickened her steps to match those of Sleeping Bird as they approached the fire pit. They settled among the women, who nestled down shoulder to shoulder with each other in an area away from the men.

"Sleeping Bird," she whispered, "where are the children?"

"In tipis, asleep. No speak!"

How am I supposed to learn if I'm not allowed to ask questions? I've been asking her that one thing ever since I arrived! I guess they leave their children alone but I'd be afraid if I were they. What if a wild animal came into the tipi and killed a baby? A little one would be defenseless against a coyote, say, and with the noise of the drums and chants every night, I'm sure they would never hear the child cry out. I just don't understand these people at all.

Mandy tried her best to follow some of the Kiowa words but in the context of a song, it was impossible. She had absolutely no idea what the songs were about and since questions weren't permitted, she let her mind wander to keep from becoming drowsy.

I wonder where Black Feather is? Sure hope he's not lurking around here anywhere. Good thing Sleeping Bird is right beside me. I'm grateful for her protection from his vicious threats. Even though it would be nice to be left alone once in a while, because of my fear of him, I'm thankful I'm seldom by myself. Such as tonight, he might discover I'm on my own and creep in there in the middle of the night and harm me. She shuddered involuntarily.

An astonishing idea struck her, one that she had never considered before. *God, is this Your protective hand on me—allowing Sleeping Bird to have the courage and ability to fend off the evil attacks of Black Feather and keep me safe?*

Mandy thought about this long and hard in the next several minutes and a peace settled over her that she hadn't felt in a long time, in truth not since coming to live here. She closed her eyes and prayed silently, asking forgiveness for not seeing it sooner and praising Him for His unique plan for protection. *Of course, if You had stopped Ken-*

ai-te from kidnapping me in the first place, it would never have been necessary. But before she got caught up in all the "whys" again, she dismissed the idea from her mind and tried to enjoy the dancing and singing. This was the Kiowa social life and, while it didn't come close to equaling what Mandy had always been used to, she found it interesting and exciting in its own way.

The beating of the drums was deafening at times and seemed to drown out everything else. Mixed with the rapid pace of the dances and the constant chants and yips from the men, it served to stir her blood in a way she never imagined could happen. Every night as she went to sleep she would hear the drums; tonight she felt she was *experiencing* them in an almost mystical way. She had become fully caught up in the mood when suddenly Sleeping Bird rose and pulled on Mandy's elbow.

"We're leaving?" Sleeping Bird's scowl silenced her questions of why and shattered the pleasant atmosphere Mandy had been enjoying. She followed, but reluctantly.

Once they were inside the tipi, Mandy asked, "Why did we leave so soon? The whole thing was fascinating. I've never seen anything like it before."

"Late. Need sleep." But she averted her eyes and Mandy had learned that meant she was keeping something from her.

"What? Did I do something wrong, is that why you hustled me out of there so fast?"

Sleeping Bird looked at her a moment. "Black Feather come. We leave."

"Oh, you saw Black Feather? Probably a good idea. Once he realized Ken-ai-te was nowhere around, things could have gotten pretty ugly."

She nodded but said nothing as she stoked the fire into flame. The two began their usual evening activity of beading and several moments passed in silence before Sleeping Bird spoke.

"Prayer Woman, your white name A-man-da Cl-ark?" Her tongue tripped over the words.

Mandy nodded, amazed she remembered. It was the first time her real name had been mentioned for weeks, since the day she arrived. The depth of her emotional reaction to hearing it spoken aloud shook her with its intensity and she caught her breath slightly.

"Who father?"

"My father's name was Josiah Clark. See, nothing horrible happens when we speak of the dead in our culture. I wish you could be free of that particular fear, Sleeping Bird. Nevertheless, why do you ask?"

Sleeping Bird waved away the question as unimportant. But deep frowns creased her forehead when she bent over her handwork once again.

Mandy decided since the older woman had brought up the subject it gave her the freedom to talk about her father some more.

"Papa and I came to Indian Territory to share Christ with the Kiowa and Comanche tribes that live in this area. It was a life-long dream of mine to do this with him. He and my mother actually started the ministry long years ago before I came along. When she died in childbirth having me Papa took me back to Ohio to get his sister Ida's help in rearing me. That's where I lived, in Trenton, until a few months ago when we came out here."

Sleeping Bird did not look up nor even acknowledge that Mandy had spoken. *Sure is odd. Not at all like her. In spite of herself, she is usually more talkative than this.* After a moment, she continued to fill the silence with her memories.

"A few weeks ago Papa was killed by a band of Indians while visiting one of the distant villages. The soldiers found his body and brought him home to be buried at the mission. He had been—" her voice broke a moment, but she cleared her throat and went on. "He had been scalped and most of his clothing removed. Thankfully, it appeared he died quickly."

Sleeping Bird glanced up at this but still said nothing. As they stared at each other, Mandy believed she saw sympathy and compassion in those blue eyes. Her heart warmed at the thought. Maybe the beginnings of a friendship instead of master and slave?

She held Mandy's gaze, then finally returned her focus to her work so Mandy also resumed sorting the beads in front of her. *Where are the yellow ones I saw yesterday? They—*

"Mother?" The question interrupted Mandy's thoughts and caught her completely off guard.

"My mother? She died giving birth to me." Then it dawned on her what the older woman had requested. "Oh, her name? Lily, isn't that pretty? Just like the flowers that bloom at Easter."

"Ea-ster?" she asked hesitantly.

"That's the day Jesus rose from the grave. Have you heard me tell Ken-ai-te that story? It's even more beautiful than the one about Jesus' baptism, when John the Baptist immersed Him in the waters of the River Jordan, in the name of the Father, Son, and Holy Ghost. Easter is considered the most glorious day of the year to Christians, that is, to those who follow Christ. If He'd stayed on the Cross or in the grave, His death would have been meaningless. But coming alive again after being buried makes Him unique, and it makes our faith stronger to know He conquered death for all of us by doing so."

Mandy glanced up and was stunned. Sleeping Bird was crying! She stared a moment, then lowered her eyes respectfully. *What did I say that brought this on? Perhaps in hearing about Jesus' Resurrection she has found faith? Oh, Lord, I do hope so!*

†CHAPTER NINETEEN†

"Restore to me the joy of thy salvation;
and uphold me with thy free spirit."
Psalm 51:12

*F*ather, whatever the struggle she is enduring right now, I pray
You will make Truth known to her.

Mandy looked up at Sleeping Bird and saw her expression change
markedly. It was impossible to read her mind of course, so she could
only guess why. She believed by remaining silent and lifting her up in
prayer she would allow God's Spirit to reveal Himself more clearly to
her without any interference.

After some time of working side by side in silence, Mandy
became so drowsy she could no longer hold her eyes open. She told
Sleeping Bird of her problem and the older woman agreed it was time
for bed. The beading put aside, they both stretched out on the buffalo
robe with blankets over them. What a treat for Mandy to get to sleep
on the robe!

*Mmm, this feels so much better than sleeping in the dirt. I had no
idea it would be so comfortable and so much warmer, too.*

Mandy's eyes closed quickly in silent prayer but somehow she
had a sense that those of the other woman remained open for some
time. Though why, she could not fathom.

†

To Mandy's great relief, Black Feather never showed up the next
day to harass her. Surely, he had taken note of Ken-ai-te's absence

125

from the campfire the night before. Then she blushed. Perhaps he believed the warrior was in the tipi with his captive? And maybe the whole village believed it, too! This whole thing about sharing a roof with a Kiowa brave really bothered her. Of course, it wasn't really a "roof" but rather a hide; either way, the damage to Mandy's heart remained the same. Something had to be done. And soon.

Her intention had been to question Ken-ai-te about this very thing when she discovered he had left the village the day before. She longed for her own tipi, as Sleeping Bird had, and in spite of what her father had taught her about Kiowa culture, she stubbornly clung to her belief that if there had ever been a good reason for a woman to have her own place, Mandy owned it. Yes, she would be on her own somewhat more but in truth, the warrior wasn't in the tipi all that much except for a brief time in the evenings and then of course while they both slept. The rest of the time, she was by herself or was with Sleeping Bird doing the many tasks required of her.

"I've just got to find an opportunity to talk to him about this," she exclaimed aloud. "He seems to trust me more now so once he hears me out maybe he will consider my request reasonable in spite of how it appears at first."

Late that afternoon Mandy was again helping Sleeping Bird flesh another deerskin when Ken-ai-te appeared and strode up to them. He looked weary but wore a broad grin ear to ear and seemed pleased to find both of them together.

"Greetings, my son," said Sleeping Bird in Kiowa.

Son? Mandy had learned enough to understand the phrase; she had suspected this relationship but hearing it spoken startled her. Then why didn't she live in the tipi with him? Chalk up another question to ask at some point.

Ken-ai-te plopped down on the ground next to Mandy and before she could say anything, he drew an item out of a bag at his waist and laid it on the ground in front of her.

It was a Bible! And not only *a* Bible, it was *her* Bible!

"Where on earth did you get this?" she cried as she hugged it to her chest.

"Took from mission. For Prayer Woman."

Her smile faded. "You stole it from the mission? Oh, please, tell me you didn't kill anyone to get it!"

His scowl darkened and the smile faded. "No one there. Took and left. It is what you ask for?"

"Oh, yes, it is exactly what I have prayed for. But I never imagined you would go all that way to get my own Bible for me. Oh, Ken-ai-te, thank you, from the bottom of my heart, thank you." She began leafing through the pages, and her eyes filled and tears spilled over and streamed down her cheeks. The fleshing forgotten, Mandy was lost in its depths for some time. Sleeping Bird didn't say a word, just resumed her task and left Mandy alone. Ken-ai-te smiled again when their eyes met briefly, then abruptly got up and walked away.

After several minutes, Sleeping Bird cleared her throat and the sound brought Mandy back to the present.

"Oh, I'm sorry, Sleeping Bird. I just got so caught up in reading some of my favorite Scripture passages, I forgot about the fleshing. We really need to finish this before dinner, I know." She put the Bible aside gently, laying it right next to her in the grass. It was her only real possession in this world and nothing could have been sweeter. Made of gold, it couldn't have been more precious to her.

Mandy worked hard the rest of the day and couldn't wait until they had finished with dinner. She had put the Bible in a corner of the tipi and was eager to start reading again. She hoped Ken-ai-te would join the men as usual that evening and prayed God would prompt Sleeping Bird to return to her own tipi when he left. This would allow Mandy time to read for a change instead of doing her work. Much to her delight, that is what happened. Settled comfortably as possible on the hard ground, Mandy closed her eyes to pray before beginning her reading.

"Thank You, Father, for the gift of Your Word. How true it is that though the flowers fade and the grass withers, yet the Word of God shall stand forever! Speak to me now through these words to encourage my heart."

Many hours later, she finally fell asleep on the ground next to the fire, her eyes too heavy to continue another page in her beloved book.

✝

Ken-ai-te quietly slipped into the tipi, trying not to disturb Prayer Woman while she slept. The flames from the fire had long ago burned down to red embers but the light was strong enough he could see her face outlined against it since this night she lay close to the fire. Usually she curled up as far from it as possible—and from him. He smiled when he spotted the Bible lying next to one hand, assuming she had probably fallen asleep while reading.

I can't pretend to understand why she wanted the book so much but the look on her face when I handed it to her was worth all the risk in going to the mission for it. With the desire I held in my heart to retrieve it for her, I believe I could have fought off a hundred white men if it had been necessary. Why do I feel so strongly about this woman? My indecision confuses me greatly. I have not taken her though we share a tipi. Everyone assumes I have done so, and with each day, the danger grows for us both because I do not. Does she also wonder why?

He lay down on the robe and gazed across the fire pit at his captive. How he longed to bring her over to the robe with him—but how? Knowing he could demand it and she could not refuse made him even more determined to find a way to convince her to come on her own, willingly. His mind briefly flitted back to his dead wife and the love they had shared, also their joy when the child was born. However, he dismissed the memories quickly because such thoughts always led him down a dark path he had no intention of revisiting—ever. For that reason, others had encouraged him to fill his bed as quickly as possible, even before his year of mourning had passed. Yet, he had waited. And waited still.

The groans grew louder and he knew it was starting again. The nightmare. She had had it every single night. He wondered about last night when he was gone and supposed so. Each time he felt more helpless. What could he do to stop it or ease her pain?

Tonight she began thrashing around more than usual, however. He rose up on one arm to watch, then sat cross-legged before the fire as it intensified. It had never been this bad nor lasted so long. She cried out and screamed one word, then said it over and over. He wasn't for sure but thought it was the man's name, the one who died during her capture. *Didn't she say he was an uncle?* His tongue played with the syllable. *Peet. Strange name for a man.*

Prayer Woman rolled from side to side and at one point it appeared she was about to roll right into the fire. Ken-ai-te knew he could watch no longer, must somehow stop her before she hurt herself. Certainly, others would hear if the noise kept up. There were few secrets in a Kiowa village. And this must remain a secret, at all costs. Wouldn't be good if others came running to help, thinking something was wrong. They would know immediately what had been going on— or rather, what had *not* been going on.

He stepped over to where she had coiled up into a ball like a snake about to strike. Without warning, she rolled toward him and he had to jump aside. Leaning down over her, he grabbed her wrists and pinned them over her head, hoping that would calm her. But instead, she kicked him hard in the stomach with her knee and he fell backwards with a soft moan, releasing her. Immediately he crawled to her side, grabbed her wrists once more and straddled her.

"No!" she screamed. More words poured out but he didn't understand them, except for the last one, that name once more. "Peeete..."

Ken-ai-te noticed her eyes were open in a vacant stare. She seemed completely unaware of her surroundings. He'd seen it before and, night after night, his confusion increased. She wriggled beneath him and shocked him with her strength. Finally, he eased himself down on top of her body and her struggles ceased. For a moment.

Suddenly Mandy blinked a couple of times and looked at him with full comprehension. Fear exploded in her dark eyes.

She screamed and jerked one hand loose. Her fist hit him on the jaw and he gritted his teeth against the sharp pain as she pummeled him on the head and shoulders. Swiftly he took hold of the free hand once more and spoke to her softly in Kiowa. He was afraid in her panic she wouldn't understand him yet couldn't think fast enough to make the words come out in the little bit of English he knew. Her screams continued to pierce the close air of the tipi. While he wasn't sure of her exact words he had a pretty good idea of what she thought was happening to her. It wrenched his heart to think she believed him capable of such an act. Somehow, he had to get through to her with the truth.

Tightening his grip on her wrists, he released one hand and placed it gently over her mouth. "Quiet," he said to her in Kiowa.

Ken-ai-te felt the rapid rise and fall of Prayer Woman's chest beneath him, her hot breath on his fingers. His breathing had escalated and not simply because of the physical effort required to calm her. It was being so close to her again. It wasn't lust exactly. He'd felt that for her and most certainly would again. No, it was something different. But what?

He became aware of moisture on his fingers over her mouth and realized they were her tears. At least she had stopped struggling so hard and her breathing had slowed. Those eyes entranced him, even wide with fear. For some reason beyond his understanding, he desired very much to hold her close and comfort her, to tell her he had no intentions of harming her. But that was not his way, the Kiowa way.

She would have to learn this for herself.

Abruptly he released her and rose up off her at the same time. She rolled away from him and scrambled to sit up and face him. Her arms were wrapped tightly around the middle of her body and the expression in her eyes had changed. In spite of the dim light he could see it— hatred, not fear. His heart sank.

Ken-ai-te hoped fervently he had not pushed her further away from the sleeping robe. His purpose all along had been to convince her to join him on it. He'd moved from in front of the entrance to the buffalo robe a couple of nights before, hoping she'd recognize his implied invitation in doing so. But forcing her? No, that was not his way, even though considered acceptable in Kiowa tradition.

He sat watching Mandy a short time longer. What was the strange spell she had cast on him? His temper flared at the thought of the feelings she aroused in him. To have compassion for her would mean betrayal of the worst kind for his dead wife, indeed, for all the Kiowa people. He could never betray them by letting his emotions rule his head.

I must remember why I took her in the first place! I will never trade her to the Mexicans for rifles as Black Feather wishes to do or use her body the way he would do. Yet I cannot allow my feelings to get in the way of my revenge. It is vital to my future to exact vengeance for my losses. I simply have to keep my eye on that and off her!

Without a word, Ken-ai-te rose and left the tipi, his fists clenched tightly and his face a solemn mask.

⚕

It was a long time before Mandy could move, for fear he would return. And there would be no more sleep this night, Bible or no Bible.

"Oh, no, my Bible! Where is it?" She searched frantically for it in the half-light. "Did *he* take it? I had it when I went to sleep, right here by the fire. Oh, God, please don't tell me it fell into the flames!"

131

FROM NOW UNTIL FOREVER

† CHAPTER TWENTY †

"But, beloved, be not ignorant of this one thing,
that one day is with the Lord as a thousand years..."
II Peter 3:8

T his day seems to be 84 hours long, not 24! Of course, without a clock, how would I know? I'm grateful I found my Bible last night, hidden under my blanket next to the fire where I apparently dropped it when I dozed off to sleep. If I'd lost it, I don't know what I would do!

Mandy had spent the morning preparing strips of meat to be dried for jerky and since the midday meal had joined about eight other women in the lovely job of tanning—by far her least favorite task because of the green goo they had to use in the process. Frequently, rotted pieces of flesh were left here and there by accident and the stench contributed to the already smelly job. Especially when the sun beat down mercilessly on them, it often required enormous self-control to keep from vomiting all over the hide! Sleeping Bird explained a few days before that because the green "goo"—as Mandy called it—turned the rough hides into soft leather it also tended to soften the skin of their hands as long as it didn't remain on them for too long. That was why it tingled. Also why they washed it off promptly!

Of course, fleshing an animal skin wasn't far behind on the list, for obvious reasons. Any usable meat had been removed before they began that job of course but again the stench from the spoiled pieces clinging to it made it almost unbearable at times. What amazed Mandy was how the soft deerskin and tough rawhide both came from such a nasty beginning.

To take her mind off her repulsive and repetitive work, Mandy allowed her thoughts to wander a bit. She recalled how the day before she had experienced her greatest pleasure since coming here. Sleeping Bird had taken her down to the river and allowed her to swim and bathe to her heart's content.

They had walked some distance down the banks until they were out of sight of the camp before the older woman allowed Mandy to disrobe behind some bushes. Removing her dingy and tattered camisole, she made the decision to use it as a rag instead of putting it on later. All this time it had been on her body, but regardless of its tie with her former life, the time had come to discard it. Her excitement over the swim made it easier.

Mandy eagerly waded out into the cool waters, splashing around like a small child and releasing every care and concern into its depths. No need to be anxious about anyone spying on her with Sleeping Bird standing guard.

She washed away all the grit and grime caked on her body, using a harsh soap that made her skin sting and turn red with its abrasiveness. Still, better than the alternative! Then she was given a shampoo made out of cactus, of all things, which left her hair shiny and soft. Flashes of memory crowded in from after her capture when Ken-ai-te allowed her into the water a couple of times fully clothed and bound during the time they crossed the prairie. She deliberately pushed them deep and focused instead on the pure delight she was experiencing right then.

"I hope I'm allowed to do this more often!" she exclaimed to Sleeping Bird upon leaving the river. The smile and nod in return gave her the expectation of doing this again soon.

Life in the Kiowa camp had seemed boring at first to Mandy but slowly she saw it for the intriguing, interesting place it became as she learned more about the routine and the meaning of each task or pastime. Everything had a purpose and reason. For instance, the sinew in an animal's legs became sewing threads and rawhide strips, which were then braided into ropes. Who would have thought to use those for that? Only the resourceful Kiowa! And Sleeping Bird had explained how to stake a hide out next to a rotting cottonwood tree and make a slow fire in it, fanning the smoke over the hide for an entire day. This gave it the soft golden color and pliable texture for making moccasins and other clothing items.

And nature's gift to them for using up the rotten wood? The smoke apparently repelled insects! Mandy wished she could have had some of it when being eaten up by the bugs on the trek across the prairie. Or bottle it and use it at night to stave off the pesky creatures annoying them while sitting under the stars and listening to the drums and exciting tales of the elders. There were poultices for this, she discovered, but the smelly and greasy substances were far more unpleasant than being wrapped in smoke would have been.

While Mandy worked, she glanced around the camp at the children playing nearby under the watchful eye of their mothers working beside her. Young girls set up their miniature tipis and fussed over their dolls, all in preparation for motherhood. It intrigued her how many already had intricate beading on the doll clothing and paintings on the small tipis, evidence they were learning many skills vital to taking their place in village society as Kiowa women someday. Some even broke branches into twigs and pretended to carry it like firewood. Little did they realize what a backbreaking task they were imitating!

Boys played with toy bows and small arrows, practicing their aim against imaginary enemies. The older ones made a game out of tying a sapling together with rawhide strips and then using the crude hoop for a target with their spears and arrows alike. It was fascinating to watch.

It astounds me how much Kiowa women cram into one day yet never seem to break a sweat. Time and again, I find I simply cannot keep up their pace. But I am trying. And I refuse, Father, to complain

*about what I have to do. You have given me new purpose in being here
and I'm grateful for that. I can't believe how my days have become
blurs but at least my nights have been more restful. The difference has
been having my Bible, I know.*

Occasionally, Sleeping Bird would elbow Mandy in the ribs to
urge her to pay more attention to her work; it surprised her how seldom
this happened compared with only a few weeks ago, however. She was
learning, slowly but surely.

*A few weeks! I've simply got to figure out some method for
keeping track of time so I can designate a Sabbath every week instead
of randomly doing so. The beading system didn't work—maybe with
colored threads? The old blanket Sleeping Bird gave me the other day
has several hues of red and blue in it so maybe I can unravel some of
those and wind them around a stick or something.*

Mandy's mind wandered through the project for the rest of the
afternoon. She was eager to get back to the tipi and see if her idea
would work or not.

A couple of hours later with the sun dipping low on the horizon,
Mandy hurried toward the tipi. As she neared it, she spotted Black
Feather watching her from several feet away. He sneered in her
direction, then disappeared. It unnerved her to have him always
creeping around the camp, constantly leering at her, and never to know
when he might appear or try to harm her. She shuddered as she recalled
the Scripture that says Satan is like a lion prowling around, seeking
whom he would devour. That's exactly how she felt with this evil man.
I wonder if the devil ever appears in human form?

Then another verse jumped forward, and she chided herself for
not having claimed it for protection all this time. "Psalm 138:7," she
whispered softly, "how well I know those words, from the earliest time
I can remember. 'Though I walk in the midst of trouble, thou wilt
revive me: thou shalt stretch forth thine hand against the wrath of mine
enemies, and thy right hand shall save me.' Thank You, Lord, for

calming my anxious heart from Your Word!"

She busied herself with preparations for the evening meal and prided herself on how quickly she could do it now. Maybe it was hunger that drove her but, in any case, she could now do many things she never dreamed she would be able to only a few short weeks ago. And any number of them were easier than they used to be. An echo of sadness tiptoed around her mind but she hushed its voice quickly.

"No time or energy for self-pity. Must get this food finished up before Ken-ai-te appears, hungry and expecting his meal to be ready."

About then, Sleeping Bird came up to check on the food preparations, grunted in approval, then sat down while Mandy scurried around with her mind on her task. Without warning, the older woman broke the silence.

"You do much for care of Ken-ai-te. Make shirts, leggings."

"Yes, I wanted to ask you about that. Won't he need those things when the weather gets colder?"

She nodded in agreement. "Also anything he desires, you make."

"Such as?"

"Clean, repair shield."

Mandy glanced in its direction, propped up on a stand directly outside the entrance to the tipi, a hide draped over its face.

"Why is it covered?"

"To show Ken-ai-te man of peace, no battle. Hide protects."

"Why not just keep it inside the tipi?"

"Important sign of warrior's power and strength. Outside tipi in place of honor for all to see."

Mandy had never seen it since it remained hidden all the time. She was grateful it had not been used since she came to live here since it was primarily designed for times of war. Maybe the Kiowa were more a people of peace than most white men believed. Her father certainly felt that way.

Suddenly she realized her thoughts had distracted her from what

Sleeping Bird had been saying.

"—and help decorate lances and arrows with feathers. Make new—" Frowning, she stopped, reaching for the right English word and putting her hands around her own neck. Mandy only caught a word or two of the Kiowa phrases she uttered but finally figured it out.

"Are you talking about a 'necklace'? He needs a new one, is that right?"

Again, she nodded. "Bone with beads. Old one fall off. I show you tomorrow."

"So it is my job to do all this for him, is that correct?"

"Also help dress when sun rises, braid hair, do feathers for day."

Mandy blushed. Apparently, Ken-ai-te had been going elsewhere daily to do all this, because she'd not seen him do any of it except arrange the feathers in his hair from time to time when they worked loose.

"Dress? Like putting on his breechcloth?" It was the only item of clothing he wore besides his moccasins. Surely, she would not be expected to touch that!

Again, the vigorous nodding.

She cleared her throat. *Oh, my, am I in trouble here! God, please give me wisdom to know how to respond. I can't say what I really want to about the subject, nor do I have the freedom to refuse to obey if commanded to help him with it. What do I do?* She took a deep breath to steady her voice.

"Well, I will certainly try to do whatever Ken-ai-te requires of me, Sleeping Bird. But it's up to him to ask. Things have been going well between us lately and I don't want to upset him unduly."

"Still no sleep on robe."

"Yes, that's right; I'm still not sleeping on the robe with him. And he has not, um, demanded I do so. I respect him for his attitude and appreciate him being such a gentleman."

"Not know word, gent—"

138

"Gen—tle—man" she said carefully. "It means uh, kind warrior."

"Ah. Respect good. Obey good. Sleep on robe good."

She sighed. *How do I make her understand, Lord?*

Ken-ai-te strode into the clearing just then, interrupting their conversation. He apparently had smelled the meal cooking and spoke rapidly to her in Kiowa, most of which went right over her head. What if he overheard what they had been talking about? She assumed he had asked about when the food would be ready but how could she be sure? Better to feign ignorance than to take a chance he had actually asked her to join him on the sleeping robe! No, better to pretend she didn't understand than further confuse an already sensitive issue.

When she stared blankly at the warrior, he pointed to the kettle and rubbed his stomach, growling the Kiowa word for "food" as he did so. Mandy replied with the phrase for "soon" and turned away from him in the hopes he wouldn't require her to speak the language any more than absolutely necessary. She recalled her solemn vow not to learn it and still resisted every attempt to force her to use the new words. And was pleased whenever her lack of knowledge of Kiowa pushed him to use English instead in order to communicate with her.

Ken-ai-te plunked himself down cross-legged in front of the fire as though taking her "soon" quite literally. She had to focus on the meal now; later she would consider pursuing further the topic she and Sleeping Bird had been discussing when Ken-ai-te joined them.

That evening she took a short stroll around the camp, simply observing the people and smells and sounds of a Kiowa village. What had been repulsive only a short time ago now brought comfort and stability to Mandy's heart. She still longed for "home" at times but less and less often.

"And that is a good thing, right, Lord?" She had wandered outside the camp a ways, feeling the need to have a conversation with her best—and only—friend.

"The one thing I cannot and will not back down on, however, is

139

giving myself to my captor willingly. Sleeping Bird needs to understand this, else I think I shall go mad! I'm tired of explaining it over and over to her. And I'm tired of the women patting my tummy and asking when there will be a baby. I want to scream at them, 'Never!' It's offensive and embarrassing. You must be horrified! I want to bring it up to Ken-ai-te but every time I try, it seems the way is blocked. Please allow me to do so, to get this straightened out once and for all. I mean, surely You don't intend for the arrangement to continue indefinitely—right?"

⚕

That woman is out of her mind! Look how she struts around talking to herself in her fancy white man's words and pretending she is so much better than all of us. The sight of her disgusts me!

Black Feather clenched his fists and worked his jaw as he furtively followed Mandy strolling among the tipis. She had to be stopped, but how? Her beauty and charm had apparently cast a spell over Ken-ai-te for he would not listen to reason any longer. The raid was supposed to have been to steal hostages so they could be traded in Mexico for rifles. Instead, this woman had replaced his sister in the tipi of Ken-ai-te.

And still, he had no more bullets for the rifle he had taken months ago, and the braves were forced to use arrows as they had for centuries. That was not the way of the future but of the past. And one thing Black Feather did not intend to do was live in the past.

"Chief Twin Fox moves slower than the black medicine I pour on my horse's wounds in getting this new weapon for our use," he muttered. Suddenly he stopped short. *I can't speak this aloud. Someone might hear and inform the chief of my rebellion against him. His time has gone for leadership. We need a new chief for our village, someone who will fight the whites and Comanche alike to keep our land and protect our people. Someone like me.* And his chest swelled with pride at the thought.

I will lead our people to get all the rifles they can carry and destroy every one of the whites who steal our land and kill our buffalo. Then I will be a hero to my people and they will name me as chief over them. First, though, I have to stop this woman!

He noted she ducked into her tipi and he stopped, realizing he stood in front of the tipi of Angry Bear. *Good name, since he's always mad at everyone around! I'm glad he's been a friend since we were young boys.* An idea formed in his mind. *Maybe he has some thoughts on how to accomplish my goals.*

While the men talked, the wife of Angry Bear worked on her beading, pretending not to listen but Black Feather knew she heard every word. Contrary to most Kiowa women, she talked a great deal and could have been called Angry Buffalo instead of Little Buffalo, due to her sour mood, which always seemed to match that of her husband. They deserved each other. Angry Bear often had grand schemes cooking, just no courage to carry them out. And besides, Little Buffalo kept her husband's friends fed whenever they came to visit and she no longer reacted with a scowl at the sight of his ugly scar like most of the women in the village did.

The scar...Black Feather's mood darkened even further. He had made that man suffer, the soldier who had given him that permanent reminder of one brief moment of distraction. And he smiled now at the thought of his screams for mercy. There would never be mercy at this warrior's hand, especially for whites. His fingers touched the red mark and he gritted his teeth. And none for this woman, either, or for any who gave her refuge!

Sometime later, Black Feather emerged from the tipi. Satisfied the two had come up with a clever plan that would accomplish his vengeance at last, he scanned the area for any sign of Prayer Woman. *She had better pray to her God because if I get my hands on her, I will make her pay. My sister is the one who should be...*

His stomach twisted in a knot. That horrible day was still too fresh in his mind. He never meant for her to get hurt, only to insist that she leave Ken-ai-te and take a husband worthy of her. *It was her own fault for defending him and threatening to tell him of my demand. But if Ken-ai-te ever found out, there would be no end to his fury.*

"So I just have to make certain he never knows the truth."

✝ CHAPTER TWENTY-ONE ✝

"Where there is no vision, the people perish..."
Proverbs 29:18

"Father, we need to have a talk!"

Mandy's frustration had bubbled to the surface once again. A few days had passed by without a single opportunity for her to speak to Ken-ai-te about the desire in her heart, which had quickly grown into an obsession to have her own tipi. She furiously scrubbed down the chopping rock she used for food preparation while she prayed, not even caring if someone heard her or not. If she didn't get this out of her system, she knew she would explode!

"I've prayed and prayed but seem to have no glimpse of why You have left me in this deplorable situation with no hope of change in sight. Your Word says it is an abomination. I cannot change this on my own, You know! It's a blessing I can share about You with my captor because of the bizarre living arrangement, but that's not the point. The important thing is that I honor You by moving out as soon as possible. So show me what it is You require of me so I can have peace in my life again."

A young mother toting her little one on her hip walked by and eyed Mandy strangely, talking away to herself in a foreign tongue, scrubbing a rock that normally never required cleaning. Mandy chuckled. *Guess I do seem to her to be acting oddly. But my chopping rock* will *be clean, regardless of what other women do with theirs!*

As the woman disappeared out of sight, Mandy added to her

prayer. "Lord, give me patience to wait on Your answer and Your timing. It's obviously not coming simply because I've asked for it." She sighed and threw a bucket of water over the rock, then wiped it down. "Wish the solution were as easy as this task I just finished." And she smiled with satisfaction for a job well done.

Mandy glanced up and her smile faded. Black Feather was watching her again, that same twisted smirk on his scarred face. She tried to stare him down, as Sleeping Bird had done a couple of times, but it didn't work. Her stomach flopping, she had to look away. Gulping hard against the fear rising from deep within, she whirled away to show him she couldn't care less that he was there. Inside, however, she was terrified.

How many times had she prayed he would go away and leave her alone? Was that the wrong prayer? Perhaps more to the point: make him hear the Lord's voice of conviction. No, he would never listen to something supernatural! It was a waste of her time to pray for him. Still better to pray for her protection from him. *Must get busy and forget those beady eyes staring at me all the time!*

That evening Mandy finally had a chance to begin working on her idea for a worship stick. She and Ken-ai-te had just come into the tipi after the evening meal and she reached for her red and blue blanket on the pile where she'd stashed it the night before. Along with it came the corner of another cloth, a piece of buckskin actually. When she tugged on the blanket further, suddenly something rolled out of the skin, right to the feet of her captor. It was a huge skull!

She shrieked and jumped back a step. "What is that doing here?"

Ken-ai-te frowned and bent to pick it up, handling it with great care, almost a reverence.

"Vision," and he finished with a phrase Mandy didn't understand.

"Sleeping Bird told me all Kiowa boys go on a vision quest, I think she called it, or at least that was the closest thing I could find to what she was saying in your language. But why a skull?" She peered at it, his copper fingers highlighted against the white bone and dwarfed by its immense size.

"Is it from a buffalo?" Instantly she felt foolish. Of course, it came from a buffalo. Its fearsome horns were still visible, making its identity unmistakable, even without the fur and other features.

He nodded and carefully wrapped it up and put it back where it belonged. She felt guilty she'd stashed the blanket on top of it, but she honestly hadn't seen it the day before when she laid it there on top of all the hides. How had it remained hidden all this time without her having seen it before? Watching him handle it as something sacred, she felt she'd disrespected it somehow by allowing it to roll around on the ground. Obviously, it meant a great deal to him.

As she began unraveling threads she asked, "Did I understand Sleeping Bird correctly in that you received some kind of prophecy about your future while on this quest of yours?"

A deep trough appeared between his eyes as he seemed to puzzle over her words.

"A vision—like a dream but you were awake when you saw it, right?"

A hint of a smile played with the corner of his mouth and the dark pools above it seemed lost in the memory. He smiled and caught her curious gaze.

"Yes. Paint on tipi."

"You painted the vision on the tipi?" She glanced around, then realized that must be some of the drawings she'd seen on the other side of the hide walls. It never mattered to her before but now her curiosity was aroused. "It's on the outside?"

He nodded. "Wife paint."

"Your wife painted it on there? She must have been very talented, Ken-ai-te. She was obviously skilled with the sewing awl," and she pointed to the bodice of her dress where the intricate beading was displayed, "and now with painting as well."

Nothing more was said for a moment, then Mandy continued quietly. "I'm sorry that I'm not as good with an awl as she was, but at least I am trying to learn. Maybe someday."

Ken-ai-te abruptly left the tipi and Mandy was disappointed that now there apparently would be no conversation about Jesus. She'd been telling him the story of the Nativity over the past couple of days and he had seemed quite intrigued by its colorful details and asked a great many questions. In fact, the only way he would allow her to go on to sleep the night before had been because of her solemn promise to finish the story the next evening. And now he had left.

"Wonder what I did, Father, to upset him like that. Maybe the reference to his wife, perhaps, and her many talents? I suppose that would be enough to upset me, if I were in his place. All I wanted to do is pay her a compliment, though. When will I learn to think *before* I speak? Please comfort him and forgive me if I have offended him again without realizing it."

After the threads of seven different colors were carefully wound on the stick Mandy had chosen, she was satisfied her idea would work. By pushing the strands of one color up on the slender column as the sun rose daily, she could keep track of the days. The following week she would simply reverse the procedure. In this way, her crude calendar would at least help her know when it was time for special worship of the Lord.

"I know it doesn't really matter to you, God, when we worship nor even how we do it, just that we do it on a regular basis. And now I can. If only Sleeping Bird were a Christian, wouldn't that be a blessing to have someone of like belief with whom I could worship every week? I wonder if she ever heard the Gospel when she was a child and living with the white people, before she came to the Kiowa village? Surely she had been christened at least before her parents were killed and she was captured, but maybe not. She just seems to reject all my attempts to talk to her about the Lord, though. Please give me an opening to bring up the subject, would You?"

Ribbons of mist swirled around Mandy the next morning as she walked to the river to collect the day's water supply. It was unusually calm and she realized that she'd grown accustomed to the frequent prairie winds. She shivered involuntarily, though not in a frightened manner. No one else had joined her yet so she dared to talk aloud in English.

"Are you speaking to me, Lord? I'm trying to hear You as this day begins and want to listen carefully to Your voice in that morning lark who is singing so beautifully from the trees, in the rushing waters below, and in the quiet air as the first streaks of the golden sunrise appear in the eastern sky, chasing away the fog."

Mandy continued her psalm of praise while turning to go back up the bank and caught her breath slightly. Staring at her from the slope above was Black Feather. Silent yet menacing, his scar more fearsome in the half-light of dawn. *God, give me courage! And protect me from this savage!*

She ignored him the best she could and made her way up to the ridge by another path to avoid having to walk near him. The chatter of some of the other women could be heard coming down from the village and she breathed a sigh of relief. *Surely, he wouldn't dare touch me with others around.* Afraid to even glance back at him, she held her head up high and balanced the jug of water on her shoulder as Sleeping Bird had taught her. The weight pinched her skin but she kept going, increasing her pace as she neared the outermost edge of the camp.

All the tipis were arranged generally in a circle and the one belonging to Chief Twin Fox sat next to the main path for entering and leaving the village. Mandy found it curious that each doorway faced the rising sun. *It seems to me they should all open onto the center of the camp. But then, little of what these people do makes much sense, in my humble opinion.* She smiled to herself upon recalling that Black Feather's lodge was much smaller than Ken-ai-te's.

I'm certain he is consumed with jealousy over that! Not to mention that ours is closer to that of the chief's, since the tipis are arranged in order of importance or wealth of each family, starting with the chief's and going down to the less affluent ones. It's interesting, too, that the number of horses owned by a brave indicates his personal wealth and those with more of them, such as Ken-ai-te, are allowed to have larger tipis. Just to glance at the camp you would think it was without order but in truth, it is not.

It pleased her to think about the scar on her enemy's face turning dark with rage as his fury burned hot about this supposed injustice. Mandy's attitude wasn't exactly honoring to God, of course, but it made her proud to belong to Ken-ai-te—if you could call it pride to "belong" to another person. And she said yet another quick prayer of thanksgiving that she had not been captured by the evil warrior.

A couple of women had finished at the river and were already gathering up firewood at the far end of the tree stand as Mandy filled the smaller bucket beside the tipi and begin mentally planning the steps for their simple morning meal. But first, she would have to scout out a few pieces of firewood for the day, though she didn't need a full load as she had some left over from the day before.

Sleeping Bird approached a few minutes later and smiled when she saw Mandy had again completed these basic chores without any prompting. In spite of herself, Mandy was happy she was able to please the woman.

That's what friends do for— She stopped in mid-thought and gasped. *Did I just call her my friend? Yes, I did. Unbelievable. But that's what she has become to me. My only friend, in fact. Besides You, Lord, of course!*

"Special day today. Visitor come."

"Who is coming, Sleeping Bird?"

"Great Chief Tohausan with his men. Go to pow-wow with Osage and Cheyenne, many warriors." And she said in Kiowa they were gathering at a mountain a great distance away.

"What mountain? I didn't understand that name."

"Snake who —" and she made a motion with her finger like a rattler shaking his tail furiously.

"Rattlesnake?" Sleeping Bird nodded. "There is a mountain called that? How did it get its name?" But the older woman didn't seem to understand her question so Mandy just let it go. And made a mental note not ever to go there on the outside chance the name indicated the presence of those vile reptiles!

"We make big feast for all our brothers and sisters this night." The first time Mandy had heard this term used she thought it meant that Ken-ai-te was related to everyone in the village. But Sleeping Bird had explained this is what Kiowa called the people of their village—and also because often they *were* all related to each other in some way.

Sleeping Bird's words brought her back to the present as she continued. "Tohausan Chief of all Kiowa, important to all Kiowa people."

Mandy stoked the fire under the pot for the porridge they usually had for the morning meal but a resentful spirit rested on her chest, almost smothering her for a moment.

Well, this man, whoever he is, is not important to me! I'm not a Kiowa so I couldn't care less who he is, unless he can get me out of here and back home where I belong. Inwardly she groaned at the thought of all the extra work this visit would require of her during the long day ahead.

And it started with Sleeping Bird requesting Mandy draw additional water for a project she had to do later. With a sigh, she once more headed down the slope. Hoping not to encounter others this late in the morning, her heart fell when she saw a small group still remained on the banks. Trying to ignore them as she usually did, Mandy dipped her large bucket down into the cool, clear stream. As she stood up, one of the women stalked over to her, her face red with fury, screeching something at her in Kiowa and waving her hands wildly.

Mandy frowned, then recognized the woman: Little Buffalo, wife of Angry Bear. *Why is she so irritated at me? She never seems to have a nice word to say to anyone, just gripes and complains about everything. Though my Kiowa is limited, I've figured this much out at least. Don't understand the little in her name, though, as there is nothing little about her! I'm sure it's because she strikes me as a lazy, bored gossip with nothing better to do than take digs at others who have what she does not, such as children and a loving husband.*

Shaking a finger in Mandy's face she shouted, "No be-long here! Go home!" Mandy hadn't realized the woman spoke any English at all.

"I would be happy to do so, Little Buffalo, if you people would release me! You make it seem as though it were my fault I'm here in the first place. I was forced, remember? I'm not here as a guest, I'm a *slave!*"

Suddenly the woman's hand shot out to Mandy's abdomen and she groped it hard. Mandy swatted her hand away and took a step backward and stumbled over the bucket, caught off guard by the ferociousness of this woman's attack.

"No baby! No be-long Ken-ai-te, to Black Fea-ther now." Then she rattled off in Kiowa, most of which Mandy missed, thankfully. But she got the gist of it. She accused Mandy of wearing a dead woman's clothes, living in her tipi, and taking the dead woman's husband for herself. And unless the words were badly garbled, she added that the spirit of this dead woman would come and haunt Mandy all her life unless she left the warrior's tipi right away!

"Skin too pale. Ug-ly. Bring shame to Kiowa!" Mandy wished the woman had not switched back to her broken English. Then she could pretend these last words had never been spoken. Crushed, she shook her head. Nothing she could say would convince these people she had not *chosen* to come here! All they had to do was point the way, give her provisions for the journey, and she would be more than happy to go home!

The women turned and headed back up the rise, chattering amongst themselves. *That's right, slink away like the skunks you are!* Mandy stamped her foot in anger but in truth, the incident had shaken her confidence once again. And reinforced her earlier defiance of these people and their heathen ways. *I wish they'd all go away and never come back!*

As the morning wore on, however, her attitude softened somewhat. In a way, it was exciting to have visitors come to the village. The extra work helped take her mind off her personal conflicts. And whether she wanted to admit it or not, she was curious to learn more about this man who seemed to be so revered by these people.

A short time later, the two women began cutting up some meat they had on hand for that evening's feast, and Ken-ai-te came out of the tipi carrying his lance and bow with the quiver of arrows over his shoulder. He walked away without a word to the women.

Mandy opened her mouth to ask but it was Sleeping Bird who got words out first.

"Ken-ai-te go with men to hunt for tonight's feast. Many foods to make today."

"Who is this chief—uh, what did you call him?"

"To-hau-san," she said slowly. "In your tongue, Little Bluff. Chief of all Kiowa, many years now. Very wise and good man. Make much peace with white men, others. Much celebration and dancing!"

Mandy welcomed the distraction in their otherwise rather boring routine. She wondered if women would accompany him and how many warriors would be with him. *And if he's chief of all the Kiowa, it would be interesting to find out if he knows there are white captives living among his people. How could he make peace treaties with the soldiers if he is aware of how the Kiowa have stolen white women and children and keep them against their will?*

151

As Mandy worked throughout the remainder of the day, an idea grew in her heart that at once excited and frightened her. Perhaps she could tell this chief that she was a captive and he would force Ken-ai-te to take her home! But did she really want to face the condemnation of her people after having lived with the Kiowa now? She was pulled in this but the hope of rescue was just too great. The afternoon wore on and she began to formulate what she would say to this chief if God gave her the chance. And the more she thought about it, the more she became convinced this was the answer God was providing for her to leave the village.

Home! She savored the word itself on her tongue and closed her eyes as often as possible to let sweet memories billow over her heart like the waves of the sea.

I just know this is it, Lord. Chief Tohausan will be the one to rescue me!

✝CHAPTER TWENTY-TWO✝

"A new heart also will I give you,
and a new spirit will I put within you:
and I will take away the stony heart out of your flesh,
and I will give you an heart of flesh."
Ezekiel 36:26

"Here he comes!"
The shout rang out around the camp as many voices joined in to echo the cry of welcome. Children chattered, the women scurried around, and even the dogs added to the din. Though the words were all in Kiowa and therefore unknown to Mandy for the most part, she had no difficulty in understanding the air of excitement surrounding the village. Her own heart rejoiced, though for vastly different reasons. Not a doubt remained in her mind by then—soon she would be going home!

Racing with several others toward the chief's tipi, Mandy frowned. *I'm confused. What is an Army ambulance wagon doing here? Did soldiers come with him?* Breathless she came to an abrupt halt on the opposite side of the fire ring from the visitors, her heart pounding. *It is an ambulance! What is going on?*

Sleeping Bird walked up behind her and touched her elbow, urging her to follow as they pushed through the crowd in order to get closer. Someone roughly shoved Mandy aside and stepped on her foot as she pushed past—Little Buffalo! Her glare shot daggers into Mandy as she disappeared quickly into the crowd. Though this incident fed her

153

insecurity even more, reminding her she didn't really belong here, Mandy tried to let the hurt go. She was only one woman, after all. Perhaps others didn't share her antagonism. Maybe she had imagined the fury in the woman's eyes.

Besides, the wagon was real and by this time, Mandy was standing next to it. She touched the rusty wheel rim of the wagon and fingered the rough canvas side with its large red cross emblazoned for all to see. Not a vision, but genuine and right here before her eyes!

She watched the driver deftly hop down from the wagon seat and embrace Chief Twin Fox in addition to several of the other elders gathered there. She couldn't believe her eyes: the warrior's dark, loose hair came well below his knees! Scattered through the long strands were a number of silver brooches of various kinds and sizes giving him a top-heavy appearance, though his easy gait never indicated any such possibility. She finally pulled her focus off him and glanced around among the other warriors who'd just arrived, eager to spot the special visitor who had created such enthusiasm in the people. All eyes, however, were on this one warrior.

"Chief Tohausan, you and your men are most welcome," said Chief Twin Fox. "All we have is yours."

And he bowed respectfully before the one with the long flowing hair. Mandy's jaw dropped in shock. He hardly looked the part of a great chief. Yet something about him spoke of strength and courage and Mandy eyed him more carefully.

Tohausan smiled. "I am most grateful, Twin Fox. You are to be honored for how you care for your family here. Your mothers and grandmothers are all well fed, your warriors are brave and strong, and your children are happy. Even your dogs join in our songs of victory this day!"

The men laughed as one, and a couple of the women threw rocks at the pack of dogs to silence them. They quieted and slinked away. Mandy turned her attention back to the two chiefs facing each other.

Her eyes wide, she stared in awe. Ken-ai-te had come forward to greet the visitor!

Mandy's jaw fell once more when he grasped Ken-ai-te by the shoulders and gazed steadily into his eyes, as though they were old friends greeting one another. They were about the same height and towered over many of the other Kiowa. Mandy wished she knew what passed between them in the soft words heard only by the two as they stared at each other somberly. A moment later, the spell broken, with a broad grin on his face Chief Tohausan, Ken-ai-te at his side, strode purposefully behind Chief Twin Fox to the fire ring, where the men were quickly seated.

With the sun sinking lower on the horizon, the food processional began. Woman after woman brought huge bowls of foods of various kinds to lay before Chief Tohausan and his men, and the feasting began. It was unlike anything Mandy had seen before in the camp.

However, her curiosity quickly returned to the Army ambulance off to one side. Maybe Sleeping Bird would know more about the mysterious wagon.

As they rushed back to their tipis to collect the foods they had prepared she asked, "Sleeping Bird, why does Chief Tohausan ride in a US Army ambulance?"

The older woman looked at her with a blank stare. Mandy wasn't sure if she didn't understand or truly didn't know. So she pointed toward it—hard to miss, sticking out like a prairie dog perched atop a buffalo hump.

"Over there, the wagon. It is intended for injured or sick soldiers, not for a Kiowa chief."

Sleeping Bird nodded and explained in broken English mixed with some Kiowa. Mandy gathered he had been presented the wagon by a group of Cavalry officers a couple of years before in gratitude for a treaty he helped negotiate between his people and the whites over by Fort Gibson. Now his pride and joy, he refused to ride a pony any

155

longer, preferring his wagon wherever he went. She shook her head in amazement. Imagine, an Indian chief owning a wagon given to him by Army soldiers, one he hadn't stolen or killed for! And one he was proud to show off to his fellow Kiowa whenever he could. Mandy had a difficult time comprehending it all.

The amount of emotion expressed by everyone toward their visitor, from small children up to and including Chief Twin Fox, made a deep impression. Obviously, this man meant a great deal to these people.

While Mandy served Ken-ai-te, following the example of the other women with their men, she tried to eavesdrop on the conversations among the warriors. She could only understand snatches but knew she could always get Sleeping Bird to fill in the gaps. When the women all gathered to one side of the camp circle to eat their evening meal a short time later, Mandy saw it as her opportunity. Because the two of them were off by themselves from the rest, she felt comfortable speaking in English.

"Sleeping Bird, can you tell me about Tohausan, why he is known as such a great chief? I mean, I gathered he is famous because of the treaty, right? But there must be more to it. Everyone here seems to love him. Does he visit often?"

"First time here."

"The first time? Then what—" The puzzled look on her face seemed to amuse the older woman, who smiled broadly—a facial expression Mandy enjoyed the rare times she showed it.

"Chief Tohausan much loved, in many stories told to children now grown. Many years as chief, loves children, has many of own."

She continued to rattle on for a bit in Kiowa, something about an attack and the cutting of heads—surely, Mandy had misunderstood that phrase! However, when the older woman repeated herself, more slowly the second time and with some English mixed in, the meaning was unmistakable. Apparently, there had been a horrible massacre of the

Kiowa people by some white soldiers years ago and all the bodies had their heads removed before being left for the vultures, the heads deposited in brass buckets like so much garbage. Her stomach clenched at the thought of the suffering the Kiowa had endured with such a ghastly experience. After this tragic event the people chose Tohausan as their chief, in large part because of the peace treaty he had negotiated with the solider general to stop the spiral of bloody reprisals on both sides. A sad time in their history, indeed, but also well-marked as the beginning of the longest time of peace they had known.

Too bad not all the Kiowa have chosen to follow this man's example. She stared at the chief for several minutes, silently amazed at how kind he appeared to be. Some of the children gathered around him with great excitement and instead of sending them away, he urged the little ones to come closer, even inviting some to sit on his lap. Mandy shook her head. Not at all the way Kiowa men usually treated small children!

She continued to stare at the warrior, still transfixed by his appearance. Two shocks of hair, tinged with grey, lay on either side of his face and created a frame of sorts for it and had the effect of softening his copper skin and stark features. Laughter rang out often as the children begged for more stories and he obliged with obvious pleasure, his face twisting into all sorts of contortions to emphasize the humor. A tall choker encircled his neck and seemed to be made of tiny pieces of bone strung together on brightly colored yarn. Dangling on his bare chest from a chain of beads hung a medallion of some sort, which he fingered often. *He must be telling the children a story about it. I wish I were close enough to hear his words.*

Turning back to Sleeping Bird she said, "I think I overheard talk of a calendar the chief had painted? Or did I misunderstand again?"

Sleeping Bird nodded. "Yes, painted calendar, tell about Kiowa in long ago times, he make himself."

"He painted a calendar about Kiowa history?" A nod confirmed

Mandy's interpretation of the words she'd heard. "I think he also said something about painting tipis, but I surely must have heard that wrong. Kiowa women do the painting on them here. What about in other camps?"

"Most done by women. Chief Tohausan great—" She searched for the right word as her brow furrowed in deep thought, her hands furiously working in what Mandy thought might be painting motions.

She took a stab. "Artist? Is that the word you are trying to say?" Again, the affirming nod. "It is inconceivable to me, a great chief who is a historian and an artist, too, just incredible! Good with children and adults alike and comfortable with Kiowa and whites. Small wonder everyone reveres him like they do."

Throughout the meal, many questions piled up in Mandy's mind that she hoped to ask Sleeping Bird later when they were alone. Most of them concerned Kiowa phrases she didn't comprehend. It frustrated her to not fully understand the language she heard all around her every day. Yet, she couldn't quite bring herself to learn it. Perhaps rebellion, stubbornness, or simple mindedness—or a bit of all three? It was a complicated tongue with many nuances that changed with the various guttural sounds. Small wonder the Kiowa words her father taught her had little meaning to her now. How she longed to hear English spoken fluently again—and not in the broken phrases used by her two closest friends. For yes, indeed, she had to admit she now counted them as friends. At least when compared with Black Feather!

Sleeping Bird had joined in with several of the women who were all chattering at once and Mandy tried again to follow those snippets of conversation. Suddenly she spotted Ken-ai-te approaching Chief Tohausan. A twinge of concern hit her.

That's odd. I never saw him leave the fire yet he must have at some point. Mental note, Mandy: pay more attention and don't let yourself get distracted again. The last thing you need is to end up without him or Sleeping Bird close by and leave yourself subject to another attack from Black Feather. If anything could ever be a recipe for disaster, that would be it!

†CHAPTER TWENTY-THREE†

"The LORD thy God in the midst of thee is mighty;
he will save, he will rejoice over thee with joy;
he will rest in his love, he will joy over thee with singing."
Zepheniah 3:17

What on earth is he doing? He's carrying something. I wish I could see better. Maybe I can move over a bit and...

Mandy gasped. Draped over Ken-ai-te's arms lay the buffalo robe she'd finished making for him only a few days before. Without Sleeping Bird's patient tutoring she never would have completed it. She had anguished over it for many days, carefully working various oils deep into its fur to soften it and then brushing it many times over until it fairly gleamed in the sunlight.

Recalling the night she presented it to Ken-ai-te, she'd been astonished at the grin on his face and the pleasure in his eyes. Her heart had swelled with pride like never before. His acceptance of her gift of friendship had gone a long way toward bringing peace to their tipi.

Perhaps he was only showing it to the great chief. However, that would be an unusual display of arrogance and vanity for a Kiowa, and in front of everyone. She felt her cheeks blaze and she gulped down her embarrassment. *What is happening?*

Another thought intruded. Mandy squirmed now, confusion fueling doubt to replace her first reaction. Did he mean to give it away rather than simply displaying it to brag on his wealth? Had he been lying when he seemed pleased? He'd proclaimed it to be his most valued possession at the time. Did her sacrifices mean nothing to him, after all?

Reverently he laid it at the esteemed leader's feet with gentle words she could not hear and bowed his head before him. Obviously, he had offered it to the visitor. Chief Twin Fox, she noticed, almost smiled. She knew this act must signify something very special in Kiowa tradition, to produce even half a grin on a man whose face often appeared to have been chiseled into stone!

Then Chief Tohausan did something quite unusual, at least in Mandy's estimation. He rose and embraced Ken-ai-te. Were they friends, then? She heard the sighs of approval from many around the two. Before Mandy could check the emotion, her heart jumped at the notion that perhaps Ken-ai-te had chosen the product of her hands with which to honor the chief and had done so in front of the elders of the village.

Wait a minute—what am I thinking? I don't want to feel something akin to pride in this savage who is holding me against my will! And she forced the feeling deep down, countering with an irritation surprisingly close to the surface. The day had been a happy one so far; however, now as clouds obscured parts of the brilliant sunset displayed overhead, her heart filled with sadness at being surrounded by these Kiowa who despised her even if they no longer showed it openly. She knew they hated her and she didn't care if they were aware of her true feelings, too.

I just have to go home soon! I fit in here more than I used to, that's true, but the thing is, I don't want to! I want to go to church and to parties and be admired by young men with pale skin and sandy hair and blue eyes that stir my heart. Mandy closed her eyes and tried to remember...but the memories were elusive and fleeting, always tinged with a sorrow too painful to bear.

The thrumming of the drums startled Mandy back to the present, her self-pity pushed aside for the moment. Dancers appeared in their regalia and Mandy caught her breath momentarily at the bright colors. The bells on their ankles and wrists echoed softly with each step, then jingled furiously as they began stomping their feet with surprising energy. The women chanted softly in rhythm with their steps, the crescendo building while more men joined in, some just in their everyday clothing. Finally many of the women rose to form another, larger circle outside of the men's and began the same swaying motions Mandy had observed before in the dances, moving around the ever-increasing ring of people celebrating their joy together. Even the children jumped up, taking their traditional places alongside their parents, the boys with their fathers and the girls by their mothers.

The exuberance in the air was contagious. *I think Papa called these big events a pow-wow but I wonder if that is what they call it. Whatever the name, it's exciting!* And in spite of herself, Mandy felt drawn into the festive atmosphere, her reluctance left behind as she eventually joined in the dancing for the first time.

Carefully following Sleeping Bird's lead, Mandy focused on the woman's feet and tried to mimic the complicated steps. It surprised her when the others laughed *with* her, not *at* her, any time she missed a beat here and there. In fact, one of the young mothers—*Isn't her name Dancing Flower?*—moved closer, flashing a broad smile at her and repeating one of the movements more slowly so she could get it right. Her heart leapt at the kindness and Mandy realized with a start that for the first time she felt truly accepted by these people, completely contrary to her earlier feelings. Perhaps it was the presence of this great visitor who engendered such obvious joy, which then spilled over even to her? She stopped trying to figure it out or counter it with her own doubts and instead released herself to embrace it.

The chanting and general atmosphere unleashed a sense of praise to God's Spirit deep within her being and without giving it a thought ahead of time, she burst forth in song, making up her own English words to fit the haunting melodies played on the flutes and accompanied by the drums. No one seemed to care what language she used, just that she had become a part of the celebration in her own unique way. Mandy *was* Kiowa now, no reservations, no second thoughts! Although contrary to everything she'd believed up to this point, the idea gave her much contentment well into the night.

Later on Mandy helped the women gather up the dishes from the feast while the men settled around the campfire to visit and share more stories with each other. They entertained the older children with their tales, amid much laughter and even serious words she failed to understand. How she longed to join them! But she knew it would not be appropriate. She had work to do.

Suddenly, Mandy spotted Black Feather's ugly sneer from the shadows off to one side. It brought her sharply back to reality. Recalling her earlier desire to ensure the great chief knew there was at least one white captive in the camp, she acknowledged the fact that not *all* of the Kiowa were such peace lovers, as he appeared to be! However, somehow her commitment didn't seem quite as important now. And besides, she didn't want to ruin the aura of this special evening. How she could even dare to approach the visitor escaped her comprehension, anyway. She certainly had no desire to bring shame to Ken-ai-te by trying. He didn't deserve that from her.

When she had completed her tasks, she slowly walked back toward the tipi, the image of the cruel face of her enemy fresh in her mind. Why did she feel so sad when only a short time ago she had been filled with such joy? Sighing she sat down on a log beside the fire ring. Her eyes were downcast and she stared at the ground without seeing a thing.

My heart is as cold as those ashes. All hope for rescue is gone, I can see that now. And on top of it all, I can't seem to avoid the constant threats from Black Feather. Why do I allow him to destroy the good God provides for me? You promised, Lord, that if my ways please You, even my enemies will be at peace with me. Yet—

"Prayer Woman, I look for you."

Ken-ai-te's voice came from the shadows behind her, sending a delighted shiver up her back. She stood and whirled around to face him. Why had he left the story-telling time to come look for her? She caught her breath for an instant, wondering if she had aroused his anger for some reason. But for what? He couldn't know her jumbled thoughts. Might he have guessed, though?

"Come." And he gestured for her to follow.

A few moments later, Mandy gasped as Ken-ai-te stopped right in front of the great chief! Her heart raced. What was going on?

"Prayer Woman, Chief Tohausan ask, meet you," Ken-ai-te said to her, and in English. Then he turned to Chief Tohausan and said simply, "*Daw-t'sai-mah.*"

Mandy's eyes widened with equal parts of fear and astonishment, but she quickly lowered them respectfully before him. *Meet me? Why?*

The warrior chief reached out and raised her chin gently, forcing her to gaze evenly into his dark eyes. To her shock, he spoke to her in English.

"Ken-ai-te tell me about this Prayer Woman from his vision quest. Fine buffalo robe you make for him, take good care of him, have many babies." At those words, Mandy blushed and instinctively averted her eyes from his when he released her chin. She took a deep breath for composure, though, and glanced up again as he continued.

"Long ago, Great Spirit promise Ken-ai-te a woman to come from great distance to change life here with new spirit in prayer. You that woman. Great honor to be woman of Ken-ai-te, my friend." His smile comforted her pounding heart in an odd way she never expected. In fact, she didn't even mind the comment about having many babies!

Mandy searched her mind desperately for the appropriate thing to reply in Kiowa but could only come up with a halting form of "thank you" and hoped fervently she wasn't inadvertently insulting him somehow.

"See you later," he said, again in English, then turned and walked away with long strides, Ken-ai-te at his side.

He had used the traditional Kiowa goodbye but in her language. As though she truly belonged here, regardless of the color of her skin. As though this were her home, forever.

Ken-ai-te glanced back with a pleased smile and her heart skipped a beat. Then they rounded a tipi and disappeared from sight.

Once more, she was alone. This time her chin was held high, not in arrogance but in great peace and confidence for being accepted on equal standing with other Kiowa women.

So the two were friends, as she had suspected. Today was not the first time they had met. Tohausan probably knew of the deaths of Ken-ai-te's wife and son as well. Yet he held no animosity for her, a white woman, in fact had only shown her respect and kindness. And what had he said about Ken-ai-te's vision? Had her coming here truly been predicted long years ago? Was that why she had been named Prayer Woman, because Ken-ai-te expected her to fulfill his destiny through her prayers? She shivered with the implications, but in excitement rather than fear.

"Father, are You telling me this is the reason You brought me here? Surely Your plan is far higher in purpose than that of a heathen, even one who is kind to me."

Suddenly it dawned on her that she had missed her perfect opportunity to tell the chief what she'd planned to say! However, Tohausan obviously knew of her heritage, did not need her to point it out to him. After all, he had spoken to her in English, not Kiowa.

"What is the matter with me?" she demanded, stomping her foot in frustration. "He pays me a compliment and I'm struck dumb like some kind of a small child? How incredibly foolish I feel! Maybe I should run after him and—"

From the deep shadows around her peeked a well-known but certainly not welcome face, mouth twisted in a snarl. Black Feather!

"No good, talk to your God. He no help." The words shattered the calm Mandy had felt only moments before. The warrior emerged from the darkness and planted his feet in her path.

"What do you know of my God? He despises those like you, who threaten innocent women and bully those who have what you do not. And He will take His revenge whereas men often delay theirs. Someday you will see His anger!"

"He see mine! You mine! I destroy Ken-ai-te, take you for me."

"Why would you want to destroy Ken-ai-te? He's done nothing to you!"

"Defile memory of wife, my sister, by have you in tipi."

"Well, your problem may be solved, then, because I intend to ask for my own tipi. I don't want to be there any more than you want me to be."

"No baby mean you mine. I take!"

Mandy paled at these words, the others having been fueled solely by emotion and certainly not by wisdom. She'd said too much and now had given him a powerful weapon he would not overlook.

She gulped and clamped her lips tightly. When would she learn to keep her mouth shut?

"How—how do you know there is not to be a baby?" she asked timidly. She'd intended for the words to come out strong but fear choked them to a squeak.

"Hear you talk. Know truth. Now all know, I tell. Destroy Ken-ai-te."

And inexplicably, he turned and strode away, leaving Mandy shaking.

"What have I done? How can he destroy Ken-ai-te? Oh, God, forgive me for blurting out about wanting my own tipi. Don't let him win because of my foolishness! Show me how I can stop him from this insanity he's planning!"

166

†CHAPTER TWENTY-FOUR†

"Now faith is the substance of things hoped for,
the evidence of things not seen."
Hebrews 11:1

"What is it you don't understand?" Mandy's soft voice hung in the silence of the tipi, her eyes focused on Ken-ai-te's face. When he didn't reply, she sighed. *Lord, help me say the right words to him. He seems to be genuinely interested.*

"Jesus die. Then alive. But how?"

"It's a miracle, Ken-ai-te. You can't explain miracles, only experience them and believe in them. And this one is for all eternity, too."

He frowned and she knew he didn't understand. She breathed another prayer for wisdom of how to explain further to him.

"E-ter-ni-ty," she said with great clarity so hopefully he would remember the word. And a sudden thought brought a smile to her lips. "The same as when you say I belong to you from now until forever. He is alive for all eternity—from now until forever!"

When he continued to stare into her eyes she added, "I don't know how to explain it any more. All I can tell you is what my Bible says happened."

"And you believe?"

"I believe. Though it sounds like it doesn't make sense, that's how I can know it is from God, when it is beyond my understanding. But it is never beyond my faith. That is His gift, eternity."

"For-ever? Fai-th?" He stumbled over the words, still unsure not only of the pronunciations but also the meanings.

"If I could explain my faith, Ken-ai-te, and if you could fully understand it, then it would not be *faith*. We use our faith, this gift, when we believe but don't fully understand how or why."

Ken-ai-te shook his head. At least she had given him something to think about, if not believe quite yet. Mandy glanced over at Sleeping Bird, her attention apparently on her beading. She hoped the words had fallen on eager ears there as well. But no indication of that—yet. Mandy continued their discussion while she worked on her sewing.

"My father used to remind me all the time, Ken-ai-te, that God draws us to Him with love and kindness and this is the very essence of our faith—the love and kindness Jesus showed when He lived here. Even our enemies love their families but when we love those who hate us, well, that's what makes us different in our faith."

The look on Ken-ai-te's face startled her. Maybe something finally got through? Her heart thrummed like the drums in the evenings, steady and rapid and beyond her control but filling her ears until she felt it rather than heard it. His facial expression now mirrored the one on the trek here so long ago, when he stopped to worship the buffalo racing across the prairie. Only, hopefully, this time it was a type of worship far different.

"Black Feather your enemy. Love him?"

Mandy squirmed under his intense stare. Would she answer him with honesty or with hypocrisy?

"Um, not yet, but I am trying. God has worked on my heart ever since you brought me here. I try to pray for him but so far, my words are empty. I do have faith God will help me forgive him someday for his evil threats against me. It's not whether *I do* what the Bible says or not, Ken-ai-te, but whether I believe God's power to do what *He says*. I'm just one person and human at that. The important thing is if I am trying to obey. God sees my heart, looks inside at my attitude and motive."

By his puzzled look, she realized she had lost him in some of the big words but she was growing desperate to explain the concept on his terms. At the same time, she felt deep conviction that his faith must come from observing as she lived hers before him, not just telling him about it. The gist of a verse in Titus came to roost in her heart, reminding her to hold fast to the words she had been taught from the Bible in order that she might be enabled to convince this man of Truth itself. And leave the rest to the Holy Spirit.

Father, doesn't he see I am no longer bitter toward him for taking me captive? That is forgiveness for my enemy, isn't it? I can't say I'm thankful for this exactly but I've tried to accept it and learn to leave the past behind. Sort of ...

Mandy felt she needed to be silent and let the words soak into Ken-ai-te's heart instead of continuing to explain further. He would ask if he didn't understand something. She would have to be patient and let God do the pricking of his mind to bring it up.

After several minutes, he rose and left the two women alone. Sleeping Bird startled Mandy by speaking first.

"Prayer Woman, mother and father have this faith, too?" She had been listening!

"Yes, they did. They came here to Indian Territory to share Christ with the Kiowa, building the mission where I lived until I came here. My father would sit with the elders in each village they visited and my mother would teach the children Bible stories. They loved the Kiowa people and my father taught me to respect them while I was growing up. And, as I've told you before, I'd always dreamed of coming here with him to continue their work."

"And mother die in birth?"

"Yes, she died giving me birth. You know, your English is getting better all the time!"

Sleeping Bird didn't smile, just nodded, then returned to her work.

169

"Are you troubled about something?" Mandy asked her, sensing conflict of some kind.

Without a word or even a glance in her direction, the older woman gathered her things and unexpectedly left the tipi without a word. Mandy furrowed her brow in concern.

"Did I say something wrong? I understand Ken-ai-te leaving because he always does later in the evenings, to join the men in their gambling and talks around the main campfire. Why you, though? Something is bothering you, Sleeping Bird, of that I am certain. But what?"

Shrugging, she laid aside her sewing in favor of reading her Bible as usual until becoming drowsy. She had almost finished a shirt for Ken-ai-te and pride in the progress she had made in her sewing ability made it difficult to stop working before it was completed. But God's Word pulled hard. She would add some feathers and shells from the riverbed and then present it to him in a day or two, no rush.

After some time of reading, Mandy closed her Bible and allowed her mind to wander a bit. Several weeks had passed since Chief Tohausan's visit to the camp and Mandy found herself often considering the monumental changes that took place in her attitude afterward. She smiled now to herself, amazed at the giant strides she had taken. One woman's act of friendship. One moment of kindness from a visitor. And now, everything was different.

As it turned out, she never had the opportunity that night to confront the chief with her question about why the Kiowa held white captives. Somehow, the idea had seemed disrespectful after their talk. Besides, it didn't matter as much anymore.

Mandy had become more accepting of the Kiowa way now, calmer and at peace for the most part. And even more tolerant of the language. Her efforts to learn the difficult words had been met with smiles and nods of pleasure from both people who were important to her, and that had increased her desire to learn more. She resolved, however, never to lose her command of English and was grateful neither Sleeping Bird nor Ken-ai-te objected to using English for the most part when they were alone.

As though speaking softly with a close friend sitting beside her—One whose presence indeed filled the tipi—Mandy lifted her chin and smiled.

"Thank You, God, for all the blessings You've given me here. I can't say thanks for bringing me here because I will never understand that. But since You seem to have put me in this place for some unknown reason beyond my comprehension, I am grateful for my new friendships and for Your continued protection of my chastity."

When she had finished, something continued to nip at her thoughts until she could no longer ignore it. In obedience, she picked up her Bible once more. Mandy flipped through the pages randomly for a few moments, then finally came to the words she knew God wanted her to see.

"Psalm 19:14: 'Let the words of my mouth, and the meditation of my heart, be acceptable in thy sight, O LORD, my strength, and my redeemer.' I do offer them to You. Use me as You will. Amen."

And with that, she lay down to sleep in peace. Daylight would come early and she would need her strength for the day's tasks ahead.

✝

As Sleeping Bird rushed out of the tipi that night, she choked back a sob. *What is the matter with me? The mere mention of my knowing English triggers tears?* A lifetime of training to control her emotions wiped out by a simple compliment—and from a white captive, of all people?

She ducked into her own tipi and closed the flap behind her. Sitting down on her sleeping robe, she retrieved a small brown item from the pile of blankets nearby where she kept it hidden. Poking around at the embers before her until flames leapt high again and chased away many of the shadows, she leafed through the pages of the weathered book and strained to distinguish the strange writing there. Ken-ai-te had told her to destroy it and she really didn't know why she had not done as ordered. Every time she looked at it, flashbacks swarmed over her like bees over a hive fully of honey, stinging her heart with their barbs until at times it took her breath away. How could she recall the memories, assuming they were indeed just that, having only been a small child when she was captured? Yet they hovered close, becoming stronger every day and accompanied by new ones all the time as well, never bidden and most times unwelcome. But still they came. She closed her eyes and this time tried hard to remember...

Someone was being held under the water in the odd vision and a cry escaped from her lips. Was the person being drowned? She didn't think so though wondered why she felt excitement instead of panic. Another snatch—warm, loving arms holding her close and singing softly. Her mother, perhaps? And another brief scene of a pair of arms holding her, but this time not with love. Fear smothered her and she gasped. Maybe the capture itself?

Her Kiowa father, a great warrior among his people, brought her home after a raid. Told often of her adopted parents' affection for her, she accepted without question the depth of their love. They lost their only child to an illness shortly after birth so her presence in their home, though bittersweet in many ways, comforted all three of them. Honest with their daughter about her heritage, they never allowed it to become a problem and so it had not been. She was Kiowa and she was content. Until now.

Was it speaking in English as much as she did with Prayer Woman that caused the unsettled feeling deep in her heart? Opening her eyes, she glanced down in her lap. Or did it come from this mysterious book and its secrets?

She flipped over to the first entry, as she always did, carefully pulled out the yellowing pages nestled there, and stumbled through the

172

words of the letter. Sadness tugged at her as the page revealed such deep love for the man's wife and his sorrow at losing her. Fingers slid over the last line, a name that once meant nothing and now meant a great deal. Then she skipped ahead to the last entry in the book and read it slowly and carefully, again stopping to stare at the two words entered at the very end. *Jo-si-ah Cl-ark.* Yes, she knew she had it right, no question about it now. There were just too many coincidences.

"Prayer Woman should read this for herself. But how can I tell her after all this time that I have it? She is becoming more like a daughter to me every day and I don't want to lose that. I also see love blooming in her tipi more with each sunrise. Nothing will ever be the same once she is told, for any of us. Would she ever trust me again if she knew I kept something this important from her? She has a *right* to know but would she *want* to?

"And what about Ken-ai-te? He will be angry with me for not obeying him. Yet he might be happy about these words, enough so the anger would be extinguished in his joy. It will change everything for these two whom I love. Can I risk it?"

Sleeping Bird had listened often to Prayer Woman talking about her parents. But that story was quite different from the one she had seen in these pages. The faded writing was stained with blood, she assumed Josiah's, so perhaps showing the book to Prayer Woman would not be a good idea, after all. Maybe she could just tell her...no, that would never work. She would have to show her before she would believe any of it to be true. And the longer she waited, the harder it would be. Prayer Woman's attitude had changed a great deal about living with the Kiowa over the last several weeks. But enough to make the secret easier to bear?

"No," she finally said aloud in Kiowa. "The time is not right. Great Spirit, show me when it is time for truth. Help Prayer Woman accept it."

Not entirely convinced the other Spirit loved by Prayer Woman would respond—knew in fact she would be terrified if He did—nevertheless, Sleeping Bird gave Him the opportunity. Bowing her head and holding the book to her heart for several moments, she waited. For what, she didn't know exactly, but it seemed appropriate to spend some moments listening. Did that mean she prayed? Whatever, the magic seemed to work for the younger woman, as Sleeping Bird had often observed her, Bible clutched in hand and eyes closed for some moments, then abruptly announcing her God had spoken.

"Will you answer me, Spirit who belongs to Prayer Woman? The Great Spirit will guide me, I know. And perhaps, between the two of you, I will know what I must do."

†CHAPTER TWENTY-FIVE†

"My presence shall go with thee, and I will give thee rest."
Exodus 33:14

"Mandy, how many times do you have to be shown how to do something before you will finally learn?"

Muttering to show her utter disgust at herself for almost ruining the morning meal, again, for about the tenth time, she stirred too hard and splashed some of the thick liquid out of the kettle. "I give up! This is impossible." She jammed the large wooden spoon into the pot and plopped down on the log in front of the fire, watching the clumps sizzle in the flames.

"What impossible?" Mandy jumped a foot when the voice interrupted her thoughts.

"Oh, Sleeping Bird, I've done it again. You are going to be so frustrated with me and I can't blame you. I let the mush burn and now—"

The older woman waved her hand dismissively and Mandy frowned.

"Not important, Prayer Woman. Today we move camp, follow buffalo. You pack tipi, I show how to take down poles and hides." Instantly Mandy's world turned inside out in more ways than one!

"Move? Where? I don't understand." Sleeping Bird simply shook her head. Mandy knew she would have nothing more to say on the subject. She rose and then stooped to gather a couple of items from the ground next to the fire. Suddenly she whirled around and called out to

Sleeping Bird before she could walk out of sight.

"Wait a minute!" The older woman turned to face her. "Did you say *I* would have to take down the tipi? Are you joking? Why doesn't Ken-ai-te do it?"

"Not job for men, for women. Pack after meal. I go pack my tipi now, come back, help you. After your tipi down, you help with mine."

"Of course, I will be happy to do so."

But instead of leaving, the older woman stood there a moment. From a pouch at her waist, she produced a couple of items, handing them to Mandy: a sewing awl and a flint. So the Kiowa *did* have flints, as she had suspected, yet she had been forced to make fire without one all this time. A flash of irritation passed over her and apparently showed on her face while she fingered the item.

"Must learn how without first. If need make fire but no—" She stopped and nodded at the flint in Mandy's hand.

"Flint. That's what it's called in English. Well, I certainly have learned the lesson well, having laid one every morning since the first day. Things would have been much simpler if you had given it to me before now."

"Learn first."

She nodded. Wise woman, if a bit cantankerous. "And thank you for the awl. I hated always having to use yours. Now I have my own!"

"More." Sleeping Bird pulled a knife out of her belt and laid it on her open palm. "Yours."

"A knife? I can't believe you would give me one." Her heart pounded.

"You need. Time right now."

Without saying another word, she left Mandy standing there utterly amazed. Tears stung her eyes and joy overwhelmed her. She gazed up at the blue sky above.

"Father, thank You for this gift of trust. I'm certain Ken-ai-te is fully aware of her action and approves. You have taken me quite far

176

since coming here to the camp. Seems I have much to learn and do today. Help me deserve Your mercy and these precious gifts. I own so little any more, it's exciting to have a few things that are truly mine."

Ken-ai-te arrived sometime later, leading six ponies. *I thought he only had five. Wonder why the sixth one?* Along with the other braves, he obviously had been rounding up his horses from where they roamed free on the prairie. Each man knew his own ponies by sight and often they would come when called by their owner. Mandy had never understood why they didn't just build corrals like the white men did to keep their horses close by, to avoid having to work so hard to locate them when needed. But it was the Kiowa way and not her concern.

Sleeping Bird came back a few minutes later with a large pack bundled on her back and a blanket wrapped around it and her to hold it in place. In each hand, she grasped several smaller bundles and Mandy chuckled to herself. She looked like Santa Claus on Christmas Eve!

"Is that all you have?" Mandy asked her. She nodded and Mandy helped her unload it so Ken-ai-te could put it on one of the ponies. While the two women worked to pull the foodstuffs, clothing, cooking pots, buckets, gourds and several hides out of the tipi and pack them up, the warrior lashed everything to the backs of four of the horses. Last, they prepared waters skins and pouches of pemmican for the journey. While they secured those in the baggage, Ken-ai-te disappeared into the tipi once again.

A moment later Mandy started to enter the tipi and nearly bumped into Ken-ai-te who emerged at the same time, war bonnet in hand. She'd never seen it up close before and its wild appearance startled her and she stumbled backward a step. Staring at it with wide eyes, she noted how reverently he carried it. Eagle feathers stuck out in every direction, reminding her of an enormous bird fluffing its wings. Except these didn't settle down, remaining erect as though on alert to danger.

Apparently, it was made this way on purpose to intimidate the wearer's enemies. *It works on me!* Shivers ran down Mandy's spine, to think of it on Ken-ai-te's head in a battle, letting out a war whoop and swinging his tomahawk. She found it curious he had not worn it the day he abducted her, though he did wear war paint. Maybe he only used it in major battles?

After Ken-ai-te had secured his bonnet to one of the ponies, he met Mandy's eyes and nodded in the direction of the structure next to the tipi. She went over to it and removed the hide and gasped. While most shields, she had noticed, were flat rawhide with various designs painted on them, Ken-ai-te's was starkly different. An eagle's head with full talons extending out from the face of it matched the bonnet, to make a fierce combination against his enemies, she supposed. Did they come from the same bird as the feathers in the bonnet? The glassy stare from the eagle held her mesmerized for several seconds. A soft grunt from behind her served as a stern reminder the warrior still waited and she carefully handed his shield to him so he could tie it in place, too.

Next, the warrior gestured for her to hand him his weapons. Mandy picked up the quiver of arrows and his bow and watched while he secured them on a different pony, the one she assumed he would be riding since it already held his food and water. Then she also gave him his lance and tomahawk and he tied those onto one of the pack animals. Her skin crawled when she saw the scalp lance propped against the tipi but, mercifully, Sleeping Bird handed it to the warrior so Mandy didn't even have to touch it.

A few minutes later Mandy, back inside the now almost empty tipi, came to her own few possessions and found a large skin pouch in which to keep them. Carefully she placed her Bible, the tiny scrap of blue fabric from her dress, her calendar stick, a small pouch of beads, and a drinking gourd among other items into it and secured it with a knot at the top. Then she slung the pack over her shoulder to ensure she could walk comfortably carrying it. Her awl, knife, and flint already rested in a small pouch at her side, and she patted them with tenderness. *When we get settled again, I will need to make a sheath in which to keep my knife, similar to the one Sleeping Bird has at her waist. And maybe add some beading on the pouch for the other two, just to dress it up a bit.* It filled her heart with joy to think about owning such important items when only a few months ago she thought life was over!

When she emerged from the tipi moments later, loud voices caught her attention above the clamor of the din around her. Sleeping Bird and Ken-ai-te were obviously arguing over a black blanket of some type that the woman kept shaking in the face of the brave. Although from that distance, she couldn't make out words, it appeared she was scolding him about the cloth. Ken-ai-te grabbed it out of her hand and threw it on the ground just as he glanced up and saw Mandy staring at them and abruptly stopped speaking. Sleeping Bird stooped over and shoved the cloth into a pack at her feet and walked away. Mandy had the impression they were embarrassed she had witnessed their spat.

Before she had a chance to ask about it, however, a frightened wail distracted her. A toddler wandered by, crying mournfully for his mother, and Mandy's throat constricted at the sight of the lost child. She recognized him so quickly swooped him up into her arms to return him to his frantic mother who ran into view just then. As the tiny boy snuggled against her neck for a moment, she was overcome with emotion. No wonder mothers smiled so much when they got this kind of a reward from their little ones! Seconds later while the mother joyfully hugged her son, Mandy returned the mother's kind expression of gratitude with a nod. And her thoughts lingered a few moments on Ken-ai-te's loss.

Turning her attention back to the work at hand, she noticed Ken-ai-te had left one pony without a load, which seemed a little odd. She became intrigued in watching the warrior quickly build a contraption of some sort using a couple of larger branches from the now-abandoned firewood stack, tying a blanket between them, and securing the long sticks to either side of one of the other ponies, so it would drag along the ground behind it. Then he lashed quite a few of their blankets on top with rawhide ropes, as well as the large cooking kettle. The whole thing took only a few minutes and it amazed Mandy how fast the three of them were able to get ready for the long journey.

Now it was time to take the tipi down. A rather complicated process, it started with removing the wooden pegs holding the skins onto the tipi poles, followed by the hides themselves one by one until only the frame remained. When Mandy started to remove the one with the strange drawings on it, painted by Ken-ai-te's dead wife, she stopped a moment to puzzle over them.

"Sleeping Bird, what do these mean?"

"Vision quest of son. Speak of you, Prayer Woman." She turned her back and walked out of sight carrying a load for the ponies.

"Me? But I don't understand. How could this be?" As the words slipped out, though, what Chief Tohausan had spoken to her came flooding back.

"What did he say to me that night? Something about a woman who was to come from afar to change life here with prayer in a new spirit, I think. Incredible! God, that means You planned my journey to becoming Kiowa before Ken-ai-te became a man, even long before we met, then inspired a woman I've never known to record it all for me to see years later." It took her breath away. Coming here was no accident, certainly not without purpose. She folded the hide carefully with trembling fingers, in awe at the insight God had granted.

Sleeping Bird returned to show Mandy how the two long sticks for opening the vent flap inside could be used to pull down the smaller tipi poles, and each fell with a crash to the ground. Then they were able to push the four primary ones, tied together at the top, over on their side. Ken-ai-te quickly rounded up all of them and lashed them to either side of the remaining pony and tied one of the larger hides between them so it would form another of the carrying carts behind the remaining horse. The two women, meanwhile, folded the rest of the hides and put them on it so the warrior could secure them, covering them with a couple of the larger buffalo robes, the fur turned inwards. Few words were spoken among them, for the most part only when necessary to instruct Mandy.

Once this had been completed, the three walked to Sleeping Bird's tipi to repeat the packing process. Mandy patted the neck of the black and white mare Ken-ai-te had led there.

"I assume this one is yours, Sleeping Bird?"

She nodded. *So that is why there is an extra one. He also rounded up hers.*

A short time later, they had managed to secure the older woman's tipi poles and hides behind Sleeping Bird's horse. Ken-ai-te led the way back to where their other ponies patiently waited and then on to join everyone else where they gathered before heading out. Stamping feet of the pack animals and voices calling out from every direction added to the noise around them as the excitement mounted.

Ken-ai-te indicated Mandy should mount the one pulling their tipi poles and her heart raced. She'd never ridden bareback before and hadn't been on a horse in some time. How did he know she could ride? When she hesitated, he gave her a quizzical look.

"I've just never mounted to ride bareback before." He quickly grabbed her around the waist and tossed her over the animal's back, not roughly but as though he'd done it before many times. Breathless, she sat there wondering if her head swirling was due more to the suddenness of his action or perhaps because of him having his hands on her, however briefly.

While she contemplated her pounding heart, he helped Sleeping Bird mount her pony, somewhat more gently, and then hopped up on his and they were ready to go.

All around them tipis were likewise being removed and readied for the trip. From her new vantage point atop the horse, Mandy was struck by the fact that in spite of the noise and chaos, the whole effort appeared to be organized and efficient. Everyone pitched in, including children and the elderly, and it surprised her how quickly the entire village was ready to move out.

She spotted Angry Bear and Little Buffalo as they struggled to get their things packed, arguing as usual, but didn't see Black Feather anywhere. Fortunately, she hadn't seen him since their ugly encounter during Chief Tohausan's visit. Maybe he had changed his mind about his plan to reveal Ken-ai-te's respect of her chastity. Probably not but she could always hope that God had heard her prayer. At least he hadn't shown his face lately. She was grateful he had disappeared from view today at least. *Hope we somehow leave him behind!*

The sight of the sparring couple served as a solemn reminder to her of the undercurrents among the ones around her. On the one hand, Mandy felt a part of the whole picture of a Kiowa village on the move, yet strangely set apart. After all, she was only a captive. In spite of herself, however, Mandy felt enormous admiration for these proud people, sitting there among all of them in the midst of such an exciting moment in their lives. It might be matter-of-fact for them but not so for this lowly slave. Her awe held her above any other emotion this day.

The long-awaited moment finally arrived. Amid great clouds of dust, the large and noisy entourage slowly moved out, with Chief Twin Fox in the lead. She hoped he knew where he was headed. Where would they set up the camp? How long would they be traveling? Mandy's mind brimmed with questions but she had no opportunity to quiz anyone as they moved, in part because of the distance between the people and also because she didn't have to be told they must conserve both energy and water for the mass exodus ahead. Talking would only drain both unnecessarily. The unknowns swirling in her mind would have to wait. She gently urged her mount forward and followed directly behind Sleeping Bird, who rode next to Ken-ai-te as he held the ropes for the pack animals.

Mandy noticed many women and children were walking; she thanked the Lord for the privilege of riding. She supposed at least from time to time they might walk to rest the ponies a bit but, for now, she was thrilled to be on horseback. The isolation from others gave her more time to pray and meditate on verses and to observe the country they passed through for the next several hours.

Maybe tonight I can get some answers out of Sleeping Bird. It has been such a busy and exhausting day and though I'm about to drop the sun hasn't even started sinking in the western sky yet. And she gasped.

When we camp for the night, will it be obvious to everyone that Ken-ai-te and I are not sharing a sleeping robe? What will happen to us if our secret gets out?

⊹ CHAPTER TWENTY-SIX ⊹

"He healeth the broken in heart, and bindeth up their wounds."
Psalm 147:3

"Sleeping Bird, are we going to stop for the midday meal anytime soon?"

Mandy's fatigue and thirst clamored for attention. All three of them had been walking for some time now, giving the horses a break from the extra weight.

"No stop. Eat while walking." And she pulled pemmican from one of the pouches on the nearest pony and handed it to her, then nodded toward the water skin hanging there as well. They shared the food and water but neither spoke again for some time. Several children came scampering by the two, laughing and enjoying the unusual routine. Their energy was enviable!

One of the little girls stumbled as she walked by Mandy and automatically reached out to grasp her hand in order to steady herself and keep from falling down. The girl grinned and seemed content to hold onto her for several minutes before finally racing off to rejoin her friends in play.

Mandy smiled at Sleeping Bird when she caught her eye as the girl ran off and managed to recall the Kiowa phrase for "sweet girl." Ken-ai-te was leading their ponies some distance ahead of them and they followed behind the last one in case something fell off or became loose. A nudge at her heart concerning the sleeping arrangements while on the trail grew until it became a troubling throb and she knew she must have an answer or her peace would never return. But could she risk someone overhearing her question to Sleeping Bird? After a few minutes, they were virtually alone so she decided to take the chance.

"Will we sleep outside tonight?" she asked tentatively. Would Sleeping Bird figure out her real question?

The older woman glanced her direction for a moment, then replied. "Yes, most will. Young children and mothers sleep with covering, rest under stars. Part of it. But men sleep around outside, protect horses and families, not with women."

Mandy breathed a huge sigh of relief. Sleeping Bird had, indeed, known the deeper need that lurked behind her simple request. At least there would be no need to pretend or fear someone finding out that so far Ken-ai-te had spared her honor. The secret was safe for a little longer.

As the two lay on their blankets under the stars that night with the other women nearby, Sleeping Bird related a wonderful tale from Kiowa history about a group of warriors who had become lost in the desert in the long ago times. Mother Sun led them by day, she told her, and at night, Sister Moon showed them the way to go, while the stars shared their stories of adventure and love to make the way easier for all on the path toward home. The story had remarkable similarities to the Biblical account of God leading the Israelites to the Promised Land. He guided them on that journey as a pillar of fire by night and a pillar of cloud by day to their new land, much like in this legend—except the one from the Scriptures was true, of course.

Home...Mandy's heart didn't linger long on it as in the past. The perfect summer evening brought too much delight to allow it to be marred and she shook it off and enjoyed the present experience. Crickets and bullfrogs echoed each other in the darkness and off in the distance a wolf howled. The sounds reminded Mandy that each tiny part of life is important to the Creator of it all, including herself. She may not know where they were, but God knew and she needed nothing more. He would lead her home when the time was right. At last, she drifted off to sleep dreaming about the stars talking to her—in Kiowa, of course!

The next morning while she and Sleeping Bird hastily made preparations to depart, Mandy asked if following the buffalo was normal or something unusual.

"Kiowa move often, hunt buffalo in fall. Fur thickest then."

"Ah, that makes sense. But it seems such a shame that Kiowa people do not have a permanent home."

"Not know this word."

"What, permanent?" She nodded.

"It means to not move around, stay put in one place all your years. Many whites live and die in the same house, in fact."

Sleeping Bird arched her eyebrows in surprise but said nothing. This seemed to be a new idea for her to consider.

"I suppose if you get tired of the old area, moving frequently is a good thing."

The older woman smiled and their eyes met for a moment of friendship between two cultures, each with something valuable to offer the other.

The second day was much the same as the first, full of choking dust and achy bones and weary feet. Mandy did notice many women managed to get in some "chatter time" while they walked. However, none spoke to her. She contented herself with talking to Sleeping Bird occasionally and tried not to nurture the hurt she felt. What did she expect? After all, no matter how much she might wish for it to be different, she remained an outsider and in fact little more than a common slave.

Shortly after midday, she asked Sleeping Bird a question that had aroused her curiosity since they started on the journey the day before.

"Sleeping Bird, how long will we walk?"

"Until chief find new place."

"Oh, I know that, but how far away will this new place be?"

"Maybe two more day?"

Mandy's heart sank. She dropped back a few paces to walk by herself.

"Great. Just what I needed, a nice long walk in the heat of summer! This is much like when Ken-ai-te brought me to the village—except I am not bound by ropes and I can eat or drink when I need to do so. And I suppose it is a good thing how I have grown in these weeks with the Kiowa. My physical strength and my stamina are much greater at least. Though I am weary I do not feel despair as I did before. Regardless of my feelings of rejection a few moments ago, the truth is I am a part of these people now, no longer merely a slave. You are so gracious, Lord. How awesome is Your plan for my life! Help me continue to be worthy of it and Your provision."

Mandy spent the rest of the long day remembering as many Scriptures as possible that would help her focus her praise on God rather than on the physical hardships of the arduous journey. It amazed her she could remember so many. On one, her tongue stumbled over it and she made a mental note to look it up that night and recommit it to memory once again. Not having access to her Bible for that brief time had taught her well the lesson of memorizing verses rather than solely depending on the written words for her comfort and wisdom. And it seemed for every one she recited, more came to mind!

Long walks, she discovered that day and the next as well, were especially helpful for this task and she learned many new passages before they finally stopped beside a beautiful stream with a forest nearby to make their camp late on the afternoon of the third day. The water flowed more sedately than those of the river they'd left behind and there were more trees here but otherwise the setting was quite similar and picturesque. They saw no buffalo but the antelope were plentiful all around them, springing into action at the slightest sound with their almost comical yet graceful leaps and twists high into the air. Mandy had felt no place could be as perfect as their last camp, but this one seemed even better in every way.

However, they had little time to admire the scenery or wildlife as now the tipis all had to be reconstructed so life could resume as before. It fascinated Mandy how quickly this process was done, each woman concentrating on her own tipi first before helping others do theirs. Except, that is, for Sleeping Bird, who assisted her in doing Ken-ai-te's since Mandy had never done it before, with the favor returned a short time later as the two finally finished erecting the other one, too.

The huge job that followed involved unloading all the ponies and other packs and putting everything away. Fortunately, Mandy didn't have to cook that night, although one more meal of the chewy yet tasty pemmican left much to be desired for an evening meal. Mandy actually looked forward to serving anything else but this the next day!

When the three had finished off their food, they got right to work before dusk overtook them. Mandy picked up a large stack of blankets from where Sleeping Bird had placed them on the ground and as she turned toward the tipi, something slipped loose from her grip. She stumbled over it and almost dropped the whole bunch.

"What on earth...?" she muttered as she glanced down. Tossing the blankets aside, recognition froze her heart in place. Mandy bent down and grasped the dusty black cloth, which turned out to be a coat. She turned it over and over in her hands, stunned at its familiarity yet unwilling to fully accept it. Gingerly smoothing the collar, she gasped at the dark red blotches on it. Folding back the lapel with trembling fingers, she stared at three small letters embroidered there and choked back a sob. Tears blurred her vision. How did *this* get *here*?

Ken-ai-te started to pass her with a load in his arms then stopped when he saw what she held in her hands. Mandy stood transfixed on the spot, hardly able to breathe much less move, staring wide-eyed at him. Anger quickly rose in her throat and she shook the coat in his direction.

"What are you doing with this coat? Tell me!" An eternity of silence passed without an answer to her question. Although vaguely aware several people nearby had stopped work to look in their direction, she didn't care who overheard.

Ken-ai-te didn't say a word yet never took his eyes off Mandy's face.

Finally, he gruffly replied, "Take in battle."

"Battle? Is that what you call killing an innocent, unarmed preacher?" She licked her dry lips and wished for something to moisten her throat as it clenched almost shut. Fury quickly overwhelmed her need for water, though.

"Answer me! This coat belonged to my father. Why is it among *your* things?"

"Kill him, take coat." His chin lifted in defiance.

Mandy sucked in a breath, then hissed between her teeth. She felt as though she had been punched in the stomach. "*You* killed my father? I don't understand—how did I end up being captured by the same vicious savage who murdered my father?"

✝CHAPTER TWENTY-SEVEN✝

"She weepeth sore in the night, and her tears are on her cheeks...
she hath none to comfort her:
all her friends have dealt treacherously with her,
they are become her enemies."
Lamentations 1:2

"Answer me!" Mandy's legs wobbled and her voice wavered but her determination remained rock solid. She deserved an explanation and would have it!

"Did you know who I was when you abducted me?" she shrieked at Ken-ai-te. "It could *not* have been an accident! Why? Tell me *why*!"

Sleeping Bird rushed up and grabbed the coat out of her fist before Mandy could stop her. She turned and shook it in the warrior's face and a string of Kiowa erupted between them, which Mandy's shocked brain couldn't comprehend. The memory of their argument the day they packed up the camp filtered back. This was the "black blanket" they'd argued about then! That's why it had seemed to be vaguely familiar. They had both known to whom the coat belonged all this time, yet neither had ever told her about it.

Ken-ai-te's voice was gravelly with displeasure, she assumed at the unpleasant display of emotion in front of everyone. Heads still turned in their direction but Mandy ignored them. Had they both known about her father all this time and never said a word? But *why*?

The more the pair fussed at each other and gestured wildly in her direction, the more Mandy's anger grew. Finally, she'd had all she could take.

Stepping between them she demanded, "I want an answer to my question and from *both* of you, and I want it now! Tell me the truth!" Sparks flew out of her dark eyes as she looked from one to the other and back again.

Ken-ai-te glared at the older woman and jerked the coat out of Sleeping Bird's hand, tossing it on the ground.

"Not important," he growled and stomped away, disappearing into the tipi without so much as a backward glance. Slowly Sleeping Bird picked it up and laid it on top of one of the bundles of hides yet to be unpacked.

"*Not important*? Is he trying to make a poor joke? This is *everything* to me!"

She couldn't hold the tears back any longer. Collapsing, sobs wracked her body. Sleeping Bird came to stand over her and demanded in Kiowa that she get up and stop her wailing.

"Task not done. Carry blankets into tipi, now." Her voice was even but firm.

Mandy couldn't care less and continued her heartbroken fit. When Sleeping Bird reached out a couple of moments later to pull her up by the elbow, however, she obediently rose, her tears finally spent...for the moment.

"He killed my father, Sleeping Bird! You knew about this, didn't you? And you never told me!"

Sleeping Bird ignored her and gently pushed her toward the pile of blankets scattered on the ground.

"Hurry," she urged her in Kiowa. "Now."

Mandy swiped at her cheeks. She thought her heart would absolutely stop beating any second, it ached so deeply. Her sweet father, dying at the hands of this butcher who had pretended to be kind to her, all the while knowing the truth! As she bent to retrieve the forgotten blankets scattered at her feet she fought with her emotions.

How can he be so callous about it? I thought he was a somewhat decent man.

A thought crashed in on her consciousness and took away her breath. *Oh, Lord in heaven! Is—is Papa's scalp among the others on the lance in the tipi? Oh, God, it just can't be true!*

She stumbled blindly to stand in front of her home which moments before had represented such pride and comfort to her. A bitter taste formed on her tongue and she swallowed hard, keeping her eyes lowered as she stooped to push through the hide flap. Her vision quickly adjusted to the dim light inside and she laid the blankets over to one side. Ken-ai-te was kneeling down constructing the bed and didn't look up at her. Gulping, she spotted the scalp lance in the shadows and pulled her eyes away and straightened a few things to keep her hands busy. Tempted to scratch the warrior's eyes out she nevertheless managed to control the urge.

When he finished, he went outside without a word. She stashed the blankets on top of the bed and unpacked some of the cooking utensils they'd brought in earlier. Ken-ai-te returned with his arms full of dry brush and proceeded to stuff it under the bed. Was that supposed to make it soft or something? Besides, wasn't it a bit too close to where the grass had already been cleared away for the fire area? What if an errant ember popped out of the flames? The whole thing would go up like a wad of cotton, followed by the tipi itself and all its contents. She shrugged. Not that she would care at this point, as long as she wasn't in it when it happened. The warrior didn't seem to notice or give it any thought, so why should she?

Next, Ken-ai-te quickly dug out the fire pit and hauled in some rocks to place around the rim. Then he unloaded some firewood that they had brought on the trek and laid the pieces in the pit. He pulled out his flint and within seconds had flames rising up from the kindling wood he'd piled there, as though it had required no effort at all.

The warmth didn't reach Mandy's heart, though. She plunked

192

herself down on the ground determined not to move another finger to help with the unpacking. As Ken-ai-te passed by her and out of the tipi, she ignored him and stared into the licks of fire. How she wished she had the courage to kick one of those flaming sticks toward the bed and watch in glee as it all went up!

Mandy felt something brush against her hand and glanced down. A scorpion crawled across her fingers and started up into her lap! She gasped and fought her first reaction to jump up and shake him off. What if he stung her before she could flip him onto the ground? Mandy wasn't certain if scorpion stings were deadly or not but she wasn't about to take any chances. The sight of its tail curled up over its back made her skin crawl. She imagined she could see the venom dripping from its stinger. She held her breath. Should she scream for help? Or flick him off her legs?

Instinct suddenly took over and she jumped up to shake her skirt hard toward the fire, screaming more out of disgust than fear. The crusty brown animal dropped into the flames and a slight sizzling sound filled the close air in the tipi. Mandy wrinkled up her nose. *Are scorpions edible? Who cares? I could never put that thing in my mouth, even dead and cooked.* Yet she could not pull her eyes off the creature, sickened at the thought of what would have happened if it had stung her.

Suddenly Ken-ai-te rushed into the tipi and she colored slightly, embarrassed to have him think she was frightened by a scorpion. Her wobbly finger pointed to the fire. His eyes followed to the blackened form, its tail still distinct, and he nodded.

"Hurt?"

"No, he didn't hurt me. I didn't give him a chance." Mandy shivered and hugged herself for a few seconds. Their eyes met briefly and she looked away. She was too crushed to give more than a quick glance at this warrior who had cut her so deeply. Yet he had come running when he thought she was in trouble. What a curious paradox this man was. Maybe, just maybe...

"Shield to be honored. Now."

The mood shattered, along with Mandy's heart, again. *The audacity—he shows no remorse whatsoever for what he's done to me!*

She brushed past him and exited the tipi. Even if this was her job, to put the warrior's shield in its place of honor beside the tipi and cover it until needed, she was in no mood to do anything he wanted her to do, much less something that would bring him pride in the village. But she had no choice. Bitterly, she did the task as quickly as possible.

Previously she had thought the shield to be distinctive and intriguing as though it somehow embodied the bearer with the power of the sacred bird preserved there. Now it appeared grotesque and ugly to her and she shuddered as she gazed at it for a moment after setting it in its spot. Covering it with the hide, she didn't even wait for the customary approval by her captor.

Instead, she hurried away from the tipi, intending to get out of sight of the shield, the warrior to whom it belonged, his tipi, and the hated scalp lance inside. Behind her she heard the voice of Sleeping Bird calling her back to work but she ignored the words and kept walking, her chin high in defiance.

Her mind consumed by anger, she was unaware of anything around her until Black Feather stepped in front of her, blocking the path. His ugly sneer made the scarred face even more hideous. He reached out and grabbed her right arm and squeezed tight. Mandy jerked out of his grasp but lost her balance, braids flying in every direction, and fell backward with a heavy thud. She groaned softly and her discomfort seemed to give him even more pleasure.

As she lay there, he towered over her with a menacing half-grin on his lips and growled something at her. His hand went to the hilt of the knife at his waist and she screamed when it softly cleared the leather sheath. The blade glistened in the sunlight as he drew it back over his head, aimed at her heart.

To her shock, fingers unexpectedly closed around his wrist and twisted the arm backward in an unnatural position, stopping the attack at the last moment. It was Ken-ai-te! Mandy had seldom seen his face such an angry reddened mask. Black Feather grunted a couple of times but otherwise remained silent as the two struggled over control of the weapon, Mandy forgotten for the moment. She rolled away from the men and scrambled to her feet.

Within moments Ken-ai-te had disarmed the evil warrior and calmly handed him back the knife, their eyes locked in a mute and somber stare-down. Only a few harsh words were exchanged before Black Feather spun around and stalked away. Another public humiliation. Mandy felt it was only a matter of time before he would succeed in harming her. Ken-ai-te couldn't be there all the time, not even with Sleeping Bird's help. What could she do to make him stop?

A thought flashed through her mind. Why didn't she think to use her knife? Her fingers flew to where it nestled inside the pouch at her waist, useless to her in a fight. She knew she must make a sheath soon and put it where it could easily be reached when needed. But could she actually stab him—or anyone? Shuddering, Mandy knew she could if that monster ever touched her again.

Ken-ai-te walked over to her and took her by the elbow to guide her back to the tipi. Vastly relieved at her deliverance from certain harm, she chose not to resist, the fight gone for the moment. But the reason it happened in the first place? Once again, her runaway emotions had distracted her from being on the alert for danger and had led her straight to her enemy. The cause, however, ate at her heart every second, relenting in its ferocity. She needed time by herself to work through this, to pray and somehow manage her fury and hurt.

Later that evening Mandy was left alone in the tipi while the other two attended the circle dancing in celebration of finding such a good spot for the camp. She wasn't about to join in the festivities with a bunch of wild savages who had killed her beloved father!

195

Mandy scooted up close to the fire and opened her Bible. She closed her eyes and placed her right hand, palm down, over the open pages of the holy book. Conviction pierced with unexpected pain. Until now, she had not brought her fury to the Lord for help. The wait had allowed hatred to sink its teeth deep and consume every ounce of her being. Would she ever find her way free of it again? She knew she had to try, to allow God the opportunity to work His healing power.

"Father, I need Your help more than ever tonight! I don't think I can manage this pain and disappointment I'm feeling right now. I know it isn't what You desire for me, know it is sin in disguise, yet I cannot help it. I'm so confused and hurt!" She stopped and took a deep breath before continuing.

"I rebuke you, my enemy, in the name of Jesus! Be gone from me and allow the peace of the Holy Spirit to settle over me. My suffering is vast and deep but I know You, Lord, are stronger than this and are able to heal it. Please, God!"

Mandy chewed her lip, lost in thought. Her brow furrowed as her mind worked furiously to put everything together. Her eyes looked upward as the tears streamed down her cheeks.

"How? How has it happened that I am living with the very Indian who took Papa's life? Was it some kind of weird coincidence or the devil's sick joke that led to my being captured by Ken-ai-te? It just seems impossible to consider that You are responsible for my being here in the tipi of the very one who killed him. For what purpose? And why allow my precious father to die such a horrible death? Surely, that couldn't have been part of Your divine plan. I cannot understand this and I don't think I'm capable of accepting it, either. Help me, I beg You!"

†CHAPTER TWENTY-EIGHT†

"And be ye kind to one another, tenderhearted,
forgiving one another,
even as God for Christ's sake hath forgiven you."
Ephesians 4:32

"Father, my heart is broken beyond repair! Just as I thought things were going smoothly, I find out he's been lying to me all this time. Bad enough if he killed Papa but then to deceive me like he has?" Her voice choked and she gave way to tears. Finally, she resumed her talk with the Lord.

Mandy's lips moved in silent prayer for some time before she opened her eyes. She had confessed every sin she could think of and reopened the path to fellowship with her Savior. But would the hurt ever go away? How could she manage to go on living with this savage now that she knew the truth? What could have ever possessed her to consider him attractive and kind when all along he harbored an ugly side only now revealed: a bloodthirsty savage bent on revenge of the cruelest sort.

Sleep, when it surrounded her that night, was restless and morning came with muscles aching and her strength gone before a step had been taken. Mandy faced the day's tasks with less enthusiasm then she had for a long time, going through the motions while her heart beat dully in her chest. Several times Sleeping Bird asked if she felt well. Mandy brushed off the questions. The last thing she wanted was to talk to her about it, would only serve to start the tears again. Finally, the questions stopped and Mandy steeped in her misery alone.

Ken-ai-te had avoided Mandy most of the day, which suited her just fine. Their daily routine usually began with her re-braiding his hair but before she awakened, he rose and left without a word. When Scriptures crowded in while she worked Mandy managed to push them aside, but her tension grew by the hour. Before long she realized only some time to confront her bitterness and pain and work through them completely would bring the peace she needed. Last night's prayers had shown her the way but with daylight, she had refused to walk in it.

As soon as dinner was over that evening, she went down by the river in the calm twilight that the earliest days of fall afforded. She relished the freedom in that small act of strolling away from the camp even more than usual as she explored the new area they now called home.

"Oh, don't get me started on that word again," she moaned.

Mandy searched a few minutes for a place to sit in the grass out of sight of the camp, then caught herself and chose one, instead, a little less secluded. *Don't want to go too far in case Black Feather shows up again. Maybe the confrontation yesterday will keep him away for a bit longer.*

She dropped to her knees, her Bible again clutched to her chest as though she could absorb the words right through her buckskin. If it had helped she would have eaten the pages themselves, her soul hungered that desperately for the comfort she sought and knew He could provide. The memory of a passage in Revelation flitted through her mind, of the angel telling John to eat the scroll. Only she was afraid she still carried too much of a burden of anger for the pages to taste like honey in her mouth as they did to John.

For some time she poured out her heart before the Lord and when the tears dried, He began answering her back. She leafed back and forth as verses jumped into her thoughts and finally she knew what He had been saying all along. To forgive Ken-ai-te's act of savagery, unconditionally and without reservation, was the sole route open to her in order to obtain the strength she longed for. Mandy could not expect forgiveness from God for her own sins until she was willing and ready to extend it to another who had sinned against her. But she also knew she didn't possess that kind of love for him as another human for whom Jesus died, to simply give up her vengeance and never take it back again. Only through His power could she manage to do that.

This was new territory for Mandy and she shivered at the prospect. *How, Father? Jesus did this for me but how do I follow in His steps?*

God spoke to her as He had done many times before, reminding her in that moment of Jesus' words, "Nevertheless, not my will but thine." And something broke deep in her heart. Mandy knew a line had been crossed in her life that would change so much. She yielded her ego and will totally in those moments and peace finally came upon her, light as a butterfly's heart.

"Lord, convict Ken-ai-te that what he did was wrong, even if he never admits it to me. Help him see that bloodshed is not the answer, You are. I don't know yet if I can ever look on him again in the same way but I do trust You to heal my pain and in time, perhaps I can. Just give me the opportunity to talk to him without others around, will You, for I know now that I must speak these words directly to him. Burn them deep into my mind as you give me courage to say them out loud."

Warm as a blanket around her shoulders, she felt the arms of her Savior. He seemed to be saying to her that this victory would be important somehow, even if she didn't understand it then. Trusting God to make it matter, she arose refreshed by her triumph over evil and self by His grace and mercy.

Later that night as Mandy worked on the sheath for her knife, she was tempted to put it aside and go on to sleep. Concentration eluded her and she kept doing it wrong, then had to start over. Suddenly, Ken-ai-te entered the tipi. She kept her eyes glued on her hands. *Why has he not joined the other men tonight?* Irritation nipped at her heels but she kicked it away. Her stomach knotted. *I won't let it get to me. It's time I found out how genuine my faith really is. Lord!*

Mandy raised her eyes to his and resisted the urge to let herself drown in those dark pools. It shocked her they still stirred her heart so deeply. She had something to say and better to get it over with before she lost her nerve.

"Ken-ai-te, I'm glad to speak with you alone. Please sit." And she patted the robe beside her. To her great surprise, he plopped down cross-legged across from her, his eyes never leaving her face.

"My heart has been aching with bitterness since you told me about Papa's death. But my God has shown me this is wrong. So I ask your forgiveness for holding this against you. I was dreadfully in error to do that." He frowned at the unfamiliar English words. She cleared her throat. "Wrong. I was wrong. I'm sorry. Will you forgive me?"

"For-give?" His tongue twisted around the word. "Not know."

"It means to put aside my emotions, to let God heal my pain, to not hold it in my heart any longer. Do you understand?" She knew no Kiowa words to explain further. She hoped the God of all languages would convey to him what she was asking, in spite of the barrier between them.

He stared directly into her eyes, then they darted over her face and hair, to her hands, and back again. She blushed slightly. It felt as though he'd caressed her physically with that look. Yet it was a warm feeling she accepted.

"Mean Prayer Woman not angry?"

"It means I'm not angry, yes. Not anymore."

"Why?"

"I told you, my God has healed my heart. When He heals, there is no resisting Him. The thing that broke it is gone."

She could see his jaw working and knew this was a struggle for him.

"Will you let God put this in our past and not have it between us?" Without realizing it at first, her eyes darted to the scalp lance in the shadows behind him but she pulled them away and refused to consider that dark thought any longer. A flicker skittered across his face and she knew he'd caught the direction of her glance. *God, give me strength to do this right!*

He nodded and a hint of a smile appeared, then widened. "Forgive. Hurt no more."

"That's right, no more hurt between us. Thank you, Ken-ai-te. It took great courage for you to do that for me."

"For-give." She opened her mouth to repeat her statement, thinking he'd not understood.

"Me." The intensity of that one little word stunned her and she stared at him for a moment without comprehending.

"Forgive—you?"

The smile faded and he nodded once more. "Not truth."

"What's not true, Ken-ai-te?"

"Not kill father. Take coat from Comanche who kill."

Her eyes widened in shock. "You didn't kill Papa? Then why did you tell me you did?"

Several Kiowa words erupted but she failed to follow and shook her head. He smiled and spoke more slowly, this time in English.

"Find out, faith real."

"You were testing me, to see if my faith was real?"

His chin bobbed up and down as the realization hit her full force. He wanted to know Truth but wasn't sure he'd found it in her. He apparently had decided this lie would prove it, one way or the other. The irony wasn't lost on her, how God had used a lie to teach the truth. From the kind smile that lit up his face, she knew she had passed this test with ease. Only it wasn't easy, in fact it had been impossible until the Holy Spirit ministered through her the ability to release her pain. *Oh, God, how easily I could have failed, had I not listened to You!*

Mandy breathed through her smile, "Of course I forgive you, Ken-ai-te, for your lie. I understand why you said it. How could I not forgive you when God has forgiven me for my bitterness against you? And you have done the same by accepting my apology."

"Words like scorpion's sting. Hurt but then gone. Good thing."

Mandy smiled in response. He understood! Oh, how her heart soared that, in spite of the immense pain she had suffered today, it had been worth it to *show* him what she had been trying to *tell* him. Yes, God had done a good thing this day.

Then a thought intruded. "Ken-ai-te, did you say you took Papa's coat from a Comanche who had killed him?"

"Meet four Comanche," and he held up four fingers to confirm he had the number correct, "one had coat on. Say he take off white man they kill that day. I make coup on him and take coat, also scalp."

Mandy grimaced at the confirmation the warrior had actually scalped his enemy but took some comfort in the fact his victim was the one who had killed her father, not Ken-ai-te. She could almost taste relief in her mouth. It wasn't Ken-ai-te! God apparently had required her to forgive him before He would allow her to find out what really happened. In other words, to trust Him so He could do the rest. *Thank You, Jesus. Your wisdom is amazing!*

She reached out instinctively and squeezed his hand and surprised herself by allowing her own to linger on his copper fingers. They felt warm and comforting. And she tried not to think of the evil they had done, only how God used them now to assure her of His presence in spite of the circumstances.

Abruptly she withdrew her hand and cleared her throat, returning her focus to her sewing. Wouldn't do to lead him on, perhaps give him any ideas about their sleeping arrangements just because God had blessed them both with forgiveness. She wouldn't relent on that point. Did he think otherwise?

A thought occurred to her and she asked quietly, "Ken-ai-te, what happened to the coat earlier? Does Sleeping Bird have it?"

He nodded. "Best away from eyes. Not hurt so much." He had given orders to have it hidden from her so it wouldn't hurt her. This warrior was, indeed, a man of great contradictions!

"If I may be permitted to do so, I would like to have the coat. I believe it will bring comfort in my hurt to have it close by." And she added "please" in Kiowa.

He nodded and replied in Kiowa the word for "later." She nodded in consent, not sure she was strong enough right now to see it again anyway. Her grief would need to heal a little more. Then it would bring her consolation, she was certain.

Ken-ai-te pulled out an arrowhead and began sharpening it on a stone. Neither spoke for a few minutes. It surprised Mandy when Ken-ai-te broke the silence.

"More about Cross, Prayer Woman. Why Son die?"

Mandy launched into reminding him about the details of the Crucifixion story, this time emphasizing the forgiveness part. He seemed to understand better now. Mandy's heart leapt again at the thought that the pain she'd suffered since the night before had been worth it if he could be made to understand God's forgiveness of sin.

"I don't know if you can possibly understand what I'm about to say, Ken-ai-te, but for the first time in my life the word 'forgiveness' has a new meaning, a personal one. My heart is different now in an important way and it is because of God's power, certainly not due to anything I've done." To her surprise, he nodded and smiled. *God, please let my words get through to Him, in spite of the language barrier between us!*

She cleared her throat and continued.

"My prayer for you this night is that you will come to understand the power of this word in your own heart, too. And of God's Spirit that makes it real when we trust Him to do so." An odd look on his face confused her. Could she dare hope he agreed?

203

Deep within Mandy knew God's voice was urging her to let it go and she battled her own will for a moment before obeying. *He's heard, now it's up to him to respond, I know.*

And she shifted subjects dramatically to ease her own tension.

"If you don't mind my asking, how did you and your wife meet?"

Ken-ai-te looked a bit taken aback for a moment. Would he want to answer such a personal question? Mandy was curious but mostly wanted to express to him her willingness to acknowledge the role she'd played in his life in the past.

He returned his attention to the arrowhead in his hand. She'd about given up hope he would respond when his quiet words startled her.

"Black Feather offer his sister to me for two rifles. I tell him no rifles. But do need wife. We argue for many moons. Then he say two horses better trade. Think he not want to feed her that winter."

"That's horrible! I—I mean, I understand that trading things for a wife is part of the Kiowa way but I thought a man offered a gift to the father, or in this case the brother, of the woman. Not the other way around."

"I see her often from small child, know love so not bad to take offer. She good wife."

"I'm sure she was. I wish I'd known her. She must have been quite different from her brother."

"He demand revenge when we take you. Not let him kill you, he want to trade for rifles in Mexico instead, not let him do it."

With tears shining, she breathed softly, "Thank you for that. I cannot imagine how hard it has been for you to stand up to him. Why was my life so important?"

"Watch for two moons. See you bury father. Decide to attack but then follow to river."

"What? You had been watching me for a while?" Mandy shivered.

Why didn't I sense his presence? What kept him from attacking all of us long before? I suppose he would have killed Jesse as well if Pete and I hadn't gone for water by ourselves.

He nodded. "Go to river, take you, but Black Feather not happy."

"Yes, I realized that when he treated me so badly that day. I just knew any moment he would plunge that blade into my neck and my life would be over. So you two were arguing over me?"

He nodded, then continued.

"Not let him. You mine." *Wish these Kiowa would stop using that phrase! As though I'm a horse or blanket instead of a human being.*

"So let me understand this, you rounded up your friends to go on a raid for the purpose of exacting revenge for the deaths of your wife and child, then changed your mind in the middle of my capture?"

His eyes met hers in a steady gaze. Then, the almost imperceptible nod confirmed Mandy's summary of the event. Her stomach flipped over at the intensity of his stare. How easily she could have met with quite a different fate, had Ken-ai-te not chosen mercy for her! She longed to pursue this further but something urged her to stop. Some things are better left unsaid. Surely, a simple thanks would be permitted, though.

"Thank you, Ken-ai-te. I don't pretend to understand but that doesn't prevent me from being grateful that I'm alive and with you right now. None of this makes any real sense to me, but I think I am finally beginning to understand it all more clearly. God never abandoned me but has used you all this time to protect me, in more ways than one."

At his puzzled frown, she concluded, "God's hand was upon you from the start—and still is—don't you see?"

⸸CHAPTER TWENTY-NINE⸸

"Casting down imaginations, and every high thing that exalteth itself against the knowledge of God,
and bringing into captivity every thought to the obedience of Christ."
II Corinthians 10:5

"Lord, why do I continue to struggle with my loneliness and anxiety day in and day out?"

Mandy scraped the skin harder than necessary, taking her frustrations out on it since no complaints would be forthcoming, and continued to cry out to the only One she knew would be listening.

"I have my Bible now and one would think that would be enough to supply my every need. And indeed, I am grateful; don't misunderstand. But a friend would be nice to have, at least someone to confide in and laugh with. Sleeping Bird is kind to me but I'd prefer someone closer to my age. Is that too much to ask? I know talking with Ken-ai-te earlier felt like it does when conversing with someone in true friendship, but how can that be true when he is a heathen who holds me captive? First, You rip away everything I know to be true about *home* and now leave me without a confidante? Why does everything have to change at once?"

She frowned, then cried out as she accidentally raked her knuckles across the rough hide. Shaking her hand vigorously against the pain, she fought back tears.

"Perhaps I should leave this task for now and come back to it later. Or never! Oh, I am *so* tempted!"

Picking up her handwork to relieve the aching in her back as well as her fingers, the beading swam before her eyes.

"Lord, I guess it's being treated like a non-person with all the talk about trading me for rifles. Both men only see me as a way to get back at the other. What if Ken-ai-te should decide to go ahead and give in to Black Feather and let him take me to Mexico? I don't think I could bear it!"

She abandoned the sewing and buried her face in her hands, sobbing for several minutes.

Without warning, Mandy felt as though something—or someone—had gently put arms around her shoulders to both protect and comfort her at the same time. An angel, perhaps? Would God consider Mandy worthy of a visit by a heavenly messenger to bring His peace in the place of her insecurity and turmoil? Yes, she had to accept He might, for no other explanation existed. Though it truly was beyond accurate description or real comprehension, she nevertheless knew an incredible miracle had taken place.

As suddenly as it had come, the moment passed. In its wake, however, she felt a new sense of calm as the anxiety melted away. God *did* see and care. And that was enough for her, for now.

That evening Mandy had an opportunity to address another of her on-going concerns: the lack of clothing on Ken-ai-te's body. Not that the sight of him scantily clad repulsed her; quite the contrary! Mandy had convinced herself if he would simply cover up more she could keep her mind clearer when around him. In fact, she had been thinking about this ever since Sleeping Bird mentioned he would need more clothes when the snows came. Why wait? Why not now?

"Ken-ai-te," she asked while ladling up his meal, "would you like for me to make you a buckskin shirt? I know you will need one when the weather gets colder but I thought I'd go ahead and do it now, if that's all right with you."

To be honest, she felt a bit self-serving with her question. It made

207

her so uncomfortable being around him dressed only in his breechcloth and moccasins. Perhaps if she didn't have to gaze on that muscled chest all the time she could better control her growing attraction for him. It didn't matter if the whole village believed they were living together as man and wife. They were not! Her feelings simply had to be conquered and with a little bit of effort on her part, not to mention a new shirt on his body, she felt they could be. Then her personal goals of friendship, keeping the peace in the tipi, and getting through the days and nights with a minimum of conflict and tension between them could be realized without adding emotion to the mix. Yes, this idea was a good one, and she hoped he would agree.

"Well, what do you think?" He finally nodded and grinned in approval. Mandy breathed a sigh of relief. One small victory at least!

"Great! I'll start on one tomorrow. I will make a special design for you in beads on the front if you like. Maybe in yellow? When it is cold and dreary with grey skies, the yellow will remind you of the sun." His grin grew larger.

Before she could stop herself, she thought how much his smile reminded *her* of the sun! What was the matter with her tonight? She cleared her throat and focused on finishing her food. Maybe she should change the subject yet again, this time to something less personal.

"The sun is important to the Kiowa, isn't it? I mean, all the tipis in the camp face the east, where the sun rises each morning. And many of the warriors have suns painted on their shields, also on the tipis."

"Mother Sun is our friend and brings life to her people," he said in Kiowa.

"Just as Jesus is my friend and brings me life." She held her breath. How would he answer? Or would he ignore what she said?

A frown appeared on Ken-ai-te's brow.

"What, do you not understand the word 'friend'?"

He said nothing for a moment. Then it dawned on Mandy.

"Oh, you mean you think it's wrong to call Him by name because

He died?" Ken-ai-te nodded. "In the first place, Jesus is not dead but was brought back to life by God's power. Do you recall when I told you that story? We call it 'Easter' and it is the most important day for one who loves Jesus." When he nodded, she continued. "So when I say His Name I'm actually honoring Him." He looked thoughtful at this but said nothing.

"I remember you told me it is disrespectful for Kiowa to speak the name of a person who has died, right?" Another nod. "Well, that's not true for Christians at all. It is the way we keep that person in our memory for all time. In fact, the Bible says for us to use His Name often because at the Name of Jesus the devil trembles and flees." Again, the frown. "Um, our enemy runs away, that's what 'flees' means."

"Enemy run away at name?"

"Yes, he does, Ken-ai-te. It's one of our most powerful weapons against him. Like your lance or your bow and arrows. And so is the Bible. It's why I read it so much, to learn the verses. Then I can use them when my enemy taunts me. Um, tries to hurt me."

He nodded, staring intently at her as though trying to absorb all of it. It was not a tense quietness between them that night, but a good one. The way a Kiowa family spends an evening together, not saying a word yet communicating volumes. And the way God's Spirit speaks without words, Mandy recalled. Nevertheless, it was all Mandy could do to hold her tongue but she knew in her heart anything further she said to him would only muddy the waters, not clear them.

Lord, I know You can use silence as much as words at the right time. And this seems to be one of those.

To Mandy's relief Ken-ai-te did not make any moves toward her when they bedded down in their usual sleeping spots a short time later. He seemed perfectly content to allow her the freedom to sleep away from him. It still seemed strange to her that he'd gone to the trouble to reconstruct the bed in the tipi yet had never used it. Maybe she'd ask

Sleeping Bird about this tomorrow. Meantime, here they were, the warrior on his buffalo robe and Mandy on the ground under a blanket a short distance away.

An odd curiosity roosted in her heart: the change in the warrior's routine. He used to spend every evening with the men, yet recently more and more often chose to remain with her, talking. Mandy was grateful she could visit with him and sew at the same time for she always had much handwork to do. Perhaps God's Spirit was drawing him away from other pursuits and to His voice? Interesting...

Before sleep came, Mandy thought about something that happened a few minutes earlier as they had prepared for bed and even now, her heart raced at the recollection of it. As she picked up her blanket and started to lie down, Ken-ai-te laid his hand on her arm, shaking his head. Then he pulled another blanket out from the stack behind him and spread it out on the ground at her feet, patting it when he finished smoothing it out to indicate she was to lie down on it. She hesitated a moment, but only a moment. When she stretched out and began to slowly pull her covering over her body, he smiled and turned away. Satisfied he wasn't going to try to join her, Mandy had lain there for a while considering the significance of what he'd done. Now she snuggled down and closed her eyes in prayer.

Thank You, Lord, for this gift. It is much warmer and more comfortable with the second blanket underneath. His kindness is such a treasure to me. Thank You for the privilege of forgiveness, both given and received. And for the blood which was shed to make it possible. Your constant presence with me offers the peace I so crave, no matter what happens. Give me a good night's sleep that I might awaken tomorrow refreshed and ready to do whatever it is You desire of me.

╫

The next morning Sleeping Bird announced she and Mandy would spend the day gathering foods from the forest area nearby. They packed up a number of gourds of various sizes, a large deerskin, and

210

some small leather pouches and headed out. Mandy's heart thrilled at the change in routine. What could they possibly find to eat in the forest, though? The thought intrigued her.

First off, Mandy learned how to collect honey from a wild hive they discovered in a rotten log and learned yet another new word in Kiowa—*ah-pean-ha*. She'd been attacked by an angry wasp once when a small child and the painful memory aroused deep-seated fear as they approached and heard the buzzing sounds around them. Not exactly eager to attempt this task, she took to heart the cautions Sleeping Bird shared to move slowly, not speak aloud, and never show fear or aggression toward the insects.

"Honor bees by using honey. Reason they make." Before they began, the older woman softly chanted in Kiowa for a few moments. A psalm of praise, perhaps? Mandy, on the other hand, repeated the name of her Savior over and over to push back her fear and, she hoped, to beg Him to calm the tiny ones whom she knew answered to the Master of the universe. Would He truly care about some bees, though? Or her fear?

Mandy would never have thought that robbing the hive of the comb could be considered an *honor*. To follow the instructions for silence and slow movements with the insects buzzing around them required all of Mandy's strength and courage and lots of prayer! Amazingly, the bees never bothered either of them.

"Taste," Sleeping Bird said to her a short time later. They had just finished pouring the honey into the gourds for safekeeping. The golden liquid's strong yet delicate flavor slipped down her throat and coated her tongue.

"Oh, yum! How I've missed sugar since my capture!" Now she had a natural sweetener to use in her baking once again. "I like *ah-pean-ha*," Mandy told Sleeping Bird with a broad grin. "It was worth the risk we took of getting stung!"

"Use in breads, berries, many foods. Good!" the older woman

declared in response.

While they walked through the forest, Sleeping Bird pointed out many roots and edible plants that they then dug up and readied for storage in the pouches they'd brought.

"These are okay to eat?" and Mandy indicated a few in her hands. She turned up her nose at some of them that didn't appear exactly appetizing in their present form.

Sleeping Bird used signs to show most would be mashed up or roasted before they could be eaten.

"Feast!" the Kiowa woman exclaimed with a smile. That was a word Mandy knew at least! She was confident they would be more tantalizing after she learned how to cook them properly and eagerly helped stash them in the small bags.

About then, Sleeping Bird paused under a tree laden with large purple fruit.

"Not many trees on prairie. When find, take foods there, also."

"Plums?" Mandy asked. But the older woman didn't appear to understand the word and Mandy wasn't familiar with the Kiowa phrase she kept repeating. "Whatever they are, they look delicious." They plucked as many as they could carry in the deerskin they had brought with them and Sleeping Bird slung it over her shoulder while Mandy took the other items, and they finally headed back toward the camp.

The two were almost out of the forest when they came upon a strange spring of some kind, with bubbles of something black as ink gurgling forth and spreading into a small pond of the goo surrounding it. The acrid smell assaulted Mandy's nose and made her blink several times in a row.

"What on earth is that?" she asked and pointed to it.

Sleeping Bird called it something in Kiowa, which, again, Mandy didn't comprehend. Then the older woman put down the skin and began scooping some of it into the one empty gourd tied to her waist.

"Important for healing."

"You put that stuff on a wound? Are you kidding? Looks like it would only make it worse."

"Horses, not men."

"Oh, okay. Still can't see how it can heal, even on a horse. You know, the other day I did see Ken-ai-te applying some to one of his ponies but had no idea what he was doing. I thought perhaps it was a bizarre type of war paint or something."

"Also to make fire if no wood."

"So it works on sores and also feeds flames? Unbelievable!"

Sleeping Bird flashed a rare smile at her, shifted her load to accommodate the extra gourd, and they returned to the tipi within the next few minutes. When Mandy kneaded the bread a short time later, Sleeping Bird showed her how to add the honey to the dough. As it baked that afternoon slowly over the fire, she was amazed at the aroma that filled the air. She couldn't wait to sink her teeth into it that evening. When Sleeping Bird told her they would be saving it for breakfast, she was quite disappointed. How wonderful it would taste to have a steaming slice of it! Her mouth watered in anticipation.

While the bread baked, Mandy learned to mash up the fruit, which indeed, seemed to be a type of wild plum. Then she added more of the honey to it, creating a type of jam of sorts. The berries they'd collected the day before were done the same way since they were becoming rather soft. She couldn't wait until morning when they could eat all of this delicious food. Dinner would be decidedly dull compared to it!

Mandy was surprised that the amount of work to be done remained the same as the days became shorter. All the women seemed to work harder and faster now, but the cooler mornings and evenings made it possible to do so in greater comfort than when the heat sucked the energy out of their bones. Fall was definitely coming soon.

Yet another season in captivity...No, I cannot think about that! This is my home, at least for now.

Later that evening Ken-ai-te joined the other men at the campfire to tell their stories and dance and sing to the beat of the drums. Mandy wondered how long he would be gone, since he no longer stayed all evening. Meanwhile, the two women gathered their beading materials and settled before the fire in Ken-ai-te's tipi.

"Sleeping Bird, I wanted to ask you about a couple of things, if I may." She continued when the older woman nodded in reply. "Ken-ai-te went to great pains to rebuild the bed in our tipi when we arrived here, yet he has never used it. He sleeps on the buffalo rug, which seems odd to me."

"Bed or rug for husband and wife, their choice. You still do not join him?"

"No, I still do not join him! I appreciate the fact that he has chosen to spare my honor all this time. But that brings up the other thing I wanted to discuss with you."

Sleeping Bird raised her eyebrows and a hint of a smile appeared on her lips. Mandy took a deep breath and plunged in.

"You and I talked about this some time ago but I've given it a great deal of thought and I'm tired of putting things off any longer. I want to ask Ken-ai-te for my own tipi."

Sleeping Bird's eyes flew wide open and she glared at Mandy, shaking her head vigorously.

"No! Not possible." Her scowl deepened and she worked her jaw hard. Mandy realized she'd done something wrong in Kiowa culture with this statement, but for the life of her couldn't figure out what.

"You have your own tipi. Why not me? Living with Ken-ai-te when we are not married is wrong. My God says I cannot do this evil thing. But I've had to do it all these months—uh, moons. And I'm tired of it!"

"Tipi earned, not given."

"Earned? Well, whatever I have to do, I'm willing to do it. How did you earn yours?"

"Comanche attack in night. I hear before they come, tell whole village. Big battle but not many warriors lost." Her expression changed appreciably to one of deep hurt. It took a moment but then it occurred to Mandy why.

"Was that when your husband was killed?" Mandy asked quietly, acutely aware of the pain showing on her friend's face.

Sleeping Bird nodded slowly, then raised her eyes to meet Mandy's. "Tipi given by Chief Twin Fox in thanks for saving many Kiowa that day. Ken-ai-te promise to look after me until death rattle comes. You no talk of this, having own tipi, Prayer Woman. No talk to Ken-ai-te. Much danger in this, make him have much anger."

"Why on earth is it dangerous for me to ask him for my own tipi? I don't understand. Haven't I earned the right, as you say, by serving him all this time? Surely, this cannot go on permanently. Besides, as I've told you before, he hasn't touched me since taking me into his tipi. Doesn't that show he has no intentions of making our arrangement permanent? He should marry again, have children, be free to enjoy his life once more. And he cannot do that with me living here. It makes sense all the way around. I really think the only reason he would be angry is that he would lose his personal slave if I move into my own tipi."

Sleeping Bird clamped down her lips and bowed her head over her handwork, her brows furrowed, refusing to meet Mandy's eyes again. Silence ruled over them for some time. But inside, Mandy was seething with fury.

If I don't get my own tipi soon, they will both know my anger as never before! No matter how kind he can be at times, he is not going to force me to go all winter sleeping on the cold ground by myself while he enjoys the luxury of the buffalo robe right next to the fire! Just you wait, Ken-ai-te. I will make my request in front of others, perhaps tomorrow or at least the first chance I get, and you won't be able to weasel out of it then. I will have my own tipi!

⸸ CHAPTER THIRTY ⸸

"A wise man feareth, and departeth from evil:
but the fool rageth, and is confident."
Proverbs 14:16

"Please, not again!" Mandy swiped the woman's hands away from her belly and stomped her foot. She'd had about all of this she could take. *How can I make them stop?*

"Problem?" Sleeping Bird emerged from behind a tipi at just the right moment. The women scattered, chattering wildly. Mandy breathed a sigh of relief, glad she couldn't understand the words. Their meaning? She sensed it all too well.

"The women won't leave me alone. They keep asking when there will be a baby in the tipi of Ken-ai-te again. Or at least, I think something to that effect. Without any provocation, they come up to me and actually pat my stomach. That's plain rude! Even if Ken-ai-te and I were married and there *might* be a child soon, I would never announce it to the likes of *them*! It's none of their business. The very idea!"

"Kiowa way. Baby come soon, once man and woman share tipi. Not so with whites?"

"Yes, it often is true. But they are married. A child is welcomed with open arms by white people as a sign of God's blessing of the union of the two. But it is wrong for them to continue to do this when they know it irritates me."

Sleeping Bird shrugged. "Ki—"

"Yeah, I know, Kiowa way." Mandy groaned. Whenever they

didn't have an explanation for something, this was the excuse they all used. Well, she had tired of their little game and simply wouldn't put up with it any longer. There had to be something she could do to stop them.

Sleeping Bird walked away and Mandy resumed carrying the water to her tipi, fuming silently. *This is why I simply have to get my own tipi.* Without thinking about it, she burst forth in angry words while she trudged through the village.

"Lord, they all think we are sleeping together, no matter how many times I've told them we are not. Even Sleeping Bird believes it. This is so embarrassing. And, God, it must be such an affront to Your holiness. Why do You tolerate it? I'm helpless, remember? It's up to You. There has to be a way for me to have my own tipi. Please show me how to get it."

Plunking down the two buckets of water, Mandy ignored the fact that she sloshed some out of each of them onto the ground. Though collected at great effort on her part, her impatience overwhelmed all else.

"So, why don't You *do* something, God? I've begged You for a solution and the only thing I can think of is to demand my own tipi. Maybe then they will all get the message, including Ken-ai-te, that there is never going to be a child between us!"

Suddenly Mandy realized she'd been speaking aloud, and the risk she ran by doing so. Glancing around, she saw no one and breathed a sigh of relief. And made a mental note to keep her thoughts on this subject to herself in the future.

✝

From behind a tipi, Black Feather smiled. He had understood just enough of the words to confirm his suspicions. Ken-ai-te had not yet taken Prayer Woman! The child by his sister had been ample proof of her willingness, whereas the absence of one now clearly demonstrated

Ken-ai-te's weakness as a man. Nothing could have delighted him more. Not only would the captive be worth more in Mexico, meantime he could use this weapon to gain some ground in his threats against her. He rubbed his hands together in anticipation and laughed softly. He must get to Angry Bear and tell him the wonderful news right away.

A short time later, he shared a hearty laugh with his friend as they made more plans regarding this new turn of events. When Little Buffalo walked in on them not long after, they told her that her efforts had been successful. But now was not the time to back off.

"You must keep it up, Little Buffalo. Tell the other women that Prayer Woman is not living up to her name, that she brings shame to Ken-ai-te by refusing to let him near her, and remind them this also brings shame to our people. She must be destroyed!"

Nodding and muttering to herself, the woman turned and left the tipi. Black Feather smiled. He had done his work for today. Leaving his friend, he emerged into the crisp morning air, his thoughts in a whirl. If his plans succeeded, Ken-ai-te would be run out of the village before long and Prayer Woman would be his at last. And if not...well, he had other plans in mind in case that happened. Whatever occurred, she would belong to him and he would have his vengeance against the whites. Just the thought of that one word *whites* brought on a gloomy spirit and whisked away his smug expression.

"Whites," he muttered. "I will not rest until they all have been wiped out!"

Black Feather stomped away from the village because he could not contain his temper any longer. But he knew better than to let anyone overhear what he said out loud so he walked quite a distance before stopping to declare his fury to the sky above him.

"I'm not as stupid as that woman," he said, shaking his fist at the sun. "I don't trust even Angry Bear or any of my friends, for if they thought they might improve their position by betraying me, they would do so in an instant. Soon, everyone will see that I am the bravest and smartest of them, not a coward at all.

"To see Ken-ai-te living in peace with that woman offends the Great Spirit who appointed the Kiowa as guardians of the prairie and protector of the sacred buffalo. Those two lie with every breath, pretending to be married and happy with each other, when I know the truth now. She would pay for being white if she were mine, every day and night, and fear would show in her eyes, not contentment!

"This scar," and he fingered it gently, "will always be here on my face to remind me of my sworn enemies. Hatred of all of them burns within me until I cannot hold it in any longer. Before long, everyone in the village will know my courage and those who have despised me will taste my anger. I am the only one here with a rifle, and the power I feel with it in my hand means that I am more fitted to lead these people than old Twin Fox or the traitor Ken-ai-te."

Here he paused to push aside the nagging reminder that he had no more bullets for the rifle so it remained useless for the time being. He should have demanded possession of the rifle of the white man killed when Prayer Woman was captured. But the one who owned it now was far away from this place, along with his weapon. Too late to do anything about that now. Though he hated the word, he knew he must be patient.

"Not for long," he vowed, again jabbing his fist overhead. "Soon, under my leadership the Kiowa will all have rifles, as well as many bullets for them, and the name of Black Feather will be feared by our enemies everywhere!"

ŤŤ

Mandy spent the rest of the morning working on Ken-ai-te's new shirt. Her sewing skills had improved but it took her so long to get a simple task like this completed, that her level of frustration increased rapidly.

"Why can't I get this right?" she muttered and tossed it aside. "Now it's lunch time and I have nothing hot to offer Ken-ai-te because I've been busy with this shirt." Tempted to give up entirely, Mandy thought better when she reminded herself why she had started it in the first place.

"If I stop he won't have a shirt and I will be forced to continue gazing on his bare chest whenever we are alone. And that is simply not an option!" Reluctantly, she picked it up and attempted one last time to finish the intricate stitching required. She was amazed that it seemed to come together much more easily now and within minutes tied off the last knot. Holding it up, she smiled.

"Not bad, Mandy. Even if I have to brag on my own work, it's still worth it in the long run." Her fingers ached from the effort but she ignored them. Relief and satisfaction replaced the dull pain. She couldn't wait to show it to Ken-ai-te that evening when they were alone.

Scrambling, then, to prepare a hasty meal, Mandy managed to get something ready to eat just as her captor came into view. She smiled at him but he seemed distracted and failed to meet her gaze.

Humpf! See if I care. He took the outstretched gourd but never sat down to eat, preferring to pace around the tipi clearing without looking at her. The silence wasn't anything new, yet it still bothered Mandy. *Wonder if he knows that will set easier on his stomach if he will sit while eating and perhaps engage in polite conversation as well.*

As soon as he swallowed the last bite, he tossed the bowl toward her and strode out of sight. Mandy blinked back tears and bit her lip to prevent them from falling.

"Why does what he says or does—or doesn't say or do—affect me so deeply? I don't care what he thinks, and I don't care what is bothering him at any given moment, either. Just so he leaves me alone at night, I will endure his bad moods and foul temper occasionally."

Just then, she reached for the bucket to pour some water into a cup and stopped with a gasp.

"My face! I look like an old woman, all puckered up like that!" She touched her cheeks and forehead, rubbing the skin gently as though to ease away the wrinkles there. Looking more intently onto the surface of the water, she tried a fake smile and amazed herself at the difference. Her appearance changed to that of a young woman, with skin as smooth as a stone washed for eons in the riverbed, as supple as a tanned hide—even though she felt no genuine joy inside. Apparently, the only thing that mattered was what showed on the outside.

"Father, I really *must* stop this frowning and replace that pout with a pleasant expression, if not a happy one. Or I'll look as old as Sleeping Bird before I know it."

Now a sincere smile spread on her lips. "That's better! No more self-pity for me today!"

Instead of eating her lunch by herself, Mandy took the gourd over to Sleeping Bird's tipi and settled beside her to talk while they both ate.

"Is Ken-ai-te all right?" she asked tentatively. "I mean, he's not sick or anything, is he?"

"Why ask?"

"He acted a little odd a while ago and I wondered if he had much on his mind or is angry with me about something or perhaps is not feeling well but hadn't said anything to me."

Sleeping Bird evaded Mandy's eyes. A sinking feeling developed in the pit of her stomach. What was she holding back?

"Please, Sleeping Bird, tell me what you are keeping from me. Is it something about Ken-ai-te? You never answered me about his health—is he okay? What else could it be?"

"Argue with Black Feather today, bad blood between them."

"Ah, I see. Um, I don't suppose this argument had anything to do with me, did it?"

The older woman nodded, then looked away.

"What? There's more?"

"Black Feather say Ken-ai-te not protect family and then refuse to take revenge for deaths. Not true but now others wonder."

"How did Ken-ai-te not protect his family? I thought they were killed while he was on a hunting trip? Didn't you tell me that yourself sometime back?"

"Yes, true. Wife go out on prairie but not tell me why. Killed while gone."

"Why did she leave the village when her husband was away? I'm assuming she had the baby with her when she left, right?"

Sleeping Bird nodded. "Think she go to find certain root which Ken-ai-te desire with deer meat, have when he return from hunt. So, deaths his fault."

"His fault? Are you kidding? How can they be his fault? He was off providing for his family, not failing to protect them. What nonsense! Surely, no one can believe this lie. They know Black Feather wouldn't know the truth if it slapped him alongside the head. How can they believe his accusations? Did Ken-ai-te defend himself?"

"Walk away. Leave Black Feather to scream. Not say a word."

"This is unbelievable. No wonder he was distracted and upset. Do you know where he is now?"

"Not say anything to me, just see him walk down by river. Why?'

"I thought I might go find him and talk to him about this. He has to respond to Black Feather's attacks! He cannot let him get away with this."

"Not Kiowa way. Leave alone. Ears have heard, now hearts must decide. Be silent or trouble come."

"But—"

Sleeping Bird clamped her lips together and shook her head, rising suddenly to clean out her gourd from the meal. Mandy knew she could do nothing and hated feeling so helpless.

This isn't fair! How could anyone believe these preposterous lies?

It might be the Kiowa way for me to be quiet but it's not my way! Ken-ai-te's reputation should speak for him, as Black Feather's should do the same. If people have a brain, they will surely know what is right. Please, God, show them truth in this, as in all things.

But she remained silent as requested. Perhaps the Kiowa way was best—for now.

A short time later as Mandy walked through the village toward the river to take a short break, she spotted Black Feather skulking around the edge of the camp. Something about the way he acted set off some alarm bells in Mandy's head and she decided to follow him. At that distance, she couldn't see clearly but he seemed to have something tall and slender in his hands, covered with a blanket. *What on earth is he doing?*

Stepping up her pace to climb the hill so as not to let him out of her sight, she realized he had headed for his own tipi. Instinctively, she hung back a few steps. She certainly didn't want him to realize he was being watched. He kept glancing around and had an odd expression on his face she'd never seen before. Every time he glanced her way, she would turn her back to him, hoping he wouldn't guess her purpose in being there. But out of the corner of her eye, she could see the ugly scar redden. A gasp escaped from her lips. No longer than she had known this evil man, Mandy knew the expression on his face could be nothing less than guilt. But guilt from what?

Ducking behind one of the tipis, Mandy peeked around the corner in time to see him pull a rifle from beneath the blanket. Where did he get that? None of the other braves here had rifles. What was he doing with one? He acted as though no one else knew about this, hiding it under the wrap like he had, but it seemed to Mandy that he ought to be proudly showing it off to the men. For the Kiowa a trophy such as a rifle was an important one.

Black Feather tossed it inside his tipi, pulling the hide flap shut. He whirled around and his eyes met Mandy's! Had he known she was watching him? She cried out softly and jumped behind the tipi for cover. It took her a couple of seconds but she knew she had to get away before he came bursting around the tipi to discover her there. The look in his eyes in that split second had scared her, a combination of fury and bitterness, and she fled on unsteady legs without giving a coherent thought to where she was headed. Suddenly she came to her senses and realized she had run halfway down the slope toward the river.

"What am I thinking? I can't let him catch me down here where we are alone!"

Whirling around she saw it was too late. The evil warrior blocked her path and strode right up to her, rage obvious on his face. Her heart froze in place as he jerked her arm and dragged her on down the hill.

"Let me go!" No matter how hard she tugged and twisted, she couldn't get out of his grasp. Her whole focus for several moments remained on not losing her footing while trying to break free.

As they came to an abrupt halt she gasped, "You are *mad*, did you know that? Absolutely crazy. If you harm me, you will have to face Ken-ai-te. And—"

"Shut up!" he screamed in Kiowa, inches from her face. Would he strike her if she opened her mouth again? Yes, certainly he would, judging from the fury on his ugly face. Mandy clamped her lips together, her heart roaring in her ears. Glancing around frantically, she realized no one had witnessed the confrontation. She was on her own—but not really.

God, help me!

✝ CHAPTER THIRTY-ONE ✝

"For he shall give his angels charge over thee,
to keep thee in all thy ways."
Psalm 91:11

hat does this maniac want from me? Jesus, You are my only defender right now!

Mandy's knees trembled but she held her chin high, hoping Black Feather would see confidence in her eyes even though she felt none in her heart at the moment.

"What you see?" And he nodded his head in the direction of the tipis above them.

"I—I don't know what you mean."

"You see rifle. Tell me!" The clenched fist he jabbed toward her face assured her it would do no good to deny it. Lies would only further incense him.

"All right, yes, I did see the weapon. But where did you get it? I have been told none of you have rifles. Does anyone else know about it?"

"Make me strong, other men weak. Have many bullets, kill many whites with it."

"Then why don't you tell the other warriors? Why aren't you the chief, if you are so strong and wise as to have a weapon of such power when the others do not?"

His face flushed and Mandy realized she'd said the wrong thing, had hit a nerve with him. As he narrowed his eyes to slits, Mandy was struck by how much they reminded her of a rattlesnake's eyes and knew he was just as dangerous. Somehow, she had to get away or attract others' attention to her predicament. No telling how far Black Feather's rage would carry him. This was the most conversation she'd ever had with the man, and she hadn't realized until now how much English he knew. A tiny prick of guilt pierced her and she tried to remember what she'd said that he might have overheard. The urgency right now pushed it aside for later.

Mandy decided suddenly to switch tactics, try to get his focus off the rifle and confront him regarding his treatment of her. She'd had all she could take. Now was as good a time as any to clear the air.

"What do you want from me, Black Feather? You harass me at every turn, threaten to harm me, and all because of the color of my skin? The others here don't feel that way any longer. Why do you alone desire to hurt me?"

"Not want to hurt, want to destroy!" His sudden burst of angry words caught Mandy a little off guard. *Destroy* her? Why?

"What did I ever do to you? I don't understand your anger at all. Ken-ai-te has more reason than you do to hate me, yet he has been nothing but kind."

"*Kind*? He not kind, but weak, forget revenge. Should take you by force, kill you. But not do a thing! No longer Kiowa, act like white man!"

She swallowed hard against the horrible words, gasping slightly. She'd suspected he felt this way, but to hear it spoken was far more fearful than thinking it. How could she answer him? How do you reason with such irrational hatred as this? By not responding, by implication she condoned his attitudes. And Mandy could never live with that.

"What do you want from me, then?" Her words sounded childish to her ears, almost whiny, but she'd intended to speak with great strength. Every second that passed meant her courage waned that much more quickly. "What?"

"You."

"Me?" she asked, feeling a bit stupid. Surely, he did not mean what she feared he did!

"Leave Ken-ai-te, be my woman." The absence of more words spoke loudly of the lack of his intention to take her as his wife, only as a slave, to do with her as he pleased. As often as he desired her.

"You can't be serious! Why on earth would I do such a thing? Because I happened to see you hiding a rifle in your tipi? I don't understand!"

"Know truth about why no child. Hear your words."

Mandy felt her blood turn cold even as her breath was sucked right out of her chest. Her eyes widened in horror. He *had* heard her! Why hadn't she kept the words to herself, instead of foolishly speaking them aloud? She tried to regroup her thoughts, the rifle forgotten in her fear. It had been his leverage so he could blackmail her with this outrageous demand. Somehow, even that seemed immaterial at the moment.

Quietly she asked, "What words?" Maybe she was wrong?

"No baby and never one to come. Not sleep on robe together. Ken-ai-te weak man, won't force you. You want marriage, white man style. Never happen, so no baby. Kiowa way shamed. You Kiowa now, no longer white. Maybe Ken-ai-te white instead of Kiowa. Cannot keep you without child. My sister give him child, I wonder all these moons why not you. Now I know." His expression wavered between fury and jubilation.

"The Kiowa way has nothing to do with this, Black Feather. It's a personal matter between Ken-ai-te and me, and certainly none of your business."

"No! Honor important to Kiowa. You shame all with lies. Tell Chief, elders truth, destroy both, then *you* belong *me*." He shrugged as though it mattered not how he got what he wanted, only that that he got

227

it: Mandy, on his terms, with no right to refuse him. And she knew in those seconds that he would never show kindness the way Ken-ai-te had. Never!

"You can't do that to him! His wife was your sister. Doesn't that count for something? You speak of honor but Ken-ai-te is the honorable one. He's everything you are *not*! And don't stand there and insult me like you don't know what I'm saying because I know you understand *exactly* what my words mean! I suspected you understood English and now I know."

His expression darkened. In Kiowa he growled, "Choose, now." His smug expression told her all she needed to know about his thoughts. He believed he had won. And indeed, it seemed he had.

Mandy's jaw flew open as the implications sank in. How could she ever willingly choose a life with him—this crude brute who had hated her from the first moment he laid eyes on her and had stalked her constantly ever since. Now, he was bent not only on her destruction but also of any others who took pity on her. *What can I do, Lord? Help me!*

"Si-lence say no. Make life mis-er-y, much bad with Ken-ai-te. Get what deserve in my tipi."

"No!" she shrieked, covering her ears with her hands to block out his hateful words, while clamping her eyes shut against the tears that sprang forth in spite of her efforts to hide them. "This simply cannot be happening!"

Suddenly Black Feather grabbed the back of Mandy's neck and forced her head upward toward his face. She gasped in pain and fear. Again, inches from his filthy breath, as so long ago when he first threatened her life, he grinned.

"Love? You *love* Ken-ai-te? He take, kill man, keep you here, you love anyway?" And he threw back his head and roared—a fake, shrill bark that hardly resembled real laughter, then shoved her away from him, and she stumbled backwards.

Her cheeks burned. *Love* him? Impossible! How could this savage sense what Mandy did not? *Surely not love! Or—is he right? Oh, God, I'm so confused and frightened!*

She turned away from him and without thinking about it ahead of time instinctively fled up the hill. He didn't try to stop her but the echo of his coarse taunts followed her back to the safety of the village and haunted her dreams that night.

Could she trust Sleeping Bird if she confided in her, or would she laugh at her predicament as well? Was love really the same as respect or kindness? Surely, it could not be *love* that nipped at her heart! She didn't want to be in love with her captor, with *any* Kiowa, in fact. *This is all so unfair! How could You allow me to be in such an untenable situation, Lord? What have I done to deserve this?*

Alternating prayer with her tears, Mandy passed the night slowly and painfully. How could she keep this to herself? Yet, how could she tell Ken-ai-te or even Sleeping Bird of the evil plans lurking in the shadows around them? Best to remain quiet and try to get through a day or two without disrupting things and see if Black Feather was serious. This strategy sounded good to her but in reality was more difficult to live out than she had figured. Only with God's strength could she manage as she claimed verse after verse to keep her going.

✝

"Prayer Woman, need more water." Sleeping Bird's voice was less of a command and more of a request. Mandy's heart warmed. They were making progress.

Inside, she groaned yet felt relief. Her hands were messy from the green goo she was using on the hide of the deer Ken-ai-te killed a couple of days before and she would have preferred to stay with the task until it was completed. It filled her with a sense of pride that she was doing her own hide by herself for the first time, from start to finish. She needed to make Ken-ai-te a second shirt and if any of the

229

skin was left, a shawl to wear around her shoulders for cool mornings. She had plans to also make Ken-ai-te a cloak for the coming snows as well as leggings and maybe another dress for herself. Ambitious plans for her and ones that would require a great deal of help from Sleeping Bird to prepare the hides and complete all those garments. For now, she tried to do the task on her own with this one. Besides, keeping busy with her hands kept her mind from wandering into the dark thoughts she tried so hard to avoid.

Cleaning her hands, Mandy took the bucket and headed for the river. It was good to be away from the camp for a few minutes at least, to have some freedom for a short time. Not too long ago, it would have been unthinkable to ask her to fetch water without someone watching her every step carefully. *As though I would seriously consider heading out onto the prairie on foot. I may only be a slave but I'm not stupid!*

Coming back up the rise, she spotted Black Feather leering at her. Involuntarily she shuddered but managed to turn away and ignore him as she hurried back to deliver the bucket to Sleeping Bird, who was busy with a group of other women in front of a nearby tipi. Mandy didn't take the time to find out why she had needed the water. Hurrying back to her place at the hide, she resumed her work.

At least doing this job allows me the opportunity to worship God as I choose and no one cares. It's Sunday again and I do, indeed, honor You, Father. The worship stick, as she now called it, helped her keep track of the days of the week, except when she occasionally forgot to move the threads upon arising daily. Again, she reminded herself it wasn't important the day or time she worshipped, just the fact that she did it on a regular basis.

For the next several minutes as her body went through the motions of the arduous task, she allowed her mind to focus on her Lord in prayer and meditation. Doing so seemed to make the job easier for one thing, and killed two rabbits with one arrow, as Ken-ai-te was fond of saying. And eased the burden of her heart as well.

Later that afternoon while preparing the evening meal, Mandy noticed an air of excitement around her and wondered if it was her imagination. She soon learned otherwise. Ken-ai-te startled Mandy by informing her of the next day's plans. Usually, it was Sleeping Bird who told Mandy what was coming up. But it seemed natural he should talk to her about these things, and in spite of this break with their established routine, she took deep satisfaction from their brief conversation.

"Buffalo hunt at morning light. You learn much tomorrow." She nodded in response and noticed him packing his quiver of arrows. Shivering slightly, she felt sadness for those animals that would die the next morning. However, their deaths meant life to the Kiowa—and to her. She shook off the feeling. How could she think about buffalo more than people when this much was at stake?

The celebration that night was particularly energized, Mandy decided as she observed the Kiowa Buffalo Dance. It was not the first time she'd seen it but the first time with a buffalo hunt anticipated for the following day. So this was different and she saw it with different eyes. Ken-ai-te tied some long tails of some kind on the back of his moccasins as he donned his regalia and Mandy vainly tried to place what animal they had come from.

"Sleeping Bird, what does Ken-ai-te have tied onto his heels?" They sat watching the men dance in rhythm to the drums and chants.

"Tail of wolf. Bring good luck with buffalo!"

Good luck...that's what we need right now all right. More, we need God's blessings to prevent the disaster Black Feather is planning for all of us.

Guilt washed over Mandy. Maybe she should tell Sleeping Bird, after all? God would give her an answer, she knew, but it would need to come soon to head off the enemy's schemes.

That night after everything finally wound down, Mandy and Ken-ai-te headed to the tipi together. She settled down for her customary prayer time before sleeping and their eyes met across the tipi floor. He smiled and gazed at her lying there under her blanket. Mandy fervently hoped her smile in return would not be misinterpreted as an invitation for him to join her. Although she would have preferred to hold his stare longer, she was fearful that to do so might stir unwanted and unintentional misunderstandings. For both of them. She closed her eyes.

Could it really be love I feel for him? Father, I cannot imagine that. My dreams of finding my one true love were so different from this. Please help me!

Shutting out everything for what she hoped would be a few hours of blessed relief, Mandy slept fitfully. Several times upon awakening, she listened to Ken-ai-te's soft snores and prayed his rest would be deep, that he would not sense her anxiety. Apparently, those pleas were heard because he never stirred. She knew he would need all the strength he could get for the buffalo hunt.

Ken-ai-te rose before first light the next morning and left the tipi without a word to Mandy. She followed him out a couple of minutes later, intending to fetch water and firewood, but found herself transfixed by the sight of the warrior in obvious worship of some kind, as he stood facing the sunrise with his arms raised to the sky. It reminded her of that time on the prairie when he was bringing her here and they spotted the immense herd of great shaggy beasts below them. She had been amazed that day when he stopped to raise his face to the heavens and she recalled praying then he would somehow learn to worship their Creator rather than the creatures themselves. Was he any closer to this yet?

One thought had refused to leave her mind since awakening: if Ken-ai-te died today, as she figured could easily happen when confronting the mammoth animals, he would never have the opportunity to come to Jesus in faith. God had done His part in providing him with a way to hear but, so far, he had rejected His love.

Jesus came to bring all men eternal life. Not just white people, not just those who attend church and read the Bible, not just those who speak English and are considered civilized. *All* men. She was frightened for him, being in such danger without having God on his side. On the other hand, by lifting him up in prayer she opened the door for God to act on his behalf with protection whether he requested it or not. She knew she had her work cut out for her this day through her fervent prayers.

Turning her attention to the tasks ahead, Mandy tiptoed away so as not to disturb him. She became intrigued to see how each woman attended to her own husband in preparation for the hunt as everyone bustled around, and it felt comforting to have a role in this exciting event.

Sleeping Bird joined her in the search for firewood and while they walked back to the village the older woman was oddly talkative. As a rule, she seldom said anything when they worked at such a strenuous job but today there was no silence between them.

After several moments of inconsequential chatter from her, she finally said, "Hunt dangerous, men often killed or hurt. Pray hard this day."

"Pray hard?"

"If Ken-ai-te not return, Black Feather take you."

Mandy stopped in her tracks, her jaw slack at those ominous words. "What are you talking about?"

A string of Kiowa words burst forth but Mandy shook her head vigorously to show she didn't understand any of it. Sleeping Bird came to a halt as well, took a deep breath, and then continued more slowly in English.

"You belong Ken-ai-te but if killed no one to stop Black Feather. He has right to you for revenge of dead sister. I tell you this long ago."

"I know you've mentioned it once or twice but I never dreamed after all this time it still might happen, in spite of that horrible man's threats against me. Sleeping Bird, I don't want to die! But even worse, I can't bear the thought of having to live with *him*!"

Mandy gulped back the tears. Between the recent threats and now this, she could no longer avoid the truth. Everything hung in the balance. If Black Feather could not get her one way, he would take her another. What if he harmed Ken-ai-te during the hunt, on purpose in order to get what he wanted? Was it really hopeless?

No! It just can't be. You are in charge, God, not that evil man!

Suddenly the silence that had fallen between them broke and jerked Mandy out of her thoughts.

"Pray. Your God listen?"

Pray? It took a heathen woman to remind me of this? Oh, Father, how I need You right now!

"Oh, yes, my God will listen all right. Of that, I am sure. His angels will protect Ken-ai-te from the buffalo," she told her as they arrived back at the tipi, their arms loaded down.

But listening to her and granting what she asked were often two entirely different things and well she knew it. She had prayed for her father, for instance, but still God took him from her. A small voice nagged within her. Whom did she trust with this warrior's life? She hoped his fate did not rest on the effectiveness of her prayers alone. Scolding herself, she realized she had to focus on who God was, not on what He could do for her. It was not solely what happened today. That decision was not hers to make. But eternal consequences also hung in the balance. And besides, she needed him.

Wait a minute! Did I just say need? *I don't want to need him...but I do.* Who would protect her from Black Feather if anything happened to Ken-ai-te? What would her future hold without this brave warrior to defend her? How could she ever hope to survive the brutality that awaited her in a life with Black Feather? Tears stung her eyes but she courageously fought them back. Yes, there were many questions on her heart but also much to do, and no time for giving in to self-pity or fear.

She must surrender those to God whenever they came to mind and give Him room to work.

Mandy hurried to assist Ken-ai-te as he painted his pony and his own body with wild colors. When he was done, she redid his braids and put the feathers in. She thrilled at the feel of his straight black hair in her fingers and blushed slightly. He smiled at her and she caught her breath. Did he know what she was thinking? He certainly acted as though he did. She really must learn to control her feelings better! It was being so close to him, feeling his warmth, smelling his breath and his sweat, staring at those dark pools that so entranced her that at times she could hardly think straight. What was wrong with her? She took a deep breath and tried to brush her emotions aside, at least keep them in check until he was gone.

As he leapt onto his horse a few minutes later, his bow slung over his shoulder and the arrows peeking out from behind his neck, Mandy took the shield from its place outside the tipi and handed it up to him. Their fingers touched briefly in the exchange of the sacred item and Mandy smiled at the warrior. He nodded toward the lance propped up nearby and she passed it to him as well. She replied the same way and caressed the side of his moccasin legging for an instant in a parting gesture. He rode away without a glance backward and she sighed.

"Lord, will I ever see him again? Do I have the right to ask that You protect him for my own selfish needs? In truth, though, there is more to it than simply that alone. I'm so confused by all this. Just please don't take him from me now!"

†CHAPTER THIRTY-TWO†

"Know therefore that the LORD thy God, he is God, the faithful God,
which keepeth covenant and mercy
with them that love him and keep his commandments
to a thousand generations."
Deuteronomy 7:9

"What would I do if anything happened to him? I'm not comfortable being so dependent on the man but it's true I am, whether I like it or not. Protect him by Your right hand, Father, and me as well while he is gone," she whispered softly. Reopening her eyes, she watched the swirls of dust rapidly disappearing in the distance.

Dogs yipped in excitement and the children whooped and hollered, envy clear on the faces of the boys not yet old enough to join the men. Ken-ai-te was already out of sight. The long day ahead loomed large.

Sleeping Bird walked up beside her and followed her gaze in the direction the men had ridden away. Mandy had forgotten about her. *Surely, she is anxious about his return, too. After all, she relies on him much as I do.*

Abruptly, as though reading Mandy's mind, she said, "Best stay busy, no worry."

"Yes, you are right," she responded with a deep sigh. God had everything under control. She tried hard to leave it with Him and not be anxious about what sunset might bring.

A couple of hours later something occurred to Mandy while going through her daily routine. The underlying tension she usually felt all the time had dissolved, as the mists of the morning do once the rays of sunlight pierce them. Her soul was full of joy, her mood even cheerful at times.

"I know it is due to the fact Black Feather is not here today, lurking behind each shadow, leering at me, and stirring up trouble with every step. If only I didn't feel such apprehension about the outcome of the hunt, I know I could fully embrace what nudges at my heart this day." Dare she call it by name? Say it aloud?

"Yes! I am happy! I'd forgotten how much easier life is when enveloped in happiness." And she giggled like a young schoolgirl, giddy with delight.

How long had it been since her burdens had felt light as a downy feather? She frowned when the memories came flooding back. Certainly not since that fateful morning when she and Pete started out for the river. And maybe not since her father died. Had God given her this insight to show her the way to finding contentment here with Ken-ai-te? Rather like welcoming home an old friend after a long absence, embracing that presence surrounding her now instead of constantly looking back on the past. And suddenly, Mandy knew Ken-ai-te's safety had become more crucial than ever for her future contentment. How, she wasn't exactly sure, but she knew it to be true.

Shortly afterward, while the two women worked on grinding up some seedpods, Sleeping Bird informed her what would happen when the hunt had been completed.

"Women do meat," and she used hand signs to indicate cutting it up.

"Butcher the meat?" Mandy asked incredulously. Surely, that wasn't what she meant! A nod confirmed her worst suspicions.

"But I don't know how to do that! I'm quite certain there must be a system for cutting up an entire animal of that immense size. Can you teach me?" Another nod.

"Much work to do if hunt good one."

"How many buffalo do you think Ken-ai-te might kill in this hunt?"

She held up two, then three, then four fingers and shrugged with a smile.

"That many?" Inwardly she groaned. *Much work, indeed. I'll be laboring until the world ends at the rate I'm learning new tasks right now.* She was grateful she had a good teacher who was more or less patient with her.

"Food, hides, tools for all year from hunt. Important to Kiowa future. Share what not needed with others not so luck-ee in hunt."

"That makes sense, so none go hungry." And the older woman nodded in response. "But how do the men tell which buffalo they killed after the hunt is over?"

"Done by color of feathers on arrows or lances. Look at each one, decide which warrior killed that one."

"That's ingenious! No way to cheat, then, is there?"

Sleeping Bird's confused look told Mandy she didn't know what the word *cheat* meant.

"Um, lie about it. Not tell the truth." Again, another nod.

Mandy wondered what Kiowa society would be like without all the nodding they did to show approval or confirmation of something. The people might actually have to speak for a change!

"I've been meaning to ask you something else. Why is it the Kiowa men here do not have rifles, only arrows and lances? I thought all Indians had rifles by now. I know many do."

"Must trade for rifles. Some Kiowa live close to white men, trade much. Others live out on prairie, never see white men. How rifles different from arrows?"

"Well, for one thing bullets will go further than an arrow, I think, and with more force so they will pierce clothing or a shield better than an arrow could. I have watched as the men and even the boys practice with their arrows, though, and am amazed at the speed with which they can draw an arrow out of the quiver and load it into the bow and let it fly. So I suppose arrows work just fine!"

Sleeping Bird nodded.

The thought struck Mandy that Black Feather could only have gotten his rifle off a white man's body at some point. But why not brag to others about his kill? Nothing about him made any sense, she decided.

"Do the men bring the bodies of the buffalo back here?" she continued in an effort to get her mind off the evil warrior. "That's a lot of work for them!"

"Women go there, cut up meat where body is." How long would it take her to remove the meat and other usable parts and haul it all back to the camp? Even with help, she imagined it would take a few days. And it seemed the meat would spoil long before then in the heat. The prospect of such a daunting task took her breath away.

"What all is involved?"

"Cut meat off bone, then dry strips or cook some, make pemmican. Smoke some of meat to keep, um—not know word."

"Preserve it? Is that what you are trying to say? So it won't spoil." Sleeping Bird nodded and Mandy continued. "You've shown me how to make pemmican and of course how to dry strips of rabbit or deer meat. But I've never had to deal with such a large amount of meat all at once like this will be. It will be a challenge to get it all done quickly. I know you keep most of the rest of the body as well but why?"

"Make, um," and here she put her arms out straight in opposite directions and signed long strings of something. "From insides."

"I'm sorry, I don't understand."

She pointed to her stomach, then lower. Mandy's face must have reflected her opinion of having to touch buffalo intestines. Couldn't be any worse, she reasoned, than the brains or liver for that awful green

239

goo she had to use in tanning the hides.

Sleeping Bird continued with a smile. "Roast, eat!"

Eat them? She gagged at the thought.

The older woman smiled at Mandy's discomfort. "Best part!" she declared to more frowns. "Also cook feet—no, not right word, hard part of feet, what called?"

"The hooves?"

Vigorous nodding as she continued enthusiastically.

"Cook in pot until soft, use for many things. Get medicines, tools from bones, many things from buffalo, *ghaul* in my tongue. Word mean 'our food' to show importance for our people. Honor him, no waste. He bring life to Kiowa."

"The word itself means 'our food'? You never told me that before. I know you use the organs for many things besides eating but I had no idea about all the rest of this. Amazing." *At least I now have my own knife for the task,* and she patted the beaded holder at her side. *Good thing I finally got the sheath finished.* She grimaced a bit considering that she would be required to remove the various internal parts and was certain it would not be her favorite aspect of this task.

However, it pleased her to contribute to the cycle of life, which the Kiowa lived with every breath. Somehow, she felt closer to God, definitely closer to nature at any rate. And who created nature if not God? Mandy offered her thanks to Him for allowing her to participate in this exciting adventure and for showing her how He lives in all of it right here in a small Kiowa village on the vast prairie.

After preparing the evening meal and still no sign of the men returning from the hunt, Mandy and Sleeping Bird sat down to eat together. As they did so in silence for some time, Mandy realized she had never asked Sleeping Bird about her life other than how she was widowed. Curious, she decided to bring it up.

"Sleeping Bird, how old were you when you were captured by the Kiowa?"

"Small child, no remember. Father say a raid by Comanche or maybe Pawnee, not sure. He find two days later, bring me here."

"So all your memories are of here? You don't recall anything of your life as a white child?"

She shook her head but averted her eyes. This aroused Mandy's curiosity even more.

"Do you have any recollection of having spoken English before you became a Kiowa?"

Again, silence. Yet Mandy persisted. She sensed Sleeping Bird was keeping something from her. How far could she push her without showing disrespect?

"Surely you do or you wouldn't have been able to speak English when I came, right? And you were the one who taught Ken-ai-te some words, at least to understand them if not speak them, isn't that correct?"

Mandy was shocked to note tears swimming in the blue eyes of her friend. She'd never seen this much emotion from her in all the time she'd known her! And then it was usually anger, never hurt. The pain was obvious from the sad look around her mouth and her drawn features. Perhaps it was the dwindling sunlight that played with the shadows to make it appear this way? No, Sleeping Bird was definitely holding back some great suffering. Was Mandy wrong to have brought it out? She opened her mouth to apologize when the older woman closed her eyes as though in great effort to remember and the words tumbled out.

"Woman held down in river, gasp for breath, afraid she never breathe again. Loving arms hold me with song and prayer. Book with names, read at night by lamp. School, learn let-ters, ci-phers, also sing and pray there. Indians come, hide under bed, hear screams, pray. Burning, choking, smoke, window. Rough hands hold me, terror. Safe." Suddenly she opened her eyes and stared into Mandy's dark ones. "All I remember."

"Sleeping Bird, that's really a great deal! Must have been your mother who held you, sang to you, and prayed for you. And the book was probably your family's Bible. Like mine," and she lovingly patted it on the ground beside her from when she'd been reading it earlier. "I wonder if the woman held down in the river might have been going through baptism? Apparently—"

"Bap-tis-m? Not know this word."

"I've told Ken-ai-te about it but maybe you weren't there at the time. It is when you have told God of your love for Jesus and a preacher takes you into the waters of a river to baptize you, show that He has washed your sins away. The Bible tells us Jesus was baptized and that we are to follow Him in doing this, too. It's to show others of your faith." She could tell the older woman was uncomfortable, perhaps in confusion or maybe in rejection? "We can talk more of this later." And she made a mental note to follow up with her on this subject at a different time.

Mandy continued her earlier thought. "Apparently, as I was saying, your family went to church. Many communities cannot afford a church and a school so use one building for both purposes. It's good that you recall learning to read though you probably have forgotten it by now. Maybe I could teach you the words again from my Bible?" Sleeping Bird didn't reply. *At least she didn't say no, so I can bring it up another time.* Mandy went on.

"The sad thing is you recall when the Indians came and killed your folks and set fire to your cabin, don't you? You must have escaped through a window and remained hidden until your Kiowa father found you. And you were the only one alive."

She nodded. "No matter. New parents love me, tell me I Kiowa now. No more English, forget. No more white. Sad but no choice. Love being Kiowa, much pride. Marry Running Elk and have long years in village before he killed."

"I'm sorry about your husband's death. May I ask why you can say his name when he is no longer living? I thought Kiowa believed it to be disrespectful to a deceased person to mention his name again."

"Only if name not passed on. Running Elk give name to our son's son when born. To son of Ken-ai-te. So okay say his name, not die with him. Only wrong for son's son since he now lay with his mother."

"Wait a minute—did you say your husband's name was given to the son of Ken-ai-te when he was born because Ken-ai-te is your son?"

"Real mother die when young. We take him to our hearts, later love wife and son like family. He promise to care for me as mother. Or I starve without husband or son."

Once more Ken-ai-te's kindness extends to others, unselfishly and generously, just amazing. Also explains why she called him her son that time. Seems there was much to learn about this man! She offered up another quick prayer for his safety.

"Cut off hair when Running Elk die but not finger."

"Cut off your finger? What are you talking about? Why on earth would you do something that horrible?"

"Kiowa way with death, show grief. Cut arms," and she gestured on her own forearm, "cut off finger, cut off hair, tear clothes, not eat. Many ways but all important to Kiowa."

"Well, I think it's a terrible way to deal with death. I respect much about the Kiowa way of life but not this custom. That's why your hair is shorter than many women your age, right?"

Before Sleeping Bird could answer, a cry went up in the camp. The men were returning from the hunt! Mandy's heart pounded. She rose on wobbly knees. *Oh, God, please let Ken-ai-te come home to me!*

† CHAPTER THIRTY-THREE †

"So shall my word be that goeth forth out of my mouth;
it shall not return unto me void,
but it shall accomplish that which I please,
and it shall prosper in the thing whereto I sent it."
Isaiah 55:11

"Do you see him, Sleeping Bird? I've seen all the others but not him!"

Mandy raced alongside the group of men as they rode triumphantly into the camp to the cheers of everyone in sight, searching frantically for the one face she longed to get a glimpse of the most. Eighteen men had ridden out and she heard someone say twenty-five buffalo had been killed. At least she thought that was the number, with her limited knowledge of the Kiowa language.

Sleeping Bird tugged on Mandy's arm in excitement and pointed off to the right of the group. Ken-ai-te sat tall on his mount, shield and lance in hand, a solemn yet proud expression on his face.

Relief flooded Mandy and she thought she would cry. *Thank You, Jesus, for hearing my petitions and for delivering him!* She pushed through the crowds to get closer to his horse. Just then, he spotted her and waved with a big smile on his face. He held up three fingers. What did that mean? After a moment, it hit her: he must have killed three buffalo. Three, all by himself?

She groaned inside. *Three* buffalo to butcher and haul to camp? However on earth would she manage? Others would be busy with their

244

own. Would anyone volunteer to help her and Sleeping Bird with this task? *Oh, who cares? He's home and that's all that matters right now.*

Ken-ai-te hopped down off his pony and scooped Mandy up in his arms. He swung her around in joy and hugged her as they both laughed before he caught himself and set her back down again, a sheepish grin on his face. She was panting from the excitement of this unexpected and uncharacteristic expression of emotion from the warrior. Or was it because once more she was close to him, this time in his arms? He stepped back a couple of paces and his smile faded somewhat.

Sleeping Bird rushed up and hugged him briefly and the Kiowa words exploded much too fast for Mandy to understand. She did hear him confirm he'd killed three buffalo, however, and grasped the fact that no one else had killed that many! Mandy's heart swelled with pride as she basked in the realization that her warrior was a hero in a sense among his friends in the village. Many were crowded around him now to hear of his brave exploits in facing the herd of great beasts.

It was enough just to have him home. There would be time for the two of them to talk later. For now, it brought her pleasure to watch everyone rejoicing with him over his good fortune. And to rest in the knowledge that they would have plenty of meat for well into winter and more than enough hides for robes and clothing. Too many, in fact, it seemed to her, so perhaps the three could share with others as well as taking care of their own needs.

In the midst of all this joy, however, a cloud of grief hung heavy over the men. One of the warriors had been killed when a cow charged him as he shot her calf with an arrow to its heart. The enraged buffalo had trampled him without mercy in its fury. Another warrior had finally shot the animal or there would have been little left of the body to return home to his family. Wails went up from several of the women in sympathy for the widow. She was bent over the blanket covering her husband's body and tears streamed down her face. Mandy felt so helpless, wanting to reach out to her yet knowing she would not receive her condolences right now. This was the time to grieve and grieve she did.

Fascinated with the customs surrounding death and feeling a little morbid in that curiosity, Mandy stood to one side and observed as the women one by one came and wailed with the young wife now without a husband. Her small boys patted her on the shoulder and courageously tried not to cry. But the smaller of the two couldn't hold his emotions in. His wails soon joined his mother's as a couple of the men gently carried the body to his tipi.

Two other warriors had been injured in the hunt as well and their family members were tending to their wounds as quickly as possible. One was in fair shape but the other had sustained some rather serious cuts and at least one broken bone, for Mandy could see the edge of the bone peeking out of his lower leg. *Ugh, I could never be a nurse or doctor.* But she knew that's what he needed right now, a doctor. Without adequate care, he would probably die within a couple of days from blood poisoning. But how could they find a doctor out here? And one who would agree to treat a Kiowa?

"Sleeping Bird, what will they do for the wounded men? I've never asked before but is there a medicine man in the village that can treat these injuries?"

"One who died. No one now to dance over hurts, pray to Great Spirit to heal." It was obvious from her grim expression that this was a serious problem for the Kiowa when there was no one to pray for them. Why did they depend on another to do this? Why not do it for themselves? She shook her head in wonder at the comfort her faith gave her in difficult times because she could go directly to God for help.

Dancing wasn't what was needed; medicine for pain and cleaning the wound thoroughly to prevent infection was what the warrior required right now. Prayer? Definitely, but not to the Great Spirit. Instead, to the Great I Am who heals all illnesses and injuries. Mandy stepped over to one side from the crowd and closed her eyes. It seemed up to her to do the needed praying, then. She remained there for several minutes in deep prayer for these two men who were suffering without someone to bring them comfort.

Suddenly Sleeping Bird grabbed her by the elbow. Mandy opened her eyes and saw that Chief Twin Fox was motioning in her direction, that she should join him at the tipi of the most severely wounded man.

In Kiowa, the chief said, "Prayer Woman, your help is needed. Yellow Eagle is badly wounded and suffers greatly. Please pray to your God for his healing." Sleeping Bird translated for her and it pleased her that she had followed most of his words. He explained that the injured warrior was a cousin and close friend of his and he was troubled that the man was in such pain. Would she pray for him?

Mandy's eyes widened. What if she did this and nothing happened? Or worse, what if Yellow Eagle died? What would Chief Twin Fox say to Mandy then? But wouldn't it be worse if she refused to pray for him? That would be hypocrisy of the worst kind. This was a supreme test of Mandy's faith in God's goodness and power, in His plan to bring her here to share Christ with these people, and in opening up this opportunity for her to live her faith instead of merely talking about it. How could she refuse?

Breathing a silent prayer for courage and wisdom and nodding in response, Mandy followed the chief into the tipi. Hostile stares greeted her from those gathered around the suffering warrior. Only a doctor could possibly hope to mend that mangled leg. How could mere words help? Mandy reminded herself the words were not important; what counted was the One to whom the words were addressed. God's power was what they needed here, Mandy only the vessel chosen to request that power to be evident. She reminded herself she must focus on this fact and stay out of the way so the Lord could act on her petition.

As she knelt over the hunter's writhing body, she could see the drops of sweat on his brow from the effort he exerted with each ragged breath to hold in his screams. She averted her eyes from the leg and gulped to hold down the rising bile in her throat, looking instead into his eyes. When she touched his hand, however, she was stunned. It was cold and clammy. He was in shock. The situation was growing more dire by the minute. *God, help me!*

A sense of peace enveloped the tipi at that moment, which Mandy would never understand nor be able to explain to anyone not present. It took her breath away for a brief second, it felt so vibrant. She closed her eyes, squeezed the man's hand tight in her own, and prayed with all her might. Her lips moved in silent prayer and then God spoke so dramatically to her, she glanced around to see if someone else had said the words instead.

Speak healing to the bone so it may rejoice.

Did that mean she was to speak aloud instead of praying to herself? She was praying in English so no one would understand, anyway. Yet, if He commanded, she knew better than to argue or hesitate.

A verse passed through her mind, she thought from Psalms, which said something about bones rejoicing. She tried to force the words forward from the depths of her brain and suddenly they came to her, crystal clear. Found in a passage regarding forgiveness of sin and being washed clean, it stated when joy and gladness are spoken this allows even the bones that are broken to rejoice. *Rejoice? He's in too much pain to understand anything right now, much less to rejoice.* But she knew what she had to do.

"Great Spirit of our Father, I claim right now healing over this bone and these other injuries that have come to Yellow Eagle this day. He was providing for his family in the hunt, not making war on other men. His bravery right now is an honor to You and to his people. The love of his family is around him and Your strength is within his heart. I ask that You give him great joy in the place of his pain and a glad heart instead of one of suffering. Let his very bones rejoice for the healing

You are doing right this minute within his body. Show us what we need to do to help this act of healing and give him rest as You work. God, I ask this in the Name of Jesus, whose body was broken for us but who is alive today. Give us hope and peace as we wait for Your miracle. Amen."

Mandy felt thoroughly drained as never before. She sat back on her heels and continued to ask for wisdom when God spoke again, telling her the bone must be straightened. Her face folded into a deep grimace at this thought, but once again, she knew she must obey. Would the men agree to do this thing? She had prayed for the suffering to end, yet was about to suggest they increase the pain many times over, however briefly. That is what a doctor would do and she knew the leg would never heal without it. Would it work? Somehow, she was aware that the Spirit had spoken to her heart, telling her that wasn't her concern, only conveying to the family what needed to be done, and now.

She managed to tell them using some Kiowa words, some English, and a lot of sign language. Yellow Eagle's eyes were round with horror when he realized what they were about to do to him but he nodded in agreement.

"Hurry!" he urged them in Kiowa. "Now."

✝CHAPTER THIRTY-FOUR✝

"Pride goeth before destruction, and an haughty spirit before a fall."
Proverbs 16:18

"Hold onto him tight, now," Mandy urged.

A couple of men grabbed the broken leg to pull on it and two held his remaining leg in place, with others grasping both arms so he could not wrestle free while they popped the bone back into place. It wouldn't be as good as a doctor doing it but it just might work. Better than the alternative, at least. There wasn't time to discuss it, just get it over with.

Mandy moved back out of the way and put her hands over her ears to block out the screams she knew were coming. And prayed with great fervor. *Please, God, let this work! How could I believe I was able to give medical advice this serious? Help me remember You are the Great Physician and I am simply following orders. Just let it be done quickly.*

Within minutes, Yellow Eagle was resting comfortably! The pain was much reduced and with the help of some herbal remedies given by mouth and a poultice put directly on the open wound, the warrior was groggy but not suffering like a few minutes before. Mandy then directed them to splint the leg using some large sticks intended for the fire, lashing them with rawhide strips so the leg would heal more or less straight. This had also come as a result of her prayers because otherwise she would never have known to suggest it. The men doing the work never questioned her, though she saw them glance nervously at each other a time or two. She certainly couldn't blame them for being skeptical.

Yellow Eagle's relieved wife hugged Mandy over and over in thanks and his children stared wide-eyed in mute wonder at the difference in their father. No one was more stunned than Mandy herself! The depth of her gratitude to God for His miracle was more than her heart could hold and the small part He had allowed her to play in it overwhelmed her until suddenly the tears began to flow.

Before leaving the tipi, Mandy felt she should say something to the family and to Yellow Eagle, provided she could speak in between sobs. Taking a deep breath for courage and to steady her voice, as well as breathing yet another silent prayer for wisdom to guide her words, which would be in English, she began.

"The Great Spirit of our Father has heard your cries for healing and for relief from pain. He uses the medicines of your forefathers and the care of your wife to bring this about. His Word commands us to rejoice over this broken bone. So, no more grieving, no more sorrow, just joy and gladness! Let it show on your faces. Let it grow in your hearts. The God of all languages will tell you this in Kiowa for I cannot. But I can tell you this in your language," and she ended by saying in Kiowa, *God loves you.*

And with that, she ducked out of the tipi into the deepening shadows of early evening, her knees wobbling and her face wet with tears. If she didn't sit right away, she knew she would fall down! How did she know to say this to them? How did she remember the appropriate verse at precisely the moment it was needed? She sank onto a nearby log by the fire ring and, realizing she was quite alone, let her praise spill forth.

"Oh, Father! You are so amazing. How can I ever thank You for giving me this privilege? Continue to heal Yellow Eagle and allow him to learn how to rejoice in You because of this day. Thank You for using me and granting me knowledge from Your heart and from Your

Word."

Sleeping Bird suddenly appeared, concern etched on her face.

"Prayer Woman, I look for you but not find. You already do prayer? What wrong now?"

Mandy smiled and wiped the tears from her cheeks. "Absolutely nothing!" Her heart was lighter than it had been since coming to live here and with a renewed fervor, she rose to accompany the older woman to join Ken-ai-te at their tipi, explaining to her as they walked.

In the few minutes it took to get there, however, word had apparently spread through the camp like the whoosh of a brushfire about Mandy's strange prayer of healing for Yellow Eagle. She didn't even have to tell Ken-ai-te for he already had heard, directly from Chief Twin Fox in fact. His welcoming smile to her was warm and kind, and Mandy's heart surged with an emotion she couldn't quite identify, was fearful to put a name to, hardly dared to consider. The last few minutes had been a bit much for her and she desperately needed some time alone.

But it was important to Ken-ai-te to share with her the result of his successful hunt, and she owed him the respect of hearing the story of his bravery, as others had already done. Besides, she truly was eager to share this moment of triumph with him, so she put her own needs aside, returned his smile, and settled down to listen as twilight descended gently upon them. Sleeping Bird eagerly joined in their quiet celebration as well, the two women hanging on every word.

A short time later when he had finished, she proudly presented the shirt she'd finished for Ken-ai-te while he was gone.

"Been busy!" he proclaimed, holding it up with a smile.

"You are pleased?" His vigorous nodding thrilled her. "Your leggings are almost done, too. Maybe another day or so?" He fingered them with another smile of approval.

"I—"

Chief Twin Fox abruptly reappeared, apologizing for interrupting their conversation.

"Prayer Woman, you are needed again. Please come." And he gestured for her to follow. She glanced at Ken-ai-te, who smiled in response. Of course, she must go. What on earth could he want with her now? To her delight, Ken-ai-te came along. Out of curiosity, she wondered, or in agreement with the purpose of her prayers?

They stopped in front of the tipi of the other brave who was injured in the hunt, Spotted Rabbit. His wounds were not nearly as severe but he did suffer from much bruising in his side, which was making breathing difficult. The chief asked her to pray to her God for him as well, as she had done for Yellow Eagle. *God, what is happening? Why all of a sudden are these people asking* me *to pray for them, and to You? I don't understand but I am grateful. And scared!*

Once more peace attended Mandy as she knelt and prayed aloud over this warrior as well. She mouthed the words, using another verse from Psalms this time, in complete awe of how the Lord had taken over her tongue for His purposes and how He was using her knowledge of the Scriptures for this prayer.

"God, allow Spotted Rabbit to have the breath of life again without pain so he might give his praise to You. Along with all who live may he praise You, Father, for as long as you grant him life. Thank you for Your hand of healing on his body and give him rest as you work your miracle. In the Name of the all-powerful God of every man, Kiowa and white alike, Amen."

Again, the difference was immediate. Spotted Rabbit's wife cried out in joy over seeing the ashen color drain from his face and the normal hue return. His breaths were coming slower now and without the previous agony.

"Give him something to eat and drink, and use the poultice you prepared on his ribs," Mandy told her. She caught her breath as it dawned on her she'd said this in English. No one seemed to care! Ken-ai-te quickly translated and the family complied with looks of awe and delight on their faces.

The two headed home but Mandy was stunned to see how many friendly smiles she got along the way. Everyone seemed to know what she had done for the village this evening and they were thanking her in the best way possible for her heart, so starved for friendship.

"You now Kiowa medicine woman," Ken-ai-te told her a short time later, "who pray to your white God. He listen when you speak. You powerful, Prayer Woman. Proud you belong to me."

He had tried to pay her a compliment and ended up reminding her of the thorn in her side here in the village. She pushed the thought aside because of her exhaustion. The fire had gone out sometime ago, apparently, and his dinner was now cold. After a long day of successful hunting, Ken-ai-te would be forced to eat pemmican instead of a hot meal! The irony cut into Mandy's heart but the fatigue was just too strong.

Sleeping Bird came to the rescue, though, and provided a rabbit stew and steaming hot bread. What would Mandy do without that woman? Realizing she'd not eaten much of her previous meal earlier, she joined Ken-ai-te in this one. As soon as they finished the older woman cleaned up and quietly departed for her own tipi, leaving them alone at last.

"All I really want right now is to rest," she said to the warrior. "I know it's early and there is much work to do but I cannot think right now. I need sleep more than anything else at the moment."

"You take night off from work. I go to circle, celebrate hunt. You rest. We talk more at daylight. Buffalo must be—um..." He stopped, obviously stumped for the correct word, his hands making a chopping motion.

"Butchered? Is that what you are saying? But won't wild animals get to the meat tonight?"

"Left men to guard to first light."

He smiled at her and picked up his dancing regalia. The drums were calling everyone to rejoice together, but Mandy's weariness overwhelmed her desire to join Ken-ai-te at the circle. A prick of disappointment played with her heart. Might the elders give her a place of honor there now that she had assumed the role of medicine woman for the village? Maybe she should go, after all.

A tiny sliver of irritation nudged at her and rapidly grew into a major shaft of anger. She had power and influence for the first time. Shouldn't she use it to get what she had desired from the first day of living here? Her own tipi lay within God's Will, it just *had* to! Nothing else made any sense to her. Then why hadn't He acted and made it happen? What on earth had delayed Him?

According to Ken-ai-te's vision, *Prayer Woman* came to bring much change to these people. The prophecy had been drawn on the sides of this very tipi by a woman now dead but who had carried in her heart, Mandy felt certain, the hope of being the one to fulfill it for her husband.

And now Mandy lived in that woman's tipi and wore many of her own clothes, even slept in the tipi with her husband. In Mandy's opinion, the whole thing didn't set well, whether you were white or Kiowa! In addition, it went against everything the Bible stood for, in particular the treasure of the family and especially of the sacred bond shared by a man and woman in marriage. Plus the fact that obedience to God's commands was more important to Him than any act of service, however special or needed. It all combined to fly in the face of everything she cherished from her heritage. No, this was just plain wrong! And it had to change.

Mandy had grown tired of waiting for God to act. He must be allowing her to do so in His place, she assumed from the absence of any action on His part.

"Now is as good a time as any to take charge and stop waiting around while my reputation is soiled more with each new dawn. Not one more day!" she declared defiantly.

She got up and smoothed down her hair. Never once did praying enter her mind, a fact that would come back to haunt her later. Her focus centered entirely on getting the justice she believed she so richly deserved—and had earned this day.

Marching toward the camp circle, she only lacked a few steps before stepping out into the light from the fire where the men danced and everyone feasted when someone blocked her way. Black Feather!

"Good time tell Chief why no baby," he announced in soft tones, his lip curled in a snarl and his voice oozing with sarcasm.

"No! You can't do that. Please! Let me—just give me a little more time."

The warrior pulled himself up to his full height before her, staring down at her with a disgusted expression on his face.

"No more time. Now! Or I take my revenge and kill you and Ken-ai-te. Your choice."

Mandy's eyes widened. Some choice! Not exactly how she had envisioned this evening, to confront the horrific demand of an evil man or lose the life and reputation of the man she cared about. Her mind was focused on her own needs, not the ones of this savage or even on those of Ken-ai-te. Yet, it was his future that entrapped her in this impossible dilemma, because of that growing realization she could no longer deny. She took a deep breath.

All right, love *then! There, I've said it. I admit it, I care about this Kiowa man whether I want to or not. If only—*

An idea nicked at her mind. Would it work? More importantly, could she force herself to do it? She gulped against the fear rising in her throat. Her heart raced and her head swirled. Still, no prayer formed in her mind.

"Black Feather, can I speak with you, away from all this?" And she gestured toward the crowd behind him. Even in the darkness, she saw his eyes light up and a slow smile spread over his entire face. He nodded. The gate of her prison slammed shut and she lowered her eyes so he wouldn't see the twinkle of her tears.

He strode past her and meekly she followed, frantically forming the words in her mind that would change her future forever. And hopefully save the dignity and life of another.

They stopped beside the river, moonlight sparkling on the surface of the gentle ripples there. Mandy glanced overhead at the stars above and longed to escape the torment she was about to endure. She felt empty and barren of all emotion except the fear that drove her to this desperate act. How could she possibly stand by and watch her captor suffer untold humiliation and perhaps even death at the hands of this animal, knowing she could have prevented it? As if that weren't enough, she would live with the assurance that it had come to him because of her presence in his life.

Mandy stared into the scarred face of the one before her, arrogance plain in the sneer on his lips and gleeful shine in his eyes and she shivered slightly. He stood with his legs apart, arms crossed over his chest, and she imagined his heart held a mixture of triumph and curiosity about what she would say. She supposed her obvious nervousness would please him all the more and strained to control her trembling knees as she cleared her throat.

"Black Feather, Ken-ai-te only desired to live again after his deep sorrow. How could that be too much to ask?"

"Not Kiowa way."

"I'm *sick* of hearing about 'the Kiowa way' as though it could excuse everything! You didn't invent revenge, you know. White people feel it, too. Indians killed my father, are you aware of that? But do I blindly hate all Indians because of this?"

She shoved deep a tiny voice reminding her she *had* felt this way at one time. No longer. While the loss saddened her, she refused to let it rot her from the inside out, willing the memory to remain in God's capable hands instead of dwelling on it until it destroyed her with its bitterness. Why couldn't this man do the same with his own grief?

He said nothing so Mandy continued quickly, the words tumbling out now.

"It's not fair to fault him that he was able to move past his pain, even though you apparently have not figured out how to do so. You've allowed the resentment and jealousy to consume you until now I honestly believe you wouldn't recognize compassion for another human being if it hit you in the head."

She could read the anger in his face. Her hope had been perhaps to talk him out of his vengeance but she could see the futility of that now. There was no other choice.

Softening her voice in spite of the fury rising in her chest, Mandy took a step toward him.

"Would you consider giving up your vengeance against your brother Ken-ai-te if I offer myself to you now? I promise to come willingly to you, as long as you vow not to harm a single hair on his head. Not with your words, not with your weapons, not with your schemes to bring him dishonor. You must let it all go, once and for all. Or the deal's off. And I reveal to everyone what I know about your rifle."

His eyes flinched slightly at those last words but otherwise his face remained impassive. Several moments of silence stretched into what seemed an eon to Mandy. Could his revenge really be so important to him that he had to *think* about this?

A sharp nod of the head sealed Mandy's future and her heart sank. She had half-hoped he would reject the offer. What had she done?

"Come now, to my tipi."

"But I need to explain to Ken-ai-te. You can't expect—"

"Never tell, just come. Or I go to chief. Make choice now!"

Now? Mandy hadn't counted on this development. She couldn't leave without saying goodbye! Yet, in that awful moment, she knew she had no other option. If she wanted Ken-ai-te to live without the danger lurking on every side, she must sacrifice herself to this monster.

Would life be worth living with—*him*? How on earth would she find the strength to carry out her promise and betray Ken-ai-te without so much as a word of explanation? What would Sleeping Bird think of her now? Mandy could not imagine giving up her chastity to this brute as he leered at her, enjoyed her discomfort, reveled in her fear. Fighting back nausea, she took deep breaths to clear her head.

Yet, she must. Suddenly she realized he had walked off without her and she hurried to catch up. What if he went to the circle and exposed the couple's secret right now? Or did he truly expect her to follow him to her fate without another word? Guilt pounded her like a hammer on a nail head, until she thought she would break apart.

Mandy wailed and lifted her face to the moon above.

"What kind of a mess have I gotten myself into with this crazy idea? Why didn't I take time to pray before I opened my mouth? How can I trust him to keep his word? He'll take me and still go after Ken-ai-te. I should have known better than to agree to do anything this insane. God, help me!"

✝CHAPTER THIRTY-FIVE✝

"The beginning of the words of his mouth is foolishness:
and the end of his talk is mischievous madness."
Ecclesiastes 10:13

God, though I don't deserve Your mercy, I beg You to give it to me now! Help me find Black Feather before everything is ruined. Stop him from speaking before the council fire and give me the words to somehow get out of this nightmare I've created with my pride.

Mandy had not moved one inch from the riverbank where she confronted the evil warrior but she knew that time was running out for her to act before all would be lost. It would take an intervention by her heavenly Father to set things right, for it was beyond her control now. Her intentions had been right but her method of carrying that out had gone outside God's protection when she failed to pray and wait on Him. She needed time alone to talk with her Father but knew she couldn't risk more than this brief moment. Even now, would she be able to prevent disaster?

Racing up the slope left her breathless. *Where is he, Lord?* She avoided his tipi and ran in the direction of the sounds of the chants of the people. The last thing she needed was to get trapped by him in these shadows before she could get to Ken-ai-te to explain. If such words even existed. From the rhythm of the drumbeats, she felt confident the dancing hadn't been interrupted—yet. Maybe she wasn't too late!

Gulping back her sobs and ragged breathing, she slowed her pace as she came into the light. No sign of Black Feather. Ken-ai-te stomped his feet and whirled with the others, totally caught up in the Buffalo Dance, undisturbed at least so far. She let out a sigh of relief. Now what?

One of the women nodded at her and she returned the gesture, trying to paste a smile on her lips so no one would suspect anything might be wrong. Catching the eye of Sleeping Bird, whose raised eyebrows expressed silent surprise, Mandy realized she would have to explain her presence after having earlier begged off the celebration due to her fatigue. She sidled through the crowd to reach the older woman's side.

In response to the unasked question, she said, "I decided I wasn't as tired as I thought."

Her eyes darted throughout the crowd, hoping to spot Black Feather yet also terrified she might. He wouldn't give up this easy. How could she possibly stop him if he showed up and demanded the opportunity to speak? A man could challenge him to a fight but not a woman. Her stomach a knot, Mandy hardly dared to breathe and tried to ignore Sleeping Bird's curious stare. This was neither the time nor the place to talk to her about what had happened. Maybe later...

In Mandy's muddled mind, she began sorting things out a little piece at a time while the flutes joined in and thick fingers of smoke swirled around them all, its acrid smell pricking at her eyelids with the tears it produced. Or could it be due to her breaking heart rather than the smoke? She blinked them back quickly. The minutes flew by and her muscles ached from the effort she exerted to try to act "normal" when her entire future was at stake. Instead of relaxing, her anxiety increased with every passing moment.

Perhaps if I go ahead and request my own tipi, as I started out to do this evening, then Black Feather won't be able to "surprise" everyone with the news that Ken-ai-te has violated Kiowa tradition. The very thing I've prayed for all this time, that my chastity would be protected at all costs, turns out to be the one thing from which my destruction, and that of the man I love, has its root. Where is Your hand now, God? I tell these people that You are the One who should be honored above all their pagan gods, yet when it is vital I hear from You—only silence!

Sleeping Bird pulled on Mandy's elbow.

"Prayer Woman, dance!"

Rising in response to the tug on her arm, she rose and her knees promptly buckled. The exhaustion she'd felt earlier had taken its toll as she sat still, and she knew she could not participate in the festivities this evening. Shaking her head, she slumped back down and wouldn't meet the older woman's eyes. If she did, Mandy knew she could no longer keep the truth to herself. Yet, what could she say?

Fortunately, the women's dance continued without incident while Mandy sat mute off to one side. Her mind was like a sea of turmoil, with waves crashing on each side without order or meaning. She managed to keep her terror at bay, but just barely. Would this night never end? Why did she leave the safety of the tipi? When would she learn that God always has a better way than any she could create and her job is to wait on Him to reveal it, no matter how long it takes?

Suddenly Black Feather stepped into sight, across the leaping flames of the fire. Mandy shuddered and clutched her arms around her body in panic. He caught her eye and glared. She felt he had pierced her body with a lance, such was the fury on his face. His eyes flitted around the circle for a moment, then came to rest on Chief Twin Fox, who chatted with some of the elders while the women settled down once more after their dance concluded. It couldn't have been any plainer had it been spelled out in a sign around his neck: he headed for the chief with his evil intent hardening his heart even as his face grew more grim and determined with every step.

It had to be now! If Mandy were to salvage anything out of her time here with the Kiowa, she would have to speak up or lose everything. She jumped up, startling Sleeping Bird who had just sat down next to her.

"Where do you go, Prayer Woman?" she asked in Kiowa.

Ignoring her completely, Mandy realized that if she moved quickly, she might head Black Feather off before he reached the chief since she was closer. Pushing through the crowd, her eyes focused on her enemy's progress. Would she make it there before him?

Words tumbled around in her head and her mouth was dry like the desert sand. Her own irritation at being forced into this action against her better judgment but in desperation to save the man she loved pushed her legs to move faster as she wove her way through the people. A few more seconds and she would be there. Yes—she would make it ahead of Black Feather. Now, how to get the chief's attention in this melee?

Mandy stopped in front of the chief and cleared her throat.

"Chief Twin Fox!" she called out in a booming voice, "I ask to speak to you in front of the elders and all the people of our village."

Her knees shook but she'd kept her head clear enough to speak in Kiowa so all could understand. Only now, she spotted Ken-ai-te sitting next to the chief, a stunned look on his face. She tried not to look at him or anyone else but the chief as she waited for his reply. His outstretched arms brought quiet to the area within moments. Out of the corner of her eye, she saw Black Feather come to an abrupt stop a few feet away. Mandy didn't look directly at him, but kept her eyes on the chief.

Knowing she had to stay in control of this or her enemy would snatch the moment away, she took a deep breath and breathed a silent prayer for courage as Twin Fox nodded at her, a look of curiosity etched on his regal face. Glancing around at the sea of dark eyes staring at her with great curiosity from the deep shadows on every side, Mandy almost lost her resolve. Then she locked onto those of Ken-ai-te and nothing else mattered except saving him!

The best she could in her halting Kiowa, Mandy spoke slowly.

"My people, I speak to you as one who has come to respect you as my brothers and sisters. I ask one thing of you for myself. Ken-ai-te has been kind to me and I thank him for that. But it is not proper for me to continue living with him any longer when we are not married. It is my desire to have my own tipi. Would you consider granting me this request for the prayers I offered today for the two warriors who were injured?"

Instant pandemonium erupted around her, with everyone shouting at once. Mandy was startled and took a step backward toward the fire circle. She could feel the heat of the flames behind her and knew she could not back away any more without being injured. Although she couldn't understand many of the words, the anger came through loud and clear.

What is wrong with these people? I asked a simple question and I deserve an answer. Why are they looking so shocked and dismayed? I'm fully dressed, I haven't violated any rules that I know of by addressing everyone like I have. What is going on?

Without a word, Ken-ai-te jumped up and strode over to her, grabbed her by the arm and dragged her away from the council area toward their tipi. Sleeping Bird trotted right behind, a grim look on her face. Mandy started to jerk her arm free but a vague uneasiness held her back. Apparently, she had, indeed, done something terribly wrong by voicing her request. Something nicked at her heart deep inside. Perhaps she should have prayed more about this first? At the very least, she managed to steal Black Feather's vengeance away. She pictured him standing there still, fury at being denied his moment of triumph deepening the color of the slash across his cheek, while frustration over Mandy having robbed him of that sweet moment of revenge bathed his face in deep furrows. How she would have liked to see that!

Suddenly Ken-ai-te shoved her into the tipi ahead of him and she stumbled to her knees. To her surprise, he stepped aside for Sleeping Bird to enter and then slapped the hide door closed behind her. Obviously, Mandy was to learn the reason for everyone's anger from her instead of from the warrior. Why did he always make Sleeping Bird do his dirty work instead of facing up to it himself? Irritation replaced concern and fed the cocky look on her face as she stood to face the older woman. What could she possibly say to her that would make any difference? No matter what it was, Mandy still would insist the chief grant her request. It was her right now as the medicine woman for the village and she was convinced of that fact. And no one could take it away from her. Besides, nobody understood how she'd been forced into this. Well, kind of. More by pride than anything but also by Black Feather. After all, *he* was the evil one in all this! If she hadn't acted when she did, he would have spoken up and the result would have been tragedy and shame for them all.

"You make demand for tipi in front of whole village. Bring much danger to you, also to Ken-ai-te, even to me. I tell you but you not listen!" Her blue eyes flashed and even in the dim light Mandy could see the woman's extreme emotion displayed on her face as well as hear it in her voice.

"You—you told me there might be problems with my plan but never told me why. I just don't believe you that it's that much of a catastrophe. How did I *endanger* all of us with this simple request? You were the one who told me the tipi had to be earned. Well, I feel I did just that by my prayers today. Surely the chief can't deny me what I want now."

Sleeping Bird jerked on Mandy's arm and pulled her down next to her in front of the fire. Glaring at her at eye level, she fairly hissed at her in a hoarse whisper as though someone might overhear.

"Now whole village know you not share bed with Ken-ai-te! Shame him, maybe have to leave camp. He kind to you, not beat you, not force you to bed. Why you do this to him?"

"What do you mean I shamed him in front of everyone? How do they know we aren't sharing a bed, anyway? I didn't say anything about that, I know better than to do such a thing. All I said was—"

"That reason you want own tipi."

"No, it's not! Well, sort of but not entirely. I'm tired of living with someone I'm not married to. I explained all this to you before, that my God doesn't permit this. I can no longer allow us to share a tipi unless we are married. And that's certainly not ever going to happen, either!"

"If sharing bed, no need for own tipi. Not have to say words, people know truth.

Mandy stared at her in disbelief as it all began to fall into place, one awful piece at a time.

"Great danger now from Black Feather," Sleeping Bird continued in an ominous tone.

"Why from him? What's he got to do with all this?" These last words rang hollow. He had *everything* to do with all this!

"I try to tell before. You not listen. Listen *now*!" Her blue eyes sparked again. Apparently, Mandy had inadvertently stirred up some kind of a hornet's nest without fully comprehending the situation. If no one would tell her the whole story, how was she supposed to know the ramifications of her request to the chief?

Nodding in response, Mandy folded her hands in her lap and tried to focus on what Sleeping Bird had to say.

"Same as when Ken-ai-te leave for hunt, if he not return. Black Feather have right to you for revenge on dead sister. Angry Ken-ai-te take you but not make baby yet. If Ken-ai-te not make baby, cannot keep you. Now, you belong Black Feather. And Ken-ai-te have to leave. I not have son without him, no way to live now. Your words not good ones. Much danger for all now."

The realization hit Mandy hard. She had opened her mouth without asking God's permission or for the words to say what was in her heart. She'd been desperate and this appeared to be the only solution to head off disaster. It seemed a logical assumption she should not be living with a man to whom she was not married since the Bible was clear on this point. Her conclusion had nevertheless resulted in horrible consequences that left her confused and hurt. How could His Will contradict His Word? This just didn't make sense. The fatigue made it even more difficult to consider all the angles. But the primary point cut through the fog and gave her goosebumps: she might be forced to leave Ken-ai-te's tipi and live now with Black Feather, after all. And in truth, she'd done this in order to *prevent* having to become Black Feather's woman, to save her captor from the very thing she had now made public. Oh, what a mess!

Tears sprung to her eyes as the shame and embarrassment flooded every corner of her body. How could she have allowed her pride to speak instead of God's Spirit? To go from being Prayer Woman and even Medicine Woman to this in just a few short hours seemed unbelievable. What was she going to do?

"Oh, Sleeping Bird, I'm finally beginning to understand now. I just wish you'd warned me earlier."

"Try. You not listen."

"That seems to be my biggest failing, doesn't it?" She covered her face with her hands and cried. *Oh, God, please forgive me for the horrible sin I've committed. I didn't do it on purpose, never dreamed this could happen. Only You can deliver me, and Ken-ai-te and Sleeping Bird as well. Help me!*

"Your God hear? What He say do now?"

"How—how did you know I was praying?" She looked up at her.

"You always pray. Why you Prayer Woman to Kiowa, *daw-t'sai-mah.*"

"Well, I certainly don't deserve that name now, do I? Not after the way I've put us all in such dire peril. To answer your question—yes, my God has heard my prayer and has forgiven me for what I've done against Him. Correcting what I've done to Ken-ai-te and to you is another thing. I honestly don't know what He wants me to do yet. He will answer me, I'm sure of that, but sometimes He chooses not to prevent suffering from our foolish words because He has something for us to learn." Even through her weariness, Mandy saw the blank look on Sleeping Bird's face. She had to keep her words simple. Or say them in Kiowa. And her brain had stopped working in that language.

"What I mean is that it may take time. Do you think the danger is immediate? Or will the men meet in council to talk first? Oh, I have to speak with Ken-ai-te right away! Where did he go? He has to know I didn't realize what would happen."

"Leave while council talk. Decision now. No time to wait."

"What? They won't even give him a chance to defend himself? I suppose Black Feather is there, though, isn't he? Spouting his venom about how Ken-ai-te cheated him by claiming me in the first place. Why did they argue over me when I was abducted? Do you know?"

She nodded. "Ken-ai-te plan vengeance raid with Black Feather for captives. Ken-ai-te claim you, Black Feather not want white man but no other to take. When you come here, they argue who has right to you. Chief decide you belong Ken-ai-te. Now may change mind. You not have baby yet, now he know truth."

Mandy sprang up and ran for the door. She turned and faced Sleeping Bird.

"I must find Ken-ai-te, to tell him how sorry I am for all this, before the chief and elders take action. Please, tell me where he went."

"To river. Hurry. Maybe can stop bad words at council, not sure. Try!"

Mandy rushed out and into the darkness. She heard angry voices from the circle and turned away, trying to block it all out. Her mind focused only on Ken-ai-te. Where could he be? *God, help me find him in time!*

In spite of the moonlight, searching for a figure in the shadows proved difficult. But not impossible. God directed her steps and she quickly spotted him in a thicket right at the water's edge. He glanced up as she approached, then looked the other way without a smile. Mandy could hardly blame him for his anger. She gulped several large mouthfuls of air to help clear her brain and stopped a few feet away.

"Ken-ai-te, please may I speak with you? I know you are angry and I don't blame you. What I did was for good reason but I went about it all wrong, I realize that now. Can you forgive me for causing you to be publicly humiliated like you were? All I wanted was my own tipi. I never meant for you to be hurt. In fact, I thought you might even be a little relieved, not to have me hanging around all the time any longer. You would be able to start your life over again, get married, have a family, whatever your heart dreams of."

"You not know my dreams. No right to talk of them. Leave!"

He turned his back to her and walked away with long, purposeful strides. She couldn't afford to let his fury with her prevent him from fighting for both their futures!

"Ken-ai-te, come back! We need to talk." She ran to catch up with him, grabbing hold of his arm and pulling him to a stop.

Whirling around to face her, fury etched on his copper face, Ken-ai-te jerked his arm free. Mandy thought for a moment he might even strike her but hoped he would think better of it, even after what she'd done to him.

"Please, I'm not asking for myself now, really I'm not. I'm pleading with you to save face for yourself. You must listen to me!"

⸸CHAPTER THIRTY-SIX⸸

"A sound of battle is in the land, and of great destruction."
Jeremiah 50:22

"I *not* listen! You not order me, woman. You slave, not forget that." Ken-ai-te spoke from between clenched teeth and his bitter words stunned Mandy, even though they truly held no surprise for her.

"It is not as a command that I speak to you, Ken-ai-te. I speak only as a friend, if you can still see me that way. You have to go back."

When he frowned, she added, "To the circle, to face the elders and fight against Black Feather's evil words that fill their ears right now. Sleeping Bird told me that even as we speak they are making the decision about—well, about me, and how that affects you as well. I was wrong to do what I did, terribly wrong. I am so sorry and if I could take the words back, I would do so in a moment. You have been nothing but kind to me ever since you brought me here, and I can see now that I owe you everything.

"You have continually protected me from my own foolishness and from Black Feather's threats without my being aware of it. I owe you a deep debt of gratitude. Please accept my apology. No matter what happens to me now, I don't want any of my stupidity to fall back on you. You don't deserve that."

No reaction came from the warrior. Did he understand? He stared intently at her so apparently comprehended enough at least. She sighed deeply and continued.

"What can I do to make things right? Is there anything at all? Maybe you could say I was out of my mind, you know, crazy, or something? That wouldn't be far from the truth. I *was* out of my mind with selfishness and loneliness and hurt and—well, you get the picture."

"Lone—what that word?"

"Loneliness?" She blushed slightly. Of all the words spewing out of her mouth right now, it would have to be that one he would latch onto. Her heart ached and she struggled for the words to explain. "It means being by myself. Feeling sorry for my being alone, in a bad way. Longing for home and friends and family."

He was staring at her with an odd expression on his face. Mandy half smiled.

"What?"

"Not know you lonely."

"How could I *not* be lonely, living here with no one to talk to or share my life with or who cares when I'm sad?" Her voice caught and she struggled to regain her composure.

"But this is not what we should be talking about right now. There isn't much time, Ken-ai-te. You have to hurry if you are going to stop the decision being made by the council right now. They can kill me or send me away, just please don't let them give me to Black Feather. I would rather die. I don't want to leave you. I've begged God already to stop this madness." She couldn't hold back the tears any longer. "Can't you do *something*?" she wailed through her tears. "I'm sorry, I didn't mean to cry, yet here I am, blubbering like a baby! Some Kiowa woman I am!"

He walked closer, towering over her. As usual, when this close to him, her breath fled. He placed his hands tenderly on either side of her head, tilted it upward slightly, and brushed her tears off her cheeks with his thumbs. He stared intently without a word. Her heart melted. Was she even breathing right now? She couldn't be sure. Warmth surged through her like a bolt of lightning and Mandy felt her knees tremble. In fact, her whole body shivered. In delight or in fear? Maybe a little of each.

She fought an intense longing to throw her arms around his neck and kiss him passionately! Not that she'd ever done anything like that before nor would even dare to consider doing it. She'd just always imagined how it would feel when you were attracted to someone and had the opportunity to do that. Mandy couldn't think straight with his hands on her face like they were, fingers caressing her skin gently, brushing strands of hair back from her face. He pulled her head closer to him and she stretched up onto her tiptoes, as they gazed into each other's eyes.

When he spoke, it was soft and her ears tingled with delight. "No hurt from your words. Only fear for you, fear I can't stop evil. Belong to me, forever."

A stick cracked somewhere in the darkness behind Mandy and abruptly broke the spell. Ken-ai-te released her at once and she took a step back, trying desperately to slow her breathing to a more normal pace. Sleeping Bird emerged from the shadows.

She didn't even look at Mandy but spoke in Kiowa to Ken-ai-te of the urgent need for him to address the council. Mandy was surprised she could follow most of it. Then the older woman reminded him they didn't have time for distractions right then. *Distraction? Is that all I am? In spite of the tender moment we just shared?*

Gulping back her emotions, Mandy silently agreed that the last thing he needed was a distraction from what had to be his priority right now. She felt even sadder, if that was possible, about the whole mess and completely helpless to affect the outcome. Her selfishness had created it but now someone else would have to face the consequences and try to patch things up. She could see how Ken-ai-te's jaws were clenching and noticed both hands were in tight fists, she assumed at being reminded of the daunting task he faced and its cause. It disappointed her at the ease with which he had moved from almost kissing her to dwelling once more in his anger at her.

How could she have felt an attraction for this man a few minutes before? He was her sworn enemy and she would do well to focus on that. That and getting out of this dilemma alive and with her honor intact. She sealed off her heart and refused to look at him.

The warrior nodded at Sleeping Bird but never even glanced over at Mandy. Without a word, he strode forward, the two women following behind as the three hurried back to the village. Mandy intended to go with Ken-ai-te to face the men but Sleeping Bird took her arm to stop her.

"Ken-ai-te go alone. Not place for woman."

It was a good thing. She feared her legs wouldn't have supported her much longer, and maybe it was best she didn't have to face the anger and hostility right now, including Ken-ai-te's. Mandy needed to spend the time in prayer, pouring out her heart before the Father that His Spirit would prevail among the elders this night. And also for wisdom for the warrior to know how to untangle the mess she'd caused because of her pride. It was a tall order, even for God.

Sometime later Ken-ai-te came into the tipi where Sleeping Bird and Mandy were sitting. Mandy was reading her Bible while the other woman was bent over her beadwork. A quick exchange with hushed voices in Kiowa took place, making the words impossible for her to follow. Her cheeks burned as they both glanced in her direction a couple of times.

Just tell *me! Don't talk about me as though I were a small child when you know how anxious I am to find out what happened!*

After several moments, Sleeping Bird left without looking at Mandy, leaving her alone to face Ken-ai-te. A rapidly growing dread caused a lump in her throat and stomach at the same time and she fought the urge to run away and hide. How could God abandon her like this—again? She hid behind that wall she'd erected earlier and forced herself to look upon this man as an enemy bent on her destruction rather than acting on her recent feelings to the contrary. Everything rested in the words he would say. Did she really *want* him to speak? Mandy realized she had been holding her breath and finally had to release it, taking in short and shallow gasps to keep from passing out. A sour taste in her mouth almost caused her to gag, but she swallowed hard to hold it back. *Get it over with!*

Slowly Mandy rose to hear the fateful words, her heart in her throat.

"Chief Twin Fox listen, I explain you want tipi of own, not live in one where dead wife's spirit live. Tell them you say wrong way, cause big problem. He listen at first, until Black Feather speak.

"He have much anger, demand you for revenge. Say he know truth from you, why no baby, reason you belong him now. What you tell him?" His dark eyes sparked even in the dim light and she noticed how he clenched his jaws while he waited for her reply.

"I—I didn't actually tell him anything, or at least I didn't mean to. He apparently overheard something I said in prayer because unfortunately I chose to speak aloud. In my foolishness I ranted against God for making me live here with you even though it violates all He holds dear and states in His Word. Yet in spite of that I admitted you had never—well, forced me to—um, you know." Could he follow all this? She hoped so. His frown made clear he did not.

"What I mean is, after Black Feather heard me say those words, he confronted me and I confirmed the truth for him without realizing he had tricked me into it. Earlier he had threatened me, promised to destroy you if I did not leave you and go to his tipi to live, something I could never do. I told him at first that I would, and I honestly thought I could, given the consequences if I refused. But when he demanded that I come to him without even telling you why, I just couldn't." Would he accept her explanation, take her side over Black Feather's?

She blinked back tears, hesitated a moment, then blurted out,

"Don't you see? I couldn't let him harm you! You have to believe me! Demanding my own tipi, then, seemed to be the only way to rectify everything and set you free to find love again for yourself. My intent was right but the way I went about it was terribly wrong. I realize that now." *Please don't let it be too late!*

And the wall crumbled. It was no use pretending any longer. The whole reason this mess happened was rooted in her newfound feelings for her captor. Her enemy at one time, yes—but no longer. Now, her protector and the one she loved. No one would consider sacrificing herself the way she almost had, had at least agreed to do, unless driven by love. Mandy covered her face with her hands and wept openly, overcome by horror and shame and fear all mixed up together.

Tenderly, Ken-ai-te lifted her chin with the fingertips of his right hand. With his left, he again brushed aside her tears, as he had done earlier, and smiled. Her heart leaped within her. Did the chief listen to him in the end or to Black Feather? Hope buoyed her sagging spirits at the look on his face and she weakly returned his smile.

"Chief Twin Fox listen to me. Not hear words of anger and vengeance. Decide you stay with me. My tipi. My woman. From now until forever. No more words on this." Abruptly he turned and left the tipi before Mandy could react.

Relief swirled around her and the tears came even more.

"God!" she cried out, her hands raised in thanksgiving for her deliverance, even as she sank to her knees before Him.

"Thank You for saving me from certain destruction! You are to be praised for Your mighty hand, which is stronger than my own will or than our enemy's vile plan. Please protect me from Black Feather's continued threats and let things go back the way they were between Ken-ia-te and me. I honor You for giving me Your forgiveness and Your continued blessing of protection and provision through Ken-ai-te. I promise to listen to You next time *before* I speak! I love You, Lord. Amen."

†̇

The next day the butchering of the buffalo began in earnest. Everyone in the camp busied themselves with various tasks associated with doing so, from the oldest to the youngest. Thankfully, Mandy didn't have time or energy left at the end of each long day to discuss with Ken-ai-te any further what had happened between them. He pretty much ignored her and she returned the favor. Better an uneasy truce between them than have to confront his anger again. Or deal with his tenderness. She wasn't sure which was more unsettling to her right now.

As soon as the women brought in the haul from the hunting ground, the men started their work of using the bones and sinews to repair and make bows, arrows, lances, arrowheads, and so forth. Mothers enlisted the aid of the children to help with anything they were capable of doing at their ages, providing a way to keep the little ones busy and close by while they worked.

The days became a blur as Mandy was shown how to butcher the first one, then left to do the second on her own. By the time she finished, she was about to drop and her stomach was queasy from all the blood and the smells that had settled in as the sun's heat bore down on the large brown and red humps scattered across the prairie by late afternoon. Flies buzzed everywhere and that turned Mandy's stomach even more.

"Too late to do third one today," Sleeping Bird said as she returned after making a haul of a portion of the meat back to the camp. "You work slow but learn well. Finish tomorrow. Pile all," and she pointed to the organs and gourds of blood that Mandy had drained from the body, "over here by bones." They would wait until the next day to take the rest. At the last moment, Sleeping Bird did pick up several of the larger and meatier ribs and tied them onto the back of the pack pony, stating they would be perfect for dinner the next evening if they started smoking them that night. Mandy's mouth watered at the thought and wished there was enough time to prepare them for today's meal.

Sleeping Bird did seem impressed with how quickly Mandy finished up the last buffalo the following day. She had, indeed, learned well!

For days upon weary days the women cleaned, dried, and fixed various dishes using the multitude of possibilities found in the buffalo the men had killed. Their meals those first few nights were a delicious feast of fresh meat for a change but most of it had to be dried to be eaten later. To her disgust, Mandy learned how to make the dish Sleeping Bird had earlier told her about, by stuffing the intestines with meat and blood mixed with flour made out of drop-seed grasses, then roast them whole. The result was a type of sausage, a Kiowa delicacy. She just couldn't bring herself to taste it, however, after seeing how it was made!

Then of course, there were the hides to tan. Portions were cut off and used for rawhide strips after the hair was removed, but on most, the fur was kept intact and scraped on the reverse side to remove all the pieces of meat clinging to them eventually to form buffalo robes. Mandy, following a suggestion from Sleeping Bird, decided to remove the hair from one entire skin and keep it for clothing or repair of the tipi walls. She was so busy during these few days that as they stretched into a couple of weeks she hardly noticed.

The women at first had been cautious again with Mandy but soon warmed up to her upon seeing how hard she worked to pull her own weight in the village after the hunt. It thrilled her to see Spotted Rabbit resume his normal duties after his ribs had healed without any further complications. Both he and his wife were quite friendly with her. Yellow Eagle still was not up and around, of course, but he was doing much better and the leg seemed to be healing properly, as least as well as Mandy could determine. He was deeply grateful for her prayers and often would ask her to come sit with him and his wife in the evenings to talk and pray with them some more.

She was excited to have this opportunity to continue sharing her faith with others in the village in spite of the unpleasantness that happened after her foolish demand. Mandy prayed it would continue and even grow wider, for she longed to be asked to assume once again the role in the village her name implied. Although the Lord had forgiven her, would He deny her that right permanently because of her arrogance? Maybe in time...

Ken-ai-te was something altogether different, however. He seemed torn between kindness and the anger she sensed simmered just under the surface whenever she was around. Would he ever be able to move past the hurt? He filled her prayers that somehow God could heal his heart enough for their friendship to be restored as before. It was difficult to know how to respond to him when she never knew what attitude he might exhibit from one moment to the next.

Often she claimed a couple of verses in Jeremiah that commanded her to forget her fear of speaking with him about God and be bold. To that, she added caution, trying hard to learn from her past failures. At times, he seemed to accept her words while at others he would turn away while she spoke, indicating he wasn't interested. She remained hopeful and prayed before opening her mouth to talk to him, eagerly sharing when she could and not resenting it when she was denied. Yes, perhaps in time things would be better.

To her shock, even Black Feather seemed unusually quiet during that period, not showing up to bother her even once. A couple of times she caught him glaring at her but chose to ignore him in the hopes that he would do the same toward her. At least one good thing came out of her terrible mistake; she didn't care why but was appreciative of God's protection.

One afternoon, however, a shrill cry shattered the peaceful routine in the village. A small hunting party had gone out to follow tracks of a herd of deer but only one man returned. They'd been attacked by a

Comanche raiding party, leaving their bodies mutilated and burned, the lone survivor wounded but able to escape and return home with the ghastly news.

As soon as he heard, Chief Twin Fox rushed to the side of the warrior who was being given water and poultices for his injuries. After talking anxiously for some moments with the man, the chief turned to face his people gathered around them. No one spoke, just waited to see what their leader would say and do. Mandy stayed toward the back of the crowd, curious what would happen next but not wishing to intrude.

His face a grim mask, Chief Twin Fox silently raised his lance high over his head. Mandy had a pretty good idea what this attack meant to the Kiowa and she was terrified. Her heart sank at the expression on their leader's face, and her blood chilled when he cried out in fury one single word. Everyone in the crowd caught it, then, repeating it over and over, each time with greater intensity than before until it was a screaming chant drowning out everything else and surrounding her on every side as she was caught up in the chaos.

"War! War! War!"

†CHAPTER THIRTY-SEVEN†

"The LORD is my strength and my shield;
my heart trusted in him and I am helped:
therefore my heart greatly rejoiceth;
and with my song will I praise him."
Psalm 28:7

God, please have mercy on us! Mandy fought back the tears as she tore herself from the mob of angry Kiowa surrounding her and raced back to the tipi. Panting, she leaned against one of the poles and began weeping.

"Will our lives ever be the same? Why must the men go to war? Why can't they just sit down and talk about it first, to see if it can be avoided?"

An impromptu war dance had broken out and she could hear the wild whoops resounding in the still afternoon air. It was unseasonably warm for this late in the fall, to the point where it was almost oppressive and made breathing difficult. Perhaps it was her imagination, fueled by the seething emotions in the camp.

"I need to get busy and quit thinking about this. Yes, that's the answer." But deep inside she knew it was not. She needed time to pray. Mandy had learned her lesson in doing something contrary to what she felt urged to do by God's Spirit, and she immediately fell to her knees, eyes closed, and bowed her head as she poured out her heart to her Heavenly Father. No one could stop the war as far as she could tell. No one was even willing to talk about it. They just all seemed determined to *do* it. But God could intervene in their hearts. He alone was capable of stopping this horrible thing from happening.

Sometime later, Mandy arose, still with a heavy heart but refreshed from her time alone with the Lord. Peace reigned, at least for now, and she would not permit fear to elbow its way back into her mind.

"My people need me right now to remain calm and focused on courage and strength, not wavering in anxiety and—"

"Wait a minute," she interrupted herself, "did I just say, 'my people'?" She stood there a moment, a smile on her lips, thinking and meditating on that phrase.

"Yes, I did! Well, they *are* my people, isn't that right, God? You brought me here, eliminated any possibility of my going home again, and have given me pride in becoming one of them by allowing me the opportunity to live the name they gave me—*daw-t'sai-mah*, Prayer Woman. My people. Yes, they truly are my people. And when they hurt, I hurt. When they grieve, I grieve. And when they are angry, I am angry. A righteous anger, you understand, but anger nevertheless. That is what I'm feeling now, that these Comanche have offended me personally by what they did. I do share in the drive for blood vengeance desired by Ken-ai-te and all the other warriors." She paused briefly.

"Um, I think I need to pray through that a little more, Father." Taking a deep breath, she sank back down to her knees. "Not sure that is a healthy attitude for me to have. Just because I am one of them is no sign I have to walk the way they do. You have called me to be different among them, to walk with honor as You have commanded."

As she prayed this time, a Bible verse played with the fringes of her mind as a breeze does with a loose hair until she could no longer ignore it. She quickly rose and went to get her Bible. After several minutes of searching, she found it.

"Right here in Zechariah 4:6: 'This is the word of the

LORD...saying, "Not by might, nor by power, but by my spirit," saith the LORD of hosts.' That is the key, isn't it, God? To let the people know they fight not by the power of their weapons nor by the cunning of their minds, but by Your strength through Your Holy Spirit—through the Great Spirit." Then another popped into her mind and she turned to it as well. "Psalm 20:7, 'Some trust in chariots and some in horses: but we will remember the name of the LORD our God.' Somehow, I have to impress on my brothers here as they go to fight in this war that they must depend on the Great Spirit's name and not on their horses' strength or that of their arrows and lances. Father, give me the right words to say to them. And the opportunity to speak."

Mandy continued to pour out her pleas for wisdom in her words to her people for some time. Vaguely she became aware of thunder rumbling not far away. So the restlessness she'd felt in the weather hadn't been her imagination after all. She hustled her Bible into the safety of the tipi and gathered up a few items from around the fire pit, also putting them away inside. A storm was coming and, at the moment, it wasn't in the form of war dances but from the sky. The wind began whipping around her and she saw rain on the horizon as she ducked into the tipi. She hoped Ken-ai-te and Sleeping Bird would both arrive soon so they would be not be caught in it.

Not long after when they got back, Mandy welcomed them with a warm fire and a hot meal to share. As soon as he was through eating Ken-ai-te dumped out a pouch full of arrowheads and began attaching them to new arrow shafts which she recalled him making some time ago, telling her they would be ready in case he needed them in a hurry. Sleeping Bird took up her beadwork without a word as Mandy cleaned things up from their meal. *I don't know why she doesn't just live here with us. There's plenty of room and she spends most of her time here, anyway. In fact, she should stay here with Ken-ai-te while I live in her tipi. That would be a perfect solution. Maybe—*

Hold on there! Mandy interrupted herself. *We are not going down that trail any more. God has it under control...but I wonder if He thought of this idea?*

Trying to get her mind off this sensitive subject, she asked Ken-ai-te about the injured warrior who had managed to survive the attack.

"Will he be all right?"

Ken-ai-te glanced up at her with a quizzical look on his face and she noticed Sleeping Bird did the same.

"Black Feather survive. Why concern for him?"

"You've got to be kidding me! It was Black Feather who lived through it?"

"You not know?" Mandy's shock must have registered on her face because they both relaxed visibly, obviously believing that her surprise was genuine.

"No, I never went close enough to see who it was. I saw the chief bend over someone who was bleeding and heard the cry for war. But I didn't stick around. Will he be okay?"

"Wound not kill him. But leg not good. Can't ride in war party."

"So you are going to war and leaving him here?" The panic in Mandy's voice was barely controlled and she swallowed hard as she looked from one to the other, hoping she'd misunderstood.

"Have much to do while men gone," Sleeping Bird said as though that solved the problem. "Hides to work, meat to dry, clothes to make for snows. No time to think."

"I know, and work will help the time pass more quickly. As long as you don't leave me alone I'll be fine."

The older woman nodded in response to Mandy's statement as a sharp crack startled both of them. Ken-ai-te had snapped in two an arrow he held between his fingers, and Mandy could see the anger on his face. Did he do it on purpose, perhaps to show what he wanted to do to this evil warrior? Mandy certainly would like to see his neck caught in those strong hands sometime. She shivered to think what might happen if Ken-ai-te ever got really angry with her. As fear's darkness spread its evil in her mind, she knew she had to talk about something else, for all their sakes.

"Ken-ai-te, I know there will be a war party sent out against the Comanches now but when will you go?"

"Men rest tonight, war dance tomorrow. Go first light next day."

"How long will you be gone, or do you know?"

"Two, maybe three days. Camp not far but they move so we not find them easy. Hunt down Comanche dogs who do this. Take many scalps for empty tipis now."

"Brother of Spotted Rabbit killed, five others, Black Feather wounded." Sleeping Bird's face spoke of her own desire for revenge.

"I'm sorry to hear about Spotted Rabbit's brother. How is it that Black Feather got away?" Mandy asked, trying hard to keep her voice even. Although she had nothing on which to base her feelings, she was suspicious of this whole thing. Maybe God was trying to speak to her, warn her or something, she wasn't sure. Or maybe it was her mind working overtime again because she didn't like Black Feather and was afraid of him and the danger he represented to her.

Ken-ai-te told her a brief summary of the warrior's account of the attack but she remained unconvinced. She wondered if he believed him or felt as Mandy did and was afraid to speak out against him without any proof. For now, she would keep her suspicions to herself. Anything else would be pure gossip. *I'll bet he rode off and left those men to die, like the coward he is. His wound might be severe but not because he was fighting to save those other men's lives.* Then she reminded herself that without more to go on than a vague feeling, she had no right to hold this against him, much less accuse him openly. She must let it go, allow God to have the revenge, if any.

To deliberately shift the focus of her thoughts, Mandy brought up something buried for a while but which now jumped to mind.

"Ken-ai-te, do you recall when Chief Tohausan came to our village recently and he first greeted you upon his arrival?" The warrior looked startled but nodded. "What did he say to you? At the time, I didn't realize the two of you were friends but Sleeping Bird told me you were, from when you were boys, I believe. I'm just curious—if you don't mind my asking, that is."

He smiled and replied, "Comfort for loss of family," and his smile faded.

"Oh, I see. I'm sorry if I touched on a painful memory. That was kind of the chief to speak of it, one friend to another." In the uneasy silence that followed, Mandy wondered if this untimely reminder would add to his fury about the upcoming war and fervently wished she'd chosen silence over words, at least those.

While preparing for bed that evening, she realized that Chief Twin Fox had not sent for her to pray for Black Feather or any of the grieving families. Perhaps it was best since she would have felt totally hypocritical doing so for the man who wanted her dead. Would she ever be asked again to pray for the people, though? The desire of her heart was still strong that God would restore that trust and allow her to once more offer public prayers for the people—her people. Until then, she would do her part to cover them with private prayers, just between her and the Father. This night she grieved deeply for their losses, lifting them up to the Lord until sleep came.

The next day Ken-ai-te spent a great deal of his time sharpening his lance and tomahawk as well as finishing up his new arrows. Mandy tried to prepare good meals for him the whole day since he would be eating only pemmican as time permitted while he was gone. She prepared a pouch of the dried meat for him to take and ensured his water skin was full. Next, she carefully checked over his clothing to see if anything needed a hasty repair but all was in good order.

Uncharacteristically, Ken-ai-te took a nap that afternoon. Then he rounded up his pony and spent some time painting his mount for war, and followed that with plenty of fresh grasses he had collected for food. Carefully staking the animal out next to the tipi, so he would not have to waste time searching for his horse before the battle, the warrior made certain there was plenty of slack in the rope. He spoke next into one ear softly in words Mandy couldn't hear and she was touched with his tenderness. The horse's brown and white coloring was now enhanced with bright yellow circles on both flanks and on its shoulders were strange red drawings like a sun with blue streaks shooting out of each one. When the warrior walked away, Mandy noticed he had saved back some paint, most likely to use on his own body the next morning, and she was struck by a sudden impulse.

She approached the horse as he grazed near the tipi & patting its neck affectionately to calm any jitters, she stroked the mane and gazed into those large dark eyes. When the animal seemed to have accepted her close presence, she turned to the small pots of various colored paints lying nearby. Pouring a small amount of the red paint onto a flat rock, she then laid her right hand in it. Shaking the excess loose, she put her handprint on the side of the pony's neck, then walked around to the other side and repeated her action.

"God, I ask that you use Your right hand of justice and protection to defend both rider and horse tomorrow as they go out into battle. Shelter them from harm and give discernment to Ken-ai-te even though he does not recognize it has come from You. Help him to depend on You instead of on his own ability to guard him from disaster. Be his shield and preserve his life. May Your angels be around him at all times!"

The special moment passed and Mandy hurriedly cleaned her hand before her deed was discovered by the warrior. Deep in her heart, she hoped her prayer for his safety would be answered with a resounding yes! She paused a moment to watch as others at each tipi in the village were busy completing the same tasks that Ken-ai-te had done earlier. Not much chatter was heard today. Everyone was busy and grim in their tasks and singular goal, to prepare to do battle to the death.

That evening just before the dancing began, Ken-ai-te asked a difficult question.

"You pray for battle, Prayer Woman? Me?"

"Of course I will. For your courage, wisdom, strength and protection."

"To kill many?" She sat there, stunned. Pray for many to die? How could she? Yet, how could she not? Ken-ai-te being shown to be a coward wouldn't be much of an improvement over being killed, she supposed. Either way, she would be given to Black Feather. To prevent that, she most definitely would pray Ken-ai-te would kill many of the enemy!

She nodded in reply.

"For shield to have much magic in war?"

"No, Ken-ai-te, that's not the kind of praying I do. I won't pray for magic. But I will pray for your safety from the arrows of your enemies, that your shield will provide protection for you when needed. My God is more powerful than all the magic in Kiowa and Comanche lands alike. I will also pray that your weapons will find their way to the hearts of your enemies."

Quietly she added, "I want you to return to our tipi victorious and unharmed."

✝ CHAPTER THIRTY-EIGHT ✝

"For though we walk in the flesh, we do not war after the flesh:
for the weapons of our warfare are not carnal,
but mighty through God to the pulling down of strongholds."
II Corinthians 10:3-4

Did I really just say what came out of my mouth? Mandy could feel her face blazing and she lowered her eyes, yet felt compelled to raise them again to look directly into Ken-ai-te's dark ones.

He smiled and nodded but said nothing. Had he heard her, understood what she said? Did she mean the words? Yes, she did. She truly hoped he would return to her safely. No doubt what she had implied. *Return to our tipi...*

The drums began thrumming softly in the distance and Ken-ai-te rose to dress for the War Dance. He started with the war paint on his face and body, dipping his fingers into the gourds of color prepared earlier for this purpose. Mandy blushed as he meticulously wove the bright hues over the muscles of his chest and arms, then did the same on his handsome face, wiping the paint off his hands when done. When he carefully removed his feathers and laid them aside, then undid his hair to allow it to flow free well below his shoulders and shook it loose with his fingers, her color deepened. Already his kind demeanor had changed into that of a fierce warrior, bent on revenge!

She knew she had to assist him in the ritual of dressing and with each piece, he put on her own excitement curiously mounted. It thrilled her when he chose his new leggings for the evening's festivities. Her plan to cover his nakedness had somewhat backfired in that he wanted to wait until colder weather to wear them on a regular basis—that, and on special occasions. Somehow, Mandy had found herself getting more used to the half-clothed bodies surrounding her, including Ken-ai-te's. Perhaps the rhythmic sound of the *tum-tum-tum* in the background added its own influence or maybe the seriousness of the whole affair finally sank in, but she could not escape the pounding of her heart that seemed to match the haunting chants echoing around them.

It surprised her that a War Dance called for different items of regalia than a time of celebration, say for a Gourd Dance for instance. Ken-ai-te would not wear much of this tomorrow, in fact, but tonight it was all for show before his fellow Kiowa. When in the final step he put the war bonnet on his head, Mandy gasped at the sight before her. Intimidating in his attire? Definitely! Handsome enough to take her breath away, in spite of his war paint and fearsome outfit? Beyond her imagination!

She had never experienced a War Dance before and found herself eager to do so, even more now that she stared at the fierce Kiowa warrior into which Ken-ai-te had been transformed in the past few minutes. Contrary to that harsh appearance, he smiled at her warmly and she returned it with one of her own.

He has seemed kinder to me the last two days so perhaps that is one good that will come out of this horrible war. Has his anger lessened against me, then? I don't know how to read his moods right now, he's so preoccupied with the war party and its potential dangers. Or seems to be. Maybe it's just that I am.

"Time now, we go." Mandy nodded and gathered her shawl to follow him into the night, to join their brothers and sisters in the traditional declaration of war against a common enemy to their people.

Sleeping Bird spotted them as they walked to the camp circle and fell into step with Mandy a few paces behind the warrior. Her face held little emotion whereas Mandy struggled to keep her feelings in control with the swirling turmoil in her heart that evening. She flew between pride and joy at being a part of these people's lives, to dismay for the purpose of the dancing and terror at what would come the next morning—and everything in between. Glancing at the men gathered around the large campfire, she wondered who would come home from the raid alive, who would be injured, and how their way of life might change with the outcome of the war.

Mandy knew no words to describe what she experienced that night. Her heart raced in rhythm with the drums, accompanied by the flutes and chants that fascinated her in their musical combinations, considering the serious nature of the dance. Though she'd been exposed to some of this before, a tangible air of excitement bubbled over from under the surface and caught her up in its aura. She literally overflowed with the contagious exuberance on every side that continued without letup through the whole ceremony.

As more men joined in, the pace picked up considerably until their rapid foot movements became almost a blur. Feathers flashed brilliant colors and when the fingers of fire leapt and swirled in their own tune of sorts, reflecting light and shadows alike on the painted bodies and faces, it lent an eerie feel to the entire scene. The women rose as a body after some time and formed the traditional large circle around the outside and began moving in time with the beat of the drums, too. Mandy couldn't begin to imitate their intricate songs in Kiowa but she did allow the robust enthusiasm to lead her in praising God for the sights and sounds she witnessed while moving along with them. The drums had never been so deep and booming, it seemed to her, and when the words of the war chants split the night sky with their shrieks and whoops, she thought her heart would burst!

By the time the last echo died away into the darkness, she felt emotionally and physically drained. Ken-ai-te remained at the campfire with the other warriors and elders to talk more of war but Mandy couldn't wait to settle into her own bed before she fell asleep standing up. She and Sleeping Bird walked back to the older woman's tipi in silence, each lost in her own thoughts. The enormity of their future weighed heavily on them both.

I scarcely noticed the passing of time this evening, yet it must be quite late. And considering the early morning departure of the men and their difficult journey, I would have thought they would have kept the ceremony shorter. How exciting the War Dance proved to be, wielding a far greater impact than I had imagined it would!

The two women parted with only nods and Mandy headed into the shadows toward her own tipi. She glanced upward at the breathtaking canopy overhead and recalled the Kiowa legend about the stars sharing love with those who were lost. Although others darted here and there, she knew she simply had to talk to God and hoped no one overheard her English words.

"Ken-ai-te is lost, Father. Please, don't let him be killed in this war. I know it's necessary within the Kiowa tradition but is it really worth it over a handful of men's lives, to risk everything we hold dear? I don't know any longer. You say not to kill yet stand back when this goes on every day out here on the frontier. How can I pray for Ken-ai-te when my heart is torn by revenge now as well?"

Suddenly Black Feather grabbed her arm sharply and hissed an angry threat in her ear. She didn't catch exactly what he said, something about killing her, of that she was certain. Once again, she'd been distracted and not seen him, another way the devil uses good in his attacks. Scrambling to stay on her feet, Mandy glared at him with fury in her dark eyes.

"Leave me alone! You aren't supposed to be anywhere near me and you know it. Now go away or I'll call Ken-ai-te to chase you back to the hole in the ground where you live." To add emphasis, her right hand closed around the hilt of her knife in the sheath at her side. Though not at all certain she could ever use it on another human being, it reassured her to know it was there. And the longer she stared at his hideous face, the more convinced she became that if it were necessary he *would* feel the cold steel of her blade!

His smug expression didn't change but apparently, her bold warning made an impact because he said nothing further. She jerked her arm out of his grasp and turned away from him, hoping he would get the message to leave her alone. He was the last person she wanted to have to deal with tonight. Fortunately, he didn't follow as she rushed away into the dark.

Ducking into the tipi she felt fear smother her, given what had just happened. No, this was her home and the safest place in the village. Mandy had called often on God's angels to be round about their home all the time, even when Ken-ai-te was not in the village, and she repeated her petition for protection now. Especially since by morning he would be gone once more and she would be alone. *Please, God, not forever!* She knew another long night of praying awaited her.

The next morning as Mandy took the sacred shield from its special place beside the tipi and handed it to Ken-ai-te, followed by his tomahawk. She gazed deeply into his dark eyes, almost lost in the streaks of war paint he had reapplied earlier. Would she ever see him again, have a chance to share Christ with him further? He asked about Him almost nightly now, knew most of the stories from His life, seemed to grasp why He had come and why He had died. What more could she say? Her sadness was oppressive and she rebuked it, claiming peace for her own shield, that he might see a smile and not tears as he left.

Ken-ai-te secured the tomahawk on his belt, then placed the war bonnet on his head and picked up the lance, bow and quiver slung over his shoulder, sitting tall on his pony and ready for battle. Reaching down with his left hand to pat the red handprint, he smiled at her briefly and nodded. *He knows I put that there! Wonder if he understands why?* She reached up to place her hand where his had been moments before and nodded in reply. Another instance of a volume of communication between two Kiowa without words!

He was as prepared as he could possibly be. What would be the outcome of this conflict? Mandy recalled the verses from the night before and once more asked the Lord for the opportunity to share them with the whole village if possible. Within moments, Chief Twin Fox approached her.

"Prayer Woman, you pray for Great Spirit to make men strong in battle."

Thank You, God! she thought, fighting down her emotions. *Make my words worthy.*

"Great Father of all," she said to them a couple of minutes later after everyone had gathered before her, "we ask for protection for our men as they go to war. Give them strong arms and sharp minds to know what their enemies will do before they know it. Help them to trust in Your Name, Great Spirit, not in their horses or weapons. Grant them courage and victory and bring them home safely. Amen."

Murmurs of approval could be heard all around Mandy when she finished and she breathed an additional silent prayer of thanks for having the privilege to share Scripture over them. And then, in a cloud of dust and to the sound of whoops and hollers from everyone present, the war party was gone. An ominous sense of fear hovered over Mandy as she walked slowly back to the tipi behind Sleeping Bird. Would her enemy never give up? She tried hard to stand in confidence rather than quivering in despair.

Day after long day passed without word from the war party. Each empty morning was difficult but the barren nights were even worse. Mandy missed her conversations with Ken-ai-te more than she realized she would. Sleeping Bird slept in the tipi with her at night, much to her relief. If it hadn't been for Sleeping Bird's company, especially when they settled down for sleep, she would have been truly miserable.

One night she mentioned to Sleeping Bird that Ken-ai-te seemed lately to spend more of his evenings in the tipi with her, whereas used to, he seldom returned until long after she had fallen asleep. When Sleeping Bird didn't meet her gaze, she realized there was a hidden reason for this, not coincidence.

"What?" she inquired. "Tell me what you are keeping from me."

The older woman's eyes darted to Mandy's face. After a moment, she sighed, as though she'd been holding her breath.

"Ken-ai-te tired of arguments. Black Feather get louder, talk against you."

"Against me?"

"Say no baby mean you his. So Ken-ai-te stay in tipi. Want to talk but want to protect you."

Mandy was speechless! His integrity was costing him dearly. Apparently, Black Feather was making Ken-ai-te's life as miserable as hers. She blinked back tears. *Why does he not confront him and stop these lies? Of course, in truth they are* not *lies!* It didn't seem to matter to the wicked warrior that the chief had spoken peace over this. He would never give up.

Black Feather's leering eyes continued to be everywhere around her but he seemed to be in genuine pain from his leg wound so kept his distance for the most part, watching but then limping away without a word to her. Each dawn she threw herself into the work with a fury so that by sundown her muscles ached and sleep came easily. But always, the silent question was on everyone's lips: when would the men return—or would they?

Late one afternoon Mandy decided to go for a swim. In spite of recent rains with their promise of cooler fall weather, the heat had returned and the pull of the water was strong. She gathered her things and headed down to the river's edge, admiring the golden leaves swirling around as her feet swished through them. Regardless of the deceptive temperatures, fall lurked around the corner. Had she really been here long enough to see yet another season pass?

The water lilies were everywhere along the shoreline, their fragrant flowers perfuming the air. Avoiding them due to the possibilities of snakes hiding beneath their leaves, Mandy walked a short distance downstream. She had often bathed here before and knew it to be secluded enough that she was hidden from prying eyes. Most people were still busy with work so she felt confident no one would interrupt her indulgence in this pleasure for both body and spirit alike. The cool refreshing washed away not only the dust from her skin but also the tension out of her shoulders. How she wished she could remain here the rest of the day!

Upon finally emerging from the water, Mandy realized she had lost track of the time, staying longer in the river than she had intended to do. She would now need to hurry in order to get the evening meal prepared. After drying herself with a blanket brought for that purpose, she pulled her dress over her head and slipped on the moccasins. Running her fingers through her hair she decided not to braid it now but instead to let the air dry it a bit first.

Picking up her things, she turned—and gasped. Black Feather stood only a few feet away behind a bush, his gaze fixed on her face. From the lust shining in his eyes, she could tell he had been watching her the whole time. The color rose in her cheeks, much to her irritation. She longed to avert her eyes but dared not. Mandy knew with a sinking feeling that she was in serious trouble.

Too far away for her cries to be heard in the village, she had few choices. Glancing around quickly for a possible weapon of some sort, a stick or large rock perhaps, she saw nothing and her heart teetered on the brink of panic. She was helpless and he knew it. Her hand instinctively went to her side where the knife in its sheath should have been but it was not there. Inwardly she groaned as she recalled leaving it in the tipi, feeling she would not need it at the river. His grin widened, the scar wrinkling in a grotesque caricature of a man's face, the expression in his eyes unmistakably intensifying by the moment.

He seemed to be feeding on her fear.

Deciding that flight was the best option she had, Mandy dropped her things and tried to run along the riverbank to get away from him. But the mud was slippery and she lost her footing, falling to one knee with a soft thud and splattering the dark goo when her hands landed in it. Before she could react, the warrior was on top of her, flattening her on her back. His legs were astride of her and one hand pinned both wrists over her head. She struggled to get loose but knew it was in vain. He showed no signs of pain from his injury now, only a frightening strength and fierce determination to have her at last. Mandy could do nothing to stop the inevitable. She screamed and he slapped her hard across the jaw, then tore viciously at the front of her dress.

"God, please help me!" she cried and turned her head to one side so as not to have to look on his terrifying face any longer. Mandy moaned softly and gulped back sobs, her shame and terror overwhelming her.

Suddenly a figure appeared out of nowhere, silhouetted against the shafts of setting sun filtering through the leaves of the trees overhead and casting a long shadow over the two of them. Both looked up at the same moment in surprise. Tears blurred Mandy's sight but relief flooded her heart. Whoever her savior was, he growled like a ferocious bear and took a flying leap at her attacker from one side and pushed him off her in one move. The two men rolled away some distance, locked in a death-grip with both yelling at the top of their lungs. Mandy scrambled to sit up and pulled her torn dress up onto her shoulder, sobbing uncontrollably.

As the pair came to a stop and they jumped up to face each other, Mandy was stunned when recognition broke through her terrified mind. Ken-ai-te! He had returned safely and had come in time to rescue her!

"Oh, God, thank You! Please help him!"

†CHAPTER THIRTY-NINE†

*"For the LORD thy God walketh in the midst of thy camp,
to deliver thee, and to give up thine enemies before thee..."*
Deuteronomy 23:14

"Ken-ai-te, look out, he's got a knife!"

Black Feather circled him, a vicious look on his face. Ken-ai-te pulled his knife out and did the same. Mandy rushed to pick up her drying blanket from where she had dropped it a few feet away and wrapped it around her shoulders to hide the torn dress. Apparently her screams had attracted attention from the village, in spite of her earlier skepticism, because several people came running, including Sleeping Bird who put her arms around Mandy to hold her back from the fight. Mandy wished she had something to throw at that ugly scarred face that threatened Ken-ai-te's life but she had nothing. All she could do was stand there helplessly.

One after another thrust his knife toward an arm, a leg, across the chest, leaving only surface cuts but never managing to get close enough to deal a stabbing blow. Each time Mandy thought her heart would stop. The minutes crawled by. Would this queasy feeling never stop in her stomach? Fear strangled her and then shame took over, regretting her decision to come down to the river to bathe when her protector was out of the camp.

God, please keep him safe, don't let him be hurt! Haven't we put up with this evil long enough? Destroy him, now! At the same time, she knew she had voiced the wrong prayer. She silently begged the

Lord to allow His Will to prevail and get this over with, yet couldn't resist pleading also for Ken-ai-te's deliverance—and her own.

Then Black Feather stumbled, giving Ken-ai-te the precise advantage he'd been searching for. It was only a second's worth but still all he needed. While the other warrior scrambled to regain his footing, Ken-ai-te managed to grasp him with his free hand and whip him around so that the blade was at his throat in an instant. Everyone expected a quick death for the loser. But inexplicably the victor hesitated a moment, frozen by an unseen force.

Between clenched teeth, he growled in Kiowa at his opponent, "You are a cowardly dog who doesn't deserve to live. You disgrace our people and the woman I love. No more!"

The woman he loves? Did I hear him right? He loves me? Mandy hardly dared to breathe, her heart was overflowing with such joy. *And he said this in front of everyone? I can't believe it, but I understood what he said. At least, I think I did.*

Her attention was ripped back to reality as Black Feather breathlessly spoke in a harsh whisper. Despite the language barrier, what he had to say stunned her with its ferocity.

"*I* am not the coward, Ken-ai-te. *You* are the one who failed to protect your own family. And now you give refuge to our enemy, this white woman who lives in your tipi. Why do you continue to defile the memory of my sister?"

Mandy saw Ken-ai-te's eyes widen with fury at these words and she caught her breath softly. What did Black Feather mean that the warrior didn't protect his family? Beside her, Sleeping Bird stiffened and her grip on Mandy's shoulders pinched deeper. Though in Kiowa, Mandy followed every syllable, to her continued surprise. Sleeping Bird had told her of the bad blood between these two and for the first time since her capture Mandy saw it expressed far more graphically than ever before. Their other encounters had been brief ones but something told Mandy this one would not end the same with simple surrender. Black Feather's attack on her a few minutes ago was not the beginning of their quarrel, but if Ken-ai-te decided to use that knife, it might be the end.

"You try to kill me to keep the truth silent!" Black Feather breathed between clenched teeth as Ken-ai-te visibly tightened his grip on the man's throat, thrusting the knife harder into his skin. Even from a few feet away Mandy knew death was not far off and recalled the feel of steel against her own neck months back. Pulling herself back to the moment, she wondered what "truth" he was referring to.

"Sleeping Bird, what is he—"

"Shhh" and she shook her head, indicating Mandy was not to speak. Did she know but also did not want something spoken aloud? *What is going on?*

Ken-ai-te suddenly spun the man around to face him and lowered his knife only a couple of inches. It was still aimed at Black Feather's heart, a fact no one present missed noting. Especially Black Feather.

"What 'truth'?" he growled from between grim lips.

"You know it was your fault my sister died."

"That is a lie!" Ken-ai-te hissed almost in the man's face.

Mandy heard a curious gurgling sound escape from Sleeping Bird's lips. Calling another man a liar constituted a serious insult among the Kiowa. What would happen now?

"She was killed by white soldiers. How is that my fault?"

"Because if you hadn't put a spell on her and corrupted her mind like you did, she would still be alive!"

"A spell? Now you speak in riddles, Black Feather." And he fairly spit the name out at him.

"You taught her white man's words and white man's ways, made her forget she was Kiowa, confused her and allowed her to live in this spell until it led to her death."

"It is good to know white man's words so when we speak with them of peace our words are understood. She asked to learn the words I knew so I taught her. *Her* choice."

"No! Your choice, not ever hers. To please you, no other reason."

It was as though the two men were locked in mortal combat but with words, oblivious to the others who continued to gather around them. Mandy was mesmerized. How would Ken-ai-te respond to this?

"How did her learning white man's words lead to her death? I don't understand you, crazy man!"

"Because—because she had to be made to see the truth of what you had done to her. I tried but couldn't make her understand. Not only you, but also *her*." And he pointed toward Sleeping Bird. Mandy glanced up to see the older woman's eyes widen in horror, her lips clamped shut in shock. Bad enough that he should blame Ken-ai-te for the deaths but now Sleeping Bird as well?

He continued spouting his venom. "Your adopted mother is white and she also added to this confusion in my sister's mind. She's to blame as much as you, casting a spell on both of you as she did! You are evil, Ken-ai-te, and you corrupted my sister until she lost her will and right to live."

"What are you talking about?" Ken-ai-te's eyes narrowed. *What does he mean "right" to live?* Mandy swallowed hard, hardly daring to breathe. Ken-ai-te took a step forward and Black Feather instinctively moved back.

"She wouldn't listen to me!" he whined, sounding more desperate to prove his point with every second that passed. "I told her I wouldn't allow her to continue to live as she was doing, bringing such shame to our people and to our family. I had to stop her, don't you see? Then she turned on me and—and—"

Ken-ai-te's face paled in the twilight. "And what?" he demanded, slowly.

Mandy could see his jaw working and the free hand clenched tight. How much longer would he stand there listening to these insane rantings without using either the weapon or his fist to stop him?

"And she threatened to tell you of my demands. I couldn't let her do that. We—we struggled and I—I hit her and she fell backward on the ground."

Ken-ai-te lunged for him, but a couple of men grabbed his shoulders and held him as Black Feather jumped out of reach.

"I didn't mean for it to happen! You have to believe me! It was an accident. She must have hit her head when she fell. The baby began to scream when she fell on top of him and I couldn't get him to shut up."

Mandy's insides twisted into a knot. Her heart almost stopped with compassion for the one who had captured her heart, as this evil man revealed the awful truth of his beloved wife's death. And at the hand of her own brother! His heart must be breaking, having to relive her death like this and in public, no less. Not to mention finding out it was not white men who had killed her, after all, but one who professed to love her.

But what of the child? Black Feather just said he was alive and crying when his mother died. Mandy's breaths came in shallow gasps. She saw Ken-ai-te's face twist into a pain-filled grimace and she didn't think she could bear to hear any more.

"*You* killed them? Both of them? And blamed the white soldiers for it? Actually lied to all of us and let us believe—" He choked and could say no more.

"I think the child was hurt but I had to think and his screams filled my ears. The rifle was in my hand and—"

"What rifle? You had a rifle?"

Black Feather looked taken aback, apparently not intending that all this should come out as it had. Now he had to tell everyone about the rifle. He glanced around nervously, licking his lips.

"Uh, I took it in a battle with a soldier several weeks before, had been practicing with it. But I only had two bullets left. So—so I used them." His voice sounded more like the squeak of a mouse than the declaration of a Kiowa brave.

301

"On my *son*? You killed my son for no reason but that he was crying? And put a bullet in my wife before you confirmed she was already dead?"

No one could restrain Ken-ai-te after this, who leaped toward his enemy with almost supernatural energy. He managed to grab Black Feather's arm before being pulled back and Mandy thought he would twist it off, he jerked it so hard. The screams were awful and Mandy clapped her hands over her ears. But even that didn't block it out and she closed her eyes. And then silence. Mandy looked up.

Ken-ai-te had released Black Feather, who was rubbing his arm, in obvious pain. With one smooth movement, Ken-ai-te reached down and grabbed his knife off the ground at his feet where he'd dropped it moments before. Apparently rethinking his decision to let the other man go, he suddenly jumped on the other warrior. He whirled him around once again and whipped the blade up to his throat, holding him fast.

Mandy's scream died before it fully formed and came out as a muffled gagging sound. Relief flooded her when no blood was spilled immediately. Yet the anxiety of perhaps watching him kill another, even one who fully deserved it, clutched at her until she could hardly breathe.

Ken-ai-te glanced around and met the eyes of Chief Twin Fox, who had earlier joined the group of people watching the fight and of course had witnessed the confession. The honorable warrior took a deep breath and nodded in the chief's direction, apparently yielding the right to decide life or death for the vanquished one to his respected elder. And waited.

Why is the chief hesitating? Surely, he won't release him after what he tried to do to me, not to mention after what he just admitted he did to Ken-ai-te's family!

"Life, Ken-ai-te. You have shown great courage in not killing him. Let him live with the shame of knowing his attack on this woman is no longer hidden in the darkness. And the terrible thing he did to his own family, to your family, is not a secret any longer. Yet, none of this can be erased by his death. Spilling his blood will only serve to keep peace from our own hearts. Therefore, let him be put out of our village, to live here no more. He cannot remain among us when he is full of so much bitterness and anger. Go from us, Black Feather—now, *One Who Shall Not Be Named*. You are not our family any longer, from this day forward."

Black Feather's eyes were wide with shock at the chief's words. Twin Fox had granted him mercy but even Mandy realized what he must be thinking: what kind of a life would it be, spent wandering the prairie without the comfort of his family around him?

Ken-ai-te released him and brutally shoved him to the ground, re-sheathing his knife as he did so. The banished one immediately jumped to his feet and whirled around to face his conqueror while screaming at the chief and all who would listen. He had one more weapon to use.

"I take my men with me when I go but I vow to return to finish the job soon. You will *all* be dead, then, and *she*," turning to point at a startled Mandy, "will be mine. Only then will my dead sister rest in peace. Ken-ai-te will not take revenge for her because he is a coward. But I will! He forced me to kill my own sister against my will, so all this is on his head."

He stomped away through the crowd and disappeared up the hill and back into the village, presumably to pack his things and leave. Ken-ai-te rushed to Mandy's side and pulled her to him in a warm embrace. She felt as though the world had stopped and let his arms shut it all out for those few precious moments. He had fought for her life and for her honor. And what was more, he said he *loved* her! In front of everyone! Strangely, she wasn't upset in the least, for she felt the same way, just had been afraid to say it out loud. Yes, it was *love*! In spite of everything, they had, indeed, fallen in love.

When he released her and took her by the shoulders to gaze deep into her eyes, he asked solemnly in English, "You o-kay? Not hurt?"

"No, Ken-ai-te, you came just in time. He tore my dress but didn't have time to do anything else."

The warrior reached up and wiped her lip. "Blood. He hit you?"

"Um, yes, he did slap me once. I hadn't even noticed it was bleeding. But it's nothing. I'm just so glad to see you! You are safe from the war, you came to my rescue, and you—"

She wasn't sure she could actually say the words out loud. Gulping for courage, she finished.

"You told everyone you love me. Is that true?"

Oh, those dark pools of liquid copper in which Mandy's heart swam right now! She couldn't get enough of looking at his face, taking in every feature as she would if she were starving and he, the last crumb of bread on earth. He was, for her! Her salvation on earth, her rescuer, her love! She picked a leaf out of one braid and caressed his black hair, so shiny in the dwindling sunlight that it took on a bluish tinge.

He nodded and smiled. "You?"

"Do I love you? Oh, yes, Ken-ai-te, I do! With all my heart. I just never realized it until today. How it has happened, going from your slave to being taken captive by your heart, is beyond me."

The warrior wiped away a tear on her cheek and smoothed down her long damp hair in mute affirmation of his affection. He pulled her to his side and held her tight as they walked back up the rise to the village. Sleeping Bird followed with Mandy's things.

At the tipi, the three hesitated for a moment to watch Black Feather and several of his friends ride out of the village in great anger. Mandy noted that Angry Bear and his wife were in the group. *So that's why her venom against me has been so strong all these weeks.* The connection hadn't clicked until right then. She felt rather sorry for the woman but she could have resisted Black Feather's attempts to manipulate her the way he obviously did in order to wreak his sadistic revenge on a helpless captive. *Well, good riddance to her, too! Maybe the other women will be kinder now without her here to goad them into their gossip.*

As Mandy watched them disappear out of sight, she shuddered to think what might be happening to her right this minute had the fight gone the other way. Suddenly her knees started to buckle. She began a slow slide to the ground but Ken-ai-te swept her up in his arms and held her close. When he ducked down to enter the tipi, he nearly dropped her and they both began giggling hysterically, releasing all the tension of the last hour. They kind of rolled together onto the buffalo robe, collapsing in laughter. Sleeping Bird caught Mandy's eye and shook her head in amusement, a smile on her lips, and nodded as she closed the hide flap and left the pair alone.

Their first kiss was passionate but tender, one never to be forgotten by Mandy. The exhilaration of that moment filled every fiber of her being and would have knocked her off her feet but she was already lying on the robe next to the warrior, clinging to him as though her very life depended on this man. She never wanted the moment to end!

Suddenly the sound of a bell rang loud and clear and she jerked her head away. *Where did that come from?* He frowned and pulled her closer for another kiss. In that instant she realized the alarm had only been in her mind. Was God speaking again? Why now, of all times?

A distinctly unpleasant feeling flooded her heart and she knew she could not ignore its warning. This was wrong, so wrong. And if she didn't stop it now, the result would be disaster for them both.

It took every ounce of her strength to pull herself up to a sitting position and scoot a short distance away from the warrior. Tears were spilling over, her voice choked with emotion.

"I—I can't! Please, don't touch me right now. Else I won't be able to resist you!"

✝ CHAPTER FORTY ✝

"Beloved, let us love one another: for love is of God;
and every one that loveth is born of God, and knoweth God."
I John 4:7

"Please, don't!" Mandy's voice was hardly more than a frantic whisper.

A deep frown marred Ken-ai-te's handsome features and indicated his turmoil at this sudden turn-about in her behavior. One moment in great passion and the next pulling away? She didn't understand it herself; how on earth could she explain it to him?

A second before their love had been so pure and full of joy. What was going on? Had it been wrong to allow him to kiss her? Something deep said yes but her heart screamed no! They had finally admitted their love, so wasn't a kiss the next appropriate and even expected step? Mandy knew in that instant there could be no more until her mind cleared and she had time to consider it further.

At least Ken-ai-te didn't press her, and she felt enormous relief. God had protected her chastity all this time and she couldn't allow sentiment to rule her head now and ruin His plan. But plan for what? Marriage? Ken-ai-te hadn't mentioned this, just seemed to assume that they could now sleep together because they had declared their love for each other. This was getting more and more out of hand by the second! She took a deep breath and prayed quickly for wisdom and strength, and the Lord seemed to confirm she had done the right thing by stopping this now. Not really what she wanted to do but she had learned that obedience is what God honors, not feelings.

"We mustn't do this yet, Ken-ai-te, as much as my heart desires it. I do love you, with all my heart, but I also love God and His Word is clear that this—what we are doing—is not permitted except within the bounds of marriage as known in the white man's society. When things calm down for us both, we need to talk. But for now, we both need rest."

His scowl deepened but Mandy's resolve hardened further after hearing the words spoken. She knew what she must do, however difficult it proved to be for them. *Please, Lord, don't let him demand what he has no right to have, nor take what I cannot yet offer to him out of love.*

Mandy rose quickly without another word and stepped over to her sleeping blanket where she stretched out, rolled over part way, and pulled it up over her shoulders, avoiding eye contact with Ken-ai-te. A jumble of disappointment mixed with anxiety threatened to strangle her and she closed her eyes tightly. *God, make my fear go away and show me I've made the right choice! I need your peace.*

Everything had changed between them, yet in other ways—the important ones—nothing had. Still shaken from the fresh memory of the near tragedy with Black Feather, Mandy's emotions were raw anyway, and now this added on top. It was almost too much. If only she hadn't crossed that line earlier, had done something to prevent the kiss from taking place, she wouldn't be going through this chaos. Did people in love always experience such confusion?

Holding her breath and hardly daring to breathe, Mandy lay there waiting. The warrior didn't say a word but she could hear him breathing hard. In the shadows, she imagined him clenching his fists over and over. The tension remained high between them as they lay in their separate places, so near and yet so far away from each other. Mandy wondered if he slept. She certainly did not. Excitement alternated with the unknown now facing her. The situation would need to be confronted and resolved soon but, for now, nothing need be done or said. Besides, wasn't it in truth Ken-ai-te's right and even responsibility to bring up marriage first? How could she hold her tongue when her whole future lay at stake? *Their* future!

The next morning Mandy was dressing when a thought hit her. She finished up and hurried outside to find Ken-ai-te sitting alone by the fire pit sharpening some arrowheads. He never looked up so she quickly put together a morning meal for them and asked him the question on her mind as she worked.

"Ken-ai-te, in all the chaos of last night, I forgot to ask you about the war party. I take it, you found the Comanche warriors who attacked our men?"

He glanced up and, for a moment, she believed she saw a flicker of something spark in his eyes. Respect, perhaps? Or maybe his frustration flaring up again? She couldn't be sure. Mandy caught her breath for a few seconds.

"Tracked to mountains but couldn't hide. Take many scalps. Peace now fill tepees of our men who die. War over." And he turned his attention back to the arrows.

Just like that? *War over.* Seemed whites could learn much from these people who took swift vengeance but once justice had been done could so easily put it all aside. This would take some contemplation for Mandy to accept.

Going through the motions of eating, the two said not a word. The wheels of Mandy's mind, however, were spinning.

Was this not the way God acted? In the Scriptures, time after time the Lord meted out His own brand of revenge without the manipulation of men but then moved right back to lovingkindness without allowing one to color the other. She shook her head but did not break the silence. The Kiowa way seemed to become more like God's way with each new revelation for Mandy. Slow steps returned her to the task of preparing for her day with a new experience added to her soul.

Yes, indeed—*war over* pounded in time with the thrumming of her heart. Even with the tension on every side, hope sang a fresh song of love to every fiber of her being and it was a good one, whether white or Kiowa and perhaps more a mixture of the two. Anytime she could hear God's voice, in fact, gave her hope. Today was another lesson in silence, yet a profound one she would not soon forget.

Over the next few days Ken-ai-te expressed irritation several times with their sleeping arrangements, yet never said much. But from time to time, she saw the muscles in his jaw working, observed the white knuckles on both fists, felt concern for his grim face and longed for a smile to ease the anxiety in her heart. And she knew his patience wouldn't hold out much longer.

The air was charged with an unexpected energy by day, however, and their joy bubbled over in many ways. Sleeping Bird's laughter came often now and Mandy found it contagious. The simplest of chores brought her tremendous joy and satisfaction. The three still went about their daily routines as before, but nothing was really as before. Love is powerful when unleashed and they were not the only ones who sensed this.

The women still asked when there would be a baby as they patted Mandy's stomach, but she was no longer offended by their curiosity. She smiled in reply and seldom said a word; just let her silence speak instead. *First, there must be a wedding, people!* Mandy wanted to scream it at them but knew they did this in love and acceptance, not to be intrusive, so she kept quiet. At least there were no more gossips prodding the others into a frenzy over this subject and that alone provided relief. Now, it seemed more like a quiet acceptance into the women's society rather than making her an object of their scorn. The more she prayed about it, the more certain she became that God would work things out if she would leave it all to Him. It was her job to be patient and wait on Him—and him!

To go from a servant position to that of an equal took some

getting used to. Working to honor her beloved rather than her master made a distinct difference in every detail for Mandy. The pleasure she experienced far outweighed her concern about the nights, in fact helped her forget them as long as the sun shone. She supposed that was a form of obeying God and exhibiting patience, not to push Ken-ai-te with limp explanations that she knew he could always ignore if he chose to do so. God had blessed her with a measure of peace and she was content to rest in that for now—in fact, for as long as He required.

Instead of focusing on the frustration she felt as the sun sank toward the horizon each evening, Mandy intensified her talks with Ken-ai-te about Christ. He seemed more open to this now than he had previously and she felt a new urgency to ensure his understanding. His questions were many and deep and they spent long hours lost in conversation even after the embers were reduced to a soft red glow. Sleeping Bird often joined them in the tipi but seldom entered into the discussions. Mandy prayed as always that she was listening, however.

One evening she and Ken-ai-te were discussing the concept of forgiveness again and suddenly his demeanor changed abruptly. He'd been eager and asking questions; now he became quiet and sober, almost sad.

"Does something trouble you?"

"Not know word but feel—" Mandy waited patiently for him while he struggled to get the words out. Expressing his feelings was not something that came easily.

"On way to village, use rope on you, not allow food and water. Right then, wrong now."

Mandy's smile faded. The memory, keen yet distant, remained one she preferred not to bring to mind. But they needed to clear this between them; that she knew with great certainty.

"Why do you say it was right then?"

"Kiowa way for enemy. Take you for revenge. Want suffering, make memory of dead wife and son easier. Not true now. Feel bad here," and he stopped to thump his chest. "How make it go away?"

"If you 'feel bad' in your heart, Ken-ai-te, it is because God is convicting you of sin. You need to consider praying to ask for His forgiveness for what you did to me. Then the 'bad feeling' will go away. If you mean it, that is."

"Will think on this. Not care for long time. Now want it different." He paused for a several moments, staring deep into her eyes. "You forgive?"

"You want me to forgive you?"

He nodded.

Sighing, she answered, "Of course I do. Our love has taken all the bad memories and brushed them out our door. Just as I had to do with my other remembrances, we have to refuse to think about them any longer. Including this. But it is not simply my forgiveness you need to seek. I shall pray for your wisdom in this."

The look he gave her in that moment made all the pain and suffering she endured on the trek to the village worth it all! She saw in his eyes shock combined with understanding and mixed with humility, topped off with a generous portion of love. *Thank You, Jesus!* And pray she would, for not only his forgiveness in this but also for his deliverance from the grip of future sin. God, indeed, seemed to be at work in his heart. As He had changed Mandy, so she believed He would do for Ken-ai-te, and soon!

Out of nowhere one day while she and Sleeping Bird worked on a hide together, the older woman startled Mandy with a declaration that stunned her, given all she had been through emotionally and spiritually. Just as she began to see God's hand working on those around her, her enemy refused to give up, insisted on nibbling away at her peace.

"Prayer Woman, you and Ken-ai-te like my family now. Much love between you. Tell my son it is good he now have wife. No more slave."

"A *wife*? He's never said anything to me about marriage."

"For Kiowa, no wedding. Just pay bride price, she go to live in his tipi. No one to pay, you already live in tipi. So already done."

"You mean I'm already married to him? Just like that? That can't be true! Don't I have a say in this at all? How can I be married without a ceremony or even our discussing the subject?"

"Tell you before—for Kiowa, no wedding."

"But what about this bride price you mentioned? He hasn't paid that yet, has he? I think Papa told me once it was paid to the father of the bride. Mine is deceased, so why isn't he required to get my permission to marry at least?"

Disappointment crushed her. All her dreams of having a beautiful wedding, surrounded by her loved ones and friends—gone in a puff of smoke, just like that. No wonder Ken-ai-te hadn't mentioned marriage to her. He had no need to do so, since they were considered already married by Kiowa tradition.

"No father, just take woman to tipi, married. Simple for our people. How whites do it?"

"They have a courting period where the young man calls on the young woman and they spend time talking and learning all about each other. When they are certain they both desire marriage, they decide on a date for the wedding and notify all their friends and relatives. The wedding itself is a solemn event, confirmed by their faith in God and held in a church. Afterwards, there is a reception that is a gala affair, usually with a huge dinner for all the guests and celebrations of all kinds. People bring the couple many gifts they need for starting their home together. Then they go on a honeymoon, to spend time alone without anyone they know around. How exciting it is when someone gets married!"

Mandy had gotten caught up in her remembering the special event that bonded a man and a woman in holy matrimony before God and witnesses of their choosing, forgetting all about the woman sitting beside her for the moment. Sleeping Bird's gruff words brought her back to earth.

"No wedding, no gifts, no feast. No time, much work to be done every day for Kiowa woman."

She looked at her in disgust. *I doubt there is a romantic bone in your wrinkled body, old woman!* Immediately she felt guilt at her harsh thoughts. Mandy couldn't blame her after having lived as a Kiowa all these years. *Oh, God, please don't let that happen to me!*

Mandy focused on the hide and tried to take her mind off what she had learned. Surely, Ken-ai-te now *did* expect her to share his bed. Why hadn't he said anything?

God, what am I going to do? How can I resolve these two cultures as well as my faith, and figure out a way to combine white and Kiowa marriage traditions within Your parameters? Surely, there is a way. Show me Your solution!

Before the hide was finished that day, Mandy had a plan. The more she prayed about it, the more excited she became, the more convinced of its value to both Ken-ai-te and his heritage while honoring her faith as well. Now, how to bring it up to the warrior and gain his cooperation?

God had, indeed, had a purpose in urging her to wait on Him regarding marriage. The distinct differences in the cultures presented her with a unique and sticky problem that needed to be handled with wisdom and great care. She realized how easily she could have botched things again had she not obeyed Him. And she knew He would open up the right time to propose the idea to her beloved, meantime preparing his heart to receive what she knew had come straight from God's heart in the first place.

Every evening Ken-ai-te's interest in Christ seemed more intense than the one before it. He was eager to hear what the Bible had to say and loved it when she told stories of battles and adventures of the brave men found in its pages. His questions became deep and personal and she knew beyond a doubt he had come under conviction from God's Spirit. Unfortunately, that also meant an eternal conflict raged inside his heart, for the devil would not give up on him easily.

In addition, because of his great intelligence and curious nature, combined with his Kiowa heritage of respect for prayer and for the acknowledgement of a creator—by whatever name he called him—Ken-ai-te insisted on thinking through every point Mandy brought up and discussing it endlessly until he became satisfied he understood the whole thing. While this was admirable, of course, it also led to many long nights with them wrangling over some relatively minor idea. She prayed constantly for wisdom to respond without arousing further doubts, to be able to explain something more clearly on his terms. God never failed to deliver and she knew it would be not long before the warrior reached a state of readiness for the next step, the one with eternal rewards.

While Ken-ai-te's knowledge of God grew, with each passing day Mandy felt a stronger attraction to the warrior. Though she had never been in love before, she knew with certainty what she felt was genuine and lasting. Far more than mere words of affection, this emotion flooded her entire being with awareness of this man—his scent, the twinkle of his eye, the sound of his laughter, the touch of his rough hand on hers. Sometimes she would catch him gazing at her and her insides felt funny as though butterflies fluttered in her stomach. When he was out of sight, she found herself longing to spot him as she walked through the village on an errand. And when he was near, she could hardly make herself focus on the task at hand.

And she could feel his love for her, too. The lilt of his voice as he spoke her name with such tenderness, the kindness in his response when she needed something right away, the security she felt in having him at her side when gathering with the other people in the twilight for dancing and celebration of life itself—they all combined to flood her soul with more happiness than she felt she deserved. Each morning she awoke with eagerness instead of dread, thrilled to see the measure of their love together grow richer and fuller. She looked forward to spending time with him, agonizing over the long daytime hours when they were apart.

He seldom went to the campfire in the evenings after the meal any longer, choosing instead to remain with her in the tipi to talk. And she knew it was due to his choice in the matter, not being forced to do so to avoid an ugly confrontation with The One Who Would Not Be Named. Most nights Sleeping Bird joined them and while Mandy hoped she listened in on their conversations, the older woman usually worked on her beading without saying a word. Mandy kept telling herself there would be time later to talk to her alone. For now, her focus must be on the warrior.

However, Sleeping Bird commented several times on the difference in Mandy's disposition as a result of the change in her attitude. It pleased Mandy her happiness showed so obviously to others, especially to this woman who had come to mean so much to her as a friend. She could sense their friendship deepening with each new dawn as well. And one day while they were baking bread together Sleeping Bird confirmed Mandy's hopes and put it into words.

"You my daughter now, Prayer Woman."

"Your daughter? What do you mean?"

"Ken-ai-te become my son, you now my daughter. My heart holds much love for you as well. No more Sleeping Bird, now Mother. Not angry?"

"Angry? Why would I be angry?"

"Kiowa way to say 'Mother' and not name. Not sure if you want Kiowa way, from now until forever. But all different now, maybe o-kay for you?"

"Oh, Sleeping Bird, I'm honored to have you as my mother. I like to think you are much like my real mother was, kind and gentle yet won't let me get away with anything!" They both laughed. "But I feel such shame that I created great danger for all of us because of my demand for my own tipi, and we're still living in the tipi together anyway. How is it any different from before, other than I'm more content?"

She shook her head, obviously lost in some of the longer words and thoughts. Finally, she answered quietly, "Just is. Love now. You luck-ee woman, have love. Most, no love, maybe never. I have love with Running Elk, luck-ee!"

Mandy blushed slightly and nodded with a laugh. Yes, love indeed! She couldn't escape the word and knew she didn't want to any longer. Love had changed everything. Playing with the syllable on her tongue, she found her heart pounding with delight at the thought of the power of those four letters. Her plan simply *had* to succeed.

She prayed fervently about it for several days and one night shortly before time for sleep, she felt the Spirit nudging her that now the time was right. Before she lost her courage, she cleared her throat.

"Ken-ai-te, I have something on my heart that I would like to discuss with you." He nodded and gazed evenly at her, a smile on his lips. "Mother told me something disturbing the other day, that we are now considered married according to Kiowa tradition. Is that correct?"

"Upset we married?" So it was true. His frown expressed his concern over her reaction to the news.

"Yes—I mean no...I mean I don't know! That's not the point here. What I'm trying to say is white people don't treat marriage between a man and a woman quite so casually as do the Kiowa. It is a sacred union, blessed by God, and not to be dealt with lightly." Oh, she feared she had gone about this all backwards! *God, help me say it right.* Butterflies fluttered in her stomach only not for a good reason this time. *Here goes!*

"If we are to continue living with each other, Ken-ai-te, whatever your customs might be, we also have to honor those of my God. And He says this is wrong. I even caused great harm to your reputation and to my own when I pushed this one issue before the people, that's how important it is to me."

She quickly went on before he could interrupt.

"Would you consider the two of us creating a ceremony of sorts that would combine some things from my culture as well as those from the Kiowa heritage? That way, we could satisfy my beliefs without sacrificing any of yours. It could be very beautiful, you know, with a great deal of symbolism in it we both could cherish always. In addition, it would provide us with a real starting point for our marriage instead of simply a continuation of our living arrangement but by another name. Although you've not said a word to me about it, I would be honored to be your wife, Ken-ai-te—but *not* until we can come to an understanding about this one point. Another thing, I know my father would never approve, either. Your bride price, therefore, can be to allow this to take place, as an honor to my heritage which will now become a part of yours."

She dared not even breathe. His answer held the key to their entire future together!

"My honor, do this ceremony with you. And after? Join me on buffalo rug at night?"

Mandy gulped. The bluntness of his question took her by surprise. She felt the color rise in her cheeks but ignored it and smiled at him, nodding in agreement, and he grinned broadly. Shivers went down her spine, not of fear but anticipation of the fullness of their relationship. She was to be married! And on her terms, without sacrificing her chastity to do it nor without offending Kiowa tradition. God's perfect plan!

"We will need to plan our wedding soon and—"

"Wed-ding? Not know word."

"The ceremony, sealing our love and making us man and wife. That is what the whites, that is Christians, call it. We don't have to use that word if you don't want to. But I've always dreamed of what my wedding would be like and I would like to incorporate many of those dreams into our own unique celebration."

"Get to dance?"

She laughed. "Yes, of course we will have dancing and drums and flutes. And a feast fit for a king! I will speak with Mother about what I need to do to prepare for our marriage so it may take a little time."

He frowned. "Time?"

"Well, there is much to do, Ken-ai-te, so it can't be pulled together overnight. You have to give me maybe one moon at least."

His face did not reflect happiness over this news but at least he didn't protest too strenuously.

Several moments later he asked, "Where sleep now?"

"Um, I will sleep where I have been. And I'm going to ask that you respect our love by not forcing me to share your bed. I'm coming to you of my own free will, Ken-ai-te, just not quite yet. Be patient! We have our whole lives ahead of us now." She reached out and caressed his face tenderly and he nodded, though his face did not exactly convey full consent. But he said nothing.

Could her heart ever be any fuller than at that moment? As she stared into those eyes, which had so captivated her from the first day, her thoughts calmed in spite of the turmoil and questions. *Strange how dreams can change, how God can mold them into His plans when we yield them to His control and timing to bring such joy! And nothing can go wrong ever again, right, Father?*

✝ CHAPTER FORTY-ONE ✝

"God...knoweth the secrets of the heart."
Psalm 44:21

"Oh, Sleeping Bird—I mean, Mother—I cannot believe I'm preparing for my wedding to Ken-ai-te! If you had told me several months ago this would happen I would have said you were crazy out of your head!"

They both laughed and kept on working. They had much to do and little time to complete everything. It felt good to keep her hands busy, to keep her from letting her mind wander into anxiety about the big step she was about to take. Marriage! And to a Kiowa—who would ever have thought!

The next afternoon while she worked on a hide by herself, she spent some time praising God for all the changes in her life over these past months. It still amazed her to consider how far He had brought her, how much she had learned, and not solely about the Kiowa way of life. Her command of Scripture had intensified beyond what she ever dreamed possible, mostly because she used her solitude to commit more and more of it to memory. To see God's hand on her all this time was more than she could comprehend.

One of the special gifts God had given her, a Kiowa mother, brought her much delight and warmth as well. Surrounded by peace now, Mandy basked in the blessing of being "mothered" for the first time in her life, letting all those deepest unmet needs from long ago wash away in a waterfall of unselfish love. Had she missed a great deal by not having a mother's love while she grew up? Aunt Ida had tried to fill the role, of course, starting the day her younger brother arrived with the motherless baby in his arms. And though Mandy would always be grateful for her sacrifice of love for her father and his infant daughter, something had always been missing. Mandy had never been able to put her finger on what, but now she had begun to understand.

"Father, help me not to dwell on the past again. I really don't want—"

Suddenly Mandy had an awful thought. She couldn't recall what her aunt's face looked like! No matter how hard she tried, no face came to mind for her. It had been crowded out by Sleeping Bird's leathered wrinkles, her wiry grey braids, and the blue eyes sparkling with love.

"God, You have been teaching me one thing above all else ever since the day I arrived here and met Mother: how to conquer my fear of the future by, well, by having confidence in the present. That doesn't mean I can't continue to cherish my past because I do, yet I no longer have to live constantly in it. My heritage will always be a part of who I am, but what I have learned as an adult is far more important. If I can't appreciate my past, I can never look to the future You've planned for me, Lord. It no longer matters what Aunt Ida looked like, only that she existed and played an important part in my life as a child. So help me leave her where she belongs."

Mandy had always imagined having a mother would be an incredible experience and it so far surpassed those dreams. Her heart swelled with gratitude for her Father's grace in this area. He had seen her need and stooped down to provide an answer, albeit a slightly different one from Mandy's original idea, which had been perhaps to love a mother-in-law someday. And strange as it may be, she actually saw that become reality because, using both the unique circumstances and Kiowa tradition, Sleeping Bird filled dual roles as mother *and* mother-in-law for Mandy, all rolled into one!

A couple of days later while gathering firewood early one morning, Mandy glanced up at the distant horizon to a ridge high above the village and for a second her heart skipped a beat. Outlined in stark contrast against the rising sun a lone warrior sat motionless on his pony.

"Surely that can't be—" She hadn't given The One Who Shall Not Be Named a thought for some time now. And what a relief it had been not to have to constantly be on the lookout for his leering face or be on guard against his taunting threats. Why did this man, whoever he was, sit there looking down at the camp like that? What did he want? Shivers crawled down her spine. Certainly, by now, The One Who Shall Not Be Named had found another place to live and had hopefully given up his hateful vengeance against her. *Please, God, make him go away.* And suddenly, he turned and disappeared out of sight. *Maybe my imagination played a trick on me and there is no danger to be concerned about. Still, I probably ought to inform Ken-ai-te.* But she busied herself with her laborious task and soon forgot all about the mysterious sight.

One evening a few days later Mandy decided to tackle the job of planning their marriage ceremony.

"We need to begin planning our wedding, Ken-ai-te."

"Tell more about. Not understand."

"Well, we will make a pledge to love each other for all eternity, from now until forever. It is called a vow, a solemn promise before God and our friends and family to love and cherish the other one always. Songs and prayers are an important part, too, and it is a beautiful time to celebrate the love that binds us together."

"Good thing, then."

"Yes, it is. I'm glad you approve. In the white culture, it is only after the wedding that the couple is permitted to live in the same house and share the same bed."

"Not same for Kiowa."

"Yes, I know. And you promised to wait until after our wedding, remember?"

"Yes. For Kiowa, it is time. For whites, wrong?"

"You are correct, Ken-ai-te. For me, it is wrong to do this thing yet. Once we go through the wedding ceremony, then the time will be right, for us both. You will wait?"

Mandy held her breath.

"For you, Prayer Woman, I wait." And he grinned broadly, scooping her into his arms in a sudden move that took away what breath she had left. He kissed the tip of her nose, then leaned in to kiss her lips as well. Unbidden, her body responded with eagerness to melt into the strength of this man she loved so much. But she knew better and put her fingers to his lips, pulling back a little in his embrace.

"Not now, but soon, I promise. I will be worth the wait!" And her eyes twinkled in spite of the frown on his brow. She gulped against the fear rising in her throat. How patient could she expect him to be?

Maybe if she turned his thoughts to something else? Her mind had jumped to something she'd wondered about for some time but had been reluctant to ask before. *Now is as good a time as any, I suppose.*

"Ken-ai-te, do you recall the time when you tried to force yourself on me?"

He frowned. "Not happen."

"Oh, yes, don't you remember? I awoke in the middle of the night to find you on top of me. Within a few days of arriving in the village."

He nodded slowly. "Ah, nightmare. Roll into fire if I not stop. You asleep but fight, hit, bite."

"I did that to you?" Mandy's eyes widened in shock.

He nodded solemnly. "Have much anger."

"Well, the memory is still fresh of how frightened I was at least, and there was a good amount of anger as well, at being held captive against my will. So, you really weren't trying to—to force me?"

He shook his head slowly this time. "Nightmare every night.

322

About death of man."

Mandy visibly paled. "Pete?" she asked softly.

"Yes. Think maybe you want to kill me for man's death. Idea of other warriors that day, not mine."

Mandy brightened. "And now? Do you still think I might harm you?"

Again, he shook his head. "I tell you, worth wait, no more anger. Now love."

Yes, indeed...love!

"Well, if we are going to wait, then I suggest you bed down in the tipi with Mother from now until our wedding. Or let her stay here with me, perhaps. We have much to work on and that way we could do so without disturbing your rest."

He frowned but couldn't hold back the smile barely underneath. Putting his head back, he roared with laughter.

"You get what you want, Prayer Woman! Own tipi. What you want, right?"

"Yes, you are right. I guess I did get it but in a backwards sort of way." And she chuckled at the thought.

He looked puzzled but she shrugged. "Oh, it doesn't matter. It's only for a short time. We need to set a time for our wedding. Maybe we can talk tomorrow."

Excitement buoyed Mandy over the next few days of busy preparation, though they still hadn't set an exact date or time. She was in love and nothing mattered anymore!

One morning she and Sleeping Bird were discussing the marriage and the changes it would bring to their lives.

"Mother, I seem to recall Ken-ai-te used as his explanation of why I asked for my own tipi in front of the elders the fact that I didn't want to live in the tipi with Ken-ai-te's dead wife's spirit, is that right?"

She nodded.

"So won't we need to have our own tipi after we are married, not the one I'm sharing with him now?"

To her nod she added, "Then, it seems I'm going to need a lot of hides to cover our new tipi before we can be married. But that could take months! And I don't want to wait months to get married. I want it to happen before the snows get here." She stopped, deep in thought.

"I know, what if we use some of the hides off this tipi? Then I wouldn't need more than a half dozen or so to complete the new covering. I have several of those ready now, and maybe Ken-ai-te could hunt some deer for the rest. Then our new tipi would be a tribute to the past and to the future, both."

Sleeping Bird laughed. Mandy could see the pleasure in the older woman's eyes and she knew she had convinced her when she nodded vigorously. She would tell Ken-ai-te right away about the need for more hides for both the tipi and for bedding. Hunting, then, would also keep him busy and not give him time to think more about the unusual arrangements, at least in Kiowa tradition, to which he had agreed regarding their union as man and wife. Mandy would spend her days cleaning, tanning, and sewing the hides into clothing and other necessary items for a newlywed Kiowa couple.

"What paint on outside of new tipi?"

Sleeping Bird's question caught Mandy off guard. What, indeed? She couldn't just copy the drawings of Ken-ai-te's first wife, of his vision quest. Her own message was of the utmost importance and would require some thought and much prayer to allow God to show her what to put on there.

"I will have to pray about this, Mother. There is time before I have to do it. God will show me, I know."

The following day as the three ate the morning meal together and chatted quietly among themselves, an alarm went up in the camp. A rider was coming across the prairie, and fast. Mandy didn't feel frightened at first but knew it had to be important, as this didn't happen every day. Quickly, however, an uneasy feeling grew in the pit of her stomach and she breathed a silent prayer for help from her Heavenly Father, whatever news the rider brought to them.

Chief Twin Fox and Ken-ai-te and several of the elders of the village took up weapons and went to the edge of the tipi circle to meet the visitor. They could tell it was an Indian but he was too far away to determine if he came in peace or what tribe he was from. As he neared, Mandy heard someone say it was Do-tan-ha, the son of one of their Kiowa brothers. He had taken his new wife to a distant place to live with his wife's sister and her family several weeks before, leaving the rest of their families behind. Why had he returned and where was his wife?

Mandy pushed close to try to hear what the man related to the chief but between her lack of knowledge of Kiowa and the breathlessness of the man from the hard ride, she didn't understand a thing. Sleeping Bird stood close by and Mandy asked her to translate.

"He say many soldiers come from fort to take away white captives. Two days from here, maybe three. Have seven women, three children, look for more. Do-tan-ha come to warn us. New words with White Father make this law."

Just then, all eyes turned toward Mandy. She gasped and felt her knees go weak.

"What? They can do that? I mean, it's what I prayed for when I first came here, that someone would arrive to rescue me. But I don't want to go now!"

Ken-ai-te heard her plaintive cry and left the men to take her back to the tipi. Sleeping Bird followed. Mandy was numb and very much afraid all of a sudden. Surely, they couldn't force her to leave. Could they?

As soon as the three were seated in the tipi, Ken-ai-te spoke.

"I fight if they come. Not give you up. Whole village fight!"

"No, Ken-ai-te, please. If you try to fight the white soldiers, you will die. They have too many men, too many rifles and other weapons they can use. You can't win. I know you are brave and are willing to fight, even die, to protect me. But if you die, then what will happen to me? Think for a moment, before you get too gallant and sharpen your tomahawk! Besides, I don't want to be responsible for more bloodshed, white or Kiowa."

"Do-tan-ha say they make strong medicine, no Kiowa can stand before it. But I not believe. They take you, I fight! You belong to me now."

"I know, from now until forever. Yes, I agree. I want to stay with you for always, Ken-ai-te. You are my chosen husband. We've been through such a great deal together. It's so unfair to stop us now, just before we finally are able to marry. Surely God has an answer we haven't thought about yet."

Sleeping Bird was strangely silent through the whole discussion. Mandy's focus was on the warrior and not on the woman. When it finally dawned on her that Sleeping Bird hadn't said a word, she turned to look at her, startled to see tears in her eyes. She assumed it was because Mandy might soon be leaving. Or perhaps because she, herself, had been born white and might be taken away as well.

"Mother, please don't weep for me. I'm not gone yet. God will find a way. And if you are concerned about yourself, don't be. As long as we keep them from seeing your blue eyes, you will be safe for they won't know you are white. Me, that's a different matter, I'm afraid."

The older woman shook her head back and forth. What was going on, with this strange behavior?

"Not worry about me. Heart heavy because of secret book. You need to read words, learn truth."

"What on earth are you talking about? A secret book? Kiowa do not have books. You aren't making any sense, Mother."

"Book will explain. You read now. Words belong to your father!"

326

†CHAPTER FORTY-TWO†

"Before they call, I will answer;
and while they are yet speaking, I will hear."
Isaiah 65:24

"**M**y father's words? What are you talking about, Mother?" Mandy was staring at Sleeping Bird now, her jaw open in disbelief. Ken-ai-te's eyes bored into the older woman but she looked only at Mandy.

She rose finally and muttered in Kiowa that she'd return in a moment, then left the tipi. Minutes later, she reappeared with an item in her hands that she carefully laid into Mandy's lap. A book! Presumably, it had been hidden in her tipi. But how did she come to possess it?

"Prayer Woman, read."

The worn leather binding was stained with something dark but it seemed vaguely familiar to her. She was afraid to touch it. Whose book was it? Why were her father's words in it?

Glancing from one to the other, Mandy tried to make sense of her confusion. What she observed only increased it. Ken-ai-te continued to glare at Sleeping Bird, fury barely concealed. She'd never seen him angry with her before, except when they argued over her father's coat that one time.

"Not destroy like you tell me to, my son." The older woman finally raised her eyes to the warrior, then went on. "Too valuable. Use to learn English writing, remember reading, many memories. Learn real meaning when Prayer Woman come to village. See name, hear same one, Prayer Woman's father—Jo-si-ah Cl-ark, right?" And she turned to Mandy for affirmation.

"Yes, Josiah Clark was my father's name. But how—"

Ken-ai-te spoke this time. "In coat. I find book, take to Mother to read. She say no. I tell her destroy it."

"But too late when I meet Prayer Woman. Good I not do it. Her book now."

Tentatively Mandy reached out to caress its worn edges. *I've seen this before, but where? Wish I could remember. Was it really yours, Papa? One crazy coincidence after another—first your coat ended up here and now this? Only You, God, could have worked that out. But why? To what purpose?*

Mandy opened the book, then recoiled when she saw the blood staining the first few pages. Her father's? Breathing a silent prayer for courage Mandy began to read. Apparently, it was a journal of some sort. But her father never kept a journal. Did he?

Abruptly, a memory came flooding back of her father slapping a similar brown leather book shut one time when she came into his study back in Ohio. He had tried to stuff it under a pile of papers on top of his desk but Mandy had gotten a glimpse of it anyway. When she asked about it, he said she shouldn't let her pretty head worry about things like that and to forget about it. Which she promptly did. Until now.

Another time shortly after they'd arrived in Indian Territory she had seen him bent over a book which could easily have been this very one, writing words in it that he then quickly dismissed when she asked what he was doing. Again, he'd told her it was unimportant. But something her father had written over a period of perhaps years certainly *would* be important to her!

Mandy scanned through the book to get a semblance of the order within, her curiosity rising with each moment that passed. It indeed was a journal, with earliest writings dating back to before Mandy was born. Every page was in her father's distinctive handwriting, sometimes neatly penned while on others it was apparent the words had been written in a hasty scrawl. How come she didn't know anything about this until today? What had her father been trying to hide from her?

Then a yellowed paper that had obviously been folded and refolded many times fell into her lap out of the front of the journal. She gently opened it to reveal a letter from her father, addressed to "My Dearest Lily"—her mother! Dated several weeks after Mandy's birth, she wondered why he would have written a letter to his wife after she died. The whole thing just didn't make sense to her.

Fingers of fear trailed down her spine but Mandy didn't have a clue why she was so afraid. What would she find in these words that could generate this terror, especially since they were all about her parents? Suddenly, she knew she had to get away by herself while she read the mysterious book.

Mandy sighed and looked up at the two faces staring expectantly at her, awaiting her reaction. But she didn't have one to offer. Numb, astounded, curious, overwhelmed—that's what she felt right now. The contents of this book were way too private to absorb in front of others, even these two who meant so much to her.

Mandy cleared her throat and swallowed hard.

"I know you both are eager to find out what's in here, although I gather you, Mother, already have a pretty good idea."

She nodded in reply and smiled hesitantly.

"From your expression, I'm assuming it contains good news but I don't share your confidence right now. Would it be all right if I took this back to your tipi this afternoon and read it for myself? I know I have a lot of work to do but it can wait. This is more important to me right now."

Ken-ai-te frowned but her mother nodded, glanced at him and

frowned, and then he reluctantly nodded as well. Mandy knew he had taken a giant leap in trusting Sleeping Bird's judgment, considering his own seemed to be in direct opposition. But he did not protest further and she was grateful.

Sleeping Bird reached out and covered Mandy's smooth hands with her own rough ones, looking intently into her dark eyes.

"Read. More words make heart lighter. You read, then you know truth."

Mandy nodded and rose, tucking the letter back into the journal and taking it to the older woman's tipi. It was quiet here, maybe too quiet.

She sat on the soft robe in the middle of the floor and positioned herself so the shaft of sunshine from the vent above fell directly onto her lap. A soft gasp escaped from her lips. It seemed the faded leather was aglow with a light source all its own! Mandy began to speak with her Heavenly Father.

"Lord, I have no idea what is waiting for me here in these pages. But You do. And I have a distinct feeling this might be the whole reason You brought me here, to find and read this book. My stomach is churning and I don't understand why. Please give me courage!"

Slowly Mandy opened the journal and took out the letter. It was this item about which she had the greatest curiosity. She read the words from long ago with almost a reverent awe. Imagine—a message from her father to her mother! Was he insane, though, to be writing to her after she died? Perhaps out of his head with grief? Reading the words aloud, she spoke reverently in a shaky voice.

"My dearest Lily, It has been many months now since you left to go be with your father and his people, and I miss you more every day that passes. Daily I pray not only for you and your safety and health, but also for the complete recovery of your parents. You promised to return as soon as they were better and yet you have not come. The dread that fills my heart every time I remember your parting vow

330

overwhelms me, for I know that only death would prevent you from fulfilling it and returning to me and to our baby daughter whom you love so much.

"She is too little, of course, to know what is happening, but I believe she misses you, nevertheless. Already she is familiar with your voice and sometimes cries in the night without cause. I can't help but feel it is for those arms that I fear shall never again hold her."

"She went to be with her parents and left me alone with Papa? They were obviously quite ill but that's no excuse! Let a doctor tend them. Why her?" The last line brought tears to her eyes. "Yes, Mama, I'm certain I did cry for you back then. Goodness knows, I cried often enough for you all those lonely years while I grew up. Why did you leave me? And why did Papa tell me you died giving birth? How could you just disappear like that?" She read on.

"In my efforts to find you, my darling, I went to the fort and solicited the assistance of the Colonel there. But he rejected my pleas and told me that he refused to risk the lives of any of his men searching for an Indian."

"An *Indian*? My mother was an Indian?" The shock left her absolutely speechless. Long moments passed without a sound. Breathlessly she repeated, "My mother was an Indian. Well, that explains why they didn't call a doctor for her parents, why she needed to go to help them, I guess." Mandy quickly returned to her reading.

"That cut deeply into my heart! May God forgive him. I cannot. Yes, I can hear your soft words even now, telling me to remember how much Jesus had to forgive and yet did it. But He was God! If only the Colonel had agreed to send out some troops, I believe we could have found you and brought you home where you belong. But then he told me something else: to forget you, because you never belonged with white people, anyway. I'd as soon forget to breathe as to forget the depth of your twinkling black eyes, the softness of your copper cheek, and the richness of your voice. I can never forget our love. I know I must, yet I cannot. A part of me has died this day, but the other part must live on for our precious Amanda!"

Eyes flashing with indignation, Mandy said, "It's unconscionable the Army Colonel refused to help search for Mama simply because she was an Indian. There is no excuse for that kind of prejudice in educated folks. What does he mean you never belonged with white people? How *dare* he! I'm with you, Papa, in that I'm not sure I could have forgiven him, either. If I'd been there I would have given him a piece of my mind!" Her heart pounding now, Mandy returned to the letter.

"One thing I can assure you, my love: your daughter shall never forget you! Every day of her life, I will tell her about you and how much you loved her. And I will tell her of the duty to family that required you to lay aside your own needs to go care for your parents who are suffering so dearly right now. Many have suggested that I take our child away from here and not tell her the truth of her Kiowa heritage but—"

"*Kiowa*? My mother was Kiowa? This can't be right! She and Papa came here together with their dream to evangelize these people. I don't understand any of this!" But the words drew her back once again.

"... the truth of her Kiowa heritage but I'm not sure it's wise to base her love for you on a lie. Yet, there is wisdom in this for people have such an intense hatred for anyone who is Indian right now, not only here in Indian Territory but also back home in Ohio. If I take the baby back there, I will have to do so without telling her the truth, and maybe that is best. Ida has agreed to help me raise her if I go but I know she would not allow Mandy in the house if she knew about you, Lily."

"*You*, Aunt Ida? You hated Indians, too? I always knew you were not overly fond of them, but would you really have rejected me if you'd known I was half Kiowa? That must be why you were so furious when Papa agreed to bring me back here with him, not the inconveniences of living on the frontier, as you insisted. Because you didn't want us telling Indians about Jesus. How *could* you? And you, Papa? Were you so ashamed of me that you couldn't bear to look on me, either? Oh, I'm so confused!" She wept openly for a few moments but soon dried her tears and went on reading.

"That she is half Kiowa is not something of which to be ashamed, as many would insist, but something of which to be proud, and she needs to grow up knowing these brave people are hers, too. There will be many who will not appreciate her rich heritage, I know, but I believe I can help her to do so."

"Not if you don't ever tell me about it! I can't accept the lies, Papa. You were cruel to do this to me, to rob me of this knowledge. Everything I have known to be truth I now find out is based on a lie— and the lies you told to cover up that first one." A cold hard spot instantly walled itself off inside her heart and Mandy felt a heaviness she'd never known before in her spirit. An odd taste was on her tongue and all joy was gone. She couldn't even pray at that moment. Strangely, she didn't cry but sat numbly staring at her father's words. Then a line caught her attention and she reluctantly decided to finish the letter, in spite of her jumbled emotions.

"I pray God will honor my decision to take Mandy back to Ohio. If you were alive, I believe with all my heart you would have found a way to return to us. Alas, I fear we shall not meet again this side of Heaven. I really have no choice but to think of our daughter's future now. Someday I shall tell her of the beautiful mother she had, who so unselfishly gave of herself to others out of obedience to the God she loved and served."

"My mother was Kiowa but knew Christ? Perhaps some of the other journal entries will explain how they met and fell in love. Did Papa lead Mama to the Lord himself?" And as quickly as the wall was erected around her heart, it tumbled into pieces. The tears came freely once more.

"Oh, God, help me understand all this." Peace seemed to fill the tipi and Mandy turned her attention back to the yellowed pages in her hand.

"When the time is right we shall return, my love, and I will not rest until I find your people and discover your fate. I feel as though I am abandoning the Kiowa, the people God called me to love; in reality I am leaving them—and you—in His capable hands. For now, I must keep our daughter safe. Should you ever find this letter, my dearest Lily, I pray you will understand my anguish in leaving and also know we will never forget you or your proud people. Remember always the verse we chose for our work in evangelizing your people, for I now claim it more dearly than ever before: Psalm 130:5, 'I wait for the LORD, my soul doth wait, and in his word do I hope.' Go with God, the Creator of our love and the Savior of our souls, until we meet again at the feet of Jesus!

Your loving husband, Josiah."

"So that's why you came back, Papa, to find her. You could have told me the truth and I would have understood. It hurts that you didn't feel you could trust me."

But even as she uttered these words, she knew why he never explained. And she was deeply ashamed to confront that ugly part of her being. She bowed her head and prayed for freedom from that horrible bondage of despising another regardless of the circumstances solely because of the color of their skin. Those early weeks of living here, she was subjected daily to this very thing herself. And, she had to admit with shame, echoed those sentiments with more than enough of her own hatred for them. Then there was The One Who Shall Not Be Named, whose fury at her because of her race was the greatest. She chuckled. *Wonder what he would say if he knew I am half Kiowa!*

"Maybe there will be more in the entries themselves that will explain things further." Eagerly she turned to the beginning and began to read her father's words.

For several more hours, Mandy continued to be absorbed in the book in the silence of the tipi, until the light began to fade. Her stomach growled and reminded her it was time for the evening meal. There was much to share with the two she loved and they would be eager to hear.

"One more entry and then I'll quit for now. I want to look ahead to the end and read the last words Papa wrote—and when." She leafed quickly through and found the entry. The words were scrawled here, not neat as throughout much of it. He'd obviously written them quickly and without much light. The date indicated the night before he was killed. She shuddered at the thought: not only his last words here but his last words on earth even.

"Light low, must save energy for ride home tomorrow. No trace found of Lily's brother Swift Eagle, whole family gone. Another mystery for Heaven. Heart heavy with regret this night, for lies I've told Mandy and for keeping her heritage a secret from her. First thing when I get home, I will tell Mandy the story of her mother and her people. Maybe let her read these words? I owe her this much. Hope she can forgive me, understand my decision, that I did it out of love to protect her. Oh, that I might have one more chance to set things right! Can hear the calls around me in the dark, know the Indians are out there somewhere, waiting for my fire to die, waiting for me to sleep, waiting for dawn to attack.

"God, give me courage! I have to find my way home so I can talk to Mandy. Nevertheless, help me to say with Paul, 'For me to live is Christ and to die is gain.' Josiah Clark, Indian Territory, 1853."

"Oh, Papa! Your words did find their way to me. God alone could have worked that out. If only I could tell you that I do forgive you!"

✝CHAPTER FORTY-THREE✝

"But these are written, that ye might believe
that Jesus is the Christ, the Son of God;
and that believing ye might have life through his name."
John 20:31

"Ken-ai-te, wait until you hear what I've found out!" Mandy's eyes were sparkling with joy as she plopped down beside him on the log in front of the fire circle. He smiled at her but kept eating his stew.

"Put that down! You won't believe this. I can hardly believe it myself." Mandy looked over at Sleeping Bird whose face was glowing in the twilight. The warrior did as told but he didn't look too happy about it. She'd better talk fast to drown out the grumbling of his stomach!

"The journal says my mother was Kiowa! That makes me half Kiowa. Amazing, isn't it? I had no idea because my father never told me. He always said the two of them came from Ohio to begin a ministry to the natives living here in Indian Territory, fell in love with the Kiowa people, and then later my mother died in childbirth. And they believed God sent them here to share Christ with our people. Uh, your people—*my* people! I still can't absorb all this."

Ken-ai-te grinned broadly. "Your God bring you here to your people. He smart!"

She laughed. "Yes, He's very smart. Incredible how He worked it all out, that I would be captured by the very one who had possession of my father's journal all this time. I didn't even know it existed until Mother showed it to me." She smiled again at the older woman. "So you have read the book, have known the secret all along?"

"No, only um, pie-ces, before you come. Saw father's name, made me cur-i-ous after I hear your name. Reason many questions, try to understand. Help me remember English words, but so hard, many not know."

"Why didn't you tell me about this before?"

"Afraid time not right. You not want to be Kiowa for long time. If find out, might throw book away, make much trouble for you. So I keep quiet."

Mandy nodded and sat in silence for a bit. She knew God had prevented her from discovering the truth until she was ready to accept it. Her own stubborn rebellion and disobedience had yielded a crop of mistakes and heartache when He had planned one of beauty and peace. Her eyes closed and she asked for God's forgiveness for all of it and thanked Him for never giving up on her.

The pair quietly waited until she was ready to continue. When she looked up at them after a few moments, both were staring at her. They had respectfully observed her prayers without interruption, though she never intended for something so private to be displayed before others, indeed had not given it a thought. Blushing she took a deep breath and smiled. The two appeared to be waiting on her to finish. Neither said a word.

"Oh, my goodness. You know what I just realized? I don't have to go back with the soldiers when they come to reclaim the white captives, because I'm half Kiowa. That means God made me as much Kiowa as He did white. So I can claim the Kiowa part and stay here!" She threw her arms around Ken-ai-te's neck, almost knocking him off the log.

"I love you, my husband!" she shouted gleefully. As soon as the words were out of her mouth, Mandy regretted them. Would he assume, simply because she called him her husband, that she now also considered them married even without a wedding to confirm it? Reddening even more, she forced herself to calm down and release the embarrassed warrior. Was it the closeness they shared in that brief moment that caused her heart to pound so wildly? Or simply her foolish words? Slowly she added, "Well, my husband-to-be, at least. Our wedding will make it official."

He nodded and picked up his stew again, his own eyes sparkling to match hers. "Eat now?"

"Yes, you may eat now," she laughed. "I was just so excited about this news and couldn't wait to share it with you both." Mandy ladled out her own bowl as she continued. "It seems that my father met my mother here in Indian Territory, fell in love with her, led her to faith in Christ, baptized her and her whole family after they also embraced Him, and then they married. In fact, with a ceremony much like we are planning, where they combined the two cultures into a new one. Wish I knew what it was like exactly. It's sad the details have been lost. But I think I know what I want to include, anyway."

"Mother do right thing, then? Show book now?"

"Yes, Ken-ai-te, Mother did exactly the right thing. And you know what, Mother? I think you are right. If you'd shown it to me much earlier I would never have been able to accept its truth like I can now. Being Kiowa is just who I am and finding out I really *am* Kiowa, or at least half of me is, has just made it that much better. God worked this all out so beautifully, don't you think?"

Sleeping Bird nodded and smiled, patting her hand with great affection. "Ken-ai-te right, your God smart."

The three chatted while they finished up dinner and then Mandy cleaned everything up, the journal forgotten for the moment. Though the winds were stronger than usual and cold seeped into her bones, she decided to go for a walk down by the river. Maybe Ken-ai-te would like to go with her?

He eagerly agreed and they both threw on robes for protection from the increasingly bitter gusts, strolling down the hill in the deepening twilight. Mandy's heart was at peace, for one thing not having to worry about The One Who Shall Not Be Named any more. Life was working out so well and now they had many dreams to share with each other the rest of their lives. She snuggled close to her beloved and held onto his arm tightly, glancing up at him, chin high, so brave and strong—and handsome! Mandy felt abundantly blessed.

While they walked the two chatted about specific plans for the wedding ceremony. But when Mandy brought up the vows Ken-ai-te frowned.

"Not understand that. What these vows?"

"It's a promise, you give your word to me and I do the same to you. And we do it in front of our friends and family, so they will know we mean it. That's all. But it has to come from your heart. From here," and she tapped his chest gently. "You say what you want to promise me for as long as God grants us breath. Our marriage will be forever, you know."

"From now until forever."

"Yes, from now until forever. You know, when I first heard that phrase I was so angry with you. It has taken some getting used to. But when I started using it to explain the idea of eternity to you, it took on a whole new meaning for me. Now it's very special."

They shared with each other for some time as they walked along the riverbanks the traditions of each culture about marriage and discovered many similarities. And the differences were simple ones that presented no problem to either one. Taken all together, the ceremony was shaping up to be a beautiful statement of their heritage as a Kiowa couple while still paying tribute to Mandy's white one, and honoring her schoolgirl dreams of a wedding, too.

A couple of days later the soldiers did, indeed, come to the village. And Mandy stood proudly beside her chosen husband and her mother as Chief Twin Fox explained to them there were no white captives here in this camp. They were all Kiowa. One of the younger men with the Army unit eyed Mandy closely so she kept her gaze lowered most of the time. Though her eyes were dark like her Kiowa brothers and sisters, she was fearful he might see some flicker in them to indicate there was more to the truth than she would admit. But dressed like the others and with her hair braided and feathers adorning one side of her face, Mandy looked the part of Prayer Woman, Kiowa Medicine Woman and wife of Ken-ai-te, the brave Kiowa warrior.

Yet, when the men rode away, Mandy breathed a sigh of relief. She felt no guilt about not admitting to her white heritage and so believed that meant God had blessed her choice to remain with Ken-ai-te. It was just good to have that behind her, to let go of one more thing from her past and to do it with no regrets this time. Only one thing troubled her and it finally came to a head one night a short time later while Mandy and Ken-ai-te were talking about salvation again.

"Ken-ai-te, you are making more out of it than it needs to be. It's really very simple. You believe that Jesus died on the Cross, right?"

He nodded.

"And you believe He loves you, right?"

Again, the nod.

"Well, do you also believe He rose on Easter, as the Bible says happened?"

Here, he hesitated.

"You do, don't you?"

"Hard to believe man dead, then alive. Not understand."

"Well, truthfully, I don't understand it, either. But I believe it all the same."

"You believe but not understand?"

"We're not supposed to understand everything until we get to Heaven, silly! That's why it's called trust. We have faith God has told us the truth in His Word, trust He won't lie to us, and then we simply believe."

He didn't reply. Mandy was getting a little frustrated with him. If he said he believed, then why couldn't he take the next step and pray what he believed? When he still didn't say anything, Mandy decided not to let it go as she usually did when they got to this point. It was time to confront him, once and for all. No more delaying or stalling. They were being married in a few weeks now and he still wasn't a Christian. That certainly wouldn't work!

"You have to do this, Ken-ai-te. Just pray and receive Christ." She stopped at the look on his face, a combination of confusion and irritation. "Now what's wrong?"

"Not know 'receive.' What mean?"

"I've told you before, you receive God's Spirit into your heart because of what Jesus did for you on Calvary, on the Cross. In other words, you believe. Nothing more, nothing less. You give Him power over your mind and heart, promise to allow Him to rule your decisions and listen to His wisdom. And you accept what He did on Easter morning by coming alive again by God's power. What more is there to know? Why are you putting this off?"

"You say must feel in heart, right?"

She nodded.

"But if not feel, why pray?"

"If you believe, then why don't you feel it? I don't understand this!" Her voice rose a bit and a dark frown crossed over Ken-ai-te's face. She licked her lips nervously. Had she pushed him too hard? Or did he need someone to do precisely that?

"Not want to talk more now," he said quietly. "Go to circle. Snows come tonight. Put hides around inside of tipi. Dirt already around outside of tipi, keep snows out and tipi warm."

"Mother showed me how to do that and yes, I will take care of it before I go to sleep. But please don't leave right now. Stay with me a little longer and let's talk this out."

But he rose and left without another sound. Was he angry with her or perhaps battling something he didn't quite know how to express? The devil could be cunning with salvation at stake, she knew, preventing people from coming to Christ simply because their minds were working overtime trying to figure out every little detail. Or maybe Mandy trusted too easily? Perhaps she needed to think things through more carefully herself.

After a moment, she said, "No, I don't trust too easily. He just doesn't know how to trust at all, is the problem. He's a Kiowa warrior. What do I expect? He might respect You, God, but I'm not sure if he is ready to love You yet. I think he will but it may take quite a bit more time. The problem is, I don't want to marry him when he's not saved, Lord!

"Please help him to make this decision without any more procrastination. Forgive my impatience. Help me keep my mouth shut when I should, speak up when I ought to, and listen for Your wisdom. I know You died for him as much as for me and I claim him for You from now until forever. Don't let the enemy snatch him away!"

†CHAPTER FORTY-FOUR†

"For the kingdom of God is not in word, but in power."
I Corinthians 4:20

"**K**en-ai-te, as I was saying last night, you really are making more out of it than needs to be. It is just so simple. I don't understand what the problem is."

He stared intensely at her but instead of his gaze melting her heart as it usually did, she grew more irritated by the moment. *He's just being plain stubborn! Although he knows the truth, he won't admit it. There's no excuse for this childish behavior.*

When he still said nothing, Mandy stomped out of the tipi. She'd had enough of his stalling and delays. If he wouldn't give in and accept Christ, she wouldn't marry him, that's all there is to it!

"Then I'll bet you'll do it," she muttered to herself.

The nagging voice became a thunderous one, and not of approval. Tears sprang up and she blinked them back.

"Oh, God, what am I doing? I'm trying to force him to believe in You. And I can't do that. It's got to come from Your Spirit, not from me. Even if he said the words right now, I'd never know for certain if it was a genuine decision or not. Stop me! This is all wrong and somehow I've got to get things back on track here." She continued murmuring to herself as she puttered around the campfire, poking at the embers with a long stick absentmindedly and mentally berating herself for going about this in the worst possible manner. "I know better!" she exclaimed to no one in particular.

"Know what?" It was Sleeping Bird and she had walked up so quietly Mandy never heard her, as preoccupied as she was. Mandy jumped backward and nearly stumbled over the cooking pot sitting on the ground.

"Oh, I didn't hear you, Mother. I'm sorry; my mind is full this morning. I think there are still a few pieces of roasted squirrel we didn't eat, if you are hungry."

"No, have eaten. Look angry."

"Well, I am, but it's a bit hard to explain. I'm frustrated with Ken-ai-te. Do you suppose that means I don't love him enough to be his wife?"

"No, mean you woman, he man!"

"Yes, I suppose it does. I didn't want to quarrel with him. Things are a little tense at times between us. I suppose that's normal when you are about to be married, is that right?"

"Normal all time for Kiowa. Not for whites?"

Mandy smiled. She felt better for having gotten it out. But now she had to go apologize to Ken-ai-te.

"Yes, for whites, too, Mother. But I need to talk to Ken-ai-te."

"I go for water," and she gestured to the skin in her hand. Then she walked away.

Taking a deep breath, Mandy dipped down to enter the tipi and saw Ken-ai-te sitting there cross-legged on his robe. He fingered the tip of one arrow as though checking it for sharpness but didn't look at her.

"Ken-ai-te, I need to apologize to you." Mandy sat down next to him but he still didn't look up. "I'm sorry for what I said. I was frustrated but it's not right to expect you to feel something you obviously do not. And you are right, you shouldn't say the words of the prayer to ask Christ into your life if you don't 'feel' it first. You can understand it with your mind and still not feel it in your heart. Will you accept my apology, forgive me for upsetting you and causing a quarrel?"

344

He glanced at her, his face an imperceptible mask and said nothing, then looked back at his arrow. Her heart skipped a beat. What if he didn't forgive her? She waited in silence, almost afraid to breathe.

"Prayer Woman, you speak many words, not always wise ones." He held up his hand in front of her face when she opened her mouth to respond, and she shut her mouth and remained silent. "Need listen more, talk less. Kiowa woman let husband speak, obey and not argue. You Kiowa now. No more talk!"

And he got up and left the tipi in a huff before she could react. Mandy was stunned.

"What just happened here, God? I was only trying to do the right thing and apologize to him. But all he wanted to do is lecture me about 'the Kiowa way.' Well, I think I understand that better than most, having it stuffed down my throat all this time. The idea of insulting me like that! I love that man, Lord, but if he doesn't stop with this arrogant attitude of his I'm not sure if I want to marry him or not."

The day went downhill from there. Sleeping Bird quickly noticed the two weren't speaking of course but didn't seem at all surprised. Ken-ai-te stayed away from Mandy for the most part and she noticed how his jaw worked constantly whenever he was around her. And she had learned the hard way that meant something troubled him. She suffered in silence and seethed with anger the entire morning.

You can forget planning a wedding with me, you beast! To treat me like that is inexcusable. I suggest you figure out a way to apologize before things get out of hand between us. I've done all the apologizing I intend to do.

That evening sunset seemed to come earlier than usual Mandy noticed as she began to prepare her stew for the meal. She huddled under a heavy robe and pulled it closer around her neck for protection. Suddenly a strong blast of very cold air hit the village and caught her by surprise, taking her breath away with its intensity. Moments later, Sleeping Bird rushed up.

"Mother," she uttered between chattering teeth, "I think this is going to bring more than the light dusting of snow we got last night, isn't it? Looks to be a bad one from those heavy clouds. I can't believe how cold it got, and so rapidly."

Sleeping Bird nodded, both of them scurrying around as they gathered everything up and stashed it all in the tipi. It never ceased to amaze Mandy how much stuff there seemed to be scattered around outside the campsite whenever it was urgent to get it all inside.

"Thanks," she said as she lighted the fire in the cold tipi. "I never could have done that all by myself before it blew away. Do you want to stay with us to eat?"

"Go to own tipi now. Have plenty to eat, hot fire waiting, many robes to stay warm, keep cold out of tipi. You have husband now, no need for so many hides."

Even her own mother believed they were sleeping together, no matter how many times she had clarified this for the older woman! She had told her repeatedly that her God would not permit it and that was why they were having a ceremony to mark their marriage. And that they were *not* sharing the same blanket until then! Her irritation grew at her mother as well and had flown all out of proportion at Ken-ai-te by the time he came back to the tipi that night.

Great, now we're in the throes of a huge snowstorm and I have to take shelter with him *for who knows how long? If we don't kill each other first, this should be a 'fun' time!*

Mandy went through the motions by ladling up his stew for him and caught her breath slightly when their hands touched briefly as she passed it to him. Averting her gaze, she avoided eye contact with him on purpose and hoped he wasn't staring at her. It appeared it would be a long night.

No matter how big Mandy built the fire that evening, it seemed the cold surged stronger than the heat generated from the flames. She had piled up some robes around the edges inside the tipi and knew

Ken-ai-te had pushed dirt against it from the outside, all in an effort to keep the snow and bitter air from seeping in so readily but it simply wasn't enough. The tipi had been designed to hold an entire extended family, not just two angry people!

She shivered through dinner, grateful for the warm stew as it slid down her throat and into her stomach. But there it lay like a large cactus plant, prickling at her from the inside instead of relaxing her as it usually did. Pulling on yet another hide, she glanced sideways at the Kiowa warrior. He hadn't said a word since entering the tipi and neither had she. She had certainly *thought* plenty but refused to be the first one to break the silence.

Mandy tried to concentrate on her sewing after clearing away the few dishes they'd used but it was no use. Her anger had reached the overwhelming point. Even her fingers felt clumsy from the cold. Sleep would never be an option like this, yet what else could they do when cooped up in the tipi like they were with a snowstorm raging outside?

The obvious answer caused her to blush, but she forced it from her mind right away. *Never in a million years! Even if we were married, I wouldn't let him touch me with an attitude like that. To not accept my apology! Imagine the gall of that man...*

She snuggled under her coverings and sat there with her knees drawn up to her chin and finally rested her head on them, listening to the wailing of the storm outside. No doubt she needed to pray. But why was it always her place to pray things through? *That's exactly the problem, Lord! He doesn't believe in You so he's not about to bring his problems to You for help. I'm the only one who can do this and I'm getting tired of carrying the load on my own.*

It occurred to her this was probably how a marriage between a Believer and a non-Believer worked all the time, with only one partner having to do all the praying through problems, then all the forgiving and reaching out, then all the making up. That was too much to expect one person to have to do. *And precisely Your point, isn't it, Father?*

You didn't design marriage to be that way but for it to be an equal partnership. Except when people get in the way of His perfect plan and mess it all up. Like they always seem to do.

That's what I've done so many times over these last months, isn't it? I could have spared myself so much heartache if I'd only paid attention to You more and not pushed my own needs so much. As Ken-ai-te said—listen more and talk less. But how can he be right when I am the Christian? Reluctantly, she had to admit that maybe it was because he'd been listening to her words and she hadn't!

Mandy fell on her face before the Lord and poured out her repentance before Him, pulling the coverings over her head. She didn't care whether Ken-ai-te saw or understood or not, just knew she had to do this to express her deep remorse. Sobs choked her until the tears would no longer come.

Softly and under the robes so as not to disturb Ken-ai-te, Mandy then confessed her sins. Her pride, arrogance, stubbornness, rebellion, vanity, selfishness, and childish behavior—everything the Spirit pointed out to her in those intensely private moments.

"None of this has been uplifting of You, and for that I am most heartily sorry. I've demanded my own way when I should have waited on You, as with the tipi. And failed to recognize the many ways You protected me through all the months past, mostly because I was so angry with You for bringing me here in the first place. Forgive me, Father, and restore me to fellowship with Your Son so I might continue to serve You in this darkness."

Mandy remained alone with the Lord for some time, refreshing herself in the waters of forgiveness and restoration, which He abundantly showered on her that evening. Surprisingly, she felt the warmth of His love flood her entire being as she did so, rather than the numbing cold whose icy fingers tried to grip her body. When her eyelids became heavy she finally ventured out from under the hides, curious to see what the warrior had been doing all this time. What she saw shocked her. Ken-ai-te was still sitting there by the fire, one robe around him for warmth, and staring into the barely pink and dying embers of the fire.

"Ken-ai-te!" she shouted without thinking. "You can't let the fire go out. We'll freeze to death if you do!" She scooted over there and pulled several more pieces of tinder out of the stack behind her and shoved them into the glowing ashes. The flames licked higher after a few moments and finally took hold, so Mandy added more fuel to the fire before sitting back on her heels to bask in the warmth. He hadn't moved a muscle, acted as though he were deaf against her frantic cry to save the fire, didn't even react to the sparks and crackles as the heat spread—thoroughly lost in his own world.

The thought crossed her mind to scramble back under the robes before she got too cold when suddenly, Ken-ai-te reached out and grabbed her by the arm, pulling her up close to him in a firm hold. She gasped, partly due to the unexpected closeness they were sharing and partly due to her concern about the reason behind his action. Their unwritten rule was being violated and it scared her. What might come next?

Mandy was a little off balance and squirmed in his grasp in order to settle herself beside him more securely. Apparently, he thought she was trying to get away because he roughly jerked her into place next to him. Now the look on his face *really* scared her.

She hadn't been this frightened of him since that night shortly after she had come here when she awoke and found him on top of her. He claimed she'd been having a nightmare and he was only trying to calm her. She hadn't believed him at the time of course but later, when the nightmare awakened her another time, she saw the truth of his words for herself. So when she questioned him recently about it, she was more inclined to believe him by then. But what was he trying to do now?

Ken-ai-te glared at her without a word for several seconds. What was he waiting for? Conviction pricked again at Mandy's heart about her recent attitude and she took a deep breath. Perhaps for her to say something first?

"Ken-ai-te, I'm sorry for the way I've acted. You are right, I need to listen to you more and talk less. God has shown me this wisdom tonight from your words. Can you forgive me? Please, let's not go to sleep angry with each other."

"Not want to sleep." The shadows on his face didn't hide his clear meaning. Mandy's heart almost stopped. But, they'd agreed, not before they were married! His stare never left her eyes. She licked her lips nervously. What was she supposed to say now? *God, help me!*

She lowered her eyes dutifully, then glanced up. Softly she answered, "I know, I don't want to, either. But we must. Just a few more days is all I ask."

"Kiowa way, now."

"I realize that," she said, swallowing a huge lump in her throat. "But it's not the white man's way when he follows God's teachings."

"Not white."

She gulped again. Was she getting through to him at all? Or was he deliberately trying to be contrary?

"I know. But I am—or at least I am *half*-white. And I am totally a Christian and that is the reason I cannot do this evil thing with you now."

"'Evil thing'?"

"Well, the um, *thing* is not evil, that is, the act was created by God Himself so it can't be evil. But it is to be shared only between a husband and wife and doing it any other way for any other reason is evil and wrong. It is sin. And we are not to sin."

"But you sin?"

"Yes, Ken-ai-te, I do sin sometimes. I have to admit that. I sinned earlier when I pushed you to accept Jesus and made it seem you were making a wrong choice by waiting. Holding off was the right decision for you at that time. And while I do pray, eventually, you will know in your heart when it is time, this is not it. God will tell you and until then, you need to wait. I sinned by pushing you and by not respecting you. I'm sorry for that and hope you can forgive me.

"But just because I sin sometimes is no reason to require this sin of me now. You and I both know I cannot stop you if this is what you want. So it will have to be your decision." She was shaking visibly and grateful she wasn't on her feet, else she would have fallen down for sure. Could he feel her trembling, as close as they were to each other? Everything depended on what he would say!

"I hope you can respect me, Ken-ai-te, as you have all this time, and not force me. What is your answer?"

⸶CHAPTER FORTY-FIVE⸶

"My times are in thy hand:
deliver me from the hand of mine enemies,
and from them that persecute me."
Psalm 31:15

"Your answer?"

Mandy waited, her heart throbbing in her ears. What would Ken-ai-te say? At last, he cleared his throat and nodded.

"Not want to make sin. Honor your God. Stay on robe tonight. But soon ..."

Relief washed over her until she was almost giddy. *Thank You, Jesus!*

"Does this also mean you forgive me for not being patient earlier? I really didn't mean to upset you and I truly am sorry."

"Me, not you. No more waiting, o-kay? Not mean to be an-gry."

"I understand. The tension is strong and I will be glad when this wait is over, too. In fact, why don't we do the ceremony day after tomorrow? I have everything we will need just about ready. What about you? Do you want to get married in two days?" She held up two fingers and he smiled.

He pulled her close and hugged her so tight she could barely breathe. When he leaned down to kiss her, she smiled and put her fingers up to his lips once more, then touched her own with them and he released her, apparently satisfied with the symbolism instead of the actual kiss. Again, he cleared his throat and the thought crossed

Mandy's mind that he had been having quite a bit of trouble lately with that odd "cough"—could holding her move him that much? The thought thrilled her!

When Mandy settled down for the night a short time later and lay staring through the shadows at her beloved, she had much to praise God for before sleep came. Once more His protection had been divine, His intervention profound. She couldn't wait for their wedding and the excitement almost crowded out her drowsiness. Almost...

The next day Mandy waded through the deep snowdrifts to Sleeping Bird's tipi, her breath crystallizing with each puff. The cold air stunned her with its intensity, for the warm tipi had spoiled her. With the white blanket covering everything in sight, the whole world seemed to be fresh and pure, without blemish or stain.

She giggled watching two dogs struggling to move, getting lost in the snowbanks until appearing again as they leapt into the air, then repeated their antics several times in order to move from one place to another in the camp. Mandy called to the older woman as she approached the tipi and was given permission to enter.

"Good morning, my mother. Were you warm enough last night? It is cold out there!"

"I am well, my daughter. The fire burned hot and I kept it going all night so I was warm under my buffalo robe and I had several other hides on my bed as well. What about you?"

"Before you go thinking anything else, I need to remind you that Ken-ai-te and I are not yet husband and wife and thus are not sleeping together. Yesterday you sounded like you thought otherwise. It is important to me that you, at least, understand. No one else around here does but I do hope you can."

She nodded and smiled. A victory of sorts? Mandy hoped so.

"Um, to answer your question, we were fine last night from the cold. Today I need help with my sewing so I can finish things up quickly for the wedding. Earlier Ken-ai-te and I agreed to hold it tomorrow morning."

Sleeping Bird's head jerked up at this and a broad grin came over her face. "Tomorrow?"

"Yes. It is time. And another thing—I would like permission from you to sleep here with you tonight. I—I have much to do yet and need your help." But she blushed as she spoke and averted her eyes momentarily. In truth, she had an ulterior motive. She looked up with a deep sigh.

"To be honest with you, it has become quite difficult for us to sleep across the tipi from each other. And I know tonight will be even worse. It is not something I can discuss easily with Ken-ai-te."

She wasn't certain how long her own resolve could hold out with both in the same tipi, let alone trust his! And needing to finish her preparations for the wedding would provide her with the perfect excuse to bed down in the tipi with her mother that night. Would she understand the meaning behind her request?

Sleeping Bird quickly agreed, to Mandy's great relief, and the ladies went directly to their sewing tasks without further discussion. When Mandy had finished all the hides for the new tipi, she inquired about the poles.

"Use same ones," the older woman responded. Perfect solution!

Later in the morning, the two emerged from the tipi to fetch water and scout out some more wood for both fires and were shocked to be greeted by the sun! As cold as it had been that morning and the night before, it had certainly warmed up quickly. Much of the snow was melting rapidly and tiny rivulets of sparkling clear water ran down the sides of the tipis in small waterfalls, often taking with them large chunks of snow that smashed into millions of pieces upon hitting the ground. Before long, the camp was awash in mud and Mandy wished once again for the pristine beauty of the snow. Such was the weather here on the prairie, changing too quickly to keep up with it!

After the basic chores had been completed and they had eaten the midday meal, Mandy sat down with her mother to finish work on one small hide. Her intention was to paint a message to her new husband on it, to become a part of the covering for their tipi. She knew what she wanted to say but not how to say it in Kiowa signs. Sleeping Bird showed her how to fray the ends of a cottonwood stick to make a paintbrush; how to make various colors of paints from an array of materials gathered a few days earlier—crushed berries, pussy willow buds, algae from a stagnant pond, and even lichens scraped off rocks; and finally how to form the complicated symbols required for the words. When completed, Mandy took a step back and admired her hard work.

"I hope Ken-ai-te is happy with this message I have painted for our new home. Do you think we can keep it a surprise until we set up our tipi tomorrow after the wedding ceremony? Sleeping Bird nodded. Mandy couldn't wait to see her husband's face!

While fixing the evening meal, Mandy made a decision about something she'd been debating with herself about all day. An urgency arose from deep within, to do it now.

"Mother, I would like to share with you what has been on my heart this day." Mandy surprised herself by saying all this in perfect Kiowa. The older woman's face registered the same emotion and she smiled at her.

"What is that, Prayer Woman?"

Switching to English, she continued. "I have decided what I want to say for my vows to Ken-ai-te, Mother. Would you like to hear them? I know you will hear the words when we say them to each other during the wedding, but I'd like to share them with you ahead of time if that would please you."

"It would please me very much, my daughter. What will you say in this vow?"

"You know, your English is getting very good! You must have been studying the journal again!"

She blushed slightly, confirming the truth for Mandy. Sleeping Bird had asked a couple of days before if she could borrow the book again, to try reading more of the words, and of course, Mandy had agreed. No more secrets between these two!

Mandy had worked for the past several days to get the words just right and that morning in her prayer time asked God's approval of them as well. Now, she prayed that somehow the Lord would use them to make an impression spiritually on this woman who had become so dear to her heart. She took a deep breath and began.

"I, *daw-t'sai-mah*, Prayer Woman, do take you, Ken-ai-te, as my husband for all eternity. I promise to love, honor, and obey you as long as I live. All I have is yours—all of my heart, all of my love, all of my possessions, and all of my dreams, I freely give to you now. My gratitude to the Great Spirit of God is deep for His plan to bring me here to live with you, and I honor you for hearing His voice guiding you to protect me, respect me, and teach me the Kiowa ways. You are my defender and friend, my brave and strong warrior, and I cherish your love for me. How blessed I am you have chosen me, and I now willingly choose you.

"As we blend our two cultures together in this ceremony and our lives in this marriage, my prayer for our future is, with God's help, a long life filled with joy, courage in our tears, many children in our tipi, and love and peace beyond measure. My parents gave me the middle name of *Soun*, which in Kiowa means Wild Grass, hoping I would grow up on the prairie where I was born and learn the Kiowa ways along with my white heritage. Today, I lovingly embrace that dream of living here as Amanda 'Mandy' Soun Clark among the Kiowa people my parents loved so much, but also promise to keep my Kiowa name of Prayer Woman, given to me by you, my husband. Now I truly *do* belong to you, Ken-ai-te, from now until forever!"

When she finished, she glanced up at Sleeping Bird and was startled to see tears streaming down her face. Yet, she had a broad smile on her lips, and framed by her white braids, it created a beautiful sight to behold even as she brushed them away quickly. *Please, God, bring her to know You someday soon!*

About then Ken-ai-te came up with a pleased grin on his face as well. He greeted them both tenderly and sat down to wait for dinner. Mandy's mind suddenly jumped to what it would be like to fix dinner for her husband at their own fire circle every night for the rest of her life. And her heart soared with joy—she couldn't wait until the wedding had taken place and they were finally living together as husband and wife!

Pulling herself back to the present from her dreams of the future, she realized there were still a few details they hadn't worked out about the events for the next day.

"Ken-ai-te, could we talk about the ceremony for a few minutes while I'm finishing up the meal?"

He nodded but frowned. "Not done?"

She wasn't sure if he meant the stew or the plans at first, then realized he was referring to the wedding.

"Well, we talked about having Mother walk me in while you wait at the camp circle for me with the chief. Is he okay with his part in this? Or did you have a chance to speak with him about it yet?" Not only he but also the entire village would be playing an important role in the ceremony the next day and she wanted to ensure they all knew this.

He nodded. At least that was taken care of. It would be interesting to hear Chief Twin Fox's blessing of the couple and Mandy hoped she would be able to understand it since it was to be entirely in Kiowa.

"After the blessing I'm going to read one verse out of my Bible, in English. I think I have it memorized but imagine I will be too nervous tomorrow to trust my memory so will read it. Do you want to hear it now?"

Again the nod.

"It is Psalm 130:5 and says, 'I wait for the LORD, my soul doth wait, and in his word do I hope.' I love this verse. This was my father's favorite and now is mine. It took some time for God to teach me how to love being a Kiowa, and while I waited, I trusted in His Word and put my hope in Him. Then of course, I also had to wait to fall in love with you until God could change my heart. And yours."

"No more wait. Past is gone, future ahead."

"Oh, Ken-ai-te, that's lovely! You are so right; the past is behind us while our future stretches out before us. Nothing can stop us now! Anyway, after the verse we will exchange our gifts for each other. I can't wait for you to see mine!" With a mischievous grin she teased, "What did you make me?"

"No, tomorrow. You wait."

"Okay, I'll wait, one more day. But no longer!" And she blushed as he flashed white teeth at her from his handsome copper face and giggles erupted from her lips.

"Anyway, changing the subject here a bit—after our gifts, we will do our vows. Have you decided what you will say to me?"

He frowned and shook his head.

"Oh, Ken-ai-te, don't tell me you still don't know what you want to say to me! I've written mine, even shared them with Mother a short time ago. I promise you, they will be special! And I expect 'special' from you as well so you'd better get going. By the way, I'm sleeping in Mother's tipi tonight as I have some more work to do on my gift for you and I need her help. Besides, according to my people's tradition, the groom isn't supposed to see the bride on her wedding day until the ceremony!"

She could tell he didn't fully understand all of that but got the gist of most of it. Especially the part about not joining him in their tipi that night. To her relief he didn't protest.

"Back to the ceremony," she said as she began taking up the stew in their bowls. It smelled heavenly and she was excited to have fresh rabbit this night instead of dried buffalo meat. Ken-ai-te had brought it to her earlier in the day already skinned and ready to be cut up for the cooking pot. She was grateful she hadn't needed to do the skinning.

"Once the vows have been exchanged—that is, each of us has spoken them to the other—the chief will pronounce us husband and wife. And I have a song I want to sing to you in Kiowa, provided I can manage to get it right and not mangle the pronunciations! I've been practicing with Mother's help but I'm also going to sing it in English. Don't worry, it's only one verse and I really do have a pretty good voice, you know."

He smiled, a puzzled look on his face. "It's a special song about God's love that we used to sing in our church called 'Amazing Grace' and I learned it years ago in Kiowa. So it is important to me that we have it as part of the ceremony. And this will be followed by the chant for good fortune, which the elders will do with the drums, and then we can all do the Joy Dance afterward. I think this will be just perfect, Ken-ai-te. What do you think?"

He smiled and caught her to him in a warm embrace. "Wed-ding fine, if you happy. After make me happy!" And she blushed. She seemed to be doing a lot of that lately.

Shortly after clearing away the dishes, Mandy bid Ken-ai-te a tender and emotional goodnight and headed toward Sleeping Bird's tipi. Against the early twilight sky, she spotted several figures sitting up on the ridge above the camp, and she gasped. It was a group of Indians, maybe ten or fifteen of them, but they were too far away and in too faint of a light to see their faces. Comanche, perhaps? Or maybe a Cheyenne hunting party? Yes, that's what it must be. Comanche would have already attacked before anyone in the village had a chance to sound the alarm.

Mandy started to look away but something about one of the figures caught her eye, framed as he was against the setting sun, something terrifyingly familiar. Her blood froze and not because of the chill in the night air. She squinted her eyes, trying to get a better look at the warrior's face. It looked just like The One Who Shall Not Be Named!

"No! It can't be, not with the wedding tomorrow morning! Surely, he would not be so foolish as to come back here after being banished. God, please don't let him make good on his threats against us!"

†CHAPTER FORTY-SIX†

"Two are better than one...for if they fall,
the one will lift up his fellow...
and if one prevail against him, two shall withstand him;
and a threefold cord is not quickly broken."
Ecclesiastes 4:9-12

"Could I have been seeing things? No, I'm sure they were there a few moments ago!"

Mandy felt a little foolish for having alarmed her mother like she did, apparently all for nothing. *I know they were real! My nerves may be on edge because of the wedding in the morning but I know what I saw.*

Sleeping Bird's eyes scoured the horizon, as did Mandy's again but neither saw any sign of warriors up on the plateau above the village or anywhere else, only the rising moon against the twilight sky.

"I tell you, they were there! And the One Who Shall Not Be Named was among them, Mother."

"Best to tell Ken-ai-te. Will know what to do."

After explaining it all to him, he assured her sentries would be posted around the outskirts of the village that night, just to be safe.

"No worry, Prayer Woman. Men protect village, you sleep. Ceremony tomorrow."

"I don't want others in danger because of his vengeance against me. Especially this night." She smiled at him and hoped he didn't think this was a ruse to get one more hug out of him before they each returned to their tipis.

Mandy wasn't disappointed as he pulled her to him lovingly. She snuggled against his chest and took such comfort from the smell and touch of his body next to hers, wondering how on earth she could have ever considered him brutal or an enemy bent on destroying her. That is what love does, she knew. It changes your perspective until there is nothing left but the emotion to rule over your head. Well, it was certainly having its way with her!

Long after everyone had settled back into their tipis, the security that came from knowing her beloved was on the alert allowed her to spend the remaining time in comfort. It also resonated with her that he had not brushed off her warning as merely the wild imaginings of a skittish bride, but took her seriously. However, now she found it even harder to get her mind off her future husband and onto finishing up the bear claw necklace she was making for her gift to him. She had traded a pair of moccasins to Yellow Eagle's wife for the bear claws that had been given to him by his father many years before, and over the last several days had worked to put this necklace together, all while keeping it a secret from Ken-ai-te.

He had one she had crafted for him months ago but it was much smaller and made out of tiny bones and beads, a poor first attempt on her part to make something for her captor. Surprising to her, he had worn it every day and didn't seem to mind its childish form. Quite honestly, her heart hadn't been in it back then, certainly not as it had in making this one. She felt deep satisfaction in it and hoped he would wear it with honor. Sleeping Bird guided her in the last few stitches to hold it together and form a loop at the back so he could easily slip the hook through it to fasten around his neck.

"It's finally done! I'm rather proud of this, you know?"

Sleeping Bird nodded and smiled.

Mandy knew she had a right to take pride in her efforts; she had learned so much since coming to live with the Kiowa. But she hoped

God would never let her become arrogant about it as she had in the past with other accomplishments. Her genuine desire was to remain humble.

Right now, my greatest need is to get some sleep!

Sleeping Bird took the dress Mandy would wear the next day out of its hiding place in the back of her tipi and spread it out over the top of some hides she had stored away. Mandy's eyes misted over as she looked at it and considered its significance. It was pure white deerskin decorated with yellow and blue beading to symbolize the rising sun on this special day, with fringes down the arms and across the bottom hem. She had made this, too, and hoped fervently that her new husband would see the beauty in her eyes because of God's love more than the beauty of her body wearing the dress. Oh, how she prayed he would come to love God the same way she did!

Sometime later Mandy spent a few minutes reading in the Bible as she struggled to focus on the words. Her excitement about the next day versus the need for rest battled in a mighty way, pulling her between. Pushing its way forward, though, a new thought demanded priority.

Given that she had caused so much heartache over disobedience in recent weeks, how could she in all good conscience take yet another step on that same wicked path of rebellion by marrying a man who refused to serve God? It gnawed at her like a rat nibbling on its prey. The words swam before her eyes and she finally closed her Bible to let sleep surround her. But it didn't work. And the longer she lay there, the more upset she became.

God, show me what You want me to do! I'm so confused. I thought Your plan was for me to marry Ken-ai-te, but he hasn't grown any closer to making a decision to accept Your gift of salvation. What am I to do? I can't refuse to marry him, yet how can I do so? She pulled the robe over her head and gave way to her tears. A soft rustling sound suddenly alerted her ears. Had her cries awakened her mother?

Peeking out, she was startled to see a tiny pinpoint of light centered on a drawing of the sun on the wall of the tipi. Blinking, she rubbed her eyes. Must be her imagination. But instead of going away, it grew steadily in size. Mandy bolted upright. What would Sleeping Bird think if she happened to open her eyes? But she hadn't stirred.

Mandy peered through the shadows as the mysterious light hovered until it covered the whole wall and a figure formed in the center. Were those *wings* fluttering behind it—or him? Mandy held her breath in fear. Then a quiet voice spoke softly.

"Mandy, wait on the Father's time for Ken-ai-te to bow his knee. God will bless you for your obedience. Have no fear!" As suddenly as the angel—or whatever—came, he disappeared. Mandy sat there breathless, uncertain of what had just happened.

She recalled a verse out of Psalms about waiting on the Lord. These words echoed that verse, yet they were spoken directly to her! Shaking her head to clear her thoughts, Mandy knew that regardless, God's message was clear. Her fear faded like a morning mist as peace filled her heart. He had sent an angel to speak to her and she must listen and obey!

He said to wait on His timing, that my obedience matters more than anything else. Ken-ai-te is the Lord's provision to me. Who am I to question God Himself? All her confusion fled and a deep sleep encompassed her, once again under the warm robe where she awaited the joy of the next morning, now free of doubts and with a calm heart ready to embrace fully what the Father had so lovingly provided in this special man.

The next morning dawned much different from the one before it. While still cold, it was clear and fresh with no new snow on the ground. Most of the deeper drifts had melted and the sunshine had dried up many of the mud holes, though not all of them. She would need to be careful where she stepped or risk ruining her new moccasins, made by Sleeping Bird as her gift to the new bride for this special ceremony.

The two women rushed through a quick breakfast of pemmican, not wanting to take the time to cook anything. Mandy dressed quickly and Sleeping Bird braided her hair, carefully working into the strands a number of small white eagle down feathers to frame her face. She wished for a mirror briefly, then let that go as something from the past, which was no longer necessary in her life. The only beauty she wanted today was that of God's blessing on her marriage to Ken-ai-te.

At the thought of his name, her knees went weak! Would her mother and father have approved of her choice for a husband? She had little doubt of that. He was handsome and wealthy by Kiowa standards, but most importantly, he loved her and would be good to her. Mandy was relieved she didn't have to dread her marriage bed that night, wondering if he would be gentle and kind or harsh and brutal. Much praise went up for the fact that the Lord had protected her chastity through all these months of captivity, so she might present herself pure to her husband. She also praised God for giving her such an honorable man and blessing her with her new Kiowa heritage and family.

Her mother had swiftly dressed while Mandy did, choosing her newest dress and moccasins for the occasion. The final touch was to fasten to her waistband an eagle fan made for her by Running Elk when she became his wife. Though old, it carried great sentiment for both women, helping to bridge the gap between past generations of Kiowa and of those yet to come.

And then, it was time for the ceremony to begin. Mandy heard the drums calling everyone to the circle to witness the special event. She had never felt such happiness or such excitement at one moment in her entire life! Sleeping Bird left the tipi and before following her, she closed her eyes and prayed one last time as Mandy Clark.

"Father, I ask that You be lifted up this day with all that is about to happen. Thank You for loving me through this awful ordeal and bringing me to Ken-ai-te's heart. I claim him for You and thank You for giving me the ability to release him into Your care. May all we say and do this day honor You above all else. I love You, Lord! Amen."

When she stepped out of the tipi, blinking against the sudden and brilliant sunlight, Sleeping Bird embraced her tenderly and gently caressed her cheek with a rough and weathered hand.

"Be good to Ken-ai-te, my daughter. He loves you much."

"I shall, believe me. And you will be right there to make sure I do so!" They both laughed as Mandy handed the bear claw necklace wrapped in a soft brown deerskin cloth to her mother. Clutched in both arms lay her precious Bible with a strip of cloth marking the verse she would read in the ceremony.

The drums steadily beat out their rhythm and she dutifully followed her mother to the circle where her new husband awaited her with all their Kiowa family. She noticed on the ground next to Ken-ai-te's feet lay a rabbit skin with the fur turned outward and obviously wrapped around an object of some kind, and Mandy assumed that was her gift from him. Alongside lay his flute, to be played later during the festivities following the ceremony. Things couldn't be more perfect in Mandy's world than at this moment!

As the bride came to her husband's side, the drums stopped abruptly. Chief Twin Fox looked solemn in his war bonnet and finest shirt and leggings. But it was Ken-ai-te who had caught her eye. He had never looked more handsome to her than at this moment! The look in his eyes was kind and love shone out to envelop her with its warm blanket. A moment before she had been shivering from the cold and nerves, but no more. Her beloved stared at her with such adoration, how could she be anxious about anything ever again?

Chief Twin Fox raised his arms over the couple and began intoning in Kiowa words that Mandy had a difficult time comprehending. She didn't care; she wouldn't have traded this for anything. He was saying a blessing over her and Ken-ai-te, and that was enough.

When he finished, Mandy opened her Bible and began in English to read the verse she had chosen on hope, praying in her heart that those who heard would be given wisdom to understand and respond to the Father of all hope. She closed the Bible and exchanged it for the gift her mother had been holding, then handed it to her beloved. Opening the skin carefully, he saw the necklace and held it high for all to see. Murmurs of approval came from all around the couple and Mandy basked in Ken-ai-te's pride, displayed in the grin he sported at his new treasure. He leaned down so she could slip it over his head and flip his braids out from under it. *Thank You, Lord, that he is happy with this gift!*

Then he handed her the object in the rabbit skin and she removed it to reveal a breathtaking eagle fan!

"It's gorgeous! I love it!" she cried in Kiowa, to the delight of not only her husband but also everyone present who shared in her joy. She mouthed her thanks to him and blinked back tears of happiness while Sleeping Bird helped her attach it to her waistband. Now she had one to match the older woman's, and just as special! Mandy scolded herself for giving in to emotion because next were the vows and she *must* have a clear voice in order to share hers with Ken-ai-te. Clearing her throat, she opened her mouth to begin speaking when suddenly someone screamed loudly in Kiowa.

"Look out! They're attacking!"

†CHAPTER FORTY-SEVEN†

"My soul melteth for heaviness:
strengthen thou me according unto thy word."
Psalm 119:28

"Ken-ai-te, it's Black—um, The One Who Shall Not Be Named! And he brings a large group of warriors with him!"

Mandy's screams were echoed on every side by many around her, fearful as they were of this surprise attack. No one was armed. What happened to the sentries who were supposed to be guarding the camp?

Arrows whizzed from every direction at once. Pandemonium reigned all around, with people scurrying for weapons and trying to protect the women and children as best they could.

Mandy grabbed Sleeping Bird's arm and they ran for her tipi since it was closer to them than Ken-ai-te's. They were only a few steps away when Mandy looked up in time to see the leering face of The One Who Shall Not Be Named bearing down on them on his horse. He had an arrow in his bow, aimed directly at Mandy!

Shrieking, she tried to dodge out of the way at the same time that Sleeping Bird deliberately stepped in front of her. The arrow struck with a sickening thud into her mother's abdomen. She collapsed with a soft groan. A gruesome flashback caught Mandy's breath and tore at her heart, recalling in an instant Pete's death so long ago.

"No!" she screamed and scooped the limp body into her arms and slid to the ground with her. At least she was still breathing, though obviously in great pain. Mandy leaned over her in an effort to protect her from further harm and glanced frantically around, trying to find Ken-ai-te in the melee. Noticing that The One Who Shall Not Be Named had galloped off in another direction, she continued to look frantically for her beloved.

"There he is!" she cried. "Oh, he's alive, Lord!"

The bridegroom had managed to get to his tipi and was now armed with his shield and lance at least. But that would only give him one shot at an enemy, then leave him almost defenseless! She had to try to reach his bow and arrows and get them to him.

Kissing her mother gently, she said, "I'll be right back." She jumped to her feet and began weaving between people and tipis in order to reach theirs without anyone seeing her, especially the leader of this heinous attack. A moment later, she slipped into the tipi and grabbed up the bow and arrows, then came back out into the sunlight. The smell of smoke was sharp in her nostrils and she saw at least a couple of tipis on fire. They weren't here to kill her. They came to destroy the entire village because of her! *God, help us!*

Within seconds, she'd made her way to her husband's side and thrust the bow close to Ken-ai-te's hand holding the lance so they could quickly exchange weapons. Then he released the shield into her hands and she helped toss the quiver of arrows over his shoulder in one seamless movement. She used the shield herself to deflect arrows as she'd seen the young boys do in their pretend battles with each other but knew unless she encountered a truly life-or-death moment she would be helpless to use the lance effectively. Her arms weren't strong enough to throw it any distance. As repugnant as the thought was to her, she thought she might be able to shove it into a horse if it came close enough. Better than dying!

Mandy stood her ground next to her husband and they fought valiantly side by side. She couldn't believe how quickly he was able to load an arrow into his bow and let it fly, and then in a strange moment of reflection amid the chaos realized she'd never seen him fight before!

Even when she was taken, he hadn't done anything except raise his lance over his head the first time she ever saw him, apparently to signal the start of the attack. But nothing more.

It seemed they were losing the battle, though. Most of the people had scattered or were dead or lay wounded. The men following The One Who Shall Not Be Named were all around them, everywhere at once, and Mandy was almost overcome by fear they might be killed. Repeatedly she gasped out her plea for intervention from God.

"Help us, Father! Protect us, don't let evil win!"

And surprisingly, little by little she realized the attackers were thinning out. Many of them had also been killed in the battle, in spite of having surprise on their side. The people fought viciously. Even with grave wounds, they never gave up. Men and women alike were grabbing any weapon they could find, sometimes off a dead body, and charging after the invaders. Mandy was sweaty and panting heavily from the effort mixed with fear but managed a quick smile in Ken-ai-te's direction. He nodded then turned his attention back to the task at hand.

Suddenly The One Who Shall Not Be Named reappeared a few feet away, once again riding hard directly toward the two, a fierce look on his ugly face. Mandy could see the war paint in wild colors, which only served to accentuate the hideous scar, not hide it. And perhaps that was the point, to arouse fear in whoever dared to look upon it.

Well, it's working! What is it going to take to kill this devil?

Wild shrieks split the air in spite of the chaos on every side. Mandy caught a word here and there, Kiowa for *revenge* and *destroy* and her stomach curdled at the innocent lives being devastated because of his irrational hatred for her.

Mandy reflexively shrunk back even as Ken-ai-te stepped in front of her for protection, loading his bow and aiming right for the tomahawk-swinging warrior. In the split seconds before Ken-ai-te had a clear shot at him, Mandy tried hoisting the lance into the air but just as quickly realized she hadn't the arm strength to launch it.

God, help me, just as you have so many others throughout history who have needed your help!

And instantly she felt a flash of unexpected strength in the midst of the confusion around her. He seemed to be telling her to hold it steady and He would do the rest, that it was His battle, not hers. She did her best with it and at the same time managed to put the shield between herself and her sworn enemy.

The sharp twang of an arrow sounded above the melee and Mandy saw it embed itself deep in the thigh of the evil warrior. But Ken-ai-te's arrow had not left the bow! From across the clearing the pair spotted Chief Twin Fox holding an empty bow and he nodded.

Oddly, The One Who Shall Not Be Named never cried out in pain, just snarled his lip up even more, if that was possible. His horse suddenly neighed and veered off to one side slightly, stumbling as he did so, and Mandy realized it had changed direction to avoid the lance she still grasped in her hand! Unfortunately, she couldn't hold onto it any longer as it clattered to the ground. It didn't matter. She had done her part and God had done what He promised. Before any of them could react, the pony had thrown the scar-faced warrior off over its head. He rolled over a couple of times to come to rest on the ground right in front of them!

Immediately he jumped up, brandishing his tomahawk with one hand and defiantly breaking the arrow off in his leg with the other. Then he whipped out his knife and advanced slowly on the two. When he lunged in Mandy's direction, she shoved the shield with both hands as hard as she could against the power of his attack. He appeared surprised at her actions and shrieked in anger at her, curling his lip and calling her a name in Kiowa, while she staggered backward a couple of steps, trying not to stumble and fall.

Overcome with fury, Ken-ai-te took full advantage of the momentary distraction to toss down his bow and pull out his knife all in one smooth motion, then jam the blade into the throat of his sworn enemy!

The One Who Shall Not Be Named gurgled and grabbed at his neck with both hands, falling to his knees with a shocked look on his face. Ken-ai-te didn't hesitate one second. He jerked the knife out of the gaping wound and finished the job by slitting the warrior's throat, then shoving him with his foot into the dirt where he died without another sound.

Ken-ai-te pulled the terrified Mandy into his arms lovingly and kissed the top of her head, gently wiping away her tears. They both were panting heavily from the exertion of the battle and Mandy's knees and hands trembled. She glanced up at the scene around them.

Just like that, the battle was over. Or perhaps only a temporary lull? A few of the attackers dotted the scene, easy to spot because they were on horseback, but all turned to flee when they saw their leader die. However, each was chased down by one or more of the defending warriors and quickly killed as well. A cry of victory went up and the battle, indeed, ceased.

The moans of the wounded replaced the sound of war and filled the air on every side of the couple while the stench from several burning tipis swirled around Mandy's nostrils, causing her to cough. People dashed to put out the flames before more were damaged. Soon little remained of the tipis that had been set on fire but smoke and ash. Fortunately, most had been left untouched.

Suddenly Mandy pulled free of her husband's arms.

"Mother! She took an arrow meant for me from him," and she pointed to the body lying at their feet. "We have to help her!"

Mandy rushed to where Sleeping Bird had fallen and found her gasping with shallow breaths but still alive. Her fingers were red with blood as they encircled the arrow shaft in her stomach. Grimacing at the sight, Mandy leaned down and tenderly caressed the beloved weathered face, making no attempt to hold back the tears flowing down her own cheeks. *Oh, God, this just can't be happening! Not to Sleeping Bird, my sweet mother! Please don't take her from me like this!*

✝CHAPTER FORTY-EIGHT✝

"They that sow in tears shall reap in joy."
Psalm 126:5

"Carry her gently, please! She's in such pain."

Mandy's tears flowed but she ignored them as she picked her way through the debris that had been their village a short time before. One of the tipis still standing intact was Sleeping Bird's and the men headed for it without a word, with Ken-ai-te and Mandy close behind. He went on in while she stopped briefly at the fire area outside to pick up a drinking gourd and a skin of water.

When Mandy stepped into the dim light, she saw they had stretched the woman out on her buffalo robe. One of the men somehow managed to break the arrow off halfway. She stared at the shattered end buried in her mother's abdomen and cold chills danced down her arms. To remove it would mean certain death from loss of blood within minutes. To leave it meant a slow and painful death when the wound festered but at least she would live for a few hours.

Rustling through the various poultice materials while trying to remember what she might need to help her, Mandy was gratified her fingers came to rest on just the right things within seconds. She also grabbed several small cloths from a pile nearby and offered one to Ken-ai-te as he knelt beside their mother. He pressed it around the wound and it immediately blossomed bright red. Mandy's heart sank.

She's bleeding too rapidly, even with the shaft still in the wound. What am I going to do? My poultices will reduce her pain but I don't

374

think I have anything that will stop that much blood.

Panic erupted and threatened to overwhelm Mandy when she knelt across from Ken-ai-te, and Sleeping Bird gripped her arm tightly. Mandy could see her jaws clenched to hold in her groans and started to tell her to scream as loudly as she wanted to. Why be brave now, with the village in shambles and her life slipping away with every breath? Certainly, no one would blame her for giving way to her pain! With trembling fingers she placed what she fervently hoped were the right powders and other mixtures into the thin leaf wrapper to make the medicine for her mother. She pressed the poultice around the arrow shaft and into the wound as much as possible, wincing at how much this hurt her beloved Kiowa mother and friend. While she worked, she asked God to use it to ease the woman's discomfort.

I must force myself to think clearly to recall all she has taught me, to be able to minister to her broken body as she has done to so many others in the past. I can't just sit here and watch her suffer while I fall apart! She took a deep breath and closed her eyes.

Father, give me courage and wisdom. Please preserve her life. You know how much she means to me. She doesn't know You. She just can't *die! Help me know what to do to ease her pain as You work to heal her body.*

Peace settled over Mandy like sunlight on a summer day and when she opened her eyes she saw that her mother had also quieted, even relaxing the grip on her forearm. With that wound, she had to be experiencing intense pain, yet she appeared to be merely asleep. Mandy reached out and brushed the wiry grey hair back from the face of her beloved mother, at once relieved it was warm to the touch, yet not feverish, and at least not already turning cold.

In Kiowa, she spoke softly to her.

"Mother, can you hear me?"

Sleeping Bird's eyelids fluttered slightly and Mandy sighed with relief at seeing those precious blue eyes focusing on her.

"Water," she whispered through dry lips. Ken-ai-te poured some water into a gourd and handed it to Mandy. She held it up to her mouth while he attempted to raise her head up just a bit. But the effort brought a groan and the water went untouched as she grimaced in obvious great suffering, and he laid her head back down again.

"You have to try. Please," Mandy begged. But the weak shaking of her head spoke volumes and she closed her eyes once more. The only sound in the tipi was that of her mother's ragged breaths, at times laced with soft moans. Until that moment, Mandy hadn't realized the other men had slipped out of the tipi at some point, leaving the two alone with her.

Mandy soaked the corner of a cloth in the water, then held it up to her mother's lips and tenderly wiped it across them. Sleeping Bird responded by licking at the cloth to soak up the moisture. Then Mandy used it to wipe the rest of her face carefully, removing the soot and dirt that clung to the weathered skin. When done, she gently grasped the woman's right hand in her own fingers.

"I remember the first moment I ever saw you and how excited I was to hear English being spoken by someone here in the village." Her heart leaped as a hint of a smile appeared at the corner of her mother's mouth upon hearing this and she nodded slightly.

"We've had our difficult moments, as you well know, but my love is so deep for you, my mother. You must fight hard to stay alive, for I need you to be present when Ken-ai-te and I are married. Did you know that he killed The One Who Shall Not Be Named after he shot you?" She knew she was chattering but that no longer mattered. "I know, I know—'no speak'—but you can't stop me now!" She kissed the older woman's brow as she choked back sobs. One tear slipped out of Sleeping Bird's right eye and coursed down her face, and Mandy's heart shattered.

"Mother, why did you step in front of me like you did? Didn't you realize it meant certain death? The arrow was meant for *me*, not you. If only ..."

"To lay down life for friend—not from your Jesus?" The strength and meaning of the words startled Mandy. Her eyes widened and she nodded as fresh tears coursed down her already-streaked face. "You more, daughter now. Protect you—" and her voice trailed off weakly.

Before Mandy could say anything further, Ken-ai-te spoke in Kiowa for the first time since they had entered the tipi.

"My mother, please listen to me carefully. The wound is deep and we cannot remove the arrow without more pain and without more bleeding. You have only a short time before you will go to lie with our fathers, regardless of what we do or do not do. If you desire for the end to come swiftly let me know and I can remove the arrow."

She gazed on his copper face and nodded, then closed her eyes once more. Mandy saw the truth in his eyes as theirs locked for a brief moment. Sleeping Bird may have understood and accepted Ken-ai-te's words but Mandy simply couldn't. Gulping hard against another sob, she had to look away or risk losing control altogether.

However, Mandy's grief was deepest that her mother now faced imminent death without a Savior. Self-pity nor even mourning had no place here. Mandy needed much wisdom and she needed it right away.

God, help me say the right words. There's so little time left. Should I press her or wait for her to ask? If her mind is alert, perhaps there is still time...

After a few moments, Sleeping Bird opened her eyes and stared intently into Mandy's face. Hope rose in her throat. Maybe God would choose to heal? She still had much to learn from her, and oh, how she longed for her to be present when the two were married. With the attack on the village, it would have to slightly delayed, of course, but she was confident it would still take place as soon as order could be restored.

It is to her credit, God, that there will even be a wedding. Surely, You wouldn't be so cruel as to take her away just as this dream is finally coming true! Immediately, Mandy regretted this thought. *Lord Jesus, forgive my selfishness. You are never cruel, only our enemy the devil. But this timing is just so unfair!*

"Prayer Woman, listen to me." The words brought Mandy's attention back to her beloved friend. "Must say this before time to lie with my fathers."

Mandy opened her mouth to protest, then clamped her lips shut as she saw the look in her mother's eyes. They both knew the truth. Arguing would serve no purpose now and might ruin the brief time they had left. Better to let it go.

Nodding, she smiled, though ground her teeth to hold back the tears.

"Yes, Mother, I am listening."

"Each time you spoke words from Bible to Ken-ai-te, my ears open, too. And wisdom comes to my heart, same as to his."

Mandy's heart pounded in her ears. Her mother *had been* listening! She had hoped but never knew for sure. And always feared asking, in case her witness would be rejected outright. With the love she felt for her friend, she just couldn't bear that thought so had remained silent. Why had she allowed Satan to deceive her like that? This woman needed Christ as much as Ken-ai-te did!

Amid more tears, Mandy forced another smile. "I'm so glad, Mother. We never really talked about it between us, and I'm sorry. That was wrong. Do you have questions?" Her words sounded almost foolish with death expected any moment, but she didn't care. She was Prayer Woman and God directed her tongue now.

With great effort, Sleeping Bird smiled faintly then grimaced as she vainly tried to speak again.

"Mother," Ken-ai-te said gently, "you must lie still, let medicine work. No need for more words now." His hands grasped her left one tightly and Mandy could see that she squeezed his fingers lightly.

Their mother stared into his dark eyes in response, then turned her head to face Mandy once more. The pressure on Mandy's hand increased weakly but enough that she managed to communicate without spoken words. One thing Mandy had learned all these months during her time in the Kiowa village jumped to the forefront in those moments: when to speak and when to remain silent. And it was time to listen.

"Your God hear me, even now?"

"Oh, yes, my mother. He hears you. What is it you wish to say to Him?"

"I understand now, my child. Perhaps because death is over me. But now I know."

"What do you know? The words are important. But if you can't speak, you can always talk to Him without words. You know that, don't you?"

She nodded, licked her dry lips, and continued.

"But I want you to hear, my little one. I know you prayed much. Pray now, for me."

"First tell me what it is you want me to pray for you. They should be your words, not mine. But yes, I will pray."

"Have much of this 'sin' you spoke of in my heart. Anger—bitterness—sorrow. But now what I feel is joy. Jesus ..." Her voice broke and Mandy held her breath. *Not now, Lord! Just a few more seconds, please!*

Sleeping Bird coughed and groaned with pain from the effort, lying still for a few moments gasping with shallow breaths. And Mandy waited. She mustn't push this, just let God lead her mother's words as He desired.

"Jesus," she finally continued, "loves me though I have sin. He wants to take it from me, right?"

"Oh, yes, Mother, that is exactly what I said. Because that is what the Bible tells us, over and over. Only He can do this but we have to ask."

"This I ask now, Prayer Woman. You fill my heart with such pride and such love—my Man-dee. Great Spirit—" She stopped and frowned.

"That's right, Mother. God is our Great Spirit, remember? He lives as a spirit and wants us to worship Him in truth. And He will bring peace when we do."

"Great Spirit has given me much with two of you." And she smiled at Ken-ai-te, who now caressed her cheek with his rough copper hand. Mandy's heart soared with bittersweet happiness at seeing the love between them. If only he could understand, too!

"We love you, too, Mother," Ken-ai-te whispered in Kiowa, choking back tears.

"Prayer Woman, you must live your name for me. Not much time left. Please?"

Mandy took a deep breath, closed her eyes, and prayed as her heart had seldom done. As the words tumbled out, she didn't realize at first that some were in English and some, Kiowa. That was fitting, since this new soul saved by grace was white by birth and Kiowa by choice. Sleeping Bird repeated each phrase after Mandy, with a strength that belied her grievous wounds and the lifeblood dripping from her with each passing second. When the last "Amen" was said by them both, Mandy was warmed to see fresh tears on her mother's cheeks. Gently, she wiped them away.

"Why tears when I am so happy?" her mother asked with a weak smile.

"Because God's Word tells us He counts each tear and puts them into a jar to hold for us, even tears shed in happiness. And these are the happiest we can have! When we leave this earth, there will be no more tears. God wipes them all away. And soon your pain will be over when you enter into His presence. I'm counting on you being there to greet me when I come to join you someday."

Mandy thought she would shout with the angels at that moment!

She had prayed so fervently for Ken-ai-te's salvation but had to admit that she had prayed only occasionally for Sleeping Bird's. And she came before he did! *Thank You, Jesus! Thank You for being faithful even when I was not. Thank You, thank You!*

Now, one more thing, Lord. Help me!

"Mother, how can I say thank you for offering your life for mine?" Her vision blurred and she gulped against the sob choking her.

"Use well, my child. No tears now. Only joy!"

⸱CHAPTER FORTY-NINE⸱

"If we confess our sins, he is faithful and just to forgive our sins,
and to cleanse us from all unrighteousness."
I John 1:9

ather, please show Ken-ai-te Your truth right this moment. Use
Mother's example to touch his heart and help him bow his knee
to You. And give me grace to accept—

Suddenly, a woman burst into the tipi. "Prayer Woman! You must come! Now, please. My father is dying and has asked for you to pray for him."

"I can't leave—"

"Go, Prayer Woman." Ken-ai-te's soft voice interrupted her. "Your prayers are needed by many. I'll stay with Mother."

Sleeping Bird nodded in agreement. "My time is much easier now. My joy stronger than my pain!"

Mandy kissed her on the cheek and squeezed her hand once more. "We will have plenty of time to talk someday, where there will be no more hurt or sorrow, my Mother. You have nothing to fear. My love goes with you and Jesus is waiting for you now. I will be back soon and change that poultice if you have more pain. Ken-ai-te will be with you until I return."

It seemed to Mandy that even her face was more relaxed, that the burden of her sin had, indeed, been lifted and it showed in her blue eyes, though clouded with the pain she was going through. But that no longer mattered, only the peace.

Thank You, Jesus! I praise You for this miracle. Now receive her to Your heart and don't let her continue to suffer. But not yet, please don't take her until I finish the work You have called me to do this day. Just a little while longer...

Prayer Woman rose and followed the woman out of the tipi. Her destiny was clear. God's Spirit had much work to do this day after the horrible attack, all right. Why did it take death to wake people up to His love?

Sometime later, Mandy headed back to the tipi, her weary heart exhausted from the scenes of death she had seen repeated several times over, eased only by the exhilaration of witnessing several come to Christ before it was too late for them. But the Good News had also fallen on hearts in whole bodies, loved ones who heard the message as well and felt the conviction of the Great Spirit that afternoon here on the prairie. She was honored to have been the instrument God chose to use to bring these souls to Him in spite of the tragedy they'd all suffered. But now she could turn her own heart back to the one so dear to her who lay dying within this tipi.

As she bent to enter, Mandy felt as though a cold wind had blown in her face in spite of the sunny day, and she shivered involuntarily.

Mother! Oh, God, not yet! Please, I want to see those blue eyes one more time!

But it was not to be. She saw her beloved Ken-ai-te bowed over the body of their mother as soft wails escaped from his lips. He glanced up with a tear-stained face full of grief and loss. Had others been present, she was sure he would have held the tears in, but it moved her heart to see him express his feelings this way.

She cried out and ran to kneel across from him, caressing the now-cool face. Both had loved her equally but he had loved her longer. She had walked by his side in sorrow as they buried his wife and young son. Had loved him through finding his way once more from that deep pit. Had been entrusted with the care and teaching of his captive under her watchful eye, which had opened the door for Mandy to love her as well. Yes, certainly, his was the deeper loss, without question.

But Sleeping Bird was also a Sister in Christ to Mandy now. And that was a bond that transcended all earthly ones, one Ken-ai-te did not yet fully comprehend. Maybe soon.

Why did You plan for me to leave her just when she needed me the most, God? You know that I wanted to be here when she stepped into eternity with You. Was she frightened? Probably not, with Ken-ai-te by her side.

After the freshest grief had swept over the pair and their wails of sorrow had ended, further time passed without any words between them. Finally, Ken-ai-te spoke up.

"Last words of you."

"Of me?"

"She say for me to love you with all my heart, that love is from God."

"That's in the Bible, yes. I'm glad that she knew Him before she died. That was my biggest fear when I saw how gravely wounded she was in the attack, that she would die without Jesus."

"Hers also. She say prayer when arrow slice into flesh that your God would grant her time to talk to His Prayer Woman."

"He granted that prayer, Ken-ai-te, gave her time to pray to Him, to talk to us both. And say goodbye."

Her voice broke and she bowed her head and held the woman's cold hand up to her face.

"Oh, Mother! I never knew my real mother but I like to think she had a heart much like yours. I believe that is one of the reasons why God led me here to meet you, so I could know the kind of woman my dear Papa had married, who had borne me and given me life and who left me with him in order to bring comfort to her own parents when they were near death. I'm so grateful that in Heaven, I will have two mothers to love!"

Ken-ai-te's hand covered hers and he touched her cheek tenderly with the other, wiping away her tears with his thumb.

"You were good daughter. Talk too much, but good daughter."

Mandy laughed. That had always been her problem. Another reason for coming here, to learn how to be silent. But it seems she didn't learn that lesson quite as well as some others!

"Walk with me." It was not a request, yet not a command. Mandy rose and followed him, glancing backward at the body lying there on the buffalo robe, so still and pale. And again rejoiced that death was not the end for her soul.

The couple walked to the top of the ridge overlooking the camp. Several families had already brought their loved ones up here for burial, and they avoided those groups so as to have some privacy without bothering them in their grief. Mandy wondered if Ken-ai-te just wanted some time alone with her or had something on his heart to speak to her about. It was hard to tell, and her weary mind didn't help in sensing the purpose of their walk together. She didn't care, just concentrated on keeping pace with the man she loved as they shared their deep grief with each other.

The death-cries of many filled the evening air, and she knew soon theirs would be added to it. The body would need preparation and they were running out of daylight. Why were they spending time walking when she should be doing this other task right now?

Abruptly Ken-ai-te stopped and put his hands on both her shoulders, staring intently into her eyes. Why was Mandy's heart beating so hard? What did this strange look on his face mean?

"You say this bap-tism must happen after believe, right?"

"Yes—yes," she stammered, "I did, Ken-ai-te. What about it?"

"Our Mother not baptized. So will not be in Heaven?"

So that was what was bothering him! At least she had an easy answer for that question.

"She *will* be in Heaven, Ken-ai-te, in fact, already is. Just as the believing thief on the Cross was promised by Jesus Himself he would be there, that very day. This is how we can know those who believe but cannot be baptized before death—as happened to Mother—can still enter Paradise."

His scowl deepened. Something else seemed to be troubling him. Maybe if she remained quiet he would share it with her. *God, help him understand! Give him faith to trust You with his eternity, so You can share eternity with him.*

"Great Spirit, one you call holy, He can enter heart of Kiowa, too?"

"Of course! That's what I've been saying all these months, Ken-ai-te. In God's sight, we are not men or women, or white or red, or slave or free men. He sees us only as people of faith in Jesus when we come before Him. Each of us is created with a God-sized hole, my husband, and the Great Spirit yearns to fill it with Himself. But He cannot and will not do so until asked by each person. He plans it for us but then patiently waits for us to come to Him so He can enter our life for all eternity. And that's what Mother finally came to know."

Could it be? Was the very thing for which she had prayed all this time about to happen? She feared if she said another word the spell of this moment would be broken. *Oh, Jesus!*

"Will He come now if I ask?"

"Oh, Ken-ai-te, He will be so happy to do that, if you will but say the words. He will give you faith to believe if you are certain that you are ready. You saw Mother do it. It's very simple."

"But she not Kiowa, born white."

"No, she was Kiowa. As I am now Kiowa. I have only been Kiowa for a short time, but she lived all her life as one. However, God doesn't care if you are Kiowa or Comanche or Pawnee—or white. We are all the same in His eyes. We are all sinners and Jesus died on the Cross for all of us. Do you believe that?"

"Yes, yes, I do. Prayer Woman, I need you pray for me now."

"I have prayed for you, Ken-ai-te, for a long time. But I will pray *with* you now if you will agree with Him that you are a sinner and tell him what you have done wrong. Then you have only to accept, to believe, that His blood can wash that sin away."

"I have had, um, desire in my heart for you, not good. And anger. Especially this day I have felt much anger. One Who Shall Not Be Named brought great sorrow to us, have much rage and bitterness against us. Am glad he is dead. And I have killed many—whites, Comanche, others, today Kiowa. Wrong, to kill men? Your God angry with me for this?"

"No, Ken-ai-te, you killed to protect your people and your family. God does not look down on that motive in your heart. The anger, yes, that is a sin. But not the killing when it is for the reason of protection of your own life or others. Being glad, as you say it, that you have done this also is not wrong, unless you hold the anger in your heart about it. And He is not 'my God' because He belongs to all of us if we have faith. Do you confess with your mouth that Jesus saves you from Hell and that you desire to spend eternity with Him in Heaven?"

She nodded to encourage him to respond.

"Yes, I do. My sin heavy in my heart." He thumped his chest a couple of times with his left hand. "How His blood wash that, don't understand. But if you say it, I believe."

"I don't say it, God does. And as I've said before, we don't have to understand a miracle, Ken-ai-te! We only have to believe in it. You say you do. That is all He requires."

And they bowed their heads as Mandy led her beloved Ken-ai-te to Christ. A new soul had been won in the eternal battle and sin conquered once more. Joy abounded and the angels sang in Heaven above!

"Hallelujah!" she cried while the tears flowed. Mandy knew her heart would explode any second with the exhilaration she felt.

Ken-ai-te erupted into deep laughter. "Mother right, have much joy now!"

He hesitated a moment. "Kiss now?"

"Now would be perfect!" And she knew in her heart it would be, that their love had been preserved as sacred and pure for this moment and for all the ones to come.

And Ken-ai-te kissed Mandy tenderly as they clung to each other there on that windy hill in the early twilight of a long and eventful day filled with profound sadness and yet indescribable happiness. She finally pulled away and raised her hands up over her head, her face staring into the heavens above her.

"God," she proclaimed, "You are to be praised above every living thing for Your wonderful plan of salvation and that it includes this man, my forever gift of love, straight from Your heart. Thank You for bringing me home at last!"

✝EPILOGUE✝

"And He hath put a new song in my mouth,
even praise unto our God:
many shall see it, and fear, and shall trust in the LORD."
Psalm 40:3

"Do not weep, my love. Heaven beautiful place with no tears, right?"

What a switch—Ken-ai-te bringing Mandy consolation instead of the other way around! She quickly dried her tears and put her hope again in the promise of that glorious place.

The two had returned to the hilltop with the body of Sleeping Bird to present her to the Father for eternity. When they finished their sad task, Prayer Woman looked around at her people who lingered to watch the sun set, warmed by the many who had prayed for faith that day.

As her chosen husband embraced her for comfort, she said quietly to him, "Ken-ai-te, there is much left to do here after this battle."

"Yes, we must rebuild tipis quickly, see to wounded and grieving."

"True, but that isn't what I meant. I was referring to the many here who don't yet know the Truth. God brought me to you and to your people—*my* people—for a reason and I have found His purpose in the name you gave me months ago. The drawing on your tipi confirmed this for me, actually, but I had to let go of my stubbornness before I could really understand. And it was only when I was finally able to release it that He could bless me with our love for each other."

"Glad you not stubborn now!" They shared yet another sweet laugh.

"Ken-ai-te, would you be willing to join with me in the effort to see Truth proclaimed to all our Kiowa brothers and sisters someday? To make it our mission, our vision of the future?"

He smiled and nodded vigorously. "Want all to know joy I have here," and he patted his chest.

"The Bible says without a vision people perish, so this is ours now. And in doing so, we can claim the same verse my parents used. It will be your very first Scripture to learn, my husband, the one I read in our wedding ceremony—was that really only this morning? So much has happened, it seems like days ago. Psalm 130:5, do you remember?" And she quoted it to him again, with him repeating the words solemnly. Nothing less than firm confirmation of what she had hardly dared to hope for, let alone dream about.

Then he frowned. "But Bible gone. Burn in tipi."

"No, thank the Lord, I had it with me for the wedding ceremony, don't you recall? I dropped it somewhere during the battle but I'm sure it is fine. We will look for it in a few minutes. Even if it is damaged, we can get another. God's Word lasts forever and nothing can destroy it! Besides, much of it is here," and she patted her heart, "and soon will be here," and patted his.

"Want this Word here," and he repeated her gesture. "You teach?"

"Yes, Ken-ai-te, I will teach you. The road to our vision will be long and not easy but it is one our God has placed us on and we dare not refuse. God will remove the stone in the hearts of the Kiowa, replace it with a new Spirit so they will be His people and He will be their God. It will be our job, my husband, to share this Truth with them." She wasn't confident he had understood all that but they had the rest of their lives for her to explain carefully.

Ken-ai-te touched the cross around Mandy's neck and she smiled, recalling how she fought him to keep it. Surely, God's Spirit had moved his heart to allow her to do so.

"Key."

"No, Ken-ai-te, cross. The cross reminds us of Jesus, remember?"

"This key for me. To your heart. To faith in your God."

Would this man ever cease to amaze her with the depth of his wisdom, no longer than he had known Christ?

"Yes, you are right. The key, indeed." She battled her emotions for control and cleared her throat, her fingers closing around his.

"Another thing, something I had planned to reveal to you at the end of our wedding ceremony but of course never got the chance, I want to tell you now. It was to be in my vows to you and I painted it for our tipi as well. It might have been destroyed but I can always do it again. I wrote this because God's Word says His Spirit gives us words to share with future generations, and these are for all who enter our home to see. The words are, 'Long life filled with joy, courage in our tears, many children in our tipi, love and peace beyond measure, to belong to each other from now until forever!'" His broad grin silently but eloquently showed his approval without any words and thrilled Mandy's heart as he pulled her closer yet.

This is where I belong, in his arms. You have given me back my home, Lord, though we don't even have our own tipi in which to sleep this night. It doesn't matter. We have each other—and You!

"I may not have chosen to come here willingly, Ken-ai-te, but I choose now to remain at your side. And when it is time, I will lie with my people here on this hill, and with you, my husband. God ordained before we were born that you would capture me and then take my heart captive as well. Who am I to question God's wisdom?"

They shared a laugh together and then she pulled back to look at him once more. As usual, she became lost in those dark pools of love shining from his handsome face and had to force herself to remember what she wanted to say to him.

"God's hand has been on both of us for a very long time. And now He is sharing with us the riches of that provision through our love. He truly has given us a new song to sing together!"

Would her father be proud? She was certain he would. And someday she would be privileged to meet her real mother in Heaven and would have the delight of introducing both her parents to not only Sleeping Bird but also Ken-ai-te. Nothing could be sweeter! Ken-ai-te was unusually quiet, even for him. Mandy didn't have to wait long to find out what he was thinking, though.

"And someday through children?" he asked her hopefully, a twinkle in his eye that matched the smile on his lips. He kissed the tip of her nose and she giggled.

"Yes, that, too. *After* our wedding. Remember, you promised? Just because it has to be delayed doesn't mean you don't have to keep your word!"

"I will. Remember, you belong me forever. I keep my word. Never forget." He leaned down to kiss her but she put her fingers up to his lips.

"Oh, I promise, I will never forget. We belong to God and to each other for all eternity. What a joy it will be to truly be yours *from now until forever*."

Ken-ai-te smiled and his lips found Mandy's.

THE END

†AUTHOR'S NOTES†

Women who have been thrust out of their comfort zone and into a different environment and perhaps even a hostile one can find genuine hope and encouragement in this novel, in spite of it being fiction. Whether due to circumstances such as divorce, death of a loved one, loss of job/career, long distance move to a new and unknown place, serious health crisis, or one of countless others where they feel abandoned and alone, by man and God alike, life often brings pain and anxiety on every side. It is my sincere belief that ***From Now Until Forever*** can make a positive impact in the midst of this confusion and turmoil. How do I dare to make this claim? Because it helped *me* face some fearsome giants, I battled while writing the book!

Shortly after making a firm commitment to myself and to the Lord to complete the work I'd begun years before, life threw several curves at me and we moved to a new location where I knew only one person, while my husband worked in another state for the first few months. As I anguished to write passionately of Mandy's ordeal, I began to sense God saying the same things to me that I was writing about my character.

"I am the same as I ever was and will always be. Trust Me and My work in you. Be obedient and faithful and your reward will be precious in My sight. Don't despair for I will love you *from now until forever.*"

Pouring my heart and soul into this project while facing this difficult adjustment in my own situation gave me great insight into what Mandy felt when she encountered her new way of life. Lost. Alone. Frightened. Angry. Frustrated. Questioning. Wanting to go

393

"home" yet aware that was no longer possible. Thus, God was able to minister peace to my heart time and again through my own words. And if He did it for me, He can do the same for others!

The Scriptures quoted throughout the book are from the King James Bible, simply because that was the only one available in the 1800s. Thus, the verses Mandy knew would have been from this version.

At the end of the book are ten Questions for Study, which are designed to be used in a group setting or on an individual basis for delving deeper into the spiritual themes of the story. It is my hope readers will find them helpful for introspection and meditation.

If you should have questions about God's sovereignty or about how to obtain assurance of eternal life for your own heart, please do not hesitate to contact me. I would love to hear from you, dear readers, and learn how this book has aided in your spiritual journey. God bless each one of you for reading it and it is my deepest prayer it has helped point you to His love.

With deepest gratitude,
Laura L. Drumb
Called to Hope...To Live in Joy!
Ephesians 1:18, Romans 15:13

†QUESTIONS FOR STUDY†

1. Although a fictitious novel, ***From Now Until Forever*** embodies a theme familiar to women everywhere. God stretches Mandy physically, mentally, emotionally, and most importantly, spiritually during her adjustment to life as a Kiowa. The following questions can be used by readers individually or as a group to delve deeper into this theme and reflect how it might apply to them personally. Have you ever experienced a violent tragedy first hand in your life as Mandy faces with the ambush? If so, how did her reaction differ from your own? Did you feel God had abandoned you when it happened? How did He help you overcome this feeling?

2. In what ways does God use extraordinary circumstances to protect us from harm without our realizing it at the time? How can they help us grow in trust?

3. Have you ever faced prejudice from those who didn't know you personally but who hated you based on race, religion, nationality, age, or other factors you couldn't control? How did God change Mandy's heart when subjected to this? Has God ever convicted you of doing so to others? Name some times in history when this type of hatred resulted in terrible consequences for innocent people. Are cultures ever totally "good" or totally "bad"?

4. Has there ever been a time in your life when you felt you were without hope and knew you couldn't go back to the way things were but neither could you imagine having to go forward into an uncertain future? How did you cope? Have you longed for "home" the way Mandy does and been denied that desire?

5. Has loneliness ever been a serious problem for you, when you felt left out of social activities and friendships? How did this emotion guide some or all of your decisions during that time?

6. What if you could never have a Bible again and only had your memory of what it says to rely on? Has your memorization of Scripture ever provided wisdom or strength in a crisis?

7. Has God ever required you to release to Him an attitude, especially one you felt was justified, before providing His solution to a dilemma as happened with Mandy's forgiveness of Ken-ai-te?

8. Explain the role of pride in Mandy's foolish demand for her own tipi and how it almost shattered God's provision for her safety among the Kiowa. How can something apparently in line with God's Word become a vessel for evil? Does God ever grant restoration after sin if we are faithful to grow in faith in spite of it?

9. Can deathbed professions of faith be genuine? How can they be used by our enemy to confuse the issue for those who are struggling to believe? How can they be used by God to spur others on to their own moment of decision?

10. How can you relate to Mandy's despair and crisis of faith? To Ken-ai-te's desire for revenge? To Sleeping Bird's long-buried memories which nevertheless have to be confronted and

resolved? To the realization that God has planned the details of your life long before you know them?

† THE STORY
BEHIND THE STORY †

More than twenty years ago, I happened to watch an old "Brady Bunch" rerun on TV and in it a Native American friend of theirs used the phrase "from now until forever" and it stuck in my mind and wouldn't go away. Little did I know at the time that it would someday become the title of a novel with my name as author!

Some years later, once I knew God had called me to write for Him but still had no clue *what* or *when* much less *how*, two names began rolling around in my thoughts and I knew that they would be at the core of whatever resulted. Mandy and Ken-ai-te (pronounced <u>*keen*</u>-*a-tay*), then began shaping their love story for me, making it clear the setting would be in Indian Territory in the mid-1800s. Around this time the title crystalized as well, as though the Lord had been patiently waiting for me to catch up with His inspiration.

In my eagerness to start this project, I plowed ahead with the writing without first doing thorough research into the history and culture of the Indian tribe I chose. Fortunately, I discovered my error before it was too late, though my ignorance did create a great deal of extra work for me in editing out the references to the wrong tribe. I then prayed that God would reveal to me the one *He* wanted and plunged into reading everything I could about the Native Americans at that time in this area. The Internet at the time was brand new but I pushed myself to learn to use its broad array of information, browsing from one website to another and taking copious notes for week after week.

One night on yet another of those countless websites, I stumbled across the true story of Millie Durgin, a white woman who was captured by the Kiowa as an infant and reared as one of them on the prairieland of what would someday be close to the border between Texas and Oklahoma. How she met Christ in her later years is a poignant tale of the Father's awesome power and proved to me, again, that God can reach across every single border people set up among themselves to divide one group from another as He answered the prayers of her family and drew her to Himself before she died. Wiping away my tears that night, I knew I had found the right tribe! If God could save Millie, then He surely could do the same for Ken-ai-te and his people in my fictitious story.

For the next couple of years I immersed myself in everything I managed to find about the Kiowa and the more I read, the more convinced I became it truly was no "coincidence" I had found that tale about Millie Durgin. You see, I don't believe in coincidences, only in God's purposes. I became fascinated with the lifestyle that Mandy would have experienced living with these people and following the buffalo herds across the prairie—the sights, the smells, the sounds, and even the harsh way of life compared to what she had been used to— and through all of these began to glimpse the destiny she would also one day find with the Kiowa. From all this the idea of her father's journal and the secret of her heritage began taking shape and with that, the characterizations for these two along with Sleeping Bird soon became a reality.

However, about this time, I realized with a shock that something vital was missing out of the plot: there was no true villain! Ken-ai-te had served that role briefly at the beginning but quickly became Mandy's hero and protector instead, then eventually her love. So he couldn't be the one trying to thwart her from being able to thrive and find happiness, let alone survive her ordeal and grasp hope for the future. It was quite obvious he was not the antagonist. Without one, there would be no conflict or tension and the whole novel would fail.

As I prayed about this dilemma, I felt God pushing me to sit back and learn to listen to my characters to see who *they* viewed as the one opposing their plans and dreams. My answer was not long in coming.

Everything began to focus on an unnamed warrior in the capture scene, who now added his voice to the discussion. Up to this point, I had been telling him who he was. Perhaps it was time to listen while *he* told me about himself. And he did!

In writing his backstory, I learned about the root of his bitterness and irrational hatred for whites and why it was in particular focused against Mandy; his jealousy against Ken-ai-te for finding the happiness the warrior desired but felt could never be his due to the hideous scar on his face that had mangled not only his body but also his soul; and the dark secret this warrior kept hidden from everyone that further fueled his anger and drove his thirst for vengeance until it erupted into a twisted scheme of revenge and destruction against all who showed Mandy mercy or kindness—much less love—including his own family and even Sleeping Bird. And Black Feather was born as the perfect villain for this novel. And a wicked one he is!

In the Acknowledgements Section I have already outlined why I sought out a primary source for information about the Kiowa people and how God led me to my friend Dorothy. As I said there, her priceless guidance and advice has resulted in a book far more authentic in its details than it ever could have been otherwise. She inspired me to write with a passion and sense of accuracy far beyond my own knowledge and for that I am truly grateful.

Another aspect that thrilled me tremendously came to light in my first interview with Dorothy. We met at a museum in Anadarko (Oklahoma) where she volunteered, the National Hall of Fame for Famous American Indians, and I found myself literally surrounded by several centuries of history on every side. I had been apprehensive about meeting her and explaining the Christian focus of the novel, not knowing if she was a Christian herself or not. I needn't have feared—

God had that well in hand, too! As we were seated she asked if it was okay while we talked to play in the background a tape of the Indian Baptist Association with 80 hymns being sung in Kiowa. What an incredible experience to soak up history and faith at the same time, for while of course I didn't understand the words, I did recognize quite a few of the tunes. It was from this that I got the idea to have Mandy sing a verse of "Amazing Grace" in Kiowa at her wedding ceremony, since it was a well-known hymn at that time.

Dorothy explained to me that the Kiowa were known for being a people who valued prayer and this made them easier to evangelize than some other Native American tribes. The Christian faith, in other words, was quite compatible in many ways with Kiowa traditions. Again, confirmation that I had found the "right" tribe! Eventually Dorothy and I worked it out together to have Mandy's new name become Prayer Woman, to emphasize this very concept. There were many such twists and turns of the plot that Dorothy walked me through over the next few months, some of which I had never even considered until she mentioned them as possibilities for more grounding in the facts of their way of life. Whenever I questioned her about certain details, if she didn't already have the answer she checked with her own sources to confirm what I knew or to inform me I was wrong so I could correct it. Her help at every step of the way was a priceless gift for which I will always be humbly grateful.

One last contribution that Dorothy made to this novel cannot be overlooked. As we talked that first day, she began telling me about her great-great-great grandfather, Chief Tohausan, also called Little Bluff. I became utterly intrigued by this fascinating man and asked a great many questions about her knowledge of him and his impact on the tribe's history. After I returned home and began writing on the manuscript again, I believe God inspired me to include him in one of the scenes. With her kind permission as his next of kin that is what I did, as a major turning point in Mandy's acceptance of her destiny as a

Kiowa and leaving her past behind.

The scene where Chief Tohausan came to the village to speak with Mandy and Ken-ai-te and their people is pure fiction. But the historical fact is, Tohausan was in real life precisely who I portrayed him to be in the novel. He was the greatest chief over all the Kiowa from 1833 to 1866 and personally responsible for the longest period of peace between his people, other Indian tribes, and the whites living in Indian Territory at the time with the many treaties he brokered among them; an accomplished artist and creator of the historic and unique Calendar Art that continues today to depict the heritage of the Kiowa people as it has for more than two centuries; a person with a unique appearance that set him apart from all others of his time; a kind and gentle man of peace who loved to be surrounded by children yet was equally comfortable with whites and Indians of all tribes as well; and the owner of a US Army ambulance wagon, a gift from a grateful Army general for a treaty he helped work out for him, and a prized possession which Chief Tohausan proudly preferred for the rest of his life when riding across the prairie rather than doing so on horseback—these are all historical facts.

I pray I have honored him and, indeed, all the Kiowa people with my words. When Dorothy finished reading the manuscript once it was completed, she seemed to agree, saying it deserved a "10" for the entire novel! Humbling, indeed.

Another exciting piece of research that I did while writing this book was in the form of a museum exhibit at the Lloyd Noble Museum of Natural History in Norman, Oklahoma, where I got to see the Kiowa Calendar Art displayed a few years back. I heard it was coming so jumped at the chance to see in person what I had studied about! The effort to repair and prepare the extensive calendar for the exhibit was overwhelming at times and the decision was made during this time to never again show it in public, due to its fragile state after all these years. That made viewing it even more special to me. I spent hours pouring over every little detail of the years around 1853 in particular, taking meticulous notes and even sketching crude drawings in some cases to help me remember a point here or there. By then I was firmly hooked on this awe-inspiring display so I finished looking at the whole thing with a renewed sense of respect for Chief Tohausan who created it in the first place. It literally tells the story of the Kiowa people from the earliest years to the present day in colorful drawings, whether battles or treaties or births or deaths or buffalo hunts. I found writing about its creator became even more important to me personally from having had this privilege.

It is my deepest prayer that God will use my words in this novel to encourage women who have been thrust out of their comfort zone by circumstances such as divorce, death of a loved one, loss of job/career, long distance move to a strange place where they know no one, serious health crisis, or many other similar situations where they feel abandoned and alone. And in facing these they often begin to wonder where God is in the midst of the chaos on every side. As a matter of fact, while writing the final few drafts of the book, my husband and I moved to a new location and I felt positively lost for months. Pouring my heart and soul into this project while facing this difficult adjustment in my own life gave me great insight into what Mandy felt when she encountered her new way of life. Lost. Alone. Frightened. Angry. Frustrated. Questioning. Wanting to go "home" yet aware that was no longer possible. And as the book took shape, so did my commitment to share with my readers what God had taught me through Mandy's story because I know first-hand how God used it to touch my heart and help me heal. And if He did it for me, I believe He can do the same for others!

Incidentally, all Scripture references in this book are from the King James Version, as that is the only Bible Mandy would have had back in 1853. So while I found numerous texts I would have liked to use, they were in more modern versions and paraphrases and thus not available for her study or memorization and therefore not appropriate for this novel.

Dear Readers, if you should have further questions about God's sovereignty or about how to obtain assurance of eternal life for your own heart, please do not hesitate to contact me. I would love to hear from you and learn how this book has impacted your spiritual growth. God bless each one of you!

Called to Hope ...To live in Joy!
Ephesians 1:18, Romans 15:1